ONE WITH THE WOLF

ONE WITH THE WOLF

THE COLDSTONE CASE FILES VOLUME ONE

JASON GILBERT

FALSTAFF
BOOKS
WWW.FALSTAFFBOOKS.COM

This series is dedicated to everyone who has supported me and been there to help me see this through. Most of all, it is dedicated to my wife and daughter: two women who have no problem kicking my ass into gear when it needs it.

I

WOLFBANE

1

J ames staggered, kept himself from stumbling by holding on to the large, low-hanging tree branch as he caught his breath. His legs were stiff from running, his chest aching and dry from the cold air. He hid in the shadows of the elm, the tree maybe a hundred years old, one of its largest limbs inches from the ground.

Running hadn't been an option. He couldn't change in town. The noise would rouse too much suspicion—damned nosy neighbors.

He looked around the area, the forest showered in blue from the bright full moon above. It wouldn't be long now.

He turned his mind to other things. Breakfast. What would he have for breakfast when he got back? Eggs? He had a few left. Some bacon left over from yesterday. He'd need to make a list for a grocery trip later that day. After breakfast.

After he was done with the change.

His mind went to less mundane, more disturbing thoughts. What if someone wandered by? Saw him shift? Would they stop for a moment and let him explain? Considering the last person who'd witnessed him turn died of a heart attack where he'd stood, James highly doubted it. He looked around the area again. He'd run far outside the city, maybe a mile. The beginnings of the change gave him a little more stamina than usual, but it didn't keep his body from feeling the effects of running nonstop for a mile. He wondered if his father ever thought to do the same thing when he was alive.

Then again, David Coldstone hadn't been one for caution.

James breathed out slowly as the creature moved under his skin, stirred as it began to wake to the light of the full moon. James felt his skin stretch, shape, and form over bones that shifted and moved, enlarged, and took new shape. Felt his mouth and nose move forward, elongating, his teeth growing longer and sharper. The night's chill suddenly didn't affect him; the silvered hair on his body slid out from behind the dark hair of his human form. His ears moved upward, every sound becoming sharper in the night.

James stood to his full eight feet and stretched his arms out to the side as he tensed his body, aware of the rippling power wrapped around his new bones.

He always kept his humanity when he turned. It wasn't like what he'd heard in the stories about his kind. He couldn't speak, of course, but he could reason. He looked around again with his new, enhanced sight to make sure he was alone before he loped into the night, fists pounding the ground, barreling in a gorilla's gait as he moved through the forest. The change always made him hungry.

He didn't allow himself into Rock Hill while he was wolf. Too much risk. Not of hurting anyone, but of getting caught.

The trees whipped by as he barreled through the clearing, his prey close. He drew the smell of panicked blood in over his tongue, licked his chops. The deer loped ahead in James's yellowed vision, darted in a zigzag, tried to lose him. James kicked out with his powerful legs. He was airborne, massive arms extended, clawed hands reaching for the animal. Tearing flesh, gnashing teeth, jaws like a steel trap around the deer's neck. Bones delicate and fragile, snapping under the pressure as the animal lost its fight and life. James tasted the blood filling his mouth, washing over his tongue and teeth, running down his jaw and chest. He'd be able to sate himself this night off this one kill. The buck was a least an eight point. Maybe ten.

He'd get some extra time running tonight.

He ate, his mind working over his path for tonight's run as he devoured his meal.

James woke in his bed, his muscles sore. He'd gotten his extra running in last night, all right. He'd gone several miles out from town, found a trail up McConnells Highway way past Eastview Road. Being directly under moonlight, the moon so large…it was intoxicating. He'd gone too long only once before. The morning sun had reversed the change, and he'd been stranded a good five miles outside of Rock Hill with no clothes. It'd taken him the better part of a day to walk back, and he was still forced to wait until nightfall.

It would be all he needed, someone seeing a naked man walking the streets toward the apartment of James Coldstone.

He rolled out of bed, started a pot of water for his coffee press, and looked out the window to the streets below. Traffic moved steadily in downtown on Dave Lyle Boulevard, people hurrying to work or wherever else. Many had children in the passenger or back seats staring out the windows or engrossed in their phones. Off to school, Junior. A senior citizen walked his dog, greeting passersby with a nod, have you read today's article?

Another morning in Rock Hill, South Carolina.

The pot on the stove whistled. James removed it, set it aside, and spooned several scoops of ground coffee into his French press before adding the water. He looked down at his naked body to make sure there were no scratches or marks that would be visible once he had dressed. His full moon runs through the countryside tended to leave behind telltale signs of not being more careful when charging through the brush. Satisfied, he donned a robe and went to the bathroom for a shower.

He rolled his eyes and stopped at the sound of a knock at the door.

Paper. Right.

He answered, expecting to bend down to pick up the morning paper and instead raised an eyebrow at the sight of Sergeant Phillip Brown of the Rock Hill Police Department standing on his welcome mat, dressed in street clothes and holding a rolled newspaper out at him.

"Good morning, Phillip."

"You have *got* to be more careful, James," Phillip said, stepping by James and into the apartment.

James sighed, pursed his lips, rolled his eyes.

"Do come in."

James closed the door, ran his hands through his dark hair as he turned and followed Phillip into the apartment. James was tall and lean, as opposed to the short, dark-skinned, and stocky Phillip. Phillip also liked keeping a short beard, while James preferred to stay clean-shaven.

The wolf had enough hair to warrant a change of pace for the human.

Phillip dropped the paper on the kitchen table and sat, running his hand over his clean-shaven scalp. James poured two cups of coffee, brought them over, and sat down across from Phillip, sliding a cup toward the sergeant.

Phillip looked at the cup and made a face.

"Coffee? A little late for that, isn't it?"

James glanced at the clock as he held up his cup.

"It's almost nine."

"I figured you'd be to beer by this point," Phillip said, gesturing at the paper. "Then again, I shouldn't be surprised at a late morning, now should I?"

James sipped his coffee, picked up the paper, and read the article Philip had circled.

Local Girl Spots Monster in Yard. Calls Police.

"She was brushed off as a child with an active imagination," Phillip said, sipping his coffee. "We sent a man out to investigate, of course, after a few efforts by me to ensure it took the officer a while to get there. Give you ample time to remove yourself from the very situation you created. Idiot."

Phillip was the only other person in Rock Hill who knew James's secret. They'd grown up together, attended Winthrop together. Phillip decided to join the force as soon as he was out of college. James opted for early retirement, having inherited millions from his late father. James felt it was a good idea to entrust Phillip with his secret in case something happened. The Coldstone murders, albeit thirty years old, were still a hot topic in Rock Hill. It was common knowledge as to what David Coldstone had been, so James was never surprised when people raised an eyebrow at him when he went to the store to stock up on steaks and beer.

"I didn't see the girl," James said, putting the paper back down on the table. "The lights in the house were out."

"Children get up to pee, James."

"Not a factor I'd considered."

Phillip scowled at James, drummed his fingers on the table.

James rolled his eyes.

"Okay, fine. I'll be more careful next time."

Phillip nodded. "Good." He took a drink of his coffee and looked around the place. "I don't understand you, James. You inherit a fortune, and you live in a damn apartment in downtown? Isn't your father's place still around?"

"It keeps new friends from showing up looking for charity," James said, flipping the paper over to read the front page. "Besides, Dad's castle is a hundred miles from here. Mario Kart 64 would be a bit difficult for us, wouldn't it?" He felt the hairs on his neck bristle as his eyes moved over the headline.

Murder in Rock Hill! Victims Mauled to Death by Wild Animal!

"The other thing I wanted to speak to you about," Phillip said, indicating the paper. "I have to ask. Standard procedure. Where did you go last night when you changed?"

"Killed a deer a few miles past Eastview Road," James said, not looking at Phillip as he read over the article. "Big one. Filled me up for the night, so I ran to the church with the big graveyard out front and howled at the moon for a while. Ways down McConnells Highway."

Phillip chortled, almost spitting his coffee back into his mug.

"Really, James? Howling?"

James glanced at him, defensive.

"It's therapeutic. You should try it sometime."

"Well, at least you have an alibi," Phillip said, shaking his head as he looked over his mug at James. "Mangy mutt."

James sat back in his chair, crossed his arms in front of him, and stared at Phillip.

"Other than asking my whereabouts from last night and chastising me for scaring a small child, what is it you want from me, Phil?"

"I need you to look at the scene," Phillip said casually as he set his mug back on the table. "Help us find out who, or what, did this."

"By us, you mean you."

"Of course," Phillip said, shrugging. "Unless you're ready to go public with your inner pet, yeah? This murder is going to draw a lot of attention your way due to its all-too-familiar nature. I need to make sure that doesn't happen."

O f course, they had to wait until nightfall. It was the only time James could enact the change without too much risk of being caught. The streets were relatively empty, the drive from James's apartment to the scene of the murder easy and uneventful.

James was no stranger to freelance police work. Ever since Phillip made detective, he'd been quick to bring his werewolf friend in on cases to make sure the supernatural element stayed low or absent altogether. There was a series of murders a few years back involving vampires. Phillip knew the telltale signs right away and had James help him find the group before things went from bad to hellish in the streets. While the police were busy dicking around about what kind of tool or machine a man would use to drain the blood from his victims, James hunted down three vampires in the city, killed them, and disposed of the bodies by fire.

The car stopped in front of a small brick house on College Avenue near Winthrop University, an older neighborhood in Rock Hill. Phillip applied the hand brake and turned to James. The sun had set only a few hours ago, and the full moon was passed.

Not that James needed a full moon to change. He was simply unable to help the change during the full moon.

"Need I be concerned as to whether or not you can control yourself?" Phillip asked. "The bedroom is covered in blood."

James looked at him sidelong.

"I'm not a complete animal. Besides, we're stopping for dinner after, right?"

Phillip nodded.

"Noted."

"Just make sure there's no silver around."

Phillip opened the car door, speaking as he got out.

"I had all silver removed earlier as evidence. In case it was...temptation for thievery."

Silver was the only thing James knew of that hurt. Even the slightest touch burned him wicked, making his skin smoke instantly.

James got out of the car and made for the house, the breeze satisfyingly cool in the warm air. Summer was on the way in, and most days were getting more humid than not. He welcomed the air conditioning inside the house, listened intently for the sounds of other people wandering their yards walking dogs or relaxing on the back porch.

"Most people are in bed at this time," Phillip said as he stepped inside behind James. "I believe there's a woman who stays up late to read, but her bedroom is on the opposite side of her house from here, so it shouldn't be an issue. This way."

James followed him through the small house, the space cramped and full of furniture and knickknackery. He tensed, kept his composure. James wasn't much for small areas. A wolf had his den, but there was a way out. Wolves were meant to be free of confines.

Phillip led James down the short hall to the end where a bedroom door sat barricaded with police tape. Phillip swatted the tape away, reached in his pocket for the key as he muttered under his breath.

Something moved outside, the growl low, surprised and frustrated. James's ear twitched as he picked up the sound. He stepped back out of the hall and into the living room, looking out the window as Phillip fought with the lock. A shadow ducked into a carport across the street. James stared at the pitch darkness, waited to see if something would move again. He could see into the carport perfectly if he went wolf, but that risked witnesses. What if someone came out of their home while a giant werewolf stalked about?

"Got it."

James turned at the sound of Phillip's voice accompanied by a lock clicking and a door opening.

Phillip breathed deep. "I can't get used to this sort of thing," he said.

James nodded. "Nor should you."

Phillip stepped aside, allowing him to enter.

The apartment defined the word "aftermath." Blood streaked every wall, some of the streaks ending in gory handprints as if someone were trying futilely to escape. The wood floor was stained dark, with deep scratches dug into the wood by something inhuman; pools of blood coagulated in the corners. The bed was soaked, the blood pooled on the mattress. The spatter and streaks on the walls trailed up to the ceiling, the white above stained with enough red to make it look like the ceiling in a Satanic temple. The room reeked with the smell of old meat combined with shit and urine. How long had the people been here before they'd been found?

James turned to Phillip. "Assuming I find anything, what do you want me to do?"

"Standard fare," Phillip said, shrugging. "I keep the department busy chasing in one direction; you go in the other and eliminate."

James nodded, stripped his shirt off and handed it to Phillip. He began to unbutton his jeans as Phillip sighed.

"Is this really necessary?"

James continued as if his friend hadn't spoken, talking as he went.

"Lest you forget, post-change I am approximately eight feet tall, I make a carnival strongman look like a stick drawing, and I'm strong enough to break said strongman like a toothpick." He grinned as he kicked his shoes off, dropped his pants to the floor, and tossed them to Phillip. "I like these clothes. Especially the shirt."

Phillip shook his head.

"Christ, James. Boxers. They're called boxers. Commonly used as underwear."

James looked down at himself, shrugged, and looked back up at Phillip as the man glared at him, his lips pursed.

"You may want to stand back."

Phillip obliged as James closed his eyes, breathing out. He concentrated, letting the wolf stir inside him, calling to it. His body begin to change as he willed it. He breathed out slowly, the breath accompanied by a low, resonating growl from deep within his throat. He opened his eyes, his vision yellowed slightly, and looked down at Phillip. He bared his teeth, licked them with his long, canine tongue, growling hungrily. His eyes widened, his features ravening and psychotic as he moved toward Phillip, putting his snarling face close to the policeman's dark features.

Phillip rolled his eyes. "Try it on someone who hasn't watched you do this since college. Now fetch."

James dropped the act, cocked his head with a grunt, turned away, and crouched down on all fours as he sniffed the apartment. All the smells were tenfold. Leftover fast food, air freshener, blood, meat going rancid. Sweat.

Fear.

It lingered in the air, the scent strong enough to make James question if there was still a witness inside the apartment. He perked his ears and listened. Phillip's stomach growling, the neighbors watching television, a cat on the fire escape.

Otherwise, nothing.

Something.

It hung in the air, stood out from the rest of the smells. James ran his large canine nose across the bloodied carpet, inhaled the odors over his tongue. Huffed. Definitely different. Not human.

Phillip stepped forward, his footstep loud in the quiet room.

"Did you find something?"

James let out a low growl that he let trail off. His way of telling Phillip to be patient.

And quit talking.

"Don't take that tone with me," Phillip said curtly. "I'll have you know that I'd planned a steak dinner afterward. Haven't eaten since this morning."

James gave a chuff as he moved past Phillip and to the blood-drenched bed. He spotted something on one of the pillows, the marks faint as if the claws had only glanced the fabric. He leaned in closer, took the scent in deep as a picture formed in his mind.

A dog. A wolf.

A man.

James gave a voluntary whimper. Another signal he and Phillip had worked out.

Not good.

Phillip moved over to the bed, standing beside James as the werewolf stood tall, looking down at the remains painted across the furniture, his eyes going back to the claw marks.

"I don't like that sound," Phillip said. "It means emails to send to someone's spam folder accidentally."

James let a low growl roll in his throat and chest, his eyes locked on the marks. He closed his eyes, concentrated on the man he saw in the mirror every morning. Tall, dark hair. Shaving, brushing his teeth. Mouthwash. What was in the paper today? On the news?

James opened his eyes, looked down at his naked, hairless body, then back at the cushion.

"Claw marks," he said, pointing them out to Phillip. "Faint, like it was just grazed."

Phillip leaned over and took a closer look.

"Still a good distance apart," he said, standing back up. "What do you make of it, then? Vampire?"

"No," James said as he held his hands out to Phillip. "It's a werewolf. My clothing, if you don't mind?"

2

How do you know it's another werewolf?" Phillip asked as he parked the car in front of James's apartment building.

James rolled his eyes. "How many times will you ask me?"

Phillip sighed, rubbed his eyes. "I don't need this, James. It's been months since the last supernatural attack. I play fucking *hell* keeping it quiet when it happens." James shrugged, opened the passenger side door, and got out. The sun would rise in a few hours, and James was longing to spend those hours asleep. The humidity in the air was up, making the thought of getting out of the car to cross the sidewalk to the front door unbearable.

Fatigue made the idea a little easier to digest.

The change made him feel as if he'd run a marathon twice when he reverted to human form. It was exhausting. After a full moon, where the change was forced rather than by choice, he would usually take the majority of the day after to sleep it off. Two changes in less than twenty-four hours, even if the second was by choice, was torture. James wondered if Phillip would let him get away with sleeping for the rest of the week.

Were there not a second werewolf roaming around, James wouldn't care one way or the other.

Phillip got out of the car behind him, leaned on the roof as he spoke. "What now?"

"Now I sleep," James said. "The sun will be up in four hours, and that's four hours of REM sleep I intend to enjoy without your company." He turned and looked at Phillip. "There's nothing more we can do. The wolf is probably gorged after all of that. Breakfast?"

"Yeah, sure," Phillip said, his shoulders slumping.

"Pick me up at eight," James said. "And get some rest. There's nothing more you can do."

J ames's sleep was restless, the thoughts of a second werewolf running around Rock Hill too bothersome to let go even for a few hours. He'd been told that he was the only one left. His mother had made sure.

So she'd said.

After her death, James spent his teen years in foster care until he was of the proper age to access his family fortune. Rather than move into his father's estate, he opted to live like the average person, thinking it would keep him under the radar. Unfortunately, people knew who he was. The Coldstone name was all over the Wolf Man Murders thirty years prior, and 2019 showed no hint of the populace moving forward other than a change of fashion and tastes in music. James kept to himself, went to the grocery store during the slower hours of the day, and was diligent about being a good, quiet neighbor.

He stubbornly stayed in bed, resting, letting sleep come and go until an hour before Phillip was supposed to pick him up. He got up, showered, and checked the news on his laptop.

No Leads for Police in Rock Hill Murder! Suspect Still at Large!

Large, James said, smirking despite his concern. *Well played.*

Who was the other wolf? James had no family left. He was alone. He'd never bitten another human being, had always fed on animals. Lycanthropy only affected humans. The other wolf would be cognizant when he turned, which made the situation worse. It meant that this other wolf knew what he was doing, that he had no remorse.

A serial killer with supernatural powers.

He skimmed the article, skipping over the usual comments and drone from the chief of police. "Best men looking into it, working around the clock, blah-blah-blah."

Nothing about the Wolf Man Murders. Nothing about the Coldstone name. Phillip had done his job.

James didn't look up from the article when a knock sounded from the door.

"Come in, Phillip," he called. "It's unlocked. And dear *God*, your cologne."

Phillip came in, shutting the door behind him as he glared at James.

"You and that damned sense of smell," he said.

"Can't help it," James said, not looking up. "Your cologne is nasty. Wash it off."

"I barely put any on!"

"My nose is running, and my eyes are tearing." James looked sidelong at Phillip, not hiding his annoyance. "Show a bit of consideration for your partially canine friend?"

Phillip grumbled under his breath as he went to James's bathroom.

"Did you see the article on *The Herald* website this morning?" he called over the sound of the water running in the sink.

"I did."

"You're welcome," said Phillip. "That article was a pain in my ass to push through." He turned off the water and stepped out, drying his face and neck with a towel. "People are already suspicious. It's too familiar."

"The bodies?"

"Mauled and partially eaten. One of the men mentioned the Wolf Man Murders. I threatened him with suspension if he mentioned it again. We don't need panic stirring."

"You're not wrong."

"Did anything come to mind since last we talked? Anyone in particular?"

"No, no one." James donned his shoes as he spoke. "As far as I know, I'm the only lycanthrope in the area."

Phillip shook his head.

"Let's eat breakfast. We'll talk on the way."

You say he's as smart as you?" Phillip chuckled. "If he's of average intelligence or has a shred of common sense, he outsmarts you dramatically."

James looked at him sidelong. Phillip never shied away from taking a jab at James. As high-strung as the policeman tended to be, at least he had a good nature.

"It's evolution, Phillip. All werewolves keep their intelligence when they turn."

Or they should. James wondered if there were exceptions. Human beings were capable of going feral under extreme circumstances. Why not supernaturals? Werewolves, vampires—they were no different, just humans with different afflictions. Changing for the first time—or the only time in the case of vampires—could be a traumatic experience.

"So how do we begin looking?" Phillip asked, stopping at a red light.

"It'll be more difficult during daylight hours, right? We wait until nightfall. Rock Hill is fairly quiet after dark. I can go hunting then. And Christ, this car is uncomfortable. How do you manage a stakeout?"

Phillip laughed as he pulled forward through the now green light.

"Am I paying you the usual fee?"

James nodded. "Please make sure the cow is cleaned properly this time. They tend to roll without noticing their own shit."

The squad car radio squawked to life. "Sergeant Brown, come in. This is dispatch. Over."

Phillip pulled his car to the side of the road, the diner only a few blocks ahead. He pulled the radio mic off the dash and spoke into it. "This is Sergeant Brown. Go ahead."

"Please respond to a possible homicide in the university area. Over," the operator said.

James looked at Phillip. The officer shook his head, raising his eyebrow.

"I've already responded to that. That was yesterday, Sheryl. Over."

"*Another* murder, Sergeant Brown. Stand by for the address. Over."

Phillip stopped at McDonalds on the way back toward Winthrop. James managed, preferring steak and chicken to fast food, but he wouldn't complain about nourishment one way or the other. He was starving.

The newest murder was at a bigger house, the street one of the more upscale locations in the neighborhood. The homes were two and three stories, many of them purchased by businessmen and salesmen who did well enough for themselves, and most of them owned by old money and politics.

"Shit," Phillip muttered. "Another family. My God."

"It's surprising," James said as Phillip drove through the neighborhood. "We're not shy creatures, but we prefer not to make a scene, either. Not unless we're provoked."

Phillip looked at him, an eyebrow raised. "Says the werewolf who stands on a church howling at the moon, then gets noticed by a little girl while trailing through her yard in the dead of night."

James shrugged. "Fair statement."

Phillip pulled the car up to the scene, stopping short of the police tape surrounding the yard, most of it blocked by onlookers. James saw a few squad cars pulled up, parked out of the way for the forthcoming county coroner's truck. A forensics crew was already in place, and a few uniformed officers worked the crowds, keeping them behind the tape and avoiding shouted questions from neighbors too nosy to stick to their business and stare like ordinary people.

"Stay behind the lines," Phillip said to James. "Listen, see if you can pick anything up. And, for God's sake, do *not* tell people who you are."

James nodded, getting out of the car and following Phillip up the driveway. A few onlookers moved out of the way as Phillip held up his badge and demanded to be allowed through. James followed to the rear of the crowd, keeping his head down as he looked around. The yard was neat and trimmed, the grass freshly mowed. He sniffed the air, letting his canine sense of smell free. Motor oil, gas, grass. Likely cut late yesterday. Damn. Tall grass was easier to track with the naked eye. He'd have to come back later and sniff around as a wolf. He glanced up, noted the street lights. That could be a problem. He'd have to see if Phillip could work out an outage with one of his contacts at the power company.

The house was a three-story modern brick with white trim and black shutters. Nothing extraordinary. James looked at the windows, noted the bloody handprint on one of the third-floor rooms. Probably a bedroom. The wolf would attack when they were sleeping, make it as quiet as possible. Bullets wouldn't kill, but they hurt like hell. Enough to make any werewolf wary of getting shot.

James cleared his head, let his ears do the work as the crowd chattered in low tones.

"No one heard anything?"

"Not a peep. Poor family. Good people."

"Oh, their dear children! Do you suppose?"

"I don't doubt it."

Someone cried softly.

"Hey! Tell us what's going on!" a small, balding man shouted from the other side of the police line. "Not any of your concern, sir," said the cop. "Please move along. There's nothing to see here."

"Oh, bullshit," the man shot back as he shook his fist. "You expect me to pretend everything's under control, do you?"

"I expect you to lower your voice, sir, and remain calm. I'm sure you have much more to do in your day than stand here making a bad scene worse." The officer's tone was firm and assertive. The man shook his head, turned away.

James made his way around, trying to catch the shouter as the man stalked across the yard and away from the scene, grumbling profanity under his breath.

"Excuse me, sir?"

The man turned, looked James up and down, seeming to note his shirt and old loafers. James would've felt out of place dressed as a lower-class working man walking around in a wealthy neighborhood if he cared at all about what people thought. He never wondered what people would think if they knew about his millions. He had much more important things to worry about than his appearance and societal acceptance.

Like a rogue werewolf.

"Can I help you?" the man said, not hiding his ire.

"As a matter of fact, you can." James pulled his wallet, flashed it quickly before putting it away. A trick Phillip had taught him. "Detective Bob Smith, Rock Hill Police."

The man looked at him again with a raised eyebrow.

"Plainclothes?"

"Yes," James said, keeping his tone polite. "Do you have a moment to answer some questions? I noticed you trying to speak with the officer back there before he turned you away." *Appeal to them, make them think you're on their side.* Another trick Phillip had taught him.

The man grunted. "Fuckin' asshole, that one," he said, gesturing toward the scene.

"Did you witness anything?"

"No, I didn't," the man said. "It happened overnight. I was up takin' a piss, heard nothing. Well, someone's dog got out, but that's about all."

James's neck hair stood up again. "Dog?"

The man shrugged. "Yeah, a dog. Someone's mutt. Sniffin' around the yards, barking. Damn near woke up my wife." He gestured at the scene again. "I oughta file a report. It's neighborhood policy, you know. Keep your fuckin' dog locked up."

"Who lived in that house?" James asked, wanting to move on before the man began to rant again. He logged the bit about the dog in his memory for later. "Did you know them?"

"Yeah, Samuel Pickens," the man said. "Big-shot lawyer. Moved in about a year ago. He don't own a dog, so I knew it wasn't his."

"Wife?" James pushed. "Children?"

"Yeah, he's got a wife...*had* a wife, I guess. Two kids. Boy and girl. Girl's a teenager. About to go to Winthrop, I think. Boy ain't far behind."

"They live at home?"

"Yeah, they do. Kids are damned loud, too." The man snorted. "Girl not as much. Just comes home late from her night shift. The boy? Hellion, that one. Threw a loud damn party last week while his folks were away. Woke up to a kid passed out on my front porch and two in the back yard screwin' their brains out. Called the cops. Damned kids. At least keep it in your own yard."

James nodded, gave a smile to keep himself from calling the man something vulgar.

"Thank you for your time, sir."

He turned and walked back toward Phillip's squad car as the man called out to him.

"Hey! Look into that dog, will ya? He left a big pile of shit in my yard!"

"Good," James muttered under his breath. "Fall into it."

He opened the passenger side and got in, leaving the door open for the fresh air while he waited on Phillip to finish up. He closed his eyes, rubbed his face as he pulled out a notepad from Phillip's glovebox and began to jot down what the annoying man had said. Dog. That was easy. The werewolf was clumsy, loud. Didn't know to keep quiet during a hunt. Probably young.

And in need to answer the call of nature.

James made sure to jot down the bit about the dog poop. It would give him a clearer scent on the werewolf. Not that he relished the thought of sticking his face in another person's shit. He'd likely vomit afterward were it not for his canine side. But it was as close as he could get to a strong lead on the lycanthrope unless the bastard started cutting himself and bleeding all over the place.

It was something.

Samuel Pickens. Why did the name sound familiar? Something that'd happened a couple of years ago, maybe? It rang a bell, but James couldn't place it. It was something big. But what?

He looked up from his notes as Phillip opened the car door, plopped down into the driver's seat, and pulled the radio from its holster.

"Dispatch, come back."

"Go ahead."

Phillip took a second, catching his breath. He looked sick. Pale. Horrified. "Send a cleaning crew with the medical examiner. They'll need buckets. Over."

James watched as Phillip rested his arms on the wheel, laid his head down, and breathed deeply.

"Are you alright?" James asked.

Phillip shook his head. "I've been doing this since we graduated college. Ten years, James. I've never seen anything like this." He sat up, leaning back and resting his head on the headrest. "That monster, whatever it is…it tore them all apart."

James looked back at the house.

"Samuel Pickens," he said. "Does the name ring a bell? Lawyer."

"I believe so," Phillip said. "In fact, yes. There was a major sting. A bust. Human trafficking. They arrested a man they figured would turn on his bosses. Pickens was his defense attorney. The evidence was too much, and he lost. Suspect ended up in jail. That was… God, that was only a few years ago. Three, I think. Yeah, three." James looked back at him.

Phillip nodded toward the house. "That's them in there, alright. Pickens, his wife, and his kid."

"Kids," James said.

"I know, right?" Phillip said, shaking his head and looking away from the house. "Tragic."

"No, I mean 'kids' as in plural," James said, looking down at his notes. "He has two. A son and a daughter."

Phillip sat up. "We only found the remains of two males in there. One female. The wife."

James pointed at the house next door. "His rather obnoxious neighbor mentioned that she's not far from going to college. It's possible she's out on a tour. It's almost the weekend, after all. The guy thinks she's looking into Winthrop."

"Wonderful," Phillip said, shaking his head. "It means I get to track her down."

"If she's going to Winthrop, it shouldn't be too difficult."

Phillip looked at him. "I could try to get a warrant to track her cell phone. It'll take some time, though. Maybe end of the day, depending on the workload."

"Get me inside," James said suddenly. He had to see it. Confirm who he might be looking for.

"How?" Phillip said. "You're a civilian. Look at you. You look like you slept in a fucking cardboard box."

James smiled wryly. "I'm sure you can figure something out."

"I'm not doing it," Phillip said, crossing his arms defiantly. "You can't make me."

You're a dickhead; you know that?" Phillip grunted. "Special Consultant! Do you know what kind of ass-chewing I'll be in for later for doing this?"

"It'll be worth it," James said. "Show me the third floor."

Phillip grunted a few more profanities as he led James through the living room and to the staircase, cursing the name "Bob Smith" the entire way.

"Bob Smith," he muttered.

James grinned.

"It's what I could come up with in a pinch."

"Yeah, well 'Bob Smith' can suck a fat one."

"Be nice."

"Blow me."

James could already smell the blood from upstairs. There was another scent, rancid and fecal. Disembowelment.

Phillip stopped at the top of the stairs on the third floor. He pointed down the hall to the farthest room.

"I've already seen it," he said, looking green. "It's all yours. Enjoy."

James nodded, walked down the hall without a word. The stench was stronger now, blood and meat mixed with shit. He reached the door at the end of the corridor, breathed out, opened it.

He'd seen worse done to animals.

The room was drenched in blood, streaks along the walls, bloodied handprints, pools coagulating on the floor and bed. Truthfully, it wasn't much different from the other house in that regard, though there was more blood since there were three victims as opposed to one.

However, parts and pieces of the victims hung from the ceiling fan, bedposts, and any other fixture in the room the killer could find. Three heads, a man, a woman, and a teen boy, were stuck onto three of the four bedposts as if put on display, their faces still carrying the pain and horror of their deaths in frozen expressions. Entrails had been strung around the room like decorations, dripping blood onto the floor.

It explained the shit smell, at least.

The scene was unnerving. Not because of the macabre nature of it. Gore didn't bother James. He saw plenty any time he went on a hunt, and he'd seen enough over the years to numb him to it.

It was something else.

"This wasn't a feeding," he said to Phillip. He turned and found his friend standing in the hallway facing the opposite direction, a cloth over his face.

"Alright," said Phillip. "If it wasn't a feeding, then what?"

James looked back at the carnage surrounding him in the room.

"This was vengeance. They consumed none of the parts, from what I can tell." James gazed at the heads again, taking a closer look at their horrified expressions. He moved over to the small fireplace in the room, three torsos stacked in the rack like wood. Bruising, lacerations, ribs protruding. "He tortured these people. Tore them apart piece by piece. Probably forced the father to pick. Made him watch. Likely the boy went first while the parents looked on. Mother. Then father."

"And you figure that how?" Phillip asked from the doorway.

James shrugged, his tone casual when he spoke. "It's what I would do."

"Nice. I'll keep that in mind next time I need a massacre."

James looked past the dresser piled high with organs, up to the intestines draped around the room.

"This is a message. We were meant to see this. You said the daughter wasn't here?"

"Yeah, that's right."

James looked out the window, off into the distance.

"We need to find her. Our killer isn't done. Not in the least."

3

Phillip agreed and dropped James off at the downtown library. He'd tried to Google the Pickens family and had found a few tidbits here and there, but something still nudged at the edge of his mind.

"They don't make everything public," Phillip had said. "The archives would probably have something if anything is missing from the internet. Might have to go old-school."

James opened the car door as Phillip finished his phone conversation.

"Right. Sure. Thanks, Murph." He pressed the "End Call" button on the screen and looked at James. "Missing daughter came back as one Clara Pickens. They're trying to locate her now."

"Winthrop, I'll bet," said James. "May take some time. It's not a small place."

Phillip nodded toward the library.

"Be discreet," he said. "I'll likely hear about bringing you in to look at the scene. It won't be so easy to explain why you're fishing around in the library archives."

James grinned.

"Simply a student with a curiosity," he said. "I do love the subject of True Crime."

"Just call me when you finish."

Phillip shook his head as James shut the door and jogged up the front steps.

The York County Public Library was small by comparison to the larger government buildings in South Carolina, but still a decent size. Large enough to accommodate any books the community might have the desire to read as well as serving as home to a proper archive in the basement. James and Phillip had agreed that James would research Pickens while Phillip dug into the Pickens's household to locate a possible lead on the daughter's whereabouts. Not all reports would be digitized for the internet, and the police also kept a section of the library archive for their closed or cold cases. Phillip had been able to get James clearance as a researcher a long time ago, providing James typed up the occasional report and published it on a blog as proof he wasn't just snooping around.

The library carpet was clean, the shelves lining the walls polished wood and full of books. James's interest was in the newspaper archives. The librarian, a bespectacled woman young enough to be a freshman at Winthrop, kindly led him down the stairs into the cold, dimly lit archive area. She instructed him on how to use the microfiche machine, how to search the online catalog for articles, and left with a flirtatious smile and a suggestion that he come to only her if he needed help.

He smiled as he flipped over the small note card she'd given him with the microfiche instructions printed on the front, noting her telephone number scrawled beneath her name.

"Right," he said to himself. "Thank you, Carly. Mr. Pickens, then."

James spent the next two hours parked in front of the microfiche viewer and computer database, scrolling through report after report on Samuel Pickens. The man had been someone of importance in Rock Hill, responsible for aiding some of the most notorious criminals. Some of the men had been accused of horrors, mostly tied to organized crime. Pickens had gotten all of them off, ensuring no time spent in jail, and some on probation for ridiculously short amounts of time. Even the terms of probation had always been arguably lax. Stay at home and watch television. Volunteer at the animal shelter.

The man had been good at his job.

Something caught his eye. He stopped on one article, noting the date placing the trial around the same timeframe as the enormous human trafficking bust James remembered from three years prior.

"Lawyer Hired to Defend Hitman."

Odd. Why would a crime boss spend the money on a lawyer in defense of an enforcer? Henchmen typically did a small amount of time while their bosses paid whomever they needed to pay to shorten the sentence. That bribe typically shaved years down to months or even days, and it was usually cheaper than hiring an attorney.

James scanned the article, suddenly remembering the details as the report confirmed his suspicions with every paragraph.

Mr. Wade Anderson, thirty-four, of Clover, SC, was convicted today after a long and emotional courtroom trial ending with a life sentence and no hope for parole. The trial comes after a major sting operation led by the local authorities that resulted in one of the largest human trafficking raids in South Carolina history.

"It took more time than we'd have liked," Police chief Brian Chesterfield told reporters. "But we managed to capture several clients and an enforcer."

"We offered a plea agreement," special prosecutor Michael Jones told reporters. "The defense wouldn't budge. We had him cold. Now Mr. Anderson will see his full sentence through."

James kept reading, the article outlining the details of the plea agreement. A reduced sentence of ten years. It was a gem of a deal considering the charges, which read like a checklist for anyone looking to be the worst human being possible. Rape. Solicitation. Child molestation and endangerment. Trafficking.

Pickens got cocky, tried to plea for a better deal. Less jail time. The prosecution wouldn't budge, and Pickens went in for "all or nothing." Anderson was sentenced within a week and sent to Livesay Correctional Institution in Spartanburg.

James clicked the next article to see if any details had been left out. All the news outlets reported the same story. He went back to the microfiche to see if the police reports said anything. Nothing. He returned to the shelf and pulled the file on Wade Anderson. He sat down, opened it, and began reading.

Prisoner Found Dead in Cell. Ruled as Homicide.

"This just got interesting," James said to himself.

The report came with pictures of the scene. A body torn to bits. Reported as prison violence. Inmates had a code. Kill, sell drugs, or assault someone. Have at it. Harm a child? Especially sexually? It was a good way to get raped, beaten, or killed in the general population.

James grunted. To anyone else, it was cut and dry: there was no feasible way Wade Anderson was the killer. Being dead tended to hinder one's capacity for murder.

James logged out of the computer, left the files and slides on the table where the librarian had indicated, and left, nodding to Carly on his way out. She wasn't unattractive in the least. He smiled as he held up the card she'd given him. She blushed, smiling as he waved. Maybe he'd call her later.

The company of the opposite sex tended to be scarce when one spent one's evenings howling at the moon.

I remember that," Phillip said, sitting back in the booth. "Fucked up scene. There wasn't enough left to make a proper identification, but Anderson had never been one to participate in shenanigans around the prison, either."

James had called Phillip with his findings. The two agreed to make up for the breakfast that had been interrupted by an inconvenient multiple homicide and met for lunch at the White Horse, a restaurant across from Winthrop University.

James nodded to the waitress as she cleared the dishes from their table and offered refills on their drinks. Phillip shook his head. James asked for more Coke.

"Shenanigans?"

"Every now and again, it gets loud and…well, let's just call it interesting in the prison blocks." Phillip fished his small notebook out of his coat pocket as he spoke. "The original warden tried to run a tight ship, but there were scuffles regularly. There's also an organized crime ring in among the prisoners. Anderson never got himself involved." Phillip opened the notebook and looked it over. "According to the guards still working there, Mr. Anderson was quiet. Kept out of trouble, and away from the rest of the populace. Anti-social."

James chuckled. "Aren't we all?"

"Well, the other prisoners still didn't like him," Phillip said. "The general population isn't friendly to guys who hurt kids. I was surprised he wasn't dead the first day when he came in."

"Yeah, you've told me before. Some code they have."

"He's not our killer. It took several buckets to carry the remains out of that cell. The door was broken in, and the inmates got hold of him."

James leaned in. "And you know better than that," he said, his voice low. "Those buckets of gore were not Wade Anderson."

Phillip lowered his voice, leaning in as well. "You believe he's our rogue wolf?"

"I've no reason to doubt it," James said. "In fact, I meant to ask you if you brought the stuff I asked you for."

Phillip passed a large manila envelope across the table. James picked it up, opened it, and glanced inside. He looked up at Phillip, his eyebrow raised.

"Underwear?"

"Best I could do," Phillip said, shrugging as he sipped his Coke.

"I find that difficult to believe."

Phillip shrugged again. "You can disbelieve all you want," he said. "But there it is, isn't it?"

James gave a small sniff, recoiling at the stench.

"They didn't bother washing them?"

Phillip grinned. "Three-year-old cock-sweat has a certain tinge to it, doesn't it?" He sat back. "They were claimed as evidence and locked away after the murder. Damn near the only thing not covered in blood, I'm afraid."

"This is disgusting."

Phillip's grin grew. "This is payback for the rather sizeable mound of werewolf shit you so kindly left in my back yard," he said, shrugging again. "And it's also the only surviving piece of Anderson's effects."

James was about to argue, then laughed despite himself. He'd been visiting Phillip at his home a few months ago when the full moon hit. James had gone on his run and was returning when the urge hit him. He was unable to change back until the moon was out of the sky, and Phillip's toilet wouldn't support a one-thousand-pound werewolf. The back yard had been the most logical place.

And, of course, a pile of shit a foot tall did not go unnoticed by the homeowner.

"Have at it," Phillip said, gesturing at the envelope. "Take it all in, Spot. Nice and deep."

James set the envelope aside.

"Later," he said. "Any word on Clara Pickens?"

Phillip shook his head, his expression returning to seriousness.

"She was last seen at Winthrop touring the campus," he said, leafing through the notebook. "I spoke with a few people out there. She was there with a man. They seemed close. Maybe a boyfriend?"

"Possible," James said. "Any idea who he is?"

"No, not a clue." Phillip closed the notebook and put it back in his coat pocket. "No one has any leads on him yet. A couple of my detectives are questioning her friends, so it's only a matter of time."

James nodded and waved to the waitress.

"My treat next time," he said.

Phillip grunted as he pulled his wallet from his coat.

"It's worth it knowing you'll be inhaling sweat fumes from another man's groin."

The waitress stopped short, the check in her hand and her mouth hanging wide open. Phillip looked from her to James and back, his eyes wide in horror.

"I...I mean..." he stammered.

The waitress raised an eyebrow as her look of shock turned to disgust. She dropped the ticket on the table. "No worries, sweetie," she said. "Adults make their own decisions."

Phillip sheepishly laughed as he gestured between him and James.

"We're not...we're not a couple."

James snorted. "I like dark meat."

The waitress walked away as Phillip glared at James, fuming.

The detectives called Phillip with no new information. The only item of interest was their recollection of Clara's boyfriend. They knew she'd been seeing someone recently, but no one knew his name. He'd just started at the university, and she'd met him during one of her trips there. The relationship was good, and not likely anything to warrant concern.

Phillip logged it regardless.

"I'd like to know more about this young man," he said to James as they drove back toward downtown. "It's interesting to me that she met him so recently and is suddenly nowhere to be found."

"One would think she'd have told her friends his name, at least," James said, reading through the report. Phillip was keeping James off the books, so the file didn't contain anything more than what the rest of the department knew. James was more interested in the photos of the bedroom and house. He studied them, trying to find anything he may have missed earlier.

That, and he was also getting an idea of the layout for later when he went to wolf for his search.

"Not necessarily," Phillip said, keeping his eyes on the road. "My cousin dated a man casually for a few weeks before she told anyone she was seeing someone. She wanted to feel it out, first. Make sure it didn't end up like the last one."

James looked at him sidelong.

Phillip cleared his throat. "It ended up like the last one."

James looked back at the photos of the carnage-drenched bedroom. Something stuck out that he didn't notice before. One of the heads, presumably Samuel Pickens's, had a strange mark carved into the side of the face, close to his ear. James couldn't make it out from the photo. The detail was too hazy.

"What's this marking next to his ear?"

"Saw that, did you?" Phillip said. "There's another photo with a close-up."

James leafed to the next photo, the marking much clearer. It looked cleaner, the photo taken in the morgue. The pattern was unlike anything he'd seen.

"Like some kind of rune or something."

Phillip sighed. "I was hoping you'd seen it before."

"No, never."

"Damn it," Phillip muttered. "Back to square one."

"Not entirely," James said. "I'll take note of it, see if I find it elsewhere in the house."

Phillip raised an eyebrow. "Another search?"

"Our killer werewolf left a sizable gift for the Pickens's neighbor," James said. "I'm wagering I can get a clear scent from it and track him down easier."

"Let me make sure I'm understanding something," Phillip said, putting his hand to his head as if warding off a headache. "You complain about smelling a pair of boxers not washed in three years, but you'll gladly stick your face in someone else's shit to get a scent?"

James looked at him, smiling wryly. "It's a dog thing."

P hillip's warning ran through James's mind one more time.

"You've got thirty minutes," he'd said before James got out of the car. "After that, you're on all fours. I can't be caught out here like this."

Phillip wasn't exactly pleased with James's twofold plan. First, look for clues the police would've missed because, frankly, the force was lacking in the lycanthrope department. And, while searching, be ready for the likelihood that the killer would return to the house looking for Clara Pickens.

The second one was more of James's focus.

Philip had given him a key and left to return to the police department to continue his search for Clara. The front foyer was large enough for James to enter the change and start his own search.

He leapt the back fence into the neighbor's yard easily, his powerful rear legs sending him over by a good six feet. He landed deftly, the sound minimal, and searched the yard with his yellowed vision. The lights in the obnoxious man's house were out, the family asleep. James lowered his nose to the ground, taking in the scents and letting them run up his long nasal cavity. He opened his mouth, let the odors in over his tongue. Grass, of course. Rubber from children's shoes. A dropped peanut butter sandwich. Grease splashed from the impressive gas grill on the back patio. Cat shit. Dog shit.

Lots of dog shit.

The smell was different. Normal dog feces had a sharper stench to it from the kibble people fed them. Obviously, Mr. McLoudmouth had a pooch. But there was something different in the yard: the duller, more nauseating smell of feces that came from something larger, and with a meatier diet.

James kept to all fours, sniffing as he went. He stopped when he got to a spot in the back corner, the smell overpowering. The grass was still moderately coated, but McLoudmouth had cleaned up the large pile earlier.

The smell was different from James's disregarded meals. It carried harshness to it. Musk. James turned away from it and bounded back across the yard, clearing the fence in one leap as he headed toward the Pickens residence. He went inside, his scent memory locked on the musk. It smelled faintly of the same aroma he'd caught when Phillip had flashed him with Anderson's underwear, though not as sweaty.

He stood to full height, his ears scraping the ceiling as he sniffed. Blood was still in the air, now duller from drying. The forensics team hadn't been able to remove it all. It wouldn't surprise James a bit if they would need to pull out drywall and flooring to fully get the smell and stains out.

James went back to all fours and headed up the stairs toward the room. He stopped at the one on the right, the door closed. Pink, glittered letters adorned the door. He looked at them closer through his yellow vision.

Clara.

He pushed at the door, found it slightly open. He wandered in, being careful not to disturb anything. Not an easy feat given his size in his monstrous form, but doable. The room was cluttered, but clean. Dolls and collectibles lined the walls, sitting on shelves amongst about a hundred books. The bed was neatly made. James moved to the dresser, sniffing as he went, trying to get a clear scent on her. He snorted, shook his head as he recoiled from the dresser, and blew air out of his nostrils, spraying the wall with dirt and snot. Dust? Not just a normal amount. He ran a clawed hand over an empty surface on her make-up table, turning it over and looking at his palm. There was an inch of dust on everything. She'd been gone longer than a few days. A person who took care to keep as much stuff in her room as she did would also dust regularly, keep her collection clean.

James moved to the four-post canopy bed. The wooden posts were lovely, ornate, the canopy made of white silk. Clara was the family princess. No doubt about it. He sniffed the bedding and could smell traces of human female on the threading of the clean sheets.

Something on the headboard caught his eye.

He moved closer to it, narrowing his eyes. A small carving, possibly the size of a penny, resided in the uppermost right-hand corner of the wooden headboard—the same symbol found on Samuel Pickens's face in the morgue.

These people were marked, he thought to himself.

Something bumped downstairs. James froze, his pointed ears perking up at the sound. He turned, baring his teeth as he listened. Another bump, a soft growl.

Every muscle in James's werewolf body tensed. He ground his claws into the carpet, bracing for an attack, readying to pounce once the killer were reached the doorway. He breathed out, waited as he listened to the telltale sound of the enormous creature climbing the stairs on all fours. He heard the wolf sniff, heard him pause on the staircase.

No, James thought. *Keep coming. Don't stop.*

The other wolf growled again, this time low and warning as it appeared at the top of the stairs. James watched the hackles stand up, watched the wolfman tense as it stood to full height and looked around the landing. The other were was every bit as large as James, its fur black and its muscles rippling under the natural coat as it sniffed with its mouth open and teeth bared.

James moved to the doorway, his yellowed eyes locked on his enemy. The other lycanthrope tensed, glared at him, sprang at him, its teeth bared. James moved in an instant, rushing the attacker. The two werewolves collided in the hall, rolling to the floor in a heap of snapping jaws and savagery. James bucked the were off, swiped at him with his claws. He missed by millimeters, and the enemy took the advantage and tackled James, bowling into him and sending him over the rail. James tumbled only a little before slamming into the floor below, the wood cracking and caving under the impact. The attacker leapt from the landing. James rolled, missing the attack just barely as he sprang to all fours and pounced. He gripped the werewolf in his large clawed hands, spun, slung him into a wall, dust and debris raining down as the wall caved. The werewolf shook his head, stunned. James bared his teeth and barked at him.

Come at me!

The wolf regarded him coolly, shook off the disorientation as he stood and bared his teeth back at James. He swung, barely missing as James ducked.

That scent. It was brief, only a split second. James glanced at the other werewolf's groin as he stood back up and made for Anderson's throat.

He knew that scent.

Anderson, he thought. *That settles that. Might not chew on Phillip after all.*

Anderson jerked backward, James's jaws snapping shut on air. Anderson slapped James in the side, raked his claws over James's ribs, bloody trenches left in their wake. Anderson bowled him into the wall, knocked the wind out of him. The wall gave, and James felt cool brick through the fur on his back. Anderson pulled him back, slammed him again, the brick cracking and bowing. James struggled, but Anderson wailed him in the side of the skull, dizzying him. James's arms felt heavier. Anderson pulled him back, snarled in his face, opened his jaws to bite James in the throat. James braced against him, kicked out, sending Anderson flying backward and propelling himself at the wall. The brick gave way, and the warm night air greeted him as he fell to the grass below.

James pushed himself up slowly, shook off the blow. The landing hadn't been nearly as hard as some of Anderson's attacks. He looked around, sniffed the air as he tried to clear his mind. He needed to leave before—

"What the fucking hell?!"

James turned, the scent of human sweat strong in the air. He saw the man from earlier, McLoudmouth, standing on the opposite side of the yard with a hunting rifle nested in his arm, a small poodle on a leash still poised in the squatting position as it deposited small turds onto the lawn. Its eyes were wide with fright, almost as wide as its owner's.

Not. Fucking. Good. James thought.

He turned and ran as McLoudmouth fired a shot. The bullet zipped by James's ear as he leapt the back fence, hit the ground on the other side, and took off on all fours at a full sprint toward the woods opposite the yard where he'd landed. It was a mere second before trees were whipping by, flora and fauna filling his senses with a cool and soothing fragrance as he churned up the moist earth. He slowed when he reached a creek, tempted to shift back into human form. He was miles from home.

Damn.

He stood tall, sniffed the air for his direction, and began his trek back toward his apartment.

4

The morning sun was beginning to bleed into the sky, the orange streaks cutting into the night, slowly spreading as James climbed into his apartment through the window. He let his human form become clearer in his mind, breathed out slowly as he began to shrink down to his height of six foot four. His skin began to cool, the fur coat fading away to bare human flesh. The morning air was crisp, biting. He quickly shut the window, found his robe, and began to wash up for a few hours of sleep before he had to face Phillip.

He shook his head. Phillip was going to go nuts.

Not that angering Phillip was something he dreaded. The policeman tended to be more humorous when he was angry. But Phillip was also working to keep James off the radar, and stunts like last night didn't help.

James finished brushing his teeth and was walking toward his unmade bed when the sound of a fist hammering on his door stopped him.

"James," Phillip called from the other side of the door, his tone rich with fury. "James! Open this door, *now!* Wake up! I know you're in there, you asshole!"

James sighed, gathered his nerves, and opened the door. Phillip stepped in, pushing James back and slamming the door shut behind him. The man's face was dark, his eyes wide with anger. His smaller stature was tense, his teeth gritted under his beard. He carried a rolled newspaper in his hand.

"You," he said, pointing the paper at James. "Yes, *you*, are a fucking *twat!* Of all the ignorant, braindead, stupid things you could do! What the hell were you thinking? Better question: *were* you thinking?"

James sighed again. "Good morning, Phillip. I've not slept yet."

"Fuck your sleep," Phillip spat. "You'll be lucky to get any *form* of rest today after what you did last night."

"What's the newspaper for?"

Phillip looked down at the paper, then back at James. He launched at him, smacking him over the head and shoulders with the rolled newspaper, emphasizing each blow with "Bad dog! *Bad! Dog!*" while James held his hands up in defense and backed away. Phillip stopped hitting him long enough to open James's laptop on the table, open Safari, and pull up the local news.

Large Dog-Monster at Pickens Murder Scene!

James swallowed back the lump in his throat. He went to the laptop and scrolled down in the article. "Well, then," he said. "I see I've made the front page."

"Jokes?" Phillip said, still angry. "You were seen, and *shot* at, and you make jokes? Are you out of your fucking *mind?!*"

James didn't look up as he scanned the article. "It's my defense mechanism."

"Stupidity isn't a proper defense."

"Chalk it up to mental illness."

James felt his skin run to gooseflesh as he read McLoudmouth's statement.

"He was big! Huge! Never seen one like that! Tremendous!" Winchester, the Pickens's former neighbor, claims to be an expert on dogs. His description, however, was deeply troubling.

Hmph, James thought. *Winchester? I prefer McLoudmouth.*

"No breed like that in my books," Winchester continued. "This thing looked like a wolf and a man all in one. Maybe a gorilla in the mix, big as he was. If he stood, I'd give him eight feet tall. Arms big as tree trunks! Believe me! Very big! Very large!"

"Write him off as mental," James said nonchalantly as he closed the laptop. "He's clearly troubled."

Phillip moved closer to James, put his hand on the table as if he was trying not to strike it with his fist.

"It's too late for that, James," he said, failing the fight to keep his tone even. "The papers are already referencing the Wolf Man Murders. They mention your father by name. The department is all over it. They're pulling every file they have on it."

James went to his window, looking out over the town as the sun continued to rise, slowly turning the sky a dull morning blue. He muttered as his mind spun. He knew it was only a matter of time before the sins of his father came back to bite him. "Shit."

"Shit?" Phillip echoed. "Really, James? I've just told you that you've screwed the pooch on this, that you may be exposed for what you are, and the best you can do is 'shit'?"

James smirked as he spoke over his shoulder. "Screwed the pooch. I like it."

"We need a plan, and we need it now," Phillip said. "You don't have long before the captain calls for you to be dragged in by your scruff."

"Then what?" James turned to him. "You'd let them?"

"You have no idea the damage control I'm having to do because of you," Phillip said, his tone dark and angry. "Vampires. Witches. Anything that moves in the dark or hides under a bed, and I'm stuck keeping the department unaware while you take care of the problem. It keeps them off your back, I'll have you know. But this is a shit storm, James. People know who you are. Who your father was. This incident last night is going to make things worse."

"He was there," James said. Phillip blinked, caught off guard. James continued before his friend could get going again. "Anderson. He's our killer. And our other werewolf."

"Am I to assume he left the scene before you could stop him?"

James nodded. Phillip cursed, smacked the back of the chair in front of him with his hand.

"A lot of good that does us," he said. "It would've been easier to turn the attention away from you. Paint him like a deranged killer."

James turned, his eyebrow raised. "What about him *isn't* deranged?"

Phillip nodded. "Fair." He stood tall, his eyes widening. James knew that look.

"I have an idea," Phillip said. "You need to come down to the station with me."

James narrowed his eyes at Phillip. He hated institutions of any kind. Schools, police departments, hospitals, they all made him nervous. They all felt like prisons to him, cold and entrapping. "I'd rather get some sleep."

Phillip waved off James's stubbornness. "If I bring you in, I can interrogate you, lowball you with easy questions, steer it in a direction that takes suspicion off you. At least in the department."

"It won't work," James said as he went to the kitchenette. He opened the cabinet and pulled out the coffee, his French Press, and his favorite mug. "They're still people." He turned and looked at Phillip. "Paranoia is a powerful thing. Coffee?"

"Please. And agreed," Phillip said. "It won't be an end-all, but it'll buy us time to stop this son of a bitch before something else—"

The radio Phillip kept on his belt crackled.

"Sergeant Brown, respond. Dispatch to Sergeant Brown."

Phillip pulled the walkie off his belt and spoke into it.

"Go ahead, dispatch."

"Another murder, sir. Stand by for location."

Phillip had changed his mind rather quickly once the call came through. James was to stay at home. Period. No going out for any reason.

"I may have need to go to the farmers' market on the corner," he'd argued, not wanting to be cooped up.

"Get over it."

It was an hour later when James's phone rang. He put down the book he'd been reading to pass the time and answered.

"A fucking *judge*," Phillip grumbled before James could say "hello." James could see the man shaking his head in his mind's eye.

"Another mess, I presume?"

"Good guess," Phillip said. "Our boy, from the looks of it. Same MO. Bodies torn apart, room decorated with their guts. He managed the entire family this time. But there's another element here you need to see."

"What is it?"

"A message. Written on a piece of paper. I grabbed it before the boys could see it and bag it."

"What's it say?"

James heard Phillip rustle something on the other end, the sound of a piece of paper being unfolded.

"Keep looking. You'll never find her."

James cursed under his breath. Of course. "I believe we can consider this extremely bad."

"Agreed," Phillip said. "Human trafficking is a deep cave to wander into, James. There's no telling where she may be. Could be here in Rock Hill. Could be on the other side of the ocean. That business knows no boundaries."

It made sense, now. Anderson's employer had paid top dollar to make sure his personal werewolf enforcer didn't spend any time behind bars. He'd failed, and Anderson had done time. It was obvious the murders were about revenge, but there had to be another element. Another agenda. Why risk being spotted? Why the carnage? Werewolves were able to maintain their human reasoning and intelligence now. They'd evolved. Anderson could've easily broken into the houses, snapped necks, and left quietly. Maybe even simply slit their throats. Simple. No gore.

No, Anderson was up to something. He wanted these murders to draw attention.

He was making a point.

But what about the first murder? He'd consumed most of the victim. The Pickens family, the judge, and his family, all had been mauled and torn apart.

"Phillip, what about the first victim? Who was he?"

James could picture Phillip shaking his head.

"No name on him yet. Some accountant."

An officer spoke to Phillip in the background.

"I've got to run. The medical examiner is here. He needs some sweet-talk to come in and look at the scene."

James hung up after the line went dead.

He could try to peg down the next place Anderson might go, fight him again. Kill him. But then what? Clara Pickens would still be missing, and the game would continue without a killer werewolf running amok.

James spent the next few hours pacing around in his apartment. He didn't usually long to go out, but he felt like a caged animal in his living room. He needed to leave, try to find anything he could. The police wouldn't know the first thing about hunting down a werewolf. If they found Anderson, he would maul all of them, their bullets useless against him. They wouldn't think to use silver rounds.

James looked around his apartment, the clutter once welcoming now confining, stifling.

"To hell with this," he muttered. "Fucking apartment."

He changed his clothes, put on his shoes, and grabbed his coat on the way out.

J ames decided to head toward the small tea shop a few blocks down, yearning for the caffeine rush to give him an edge over his sorely neglected sleep. The place was low-key, quiet, the clientele generally college students looking for a decent place to study while they overdosed on caffeine to keep themselves awake for whatever final examination lay ahead. The shop also had a generous assortment of pastries. James's tastes typically turned toward meat, preferably rare, if cooked at all. But he had a weakness for a homemade pastry, and The Coffee Bean had the best orange scones in York County.

At least in James's humble opinion.

He sat in a far-off booth in the most remote corner of the shop, his back against the wall so he could see who came in and out. He had a clear view out the window next to him. There were only two other people in the café besides him and the barista. The two customers were college students, one of them looking as if he might lay his head down and sleep at any moment. The girl a few tables down pored over books, taking notes diligently as she turned pages, then switched to another open book on the opposite side of the table.

James glanced at the barista, who looked away quickly, busily cleaning a coffee cup as she walked to the opposite end of the counter from where he sat. He looked out the window. He wasn't an unattractive man. He'd gotten used to women looking at him long ago. He wondered, at times, how a woman would feel about him once she'd discovered his more... animalistic nature when the moon was right.

Or the mood.

He glanced her way again. She looked away once more, her hands shaking as she wiped down the countertop for a second time. Or was it a third? She refused to look up, purposefully keeping her eyes averted. She pulled out her cell phone, wrote a text, then put it back in her pocket. James let his sense of smell open a bit, drew in the scents around him. Coffee, sweets.

Sweat. Fear?

The hackles rose on his neck. Fool. Idiot. He hadn't thought about the ramifications of the stories in the paper. The people in the community knew they lived near David Coldstone's relative. The paranoia would be...*shit*.

James stood, approached the counter. He had to do something, *say* something to dissuade her fear. He kept his tone even, friendly, putting a smile on his face.

"Excuse me, miss?"

The girl startled, dropped her towel, turned to him. Her eyes were wide with fright, her voice wavering as she spoke. "Yes…yes, sir?"

James held out his cup. "Can I have a refill on my coffee, please?"

"Right," she said, approaching him cautiously. "Sure." She picked up the cup, moved quickly to the coffee dispenser, and emptied out the small amount he'd left in the cup before pouring a fresh brew. James glanced over his shoulder. The male college student had given in to sleep; the female kept her eyes on her books.

She glanced in his direction with her eyes, her face still pointed at the pages. She was checking him.

James turned back to the barista as she placed the cup down on the countertop. He reached into his pocket, but she waved her hand.

"It's okay," she said.

James looked at her, bewildered. "A refill costs, does it not? I don't mind paying."

"It's okay," the barista said. "You…I mean, you're in here so often. Why not?"

James smiled pleasantly at the girl. "Well, then. Thank you."

She nodded, glanced at the door, then back at him.

A young man walked in, possibly the same age as the barista. He was almost as tall as James, stocky as if he spent most of his time in the gym. He looked at her, nodded, then nudged his chin at James as he approached the counter.

"This him?" he said.

She turned away, keeping her head down as she went to the sink to wash a coffee pot that didn't need it—anything she could do to stay away from the situation.

James looked back at the tough, who stood tall and puffed out his chest.

"Hey, you," the man said. "Time to go."

James put on a grin as he looked from the ape to the barista and back to the ape again. "Sorry," he said, keeping his tone friendly. "I'm not sure I understand."

"Bullshit, you don't understand." The man took a step forward, moving a stool out of his way. James glanced at the two college students. The girl sat straight, watching the scene intently. The boy was waking up, rubbing his eyes as he looked around to see who was shouting.

James held his coffee in one hand as he placed the other to the side, palm open to show he wasn't armed. "I assure you, I'm confused. Have I done something?"

"You've upset my sister," said the man. "I get a text from her telling me James fucking Coldstone is in here, and she's scared out of her mind. Should be locked up. All of you. And shot."

"Not following."

"You mean to tell me you don't know anything about the murders?" The man took another step forward, balling his large fists as he went. "Look a bit familiar, don't they? Like something your old man would've done?"

There it was.

James bristled, forced his pleasant smile back into place. "I assure you," he said again. "I mean no trouble. Just came for a cup of coffee. I'll head out."

James made to walk by the man, but the tough stepped in his way, his beady eyes locked on James's. James tried the other way, but the tough slapped his hand down on the counter.

"This is counterproductive," James said with a grunt, his politeness more forced, his agitation showing.

"I think I'll make sure you don't bring your bone-chewin' ass back in here," the man said with a snarl.

"Bobby, please," the barista said, pleading as she stepped up behind the cash register. "Just let him leave. It's all I want, is him gone."

"Not without teaching him a lesson," Bobby said, tensing his not inconsiderable muscles.

James nodded, then looked at Bobby sidelong, his eyes hard as he stared at the younger man. "I would like to leave. I never intended to upset the young lady. But do not force me to do anything you might regret."

Bobby stepped even closer, his face inches from James's as he spoke in a low, threatening tone.

"I know what your daddy was. What your mother likely was." He looked James up and down. "What you likely are. Think I'm afraid of some big dog?"

Something inside James moved. The wolf shifted around, made a low growl in his mind. Something wasn't right. It wanted out. No.

It was being *pushed* out.

James broke into a sweat. He looked outside, saw the sunlight. He usually only shifted at night, and that was after a rest. The full moon had to be visible for him to be forced to change. But that was what he felt. The wolf wasn't being asked to come. It was coming.

"This is your final warning," James said, feeling the wolf being dragged from its rest in inside his mind. "Let me by."

Bobby stood his ground, holding his arms out as he glared into James's eyes. "You gonna move me, wolfman?"

James's vision yellowed, his teeth went sharp as he glowered back down at Bobby. The man's face went slack, his eyes wide in shock as James spoke around teeth growing too large for his mouth. "I just may."

The shift was painful, hard, slower than usual. His body grew to his eight-foot height, his muscles swelling around bone and bulging under skin instantly covered in a thick gray coat. His chest swelled, his legs elongating into powerful canine rears. His clothes ripped and shredded under the strain of his new form, his shoes splitting as clawed feet burst forth. His face stretched into a muzzle, his teeth fully grown and sharp. He looked down, turning his massive clawed hands over and back as if he'd never seen them before. He looked at Bobby, the now even smaller man cowering back, eyes wide in terror, mouth working as small high-pitched croaks escaped his throat. The smell of feces and urine was thick in the air, accompanied by the large soil spot growing down Bobby's jeans leg.

James looked at the college students. The girl had fallen back in her chair, was weeping as she scrambled to get to her feet. The girl behind the counter had fled to the back room, the door still swinging.

The boy sat, his eyes wide, observing.

Something stirred in James's mind. He heard a low growl deep from within the recesses, felt it cling to him. A wolf entering his mind's eye, its yellowed eyes staring at him, wide and focused with dominance. Hunger.

Freedom.

James tried to force the change back, but the wolf wouldn't budge. He heard the barista in the back on the phone, weeping as she spoke to the police. He looked back to Bobby, the boy's jeans now completely soiled, and his fists up and shaking.

James sighed.

Might as well make the best of it. I'm truly fucked here.

James hunched, his shoulders up as he tensed every muscle in his giant were body and held his arms out to the sides with his clawed fingers spread. He snarled, the sound like a roar. Bobby screamed, the sound shrill and high as he turned and ran, knocking over tables as he went. James reared back, raised his muzzle high, and unleashed his howl. The humans clamped their hands over their ears, the college students fleeing for the door. The boy stopped and looked back at James.

He was grinning.

5

J ames made after the boy, hitting all fours as he loped at the door. The kid darted out, cut a hard right and took off. James went through the door, glass and doorframe giving way like paper, the metal fragile, and the glass bouncing harmlessly off his thick coat. He saw the guy sprint across the street, cars stopping and honking at him.

I've got questions for you, James thought at the kid. He made for him at top speed, the distance closing quickly. A school bus slammed on the brakes as James crossed the street; cars stopped in front of him. He leapt over them easily, the screams of the people inside matching the shouts and shrieks of those on the sidewalks who caught full sight of the massive werewolf chasing down a fleeing college student.

The kid ducked right into an alleyway. James followed, barreled through a couple of trashcans the boy had knocked over in a futile attempt to slow James down.

The kid ran up the tall wood fence at the end of the alley, grabbed the top, and flipped over without losing his pace.

Agile, aren't we? James thought. *It won't save you.*

James kicked out with his powerful hind legs, caught the fire escape high in the air on the left, and swung over the wall, landing at a run. He kept moving, saw the kid duck behind the Cobb House apartment building.

"*Now!*"

The voice startled James, giving him pause just before a hail of gunfire peppered the wall next to him. He doubled back and hit the fire escape again, this time climbing to the top as more rounds whizzed by him. He looked around the roof, the closest building easily reached with his wolf form. He made for the ledge, leapt, landed squarely on the roof of the next building, rolled, kept moving. His tongue lolled over his teeth as he panted, his heart racing. He jumped again. Church. More buildings. Fine Arts Center. McHale's. The City Club. He leapt to another rooftop, landed on top of the Wells Fargo building, stopped to gather his surroundings.

His apartment was close. On the corner. One more good leap.

He moved to the ledge, stared down at the window that looked into his living room. He tried to shift again, but the wolf wouldn't budge.

His leg erupted in sudden agony, the pain taking him down onto his side. He looked down, saw the exit wound at his knee. The flesh was already healing back, the wound closing quickly.

Not silver, he thought. *Still fucking hurts.*

He looked in the direction the bullet had come from, his yellowed eyesight picking up the figure on the far rooftop as it ducked down behind a ledge, pulling the rifle with it.

Sniper. Outstanding. James got to his feet again as the wound finished healing. He turned and ran for the ledge, bounding across and landing on the roof of his apartment building. He ducked down and moved behind a large air conditioning unit. Another round would slow him down again. He needed to get to safety before someone smarter than the rest of them figured out what they were dealing with and loaded their guns accordingly.

His apartment was out. They would already be waiting for him. He needed to find Phillip. Try to explain things.

If he could shift back.

James tried again, focused on his human form. If they found a naked man on top of the building, he could fake a psychotic episode. He'd done it before, gone full bore. He'd even drooled on himself and soiled his pants once in college. Phillip had been humiliated.

Good times.

The wolf clung on, frustrated, snarling in his mind. It didn't like being trapped, either.

James braced at the sound of the roof access door being kicked open. SWAT team members filed out, their rifles aimed as they shouted to each other.

"Over here! Footprints!"

"*Big* fuckin' monster! Son of a bitch is *huge!*"

"Dial it down, Hudson! Fan out, people. Check those corners!"

James could hear them coming closer, boots crunching on gravel. He looked around. The roof across the way wouldn't be far for him. Two good bounds if he kicked off right. The bullets would hurt, but he'd live.

He tensed his legs, the muscles powerful, rippling as he crouched. He pushed off; his body launched into the air. Shouts. Gunfire. Bullets zipped by him, barely missed as he flew toward the other rooftop. Almost there. Falling.

Too soon.

James reached out, grabbed the ledge to stop himself, slammed into the side of the building. The shelf gave under his large hand, the mortar crumbling. He slid down the brick, scrambling to find his grip as the building wall crumbled and chipped from the scraping. He hit a fire escape, the pain in his back jarring a yelp out of him, the metal railing bending under his weight. He toppled over onto the platform, the ladder shaking loose, the bolts in the brick pulling out from the force of his landing. He got to his feet, made for the nearby window as the fire escape gave out. He bowed his head, blowing through the window with his shoulder. He landed squarely on a carpeted floor and stood to full height, looking around quickly. The woman sitting in her chair screamed hysterically, scrambled up and over the back of the chair trying to get away as James looked down at her. He tried to speak to her. Calm her.

The loud, deep bark and whine seemed like less of a good idea than he'd initially thought.

Well shit, he thought as the woman ran for her bedroom, slamming the door behind her.

He looked around the small apartment. It wasn't much different from his, though he had to credit the poor woman on her housekeeping. Her apartment was immaculate, contrary to the sty that Phillip often referred to as a "crime scene."

Phone. He could dial Phillip. Maybe catch him at his office. Leave a message. Something.

James spotted an old-style house phone on the small table near the chair once occupied by the rightfully terrified woman. He tried to pick up the receiver, his claws making it hard to grip the little plastic thing. He managed to grip it and began to fiddle with the buttons, using his index claw to dial Phillip's desk number at the department.

"Rock Hill Police Department Operator," a woman's voice squawked over the handset. James barked into the receiver, followed it with a few mewls.

Need help. Something wrong.

"Hello? Is this some kind of joke?"

James repeated the sequence. He followed by two loud barks.

Urgent.

"Look, I don't know who this is, but I can assure you this isn't funny."

James growled, frustrated, and threw the phone to the side. It shattered against the wall. His ears perked up at the sound of boots on stairs. Guns were made ready. A man called from the other side of the apartment door. "Stand down! Is anyone in there?"

The woman shrieked from the bedroom. "Help me! It's in here! It's rabid!"

James huffed at the bedroom door. *Your mom's rabid.*

The apartment door shuddered under the force of a blow. Another would break it down. James looked out the window, saw the snipers on top of the building. He was immune to non-silver human weapons, but getting shot during a jump would slow him down, make him vulnerable to capture.

And it still hurt like a sonofabitch.

He couldn't risk it. He had to find a way to change back, tell Phillip what was going on.

He looked at the door as the SWAT team readied to break it down. He bared his teeth into a grin.

Hell with it. Could be fun.

James crouched down, gave a roaring howl, and charged the door. The wood splintered under his weight, rained down in the corridor as he crashed into the opposite wall and swung out with clenched fists. Armored men went flying against the walls and down the hall, others shouting. Someone fired at random, the rounds blasting a hole in the ceiling.

James plowed through the group, shoving men aside as he ran down the corridor. He dove down the stairs, the front foyer coming up fast as he gained speed. He crashed into the door, the heavy wood cracking as glass shattered and crumbled to the floor. James was up, out the door, and into the street. He ran at his heightened speed, tore down Dave Lyle Boulevard, traffic whipping by in both directions as he hit Mount Gallant Road and took a hard left. He heard police sirens sounding all over the city, cars trying to chase the massive gray beast. Anderson. Cherry Road. Celanese. He stopped just past the Food Lion Shopping Center, looked to his right, saw the woods on the other side of the small housing development.

His path.

He ran for it, the small houses and yards whirring by as he leapt fences and cars in driveways. He rounded the corner of a yellow house, pressed his back to the wall, and waited, listening for the police.

"It's you."

The small voice startled him. He whipped his head around, his yellowed gaze falling on the little girl in the swing on the other side of the yard. Her eyes were wide, cautious but not fearful. She wore a pretty yellow sundress, her tiny hands clasped around the chains that held the swing to the bar above. A headband kept her brown hair out of her face, a yellow bow on top of her head, maybe all of nine years old.

James cocked his head to the side.

"I saw you. The other night."

James looked back, the sounds of men shouting a few blocks down carrying on the wind. They couldn't find which way he went. At least for now.

"You don't scare me," the girl said. "I like doggies."

James crouched down as he went to her, careful to move slowly. He didn't want to frighten his one chance at help. He could find a way to get her to contact Phillip. It was stupid, far-fetched. He was getting desperate, panic beginning to take over.

Get a grip, Coldstone, he thought to himself.

"I've seen you a bunch of times," the little girl said as he approached. "You scared me at first, but not now." James lowered his head further as she got off the swing and stood. She rubbed the thick fur between his ears. "There, now. I was right! You *are* nice! Just big." He glanced up at her as she looked him over. "*Very* big."

James looked toward the house, then back at her, giving a low mewl.

Inside. Phone.

"You want a treat?"

James licked her hand and grunted.

Yes. Treat. Steak. Doggy biscuit. I don't care, just get me inside!

A familiar scent filled the air. Cologne? Aftershave. Cheap.

"There!"

James craned his neck at the sound of the man's shout. An armored

SWAT officer stood at the end of the driveway next to the corner of the house, his rifle aimed. More ran up the drive as he began to shout.

"Get away from her!"

The girl stepped around and put herself between James and the gunman. "He's my friend! Leave him alone!"

The man shouted again, ordered the little girl to step aside. More showed up, weapons aimed.

James barked. *Put those fucking guns down! She's a child, for Christ's sake!*

More surrounded the house, stood at the fence, their weapons pointed. Someone shouted at them to stand down, cursed at them.

Phillip emerged from behind the gunman and stood next to him. He looked at James, his eyes wide as he crossed himself.

"Sweetie," he said to the girl, his voice calm. "We need you to step away from the monster, please."

"No," the girl snapped back, her lower lip out and defiant as she spread her arms to the sides, shielding James. "You'll hurt him!"

"Fucking *move*," the man next to Phillip shouted. James heard the tell-tale sound of a chambered round.

Phillip kept his eyes on James as he spoke to the man.

"Watch your language; there's a child," he said. "And keep your mouth *shut*."

James smelled something else. He focused on the man, saw the rifle shaking slightly, the scent on him sweet and rancid all at once. Not fear. Something worse.

Panic.

It all happened in a second. James baring his teeth. Phillip shaking his head, his eyes wide. The rifle fired. The round was low. Too low. James hunched, swept out with his arm as he scooped the girl under him, turned his back. The pain was searing, hot and hateful, the round buried in his back. Just low enough. It could've been her head.

Two more shots, two white-hot points of pain in his back. Men shouting. The little girl screaming, burying her face in James's chest, hiding. James looked around, saw Phillip grab the rifle from the officer. The officer lunged at him, but Phillip stopped him with a quick rap to the temple with the rifle stock. He looked back at James.

The little girl sobbed loudly, shaking, James's fur clenched in her hands. He had to get out of there. He couldn't risk running and leaving her behind. More of them might fire. He couldn't chance her catching a bullet.

He stood, tucking her into his chest as he dashed for the woods. More men shouted, but James could hear Phillip ordering them to stand down, damn you.

James kept his pace quick, but not fast enough to frighten the child in his arms as he moved through the brush. He'd worn a path of sorts at some point during his full moon runs, knew the area inside and out. He moved off to the left toward a rock he knew. The ground was cool, canopied by the trees. He looked back; his ears perked as he listened. He heard the men calling to each other as they fumbled through the brush. It would be only a few minutes before they were on top of him. They would find the girl quickly.

A large tree had fallen a few months ago during a severe storm. The leaves were falling off, though the larger branches were still intact. He set the girl down on one low enough to where she could easily hop down on her own if needed. He pulled back as she reached for him, her face tear streaked.

"No, doggy, don't leave me!"

The shouts came closer. This way. Through here. Dear, *God,* look at the size of those prints. James glanced in their direction, gave a low growl, then turned back to her. He leaned down, sniffed her fingers, ran his long canine tongue up one side of her face. She giggled, pushing away at him playfully. He looked back as the shouts grew closer, then took off into the brush, her scent locked into his memory. If they harmed her, if anyone harmed her, he would know.

There would be hell to pay.

James stopped short as Phillip came out of the bushes. He looked James up and down, tried to catch his breath. His eyes were wide, his body tense.

"James," he said.

James looked at him and barked, followed by mewling. *Help. Urgent. Something wrong.*

Phillip looked over his shoulder as a few shouts came through the trees. He looked back at James. "Get out of here," he said. "We'll meet up later." He swatted at him. "Go. *Go!*"

James took off into the woods, the trees whipping by.

He overheard Phillip's voice growing more distant as he spoke to the girl. "Are you okay, sweetheart?"

T he rounds had worked their way out of his back a while ago, the pain subsided. James moved quickly through the brush, still in wolf form. He felt its grip begin to relax, but he still couldn't change back. James gritted his teeth, uttered a low growl as he swatted a chunk out of a nearby tree.

That college student. He had something to do with this. Had it been Anderson? No, Anderson was dead.

Or was he?

If the body had been torn to pieces, made unidentifiable, it was entirely possible Anderson had faked his death. Werewolves aged slower than humans. James, himself, appeared to be in his late twenties, early thirties. Had David Coldstone lived, he might still look to be in his fifties. They weren't eternal, like vampires, but life was long. James had read once that an average werewolf's lifespan was at least a hundred and fifty years. Some had lived to two hundred.

Of course, since society believed werewolves and vampires to be creatures of fiction, most of his research had to be taken with a grain of salt. He'd been able to find some lore with credible backing, but not much.

The sun was beginning to set as James loped up the hill to his usual howling spot. There was an abandoned trailer near the church, deep enough in the woods to be out of sight. He used it occasionally if he lost track of time and reverted to human form after a full moon. Or if he overfed during a run and needed a nap.

The trailer still stood, the roof intact enough to keep rain out if need be. He settled in, looking out the window at the woods. He was miles out from town. Far enough down McConnells to be outside of the RHPD's jurisdiction. The little girl came back to mind. She'd seen him often enough not to be afraid of him. He didn't know if he should be relieved or worried. His common sense told him to be concerned that he'd been so careless. She was young, likely not aware that she need not inform the RHPD as to how often she'd seen a giant werewolf travel through her yard in the early hours of the morning.

The Coldstone murders would resurface. It meant that his next encounter with the RHPD SWAT would feature silver bullets in their guns instead of the standard-issue lead rounds.

Brilliant, he thought. *Shit.*

He'd have to stay in the trailer for a few days and hope that he could eventually change back. What had that boy done to him? How? He'd never heard of a change forced on someone. How long would it last?

His stomach growled. He searched the area, his yellowed vision growing sharper as the sky began to give way to night. The air was brisk, which meant the prey would be frisky. Under normal circumstances, he would enjoy a good hunt. Playing with his food, as it were. Considering the circumstances, having fun could wait.

Something moved in the brush several yards from the end of the trailer. He could smell its musk through the cracked window, sense its alertness. He held quiet, taking his breaths slow and steady to keep from alerting his dinner.

The deer stepped out into the open, looking around, pensive as she lowered her head to the grass and began to eat. She moved to a small patch of clover nearby, sniffing at it before looking up again. She was alert. She would be fast, her reflexes sharp.

James Coldstone would be faster, his reflexes sharper.

He bared his teeth, every muscle in his body tense, his claws out, razors ready to tear flesh and sweet meat as he slinked out the back door and hit the ground without a sound. The deer looked up again, its head only centimeters from full height before James was on her. She gave a loud call cut short by the jaws clamped around her neck, crushing throat and bone. James slammed her to the ground, used his teeth to tear a large hunk of meat from her shoulder.

Something moved in the brush. James sat up, tendrils of meat hanging from his jaw as he sniffed the air, his ears perked and alert. There was a scent. Different. Not human.

Cat?

He'd heard of wild cats in the woods in York County, but he'd never come across one during his full moon romps. Then, of course, there was the legendary Rock Hill Panther. Bullshit, of course, but still...

He crouched down low, sniffed the ground. The deer, his own musk, a few smaller woodland animals.

Cat.

He sniffed again. It was feline. Bigger than a housecat. Definitely one of the larger animals. He braced, waited for the animal to attack. No matter how big it was, he was bigger. It wouldn't last more than a few seconds. Grab it, a quick jerk, crush its neck or skull in his jaws. Done.

Silence.

Rain fell, coming steadily, the ground already wet, the smells of mildew mixed with the metallic scent of rainwater from above. What would draw a wildcat out into this weather?

James stood tall, his muscles tensed as he sniffed the air again. Where was it? Close. The scent was stronger. Above him. He looked up, saw a shape in the trees.

The dart was in his neck before he heard the shot. He snarled at the shape, made for the tree, digging his claws into the trunk as he climbed, his eyes fixed on his new target. His vision hazed, blurred as his muscles began to relax against his will. His body was heavy, his arms weighing too much to reach, to hold on. He tried again, extended his right arm up, reaching for a nearby branch as his legs gave. The ground came fast and hard as sleep overcame him. Something stood over him, looking down the rifle in its hands. It crouched down over him, a woman's voice fading as he drifted off.

"My, aren't *you* a big one?"

6

James opened his eyes slowly, his body aching, stubborn to wake. The ground underneath him was different, soft and padded. He sat up slightly, looking down at the blanket that covered his body. His very human body.

When had he shifted back? He rubbed the spot where the dart had gotten him, but there was nothing there. He'd apparently shifted after he'd healed. The cot he was laying on was warm, more comfortable than his couch, the sheets and blankets freshly washed. He looked around the room, the sunlight coming in through the windows brightly lighting the place up. The house was small, the living room also serving as the bedroom. He surmised that the kitchen was likely also the wash, and the bathroom would be no larger than a walk-in closet.

His eyes ached, seeming to complain about being open. Whatever had been in the dart was potent. How long had he been out?

He sniffed the air. His sense of smell was still keen, though not as sharp as when he was the wolf. He detected the tinge of the scent he'd gotten in the woods. Cat. Not offensive, but the scent one got when cuddling a housecat. Except with a wild edge to it.

Maybe the owner had a cat they weren't supposed to have?

A woman poked her head out from the kitchen. James looked at her, noted her red hair and bright green eyes. Her face was freckled, her lips full and heart-shaped. He was instantly curious as to what the rest of her looked like.

"Good, you're awake," she said, smiling. "I was beginning to wonder how long you might sleep. Everyone reacts differently to tranquilizers."

"Where am I?" James asked.

"My home," the woman said. "It was a chore getting you here. You're not a light person when you're a human, and I wasn't about to try dragging you up here in your other form."

James didn't know how comfortable he should be with her casual and relaxed tone concerning his lycanthropy. Still, he decided against shifting. He didn't want to risk another episode of not being able to change back.

He had a sense about the woman. Then again, he also couldn't help himself when it came to attractive women.

"I guess I've no secrets with you, then," he said, looking down. He shifted, lifting the blanket and looking down at his body. "At all."

The woman's smile went wry, her eyes flashing. "Big secrets are best shared."

"I'll need clothes."

"I'll get you some. I've got a few things around. I think my last roommate was your size."

James nodded. "Next question, then. Who are you?"

The woman stepped out of the kitchen, and James took a split second to admire her figure. Her body was fit, her jeans tight enough to highlight her small waist and long legs, her plaid shirt unbuttoned at the top, exposing just enough cleavage to keep him interested. Her freckles traveled lightly down her chest, and he wondered how much more of her shared the wealth.

Forget the librarian, he thought.

"I'm Angelique," she said. "Please, call me Angel. It's less of a mouthful."

"James. James Coldstone."

"Coldstone?" Angel raised an eyebrow. "I know the name. Can't say I'm shocked to know you are what you are." She nodded. "Not to worry, your secret is safe with me. I've my own, so it's in my best interests not to mess with yours. Especially with so many police and SWAT roaming the area."

Phillip, he thought suddenly. *Dammit! I need to call him.*

"Right," James said, tossing the covers aside and standing. He relaxed and looked at Angel, who stood there grinning. "Can I use your phone?

Mine got lost when I turned. And I'll gladly accept those clothes you offered. Or should I wander back to town like this?"

"No phone. Too expensive, and I like my privacy," Angel said. She looked him up and down, raising an eyebrow. "I'll see to that clothing. Please, make yourself comfortable."

James looked around as Angel went to the closet and sifted through the hanging clothes. The place was sparsely decorated, neat and clean beyond his comprehension. The contrast between his apartment and Angel's cottage was stunning. The walls were plaster, the ceiling vaulted, rafters exposed. The windows were small, the drapes black. He thought about the times he wanted to completely shut out the daylight, sit in the dark and quiet, and enjoy his coffee and his thoughts.

Black curtains. Novel idea.

"Why were you out in that form last night?" Angel asked as she dug through the closet. "The moon wasn't full."

"I had no choice," James said. "Something happened. I couldn't change back."

Angel nodded as she turned to him, a pair of jeans and a shirt draped over her arm. "It was at least an hour before you reverted to your human form. I had to wait before I could bring you back here." She made a face. "In the rain."

James blinked. Any time a werewolf was incapacitated, they would turn back to human form. Be it knocked out or killed, the wolf would shed away. Whatever that college boy had done to him had affected even that minor natural fact.

"I'll level with you," James said, taking the clothes from her. "Even as a human, I'm not a small man. And you're taking the fact of what I am really well for a human, which makes me wonder if you're a werewolf as well."

Angel's smile grew as she stepped closer to him, leaned in as if sniffing him. He thought he detected a slight purr in the back of her throat.

"I'm more of a cat person." She turned away and headed to the kitchen. "I've got breakfast ready. Get dressed so we can eat."

"Cat?"

"It's arrogant to think that wolves are the only weres in existence," Angel said, stopping at the doorway and turning to him. "You don't strike me as arrogant, so I'll just assume ignorance."

James chuckled at the jab.

"You don't seem awfully surprised at my problem last night." James began to dress while Angel turned away and went back to the kitchen. He could smell bacon and hoped eggs and toast would follow suit.

"Because I'm not," Angel called. "In fact, I was expecting it. I come from a long line of collectors. Rare artifacts interest me, and there's one, in particular, I've been after for quite some time."

Angel returned from the kitchen with a plate of food as James finished getting the clothes on. He could deal with the lack of underwear. He didn't plan on being there long.

"Do tell," James said, accepting the plate from her. *Yes! Eggs!*

"There was a ring that once belonged to Vlad Tepes," Angel said as she sat down in the chair next to the couch where James had spent the evening. She crossed her legs and arms, eyeing him as he sat down and ate.

"Count Dracula?" James said between bites, raising an eyebrow. "Seriously?"

"During his second century of life, the Carpathians were overrun with werewolves. He tried to control them at first, bend them to his will. It proved impossible unless the weres were bitten, which didn't bode well for anyone. The vampire infection didn't mix with the lycanthropy in one's blood, and the werewolves would die. The same for vampires who were bitten by lycanthropes. Once other types of weres began to show, particularly werecats, things began to get out of hand."

James paused in thought. Something didn't quite add up.

"But if he forged a ring that could force a change, that would compound his problem," James said. "Back then, lycanthropes would go feral in their animal form. The human form is much weaker."

Angel narrowed her gaze at him, tilted her head. He'd said something. Caught her by surprise. He sat forward, swallowing the last bite of bacon. "What?"

She shook her head.

"It's nothing," she said, looking at him. "I just…it's interesting."

"What is?"

"Nothing," Angel said, waving it off. "At any rate, Dracula wore the ring right up until his demise at the dawn of the nineteen hundreds. Dr. Van Helsing took it and locked it away. Until recently, so it would seem." She leaned forward. "Whatever happened to you, it seems to be in line with the powers that ring bears."

"Some college boy," James said. "It happened yesterday. I went for coffee, and he was in there. Left before I could catch him. I think his name is Wade Anderson. Does that ring a bell?"

Angel stiffened in her seat, her face suddenly hard and angry.

"Anderson?" she said. "That little son of a bitch is still alive?"

"I caught his scent at a crime scene," James said between bites. "He relieved himself in a neighbor's yard. My friend on the police force had some of his effects from his stay in prison, and then I encountered him in his wolf form. All three matched up."

Angel huffed. "Piece of shit," she muttered.

"History?"

"Quite." Angel stood, went to the kitchen, and returned with two cups of coffee. "Anderson was tied up with human trafficking until there was a big bust. He took the fall for his boss, who was supposed to walk, but the lawyer got big-headed."

"I've read the articles," James said, nodding and thanking her for the warm cup of coffee. "Samuel Pickens. Tried to walk him clean. Instead, Pickens lost the case completely, and Anderson wound up with a full sentence."

"They took my cousin."

James paused, the cup at his mouth as he was about to sip the coffee. Angel held her cup in both hands as she sat back down, crossed her legs, and looked toward the window. She cleared her throat and spoke again.

"It's been ages. Years. She was thirteen. Well, thirteen in human years. She looked more like she was ten."

"Where is she now?"

She cleared her throat again, shook her head.

"She was killed in the raid that ended with Anderson's arrest. The client who'd purchased her that evening."

A wave of revulsion hit James. A child. Someone had purchased...a *child*. For...he couldn't make himself finish the thought. "I'm sorry."

They both startled at the knock at the door. Angel stood, dropped the cup as she began to grow. Her clothing shredded, her skin breaking out in fine, ginger-colored fur as her ears moved to the top of her head and became pointed. Her face molded, her mouth and nose moving forward as her upper lip split. Her fingers sprouted long, curved claws. Her teeth elongated into fangs, and her eyes turned to green, diamond-shaped cat's eyes. She was at least seven feet tall, growling and poised to attack whoever was knocking.

James let some of his wolf slip forward, sniffed the air, and caught a familiar scent. He stood, putting his hand out as he put himself between the door and the angered werecat that stood before him licking her lips hungrily.

"Wait," he said to her.

She growled again, hissed at him.

James opened the door a crack, looking out as Phillip stepped back. "How did you find me?"

Phillip rolled his eyes.

"I'm a deer hunter, you idiot," the policeman said, annoyed. "You're not the only one who can track. Whose house is this?"

Angel yowled behind James. He glanced over his shoulder, then back at Phillip.

"Now isn't an ideal time," he said. He tried to speak again, but a sizable clawed paw smacked him in the shoulder, sending him sprawling. Angel yanked the door open, grabbed Phillip by the shirt, and pulled him inside, slamming the door closed. She threw him across the room and onto the couch, which tipped over, dumping Phillip into the floor. James got to his feet as Phillip did the same, his gun drawn. James started to let the wolf come forward, then stopped.

Two weres could make this worse. Damn it.

He put himself between Phillip and Angel again, his arms out as he looked up at her.

"I know this man," he said, keeping his tone firm. "He's with us. He knows my secrets, and now yours. He's a friend." He looked over his shoulder at Phillip, who had his revolver out and pointed at Angel. "Phillip, put the gun away."

"Move, James!"

"She's a were! Drop the fucking gun!"

Angel moved toward him, her claws out as she hissed at Phillip. James stepped close to her, his eyes locked on hers.

"Stop. He's a *friend*. He won't hurt you." James looked over his shoulder as Phillip slowly lowered the revolver. "Better. Now put it away."

"Fuck *me*," Phillip muttered as he put the revolver back in its holster.

James looked back at Angel. "This is unnecessary. Shift back."

Angel growled at Phillip, looking from him back to James. She shuddered, her skin rippling as she shrank down in size; fur retreated into pale skin. Hands, arms, legs all returned to normal. It was mere seconds before Angel stood before him, the top of her head almost coming up to his shoulders, her red and voluminous hair draped around bare shoulders.

James looked her over before he could stop himself.

The mystery of the freckles was now solved.

"How did you find my home?" Angel snapped at Phillip.

"I followed the trail James left behind," he said. "I'm aware of his path he takes during his runs. Your place isn't far from his trailer. I decided to check here first. See if the homeowner may have seen anything." He motioned to her. "I guess my question is answered." He turned back to James. "We need to talk. *Now.*"

"I'm going to get some new clothes on," Angel said, glaring at Phillip. "And you owe me a new outfit." She turned and sauntered off to the bathroom, grabbing clothing from the closet along the way. James watched, admiring her perfect buttocks as she went.

"Try not to think with your dick for a change," Phillip said, giving James a shove. "What the hell happened to you yesterday?"

"I couldn't help it," James said, moving to the couch. He began to straighten up the room. "There was an incident, and I got turned."

"*Got* turned?" Phillip shook his head as he motioned James to help him set the couch upright. "How is that even possible?"

"Some trinket. I believe Anderson was involved."

Phillip sighed. "In other news, Mindy Robertson sends her affections."

James raised an eyebrow.

"The girl, you twat," Phillip said. "The one you ran off with yesterday. Which, by the way, doesn't help your case considering the rest of the fuckery you carried on with."

"What fuckery?" James asked, feigning innocence. "I simply tried to go back to my apartment."

Phillip glared at him. "You wrecked a coffee shop and made a man shit his pants before you led police on a chase all over downtown Rock Hill. Dickhead." Phillip rubbed his face as he paced, turning away from James.

"I couldn't change back," James said. "Besides, that guy threatened me. He needed to shit his pants."

Phillip rounded on James, his face red. He moved closer to James as he spoke.

"Oh, that's right. Make jokes, you fucking *idiot!* I'm up to my tits at the department trying to cover for you, and you piss it all away by going on a rampage that ends with you kidnapping a child. A *child!* A damned ten-year-old, who doesn't understand the difference between a large dog and a *dumbass* that can turn into a fleabag!"

Phillip was so close to James their noses would likely touch were the policeman not a head shorter. James regarded him coolly, trying to come up with an excuse or a witty remark.

He let it go. Phillip was right.

"I'm sorry," he said, stepping away and sitting down on the couch. "I didn't mean to cause you trouble. Or endanger the girl."

Phillip sighed loudly. He spoke, forcing calm. "Okay. Fine. Just tell me what happened. And who the hell your new girlfriend is."

Phillip listened intently, helping put the room back together as James recounted everything up to waking up on Angel's couch. Angel had wandered back in from the bathroom, still glowering at Phillip as she cleaned up the two shattered coffee cups and went to brew another pot. She returned with three cups, handed James and Phillip theirs, then sat down in her chair, her eyes still trained on the cop sitting on her couch.

"Was it Wade Anderson?" Phillip asked.

James shook his head.

"Not very likely. According to what Angel has told me about this ring, Anderson would have been forced into the change as well."

"Then it's possible that our young friend works for Anderson," Phillip said.

Angel shook her head. "Wade Anderson was a low-level enforcer. He wouldn't have people working underneath him."

"Unless he carries a certain level of clout," James said, looking at her. "Which could be likely. His abilities might give him some extra pull in the organization."

"If he has Clara Pickens, then there's a possibility we may never see her again," said Phillip. "The world of human trafficking is massive. She could be anywhere."

"Or dead," said Angel. "It depends on the circumstances. Either way, we have to act."

Phillip bristled. "We?"

Angel nodded. "I've been after that ring for ages. Decades. It only activates when worn, but it affects any were in the vicinity, including the wearer if he or she happens to be a lycanthrope. As far as the criminal element, I leave that in your court, officer. I only want the trinket." She turned her eyes to James and smirked. "Well. Mostly."

James rolled his eyes and muttered. "Cats."

"Well, I think you can forget going back home," Phillip said, looking at James. "Your apartment is being raided. I was able to get a warrant to limit the search, but not by much. Hopefully, you don't have anything I should know about in there."

James shrugged. "Just my cocaine."

"Fuck you."

James grinned as Phillip pulled out a photograph and handed it to him. James looked at the photo, his hackles rising.

"That's him," he said, the college kid from the coffee shop looking smug in the picture as he held up his new inmate number. "The boy that ran from me."

"That's Wade Anderson," Phillip said. "And that would be impossible. That photo is years old. His first college campus rape."

James shook his head as he handed the photo to Angel.

"It makes no sense," he said. "I saw plenty of photos in the articles I found, but they were all of an older guy. Man had a beard."

"Chances are, his bosses had them doctored," said Angel. "I wouldn't put it past them. But if it was him you saw in the coffee shop, we have bigger problems."

"Such as?"

"The ring should have forced him to change as well. It didn't. It means he's not a lycanthrope."

Phillip grunted.

"Then what is he?"

"Something else," said Angel. "Something I've never seen."

Phillip looked at James.

"Alright, you dumb dog. I need you to be productive for once."

James chuckled, bowing dramatically.

"Anything for a dear friend."

7

James crouched low in the dark, hiding in the shadows as the moon rose overhead. It was waning, no longer full, but still turning a shade of orange. He glanced over at Angel, who leapt deftly across the rooftop above and looked down on the street from across the way. She licked her arm, her cat's eyes glinting in the moonlight.

He'd be lying to himself if he said he didn't find her amazingly attractive.

"Keep it simple," Phillip had said earlier. "Get to the campus and sniff out Anderson's trail. Do not engage. We simply want a hint as to where he is staying. And keep your girlfriend in check."

"Girlfriend?" James shook his head. "I barely know her."

"Oh, please," Phillip scoffed. "You two have been screwing each other with your eyes ever since I've been here."

"She's not unattractive."

"You're a dog."

"There is that," James said. "But I also don't know if I'm ready to keep the litter box up."

James lifted his head and sniffed the air, let the breeze in over his tongue, took in every aroma. Trash, food cooking at a nearby all-night diner. Car exhaust. Rain coming. Damn. A good storm always made him sleepy.

Something else. Familiar.

He gave a quick bark at Angel, darted across the empty street and into the alley in a flash. They hadn't made it to the college yet. No need.

Anderson was near.

It also meant he might have his ring on him. He hadn't had it when they'd first met and fought. James had been able to shift back with ease. It meant the boy had acquired it soon after. That, or he'd been negligent, hadn't expected James to show up in wolf form to investigate the place.

James put his nose to the ground and sniffed. Anderson had been here. There was no doubt. He locked in on the scent. He looked around, tried to spot his prey. Nothing. It was likely the bastard had come through here, then moved on.

James dropped to all fours, moving along as he sniffed the ground, sorted out the smells so he could single out Anderson's stench. The trail tracked down the alleyway, turned the corner. He gave another bark at Angel. *Follow.*

She leapt down off the rooftop, hit the ground without a sound. She let out a low growl as she sniffed the air, moved to James, a purr escaping her throat as she licked her feline lips.

James gave a whine, rolled his eyes, and went back to tracking. Phillip would kill him if he let himself get distracted.

The scent grew stronger as they moved through downtown, down Albright Road toward Leslie Highway. The buildings were getting older, the neighborhoods less savory than where the two weres had been only moments before. James considered it lucky the streets were empty, though it helped that it was two in the morning.

A sound carried on the wind, faint but clear. Two people, men, voices raised. He gave a quick bark to Angel, then took off down the highway at a lope, his ears perked as he tracked the sound. He didn't bother to check that Angel was hot on his heels. He knew she would be.

He stopped, ducked into the empty school building across from an old motel. The sign still burned, letting passersby know there was a vacancy. There was no name to the business—only the sign welcoming new patrons.

The scent was strong; the sound of yelling came from inside.

"I did exactly what you said!" The voice was young, the tone a boyish twenty-something with a hot head and no brain. "It's not my fault he went fucking psychotic!"

"You were supposed to incapacitate him," said an older man. James could tell by the way his voice resonated that the man was large. "We don't need two of you running around here, do we? Especially one that runs around with the goddamned cops!"

"Fucking cops went after him," said Junior. "Tracked him back to his apartment. Tore the place up, didn't find a damned thing."

"You have to understand my frustration, Wade," said the older man. His tone was forced and friendly, almost fatherly. "You were supposed to follow him, make him shift, and let the cops get after him. Make sure they caught him. That's why you were supposed to disable. As far as they know, he's the killer."

"Seems like he's like me. Keeps his shit together when he shifts."

That one caught James by surprise. Why *wouldn't* keep his shit together during a change? It was evolution. All weres maintained their rational, human thought during a change.

James glanced around, saw Angel crouched behind him, her eyes flashing as she flicked her tail in agitation. He gave a low grunt. *Stand down.*

A low, moaning growl sounded from the back of her throat. James shifted, narrowed his eyes at her as he bared his teeth slightly. *I mean it.*

Angel's ears went flat, the rest of her body relaxing as she stood and moved to a nearby window. She looked out at the other building, and James went back to listening to the two men speak.

"...didn't work out that way," Anderson was saying. "But he did manage to distract the cops off us for a bit, right? C'mon, Santiago, you've got to see the opportunity here."

Santiago sighed. "For what? Another monster like you roaming around? Not like this one's hirable. Seems more interested in snooping around the Pickens murders."

Now we're getting somewhere, James thought.

Santiago spoke again. "What I see is that I've got a girl with big tits, areolas the size of dinner plates, and a tight ass that I've got to ship out of here and into work *now* before they close in on us. And now she's missing. And you're too busy screwing around with magic toys to notice that the cops are right up our asses." Santiago's voice was getting louder as he spoke, his tone angrier. "While you've been fucking around with that bastard Coldstone and leaving messes, I've been up to my ass in clients who can't wait to start putting in bids for her. So, remind me again as to why I pay you. Please. I need that."

James heard Anderson respond, his tone low, bitter.

"I don't deserve the money you give me. *Sir.*"

"You're goddamned right you...*what the fuck?!*"

James shot to his hind legs, standing straight, as he heard a crash in the other building. Glass breaking and scattering. Shouts. Gunshots. He looked at Angel.

At the open window where Angel had been standing.

He bolted from the school toward the motel, his yellowed vision hazing to red as he saw the broken window on the ground floor near the entrance. The motel manager's office. He kicked out with his right leg, launched himself into the air toward the window. He turned, his shoulders barely clearing the window as he spun and landed hard into position, the impact from all fours shaking the boards.

Angel yowled as she swiped at Anderson. The kid ducked, rolled as the savage werecat hissed at him, pounced. Missed. Anderson tucked and sidled out of the way, ran up the wall, spun, and landed a kick to her face.

An older fat man with perfectly-combed white hair, bushy eyebrows, and a suit that might cost James a quarter of his family fortune stood at a large oak desk. His jowls worked overtime as he opened and closed his mouth, his eyes wide as he took in the giant werewolf that loomed over him, looked down on him as it licked its teeth, sending drool to the floor in long tendrils. James had practiced that look to perfection over the years: the insane canine grin, the wide, crazed yellow eyes, the loud, hungry mouth-breathing as he tensed his large wolf muscles and flexed his claws.

It helped get his point across: dinner.

James made to lunge at Santiago, his arms and claws out as he snarled at the old man. He held back slightly, gave Santiago the opportunity to duck and dodge. He didn't want to kill him or hurt him. Yet.

No need for him to know that.

James shifted to human form quickly as Santiago scrambled to his feet. He grabbed the man by his expensive coat, shoved him into the desk, putting his face inches from the sweaty old fart.

"Where is she?" James shouted. Santiago sputtered, his eyes wide with fear. James jerked him, slapped him across the face. *"Where is she?!"*

Light flashed in James's eyes, the blow to his head sounding like a loud slap from inside his skull as his world spun. He hit the far wall, caved in the plaster before he hit the floor. He looked up as Anderson charged him in wolf form. James shifted back just as Anderson hit him. He grabbed the other were, rolled as jaws snapped in his face. He grabbed Anderson's head and slammed it into the floor, disorienting him enough to give James a chance to push himself away and finish recovering from the blow. He looked around and saw Angel picking herself up off the floor, shaking her head.

"You're too late, Coldstone," Anderson said behind him. James turned as the kid picked himself up off the floor, now nude from his shift. He chuckled as he rubbed the back of his head. "You pack a damn good punch."

James snarled at him, put his teeth close enough to Anderson's face to taste the smell of sweat.

"She's gone," he said. "Moved somewhere else." His body shuddered, his skin moving as if something crawled underneath. James stepped back, watching as Anderson began to grow, hair sprouting all over his body, his muscles enlarging, his arms and legs changing as his face took on a new shape, his nose growing longer, taking his mouth with it. The fur was orange, striped. His spine lengthened, his hands folding into large clawed paws.

The tiger roared at James, turned, and made for the window. James froze, his mind spinning, trying to sort out what he'd just seen.

What kind of were is he?!

Anderson leapt through the window, Angel hot on his heels. James barked at her, the sound loud and deep. She stopped, turned to him, hissing. He barked again. She glared at him, giving a low growl as she moved toward him.

Santiago cowered in front of his desk as the two weres approached him. James shifted back to human form, crouched down in front of the man. Santiago sputtered again.

"Oh, come on," James said. "What's a naked man and woman going to do to you, hmm?"

Angel stood over him, now in human form, glaring down at James. He stood and faced her.

"You'd better have a damn good reason we just let that piece of shit go," she said, putting her face close to his, her eyes filled with hatred.

"Because we don't need him." James nodded to the squealing man on the floor. "Not yet. Mr. Santiago is going to tell us what we need to know. Starting with what the hell just happened here."

"He's…one of you, right?" Santiago said, stammering. "I mean…all of you. Animals. Oh…God, please don't hurt me!"

James crouched back down in front of him, his tone low and even as he spoke.

"We're going to have a small Q&A session. I'm going to ask you a series of questions. You will answer them. If you refuse, my feline companion and I will play with your entrails. Shall we begin?"

I still would've eaten him," Angel said as she sat the tray of coffee and biscuits down next to James. "And you're a bastard for letting that asshole go."

James sat in the chair, slumped with his head back as he stared at the ceiling. They'd returned to her house after interrogating Santiago and leaving him tied up for when the police would arrive. The man hadn't been a wealth of information that James hadn't already caught on to. James was supposed to take the fall for the murders. Anderson was to keep the police at bay.

"I don't know where she is," Santiago had said, his hands up as he cowered away from James. "I swear."

"We still don't know what kind of were Anderson is," James said, still staring at the ceiling. "And he knows where Clara Pickens is. We need him alive."

"It means we have to track him all over again," Angel said, sitting down on the couch with her coffee cup. "I'd have rather finished things last night."

"It is highly unlikely we would find Clara as easily as we will now had we followed your brilliant plan," James said, not hiding his annoyance. "We have her scent from the crime scene, but it won't be much help if she was carried or driven to wherever she is. Tracking her will take weeks. Anderson will come for us." He paused. "Well, he'll come for *me*, anyway."

"What makes you sure of that?"

"Because I am still part of the plan," James said, sitting up and reaching for a biscuit as he spoke. He took a bite. "Excellent. Do you make your own butter?"

"Part of the plan?" Angel said, ignoring him as she sat forward. "To frame you? I'm not sure if you're confused, but we just sent the ringleader to your friend with the police complete with a confession and soiled pants."

James shook his head as he took a sip of his tea. "He's not the ringleader."

Angel looked at him, her eyebrow raised. "He did mention that he was paying Anderson."

"And I'm sure he was, but not out of his own pocket." James took another sip of tea before he spoke again. "A ringleader would've been much cleverer in his confession than Mr. Santiago had been." He grunted. "If that's even his real name. Wade Anderson would've made more of an effort in defending him from us. You should know as well as I do that a lycanthrope's loyalty is nothing to fool with. We'll go to our graves to protect those to whom we are loyal."

Mindy. His mind stirred. Why was he still locked on her? Something about the girl fascinated him. Why? What was special about her?

James looked up at the sound of the knock at the door. Angel got up and answered.

"More good news," Phillip said. "James, we need to speak."

Angel rolled her eyes and stepped back as Phillip entered. "You do know how to ruin the mood," she said as she shut the door behind him. "Humans. Ugh."

Phillip looked at her, a smirk on his lips. "What's got your mood this morning? James forget to scoop your litter box?"

James spoke up as Angel's eyes turned yellow, her skin starting to sprout hair.

"That's enough, you two. Phillip, sit down. I believe I have discovered Miss Angelique's true gift." He held up his half-eaten biscuit. "My own mother wasn't able to make biscuits like this."

Angel calmed down, her eyes and skin returning to normal, her glare still fixed on Phillip as he took a seat on the couch nearest James. "I'll get another coffee," she said. "Arsenic, anyone?"

"No, thank you, just sugar," James said, raising his cup.

Phillip put up his hand. "No, thanks. Coffee turns you black."

James snorted. Angel left the room in a huff as Phillip spoke. "Your catch last night proved both fruitful and a dead end."

James raised an eyebrow. "Do tell."

"Michael Santiago," Phillip said as he pulled an envelope from his trench coat and handed it to James. "He's not our boss, but he is a higher rank in the organization, apparently."

James huffed. "Told you," he called to Angel. He looked at Phillip. "What did he have to say?"

"The hotel was to be another trafficking house. Wade Anderson was to meet him there to discuss the murders and tying you to them."

"I'm assuming the interrogation wasn't entirely public?"

"Good guess," Phillip said. "I turned off the mic and told him it was off the record, though you're still up there on the suspect list. A *lot* of eyewitnesses have you turning into a werewolf right in front of them. Thankfully, the security camera in the coffee shop was on the blink. Without camera footage, it's only word of mouth for now. It's not enough to gun for you, but the suspicions are there. The department is actively looking. I'm doing my best, but you can't go back to your apartment. Ever."

"Our problems were compounded last night, I'm afraid," James said. "Anderson changed during the fight. He's not a werewolf."

Phillip blinked, shaking his head. "Wait a minute. You said you fought him, as a were, while you were sniffing around the Pickens place." Phillip looked up as Angel returned with his cup of tea. He thanked her, then looked back at James.

"He's not any kind of were I've seen," James said.

"He's something else," Angel said, sitting down on the opposite end of the couch from Phillip. "I'll have to look through my family research, but I remember my father telling me about a type of creature that can shift into any animal of their choosing. Some refer to them as changelings."

"Which may explain why the ring didn't force a change on him when he used it on me," said James.

"Exactly," said Angel. "He's not a lycanthrope." She winked at him. "Smart *and* attractive."

Phillip raised his hand slightly. "I wish to debate you on the former of those two descriptors."

"Did Santiago have an idea as to Anderson's current whereabouts?" James said.

Phillip shook his head. "Not a clear one. But he did give me a few places Anderson tends to haunt. He doesn't stay still for long. Likes to keep on the move. He's wily."

"Santiago has a northern accent," James said. "Sounds like he's from New Jersey. Why would someone from up north be involved with this?" James asked.

"Human trafficking rings are rarely isolated to one place," Phillip said. "It'd be too easy to track them. Too easy to break them up and find the victims." He leaned forward, setting his cup down on the coffee table and touching his fingertips together as he looked at James. "You have to understand something: human trafficking is a world separated from our own. It's a dark world. Sick. Demented. Once someone is taken into that world, it's highly unrealistic to expect to ever see them again. There's a chance that Clara Pickens is here in Rock Hill. There's a more likely chance she's already been shipped out of the country. Even Santiago may not know if she's still here. If someone from the New Jersey mob is involved, then that puts an entire nation onto our search grid. And, frankly, that narrows it down from the entire world. So, believe it or not, it helps."

"Who runs the organization?" Angel asked.

Phillip shrugged. "Even Santiago doesn't know who he works for. Again, I'm not surprised. The heads of these rings like to keep a low profile. The fewer who know the identity of their employer, the safer they are. Santiago is a prime example. The boss sends him money to pay his enforcers, speaks through him. Everyone thinks they work for him, not realizing that they work for someone much more powerful. Much darker. If that's what we're up against, then this ring is massive. One thing that may work for us is that a lot of people move from the north down here and end up living in Fort Mill. It's not much, but it's something."

"And they've put a monster in their employ," James said, shaking his head. "If we find Anderson, we'll be that much closer to Clara Pickens. Do you have that list?"

Phillip nodded, pulling his notebook out of his pocket. He tore out a page, handed it to James.

James smiled. "Also, I'd like another word with this Santiago."

Phillip huffed. "As if you didn't interrogate him before you hung him up in that hotel like a pig waiting for slaughter. You're unbelievable."

"He was panicked," James said, his tone casual. "Angel and I may, or may not, have had something to do with that. I intend to make amends."

"Bullshit," Phillip snapped. "You intend to question him again."

"While I'm making amends. I did threaten to eat him, after all."

"I thought you didn't eat people."

"Too chewy."

"You're revolting."

"Thank you."

Angel looked at Phillip. "I could go," she said. "He might be more open to speaking with a woman." She winked at James. "Besides, breasts can be quite persuasive."

Phillip looked back and forth between them, letting out a loud sigh.

"I thought my life was shit enough with *one* of you. Fine. I'll set it up."

8

Y ou're in luck," Phillip said. "I've arranged a prisoner transfer to a safe house."

James raised an eyebrow. "Just like that?"

Phillip shrugged. "Paperwork. The world revolves all around it."

Phillip had left Angel's and gone back to the police department to figure out a way to have James and Angel speak to Santiago that didn't require James walking through the police department like a moving target. There was a manhunt out for him, and Phillip already had his hands full with keeping the search away from Angel's place in the deep country area of McConnells. He was adamant that his hands would be tied if James was seen and apprehended.

James's mind went back to Mindy Robertson. He wondered how many police officers had been to her home, disturbed her family, and searched her yard. All because of him. He felt guilty for drawing the attention to the Robertson family. When it was all said and done, he planned to speak with Phillip about pulling the search away from her and hers.

"Michael Santiago," Phillip said, sitting down at Angel's kitchen table and pulling the transfer form from his coat pocket. "He's considered a high-profile suspect. Since he's a ringleader, he'll have information on the operation. Including Anderson's role. He's offered to flip on certain individuals in exchange for immunity."

"It means he's scared," Angel said. "Rats typically turn on their own when they fear the ship is sinking."

Phillip pointed to her, winking and nodding.

"They call him 'Santa Mike,'" he said. "His responsibility is acquisitions. He wasn't the one who funded Anderson's lawyer, but he certainly has something to do with the murders. Likely, his direction was to order Anderson to kill everyone involved in the trial. Punishment for Anderson's incarceration. I'm certain Anderson was much obliged to carry out the acts."

"Right," James said, distracted by his thoughts. It was all wrong. Why was it so wrong? What wasn't adding up? Anderson had been at the Pickens's home. More than once. He'd been in wolf form. A large, wild animal had destroyed the families. It all pointed at Anderson, while Anderson had taken steps to point it all at the resurgence of the Coldstone murders.

It all seemed wrong. Wrong path, wrong direction, and no stopping the bus. Anderson's motives had to run deeper. Even during their brief encounter, Anderson didn't strike James as a psychopath.

"The transport leaves out for McConnells this evening," Phillip said, standing. "It's best to move at night. Fewer cars on the roads means less likelihood of an interruption in the transfer process. Plus, the population here is about two hundred and eighty people. It means not a lot of questions asked or people snooping. The arrangement is dark to the press. They don't even know that we have Santiago in custody. The entire operation is dark. I'd prefer to keep it that way indefinitely. If we reveal who we have and what we know, the trafficking organization will be quick to cover up and shift around. Santiago will be forgotten, and every lead he gives up will be a dead end."

"Understood," James said. He looked at Angel. "May I have a moment alone with Officer Brown?"

Angel snorted. Phillip looked at her.

"Yuck it up, kitty-kitty," Phillip said. "A black guy named 'Brown.' Lots of laughs."

Angel put her hands up innocently. "I was going to comment on how sexy it is to see a man who keeps his head neat and shiny."

James stifled a laugh. "That's enough, you two. Angel, please."

Angel nodded, stood, and stepped out through the back door. James looked at Phillip, his humor dissipating quickly.

"I don't like any of this."

Phillip looked at him, confused. "What's to like?"

"I mean to say that it's too easy. It all adds up. It's wrong. Nothing should be adding up. There's too much risk involved to the organization. You know more than I do about human trafficking, but I know enough to know that they do *not* want to be caught. They're making too much money to give it up."

Phillip nodded, agreeing. "Millions. Annually."

"At least. Yet we have one of their leaders in our hands and Anderson not far from being cornered. Do you not find it unsettling that the only real question is what Wade Anderson truly is?"

Phillip nodded at the door. "Why not express all of this in front of Angel?"

"Because she is far too close," said James. "I don't trust her to hold back were she to get hold of Anderson. It's gone from us needing to kill him to us needing information from him. Particularly his motivation for working for this organization. Nothing is fitting in a puzzle where every piece is falling into place."

"Do you think she's a threat?"

James shook his head. "I believe we can trust her not to betray us. I also believe that she is angry. I can't say I can blame her. Her cousin is dead because of Anderson."

"So, what do you suggest?"

"That we keep her involved, but make sure that she does not come along when we make the move directly for Anderson. Above all else, we need him alive." James leaned in. "And we give her Dracula's ring for the trouble."

The breeze in the night air didn't affect James at all, his skin kept warm by thick fur, his blood running hot as he waited for Phillip to drive by in the transport. Angel waited on the other side of the road, also shifted into her werecat form. Phillip had organized the transfer so that he would be riding along in the van. Needed to be careful, calculating in the ambush to not harm him. Much.

James wagered he still owed Phillip for the dirty boxers.

The safe house was in a remote area in McConnells, the highway heavily wooded except for one home not far from the intersection, and the safe house several miles down the road. Stationed guards would see anything coming their way. Phillip had also confirmed the use of silver bullets. James and Angel would have to tread carefully.

Though he'd spoken to Phillip about his concerns, he still carried them, the ease of the entire thing weighing hard on him. It didn't feel like a trap, like he was walking into an attack, but it did feel like he was building up to miss his target by a mile. Phillip's comments about trafficking organizations stuck with James, altered his outlook on the situation. They were cloaked in shadow, lived in the dark. Once discovered, the evasion tactics could be quick and quiet, or brutal and bloody.

"They don't care about killing the girls they take," Angel had said while she and James were getting ready to meet Phillip. "The people they run into. Stand in their way, and you've essentially committed suicide."

"Wouldn't killing the girls prove counterproductive?" James had asked. Angel shook her head. "They always have their eyes out. There are ten girls they have lined up to replace the one they decide they no longer need."

James heard several vehicles approaching. He looked down the road toward town, saw two sets of headlights approaching. The squad cars pulled up, turning to block the way. His hackles raised, his pulse quickening. This wasn't part of the plan. He looked across at Angel, her eyes hard on the officers as they got out of the cars, four of them armed with pump-action shotguns. One lit a cigarette, blowing smoke into the air casually as another vehicle approached.

It's a trap. James growled low at the fake cops as the transport van stopped in front of the barricade. Phillip stepped out on the passenger side.

"Hey! What is this?"

"Checkpoint," the leader said. "We need to see the prisoner, please."

Phillip blinked at the man. "I don't know you," he said. "Who authorized this? You're interrupting a prisoner transfer. Please step aside."

The three officers readied their shotguns, aiming them at Phillip. James fought to stand down, his heart racing. He didn't want Phillip accidentally getting shot.

Phillip stood still, his eyes locked on the leader.

The man nodded. "Everyone out of the van."

Phillip motioned to the driver to step out. The guard riding in the back with Santiago also stepped out, his shotgun gripped in his hands.

"Weapons."

Phillip drew his sidearm and set it down, motioned to the driver and guard to do the same.

James clenched his clawed fist. Dammit.

He heard something shift across the way. He stood as Angel wandered out into the road, completely nude, staggering. She held her side, blood running over her fingers, her lip swollen and bleeding, her eye blackened.

"He…help me," she moaned.

"What the hell?" Phillip said, moving to her. The head officer nodded to the other three. They went to the van as Phillip rushed over to help Angel. She fell to her knees.

One of the fake officers went to Phillip, pointed his shotgun at him.

"On your feet."

The driver and Phillip's guard stepped back, their hands up. Phillip looked over his shoulder.

"She's injured, asshole," he said. "She needs medical care."

The gunman stepped forward, pressed the barrel to the back of Phillip's head. "Now, dickhead."

Phillip nodded, standing slowly. Angel looked up at him, winked.

The gunman looked down at her. "Get up," he said.

She stood, no longer acting as if she hurt. Her skin rippled as she approached him. James could smell the man's pheromones go into over-drive as she moved closer to him, took one of his hands and placed it on her breast as she leaned in closer to him.

"Meow."

She entered the change, growing as the guard screamed in terror. Phillip backed away as Angel lifted the man off the ground and roared in his face. James thundered from his vantage point as the other guards moved out of the van, their shotguns aimed at Angel. He snarled as one turned to him, fired wide, the shot missing James by a mile as he crashed into the panicked guard. He lifted the man by his face and slung him off to the side. Santiago screamed in terror as the other guard aimed and fired at James. The rounds grazed him, nothing embedded, but the pain was white-hot, the sudden fire drawing a quick yelp from him.

Silver, he thought. *Lovely.*

James pounced on the guard, grabbed him before he could chamber another shot. He slammed the man into the side of the van, dropped his unconscious body to the ground. James turned toward the man Angel had choked and gagged. She had him by the throat, lifted him high as she squeezed the life out of him. James took a step to stop her, but her claws flashed in the night. The officer writhed in her grip as his entrails dropped to the ground. James heard bones crunch, cartilage pop as she squeezed the man's neck. She dropped his lifeless form like a sack of bricks, spun on the leader of the group.

James rushed her as she barreled down on the man, tackled her to the ground. He was up instantly, his arm out wild. The back of his fist connected, and the man went down in a heap.

Angel stood and lashed out. Her claws raked across his chest, five deep scratches open and bleeding. A warning.

Another shot. James knocked Angel out of the way, ducked as the round disintegrated the light atop the police car. He looked up as the man chambered another round.

"There's a good doggy," he said. He aimed.

The loud smack came just before the man crumpled to the ground. Phillip stood over him, dropped the shotgun as he looked to James and Angel.

"Best way to judge a good gun stock," he said.

James shifted back into human form, the cuts across his chest healed as he worked to get the man he'd knocked out to his feet. Angel went back to human form, shoved him as he tried to bend down. James stood and looked at her.

"What the hell was that?!" she shouted at him.

James got back in her face. "We do *not* kill," he shouted. "What the fuck were you thinking?!"

Phillip spoke behind them, standing over the remains of the man Angel had disemboweled. "This is not good."

James moved to the van, pulled the two duffle bags Phillip had stowed in the back. He tossed one to Angel, opened the other.

Angel caught the bag, glaring at James as she opened it and began to dress.

"It was them or us," she argued. "This wasn't part of the plan."

"Neither was spilling a man's guts on the road," James shot back, pulling on a pair of boxers and searching the bag for jeans and a shirt. "*Christ*, you've just caused a real fucking problem!"

"You said it'd be an ambush," Angel said as she fastened her bra and pulled a shirt over her head. "These four showing up weren't part of the plan."

James moved close to her, his face inches from hers as he shouted. "Neither was gutting them in the fucking street!"

"Alright, both of you knock it off!" Phillip put his arm in between them, nudging James back. "We'll deal with it. Right now, we need to get Santiago out of here." Phillip stepped back, looking around. "Where the hell are my driver and guard?"

"Here, sir," a voice said from behind the van.

James saw the shotgun aimed at them before he saw the rest of the guard. The driver got back into the van, started it. James began to let the wolf come back to play, clothing be damned. Phillip grabbed his arm, shook his head.

James sighed, pushing the wolf back down.

The guard chuckled.

"Good puppy," he said.

"I'll be reporting this," Phillip said.

The guard grunted. "Go right ahead, then," he said. "Tell 'em how you rode along on a prisoner transport with two men you've never met, let four more ambush you, and wound up with a dead body in the road. Meanwhile, I wager I could save us all some trouble, pumpin' Fido and Whiskers here full of hot silver."

"You can have the old man," James said. Phillip blustered, but James ignored him, stepping forward. "We're looking for Clara Pickens."

The guard cocked his head to the side, looking confused. His mouth broke into a smile as he nodded. "Right," he said. "That one. Pretty girl. Big chest. Lots of energy."

"Where is she?"

The guard climbed into the van without a word, looking back out at them.

"Somewhere you'll never find her. Now, if you'll excuse me, the Powers that Be would like a little chat with Mr. Santiago, here." He slid the rolling door shut just before the wheels on the van spun out. The vehicle cut a U-turn and sped back toward town, Phillip's cursing becoming more audible as the sound of the engine faded in the night.

"This is some *fine* shit, here!" Phillip paced, running his hand over his scalp. "Fuck. *Fuck!*"

"We know something," said James, watching the taillights on the van grow smaller in the night. "Three things, actually."

"Oh, do enlighten me," Phillip snapped. "Please tell me how this storm of solid shit could be any better. I'm dying from anticipation, James."

"Their leader is in Rock Hill," James said, smiling. "Lycanthropes can run at hellish speeds, and you've got enough handcuffs on you to cuff three unconscious traffickers while you cook up a brilliant tale of how the fourth met his grisly end." He turned and looked at Phillip. "I can catch up with them."

"I'm going, too," said Angel.

Phillip and James spoke in unison. "No!"

Angel glared at them. James shook his head. "It's out of the question. We can't afford to leave a trail of bodies in our wake. Phillip already has his hands full enough explaining away what happened here tonight."

Angel stepped up to him, her eyes steel as she gritted her teeth.

"I'm not asking," she said. "I won't kill anyone. Fine. But you can't stop me from coming along, either."

It happened before James could blink. The syringe was in her neck; the plunger pushed down. James caught her as she dropped, her body completely limp. Phillip stepped back, tossed the syringe to the side.

"Little insurance," Phillip said, looking down at Angel as James eased her to the ground. "Swiped it from the nurse's office at work. She'll be out for a while."

James looked up at him. Phillip nodded in the direction of the van. "What the hell do you need? Scooby Snacks? Go get that van!"

James nodded, stood, and took off after the van at a sprint. He released the wolf, his body shifting as he pumped his legs harder, the wind picking up as the road sped along underneath him, the trees whipping by faster as he grew, his back hunching over, his shoulders and arms powerful as he went to all fours, his vision going to a deep yellowed hue as the headlights ahead, now a small dot in the distance, taunted him on their way back into town.

James had raced a car once. He'd wandered to the highway late during a full moon. A boy was out in his sports car, speeding to impress the young lady in the passenger's seat. James had fallen into pace with him easily, having to make himself not run ahead.

He opened his mouth, took in the night air over his tongue as he shot toward the city, the small taillights locked in his line of sight.

Rock Hill was quiet, dark as James leapt across the rooftops. He stopped, perched on a chimney as he pointed his nose into the air and sniffed. He hadn't had a chance to lock onto the van's scent. Tracking would be made more difficult.

Damn.

He'd seen the van turn down a street just before he'd reached the city limit. The neighborhood was small, the houses close together. It was easy for him to stay on the rooftops and avoid trailing through yards.

He was thankful it was on the side of town opposite Mindy's home.

He looked around the yards, making sure no lights shone through house windows before he leapt down to the ground and out into the street. He sniffed the asphalt, found a set of tire tracks still warm. Right. The bastards had gone right.

He broke into a run, headed toward downtown. His apartment would be another street over. He felt a small tinge of exhaustion, a longing to sleep in his bed. Phillip had been right: maybe moving into the old Coldstone Keep wouldn't be a bad idea. Get out of Rock Hill.

Then again, there was a likelihood that the police had also ransacked the place after James's little rampage through town.

The sound of the van's engine broke his train of thought. He rounded a corner, bounded down an alleyway, scaled up onto a cast iron drainpipe, and climbed to the rooftop in a flash. He focused on the noise. Louder this way? No, that way. Left. Now right. He pushed out with his powerful hind legs, propelled himself forward and across the gap to the next rooftop. He stopped short on the fourth building and looked down.

The van moved slowly, turned into a parking lot. They were on Cherry Road. Near the stadium. Not far at all from the Winthrop campus. The store was closed for the evening, the lot empty. The van came to a halt, and the guard got out, pulling Santiago with him as the driver stepped out of the front.

"Alright, then," the driver said to the guard. "What's the order?"

"Keepin' it simple," the guard said, shoving Santiago to his knees. He pointed the shotgun at the old man's head. "Hard to flip when your brains are out." He gave the shotgun a pump, his finger on the trigger.

The attack came too fast for James to react. The other were barreled into the van, knocked it over. The guard and Santiago fell away before it could land on them.

The driver was not so quick.

Anderson climbed atop the toppled van and over. The guard fired at him, missed.

James leapt into the air, landed on top of the van with enough force to shatter every window and cave the side in a decent twelve inches. He stood tall, his arms out to the sides, his large muscles tensed as he reared back and howled into the night—a challenge.

The guard got to his feet, aimed his shotgun. Anderson swatted it away, grabbed the guard by his face, and crushed his skull against the asphalt. James slammed into Anderson, took him to the ground. The other wolf yelped in pain, growled, kicked James off. James was barely to his feet again when Anderson tackled him, swinging back and forth with his claws extended. James bucked, grabbed Anderson, grappled him over as he snapped with his jaws again, his front teeth barely missing Anderson's neck. Both barked and snarled. An ear bitten, the blood hot as it ran down James's jowl. Teeth sunk into an arm, the blood splashing into James's mouth. Anderson smashed him in the side of the head with his large paw. Another blow. James fell to the side, dazed as Anderson stood and kicked him in the face.

James opened his eyes, pushed himself up as Anderson closed in on Santiago. He lifted the old fat man into the air effortlessly, tossed him down next to the dead guard. Santiago's eyes were impossibly wide; his mouth opened in a shrill scream as he stared at the dripping remains of the man's skull.

Anderson gripped Santiago by the front of his orange prison uniform and jerked him bodily to his feet. James watched him shift into human form, still holding onto Santiago as he screamed in his face.

"*Where is she?!*"

James caught a glimpse of Anderson's hands. No ring.

He shifted to human form as Anderson screamed at Santiago again.

"*Answer me!*"

"Drop him," James called out. "Back off of him, Wade!"

Anderson looked at James, his face contorted in rage. "You back off, Coldstone! He's mine!"

"Not according to what I witnessed earlier," James said. "You work for this man."

"Now I don't," Anderson spat. He turned back to Santiago, jerked the man close to his face. "Got himself caught. He's on the outs, now."

"Let me go," Santiago pleaded. "Oh, God, please! I'll...I'll tell you anything you want! Anything!"

"Start with Clara Pickens," James said, moving up next to Anderson. "We'll move on from there."

Santiago opened his mouth, stammered, shook his head. His body began to tremble.

Anderson shook him again. "Answer me first!"

Santiago shifted his terrified gaze back to Anderson.

A click. A round chambered.

The back of Santiago's head blew outward from the force of the bullet that entered through his eyeball, showered brain matter and blood onto the street. James and Anderson ducked as another round sailed by, smacked into the lamppost next to them. They moved around to the other side of the van, took cover as a third round zipped by James's ear, clipped it. The sting was sickening; the entire side of his skull felt as if it were on fire.

Silver.

Anderson cursed, looked at James as if he might run. James shook his head, motioned for him to stay quiet. He shifted into wolf form and peered out over the edge of the van, looked over the rooftops with his lycanthrope sight. Windows. Doorways.

His ears perked at the sound of footsteps running off, someone climbing down a fire escape. Landing on a dumpster. Ground. Gone.

He shifted back as Anderson stood.

James looked at Anderson as the boy raised his hands.

"You're looking for Clara Pickens."

Anderson smiled. "She's all that's left. No one locks me in a cage and gets away with it."

9

James looked at Anderson, waited a second to see if he would make a move. Nothing. The boy smiled at him, his lithe form weak in comparison to his more muscular build as a were.

Or tiger. Or whatever the hell else he could change into.

"What are you?" James asked. "You're no lycanthrope I've ever seen before."

"I'm no lycanthrope, period," Anderson spat, his tone thick with disdain. "I'm an actual magical being, not some disease-carrying mongrel. Shape-shifting requires full control of every cell and molecule of the body, not some virus passed down from generation to generation or transferred by a bite on the ass." He put his hands down as he spoke. "And I smelled my target on these bastards. I know where she is."

"Then tell me," James said, clenching his fists. "Don't make me have to hurt you."

Anderson threw back his head and laughed. "Hurt me? You can't even manage your own fleas. You live in filth in a shit-hole apartment in downtown, you don't even bother with your family fortune, and you haven't set foot in your father's house since the day you were born."

James took a step back, his muscles tense. Anderson grinned at him.

"That's right, Coldstone. I know all about you."

The sound of a police siren echoed in the streets, the car off in the distance and closing. James looked over his shoulder in the direction of the noise, then back at Anderson. The kid shuddered, his skin crawling as feathers sprouted from every pore. He shrank in size, his wingspan wide as the hawk flew into the night sky.

"Dammit," James muttered under his breath. Three corpses, no answers, and the cops on their way.

The night just kept getting better.

He stopped short, sniffed the air. That sniper couldn't have gotten far. Not unless he was were, which was unlikely.

James shifted, made for the direction the bullet had come from, and picked up the scent of freshly used powder. Cologne. Bar soap. Sweat. He climbed the building effortlessly, breathed the scents in. North. The sniper had fled north.

He bounded across the rooftops. Sirens faded in the distance. Footfalls. Grunting. Cursing. Where the hell was the car?

James moved right, leapt onto the side of an apartment building, and scaled down the wall, using the windows as ledges as he lowered himself to the ground. The sniper turned, the man dressed in a black bodysuit and ski mask, the bolt-action 30.06 still gripped in his hand. He aimed it at James and fired. James dodged the bullet and closed in on the shooter. The man made to clock James with the butt of the gun, but James swatted lazily, and the rifle went flying. He reached out, gripped the man by the shirt, and threw him into a nearby garbage can. The can went over, spilling James's victim onto the sidewalk. He scrambled backward as the giant werewolf approached. James sent the wolf back, his body shifting to normal as he knelt over the panicked shooter.

"Information. *Now.*"

The man nodded.

"Why did you kill Santiago?"

"He was going to talk," the man said.

"Clara Pickens."

"C-Coldstone Keep," he stammered. "Been abandoned for years. Took the place a year ago."

James swallowed down his anger. Not only at the traffickers, but himself. If he'd been more attentive…damn.

"I'm not going to kill you," he said, moving his face close to the sniper as he brought the wolf back forward gradually. "But I can't have you following me, either." He let the change happen, the man screaming in terror as James snarled at him. He lifted a heavy foot and brought it down on the sniper's knee, the satisfying sound of bone and cartilage crunching loud in the air. The man screamed again, the high-pitched wail likely nothing compared to the amount of pain. James took back to the rooftops and toward the edge of town. He had to get to Phillip.

A squad car turned the corner below. He looked down, an idea forming in his mind.

I'm screwed anyway, he thought.

He leapt down, slammed to the ground in front of the vehicle. The driver hit the brakes hard enough to scrape the tires on the asphalt, the car stopping inches from James's knees. The officers got out, their weapons pointed. Both shook in terror, their eyes wide. James could smell the stench of fear on them.

He snarled at them, reared back, and released a howl. He pushed harder, his vocal cords vibrating as he flexed every muscle in his body.

The officers dropped their weapons as James climbed onto the car, his eyes fixed on them as he licked his teeth and snarled. The passenger turned and ran while the driver stood frozen, his eyes wide and locked on James.

James jumped off the car, landed in front of him, sniffed him. The man stood stock still, gripped in terror.

James grunted, cocked his head to the side.

Well, now. That's new.

He picked the man up by the shoulders and set him aside like a standing lamp. The man was stiff as a board, completely frozen with shock.

James reverted to human form, got into the squad car, and drove off into the night.

His father's castle.

Damn.

"About fucking time," Phillip spat as James got out of the car. "And I assume you'll need clothing again? And how the hell did you get a police car?"

"No time," James said. He looked around the highway. Phillip had moved the bodies off to the side of the road and had Angel sat up against a rock, positioned to where she looked comfortable. "I see you've been busy."

"Well, this highway does see traffic every now and again," Phillip said.

"I couldn't very well let them see a man surrounded by what looks like dead bodies, one of them actually dead."

"My father's castle," James said. "They've got Clara Pickens there."

Phillip blinked. "What the...hell? Why there?"

"I've never been there," James said. "I was letting it go. Never needed it. Get her in the car. I'm going to get some clothes."

"Hang on," Phillip said. "Letting it go? It's a fucking castle, James."

James rounded on Phillip, his anger boiling. "I've spent my adult life trying to separate myself from David Coldstone. I don't want his money, I don't want his legacy, and I don't want his fucking estate." James breathed, fought to calm his nerves. "I want nothing to do with my father."

"We can't help who our parents are," Phillip said. "It's not our choice. Our only choice is what we do."

James nodded, pushing away the urge to argue. Clara Pickens was being held at Coldstone Keep. There was no negotiation. He had to go.

James found an unconscious man whose clothes were the same size he wore and stripped him while Phillip gathered Angel's petite form and loaded her into the back seat of the car. He dressed, noted the pinprick in the man's neck.

"Why on earth are you carrying drugs with you?" he asked as he approached the car.

Phillip finished buckling Angel in and stood.

"Mostly for her," he said. "Like I said earlier: insurance. We couldn't have her getting loose in the city, could we?"

James shook his head. "She's not likely to be pleased when she wakes."

Phillip patted James on the arm. "That's why *you're* riding in the back with her."

"I call shotgun."

Phillip moved by him and climbed into the driver's seat. "Absolutely not."

"Why not?"

Phillip went to pull the door shut and stopped, looking up at James.

"Firstly, because I want you back there to keep her under control when she comes to. Secondly, it is recommended by the York County Department of Road Safety to always have your pets ride in the back."

He shut the door as James shouted back at him. "You made that up!"

Phillip shot him the finger and jabbed a thumb toward the back seat.

"Dick," James muttered as he got in.

———

A ngel stirred, groaning as she rubbed her forehead and stretched. James could tell from her grimace that she was in pain.

And, as anticipated, not particularly happy.

"You fucking bastard," she said, glaring at Phillip through the wire mesh that separated the front and back seats. She gripped the mesh, leaning close to Phillip's ear as she hissed at him. "I'll take that needle and shove it so far up your ass..."

"I see your girlfriend is a morning person," Phillip said over his shoulder.

James raised an eyebrow. "I don't believe she'd be willing to share a litter box with me," he said as he put his hand on Angel's shoulder. "Relax. We can explain."

If looks could kill, Angel would have murdered him a thousand times over. He moved his hand.

"You drugged me to keep me from chasing after Anderson with you and stuffed me into the back of a fucking police car to drive me out into what looks like the middle of nowhere."

James opened his mouth to speak, then closed it and shrugged. "Yeah, I'd say that covers it. Phillip?"

Phillip nodded. "Yup."

Angel crossed her arms in front of her. "I should kill both of you."

James grinned at her. "Then you'd never find Anderson," he said. "We've got him. We're headed right to him, now. Along with Clara Pickens and what looks like the current headquarters for our local trafficking ring."

Angel looked at him sidelong. "At least you've been productive."

"I try."

"We're a few miles out," Phillip said. "Anything I should know about this place, James?"

"As I said before, I've never been there. I've seen pics, but that's all."

Angel laughed. "Coldstone Keep? We're going there?"

James nodded. "We are. It's where Anderson and his group are hiding out. We're ending this tonight."

"I just find it fascinating that you know nothing about your ancestry," Angel said. "Coldstone Keep goes much further back than you think."

"I don't care," James said, turning away and staring at the window.

"Do go on," Phillip said up front, mocking enthusiasm. "I love a good history lesson."

James made a note to shit in Phillip's yard again when they got back to Rock Hill.

"Lance Coldstone came here four hundred years ago after escaping the Carpathians," Angel said, ignoring James as he rolled his eyes. "Once he found out the true dangers of Dracula's ring, he wanted to move his family away rather than make them vulnerable. If Dracula could force a change, then they could be exposed and hunted by the locals."

"Which explains his reason for making the thing in the first place," Phillip said. "Have frightened villagers do his dirty work for him."

"Yup," Angel said. "My father suspected the ring was capable of more, but that seems to be its primary purpose. Coldstone was one of the last of the lycanthropes to be driven from the Carpathians. He managed to bring a few artifacts with him. My father and I found one or two things, but I've never been to the estate." She winked at James. "Care to see them when we get back?"

"David Coldstone took the place over generations later," James said, shooting Angel a look. She smiled as he spoke. "He'd moved to Wales on business and returned when my grandfather passed away, leaving him the castle and the family fortune." He rolled his eyes again. "I want nothing to do with that place."

"God, you whine like a child," Phillip said.

"My father was a feral murderer," James said, his anger rising. "He knew what he was, and he made no effort to stop himself from killing everyone near him."

"So, you try to make it all better by avoiding killing humans?" Angel said. "That's why you were so angry at me for gutting that guy?"

"Actually, that one will make things difficult on me as well," Phillip said, looking in the rear-view mirror at her. "Investigations, animal attacks, and fuckery. Lots of paperwork and a cover story. I appreciate that. Bitch."

"So, what's the plan, babe?" Angel said, ignoring Phillip as she smiled at James.

James stared out the window. "I'm working on it."

Coldstone Keep sat in a valley surrounded by hills and forest, a lone road the only way in or out of the property in the furthest countryside of York County a person could get without hitting Cherokee County. A small, rural community called Smyrna. James had a vague idea of the area based on what his mother had told him, but nothing concrete. He did recall that the road up to the house was at least a mile long, and he had Phillip park on the side of the highway to keep the sound of a car on the drive from alerting any guards that might be present.

James looked around, sniffed the night air as he closed the car door behind him. He let the wolf forward just enough to let him smell things beyond human ability. The scent of wood smoke permeated the air, carried by the light breeze.

They were there.

"We go in dark," James said, turning to Angel and Phillip. "We use stealth, quiet. Hit hard and make sure you're not seen."

"I'll radio in for backup," Phillip said. "It'll give you an hour. After that, the place will be crawling with cops."

"We do not kill," James said, looking directly at Angel. "I don't care who it is or what they're doing. Incapacitate only."

Angel pouted. "You're no fun."

James ignored her and looked at Phillip. "Angel and I will shift and head up the road. Give us a ten-minute head start, then radio in."

"How do I explain the car?" Phillip asked, raising an eyebrow.

James looked at the car, then back at him. "Radio in as anonymous."

Phillip laughed. "It doesn't work that way," he said. "I have to identify myself. I have to give a badge number. I can't just call in and say, 'Yeah, I don't want to give my name.' There's protocol to follow."

James looked from him to the car and back again, his expression not changing. He did it again.

Phillip shook his head, closed his eyes, and breathed out as if to keep himself from yelling. He spoke through gritted teeth. "I'll figure it out."

James and Angel made for the road without a word. James was almost off the highway when Phillip called to him.

"Alpo's on sale if you make it back."

James stopped and looked over his shoulder. Phillip's tone carried no sarcasm behind the joke. He saw Phillip watching him, his face drawn with concern and worry.

"Just make it back."

James nodded. "I will."

He turned away and jogged after Angel, following her down the dark path toward the castle.

The trail was growing darker, the branches high above starting to block the moonlight. The moon was still fresh off its cycle, only a shade shy of the fullness that could force a change. James considered himself lucky. He needed complete control, to be able to shift and revert when necessary.

There was no sign of Angel. She'd run ahead.

Christ, he thought. He knew he couldn't trust her not to run ahead. She'd likely shifted and was already near the castle.

He'd have to be quick.

James stripped, moved to a nearby tree to hide the clothing. Something seemed off in the moonlight. He knelt and moved aside the pile of leaves.

Angel's shirt. Pants. Bra and panties. Torn to shreds.

Fuck me, he thought to himself.

He shifted, his yellowed vision rendering the moonlight unnecessary as he broke into a run, falling forward and using his powerful arms to gain more speed as he loped down the road. He let the scents come at him full bore, picking up on Angel's unmistakable musk as he went. She was in cat form. He cursed himself again. He should've given her another round of sedative and left her in the fucking car. He picked up speed, heard someone calling out ahead. *Keep an eye. Watch the girl. They'll be coming.*

James darted to the left, found a large fallen tree to hide behind as he peered through the branches, looking ahead at the looming and ominous Coldstone Keep.

The keep was tall, looking from the outside like a modest castle with four gables, each connected by a wall. The structure was made from large stones set in place and secured hundreds of years ago, the front gate formed of iron inlaid into thick wood. Large sconces burned on either side of the gate, and men walked around carrying torches, likely forgoing flashlights to avoid attention should a helicopter wander by. James could see men posted on guard, two at the gate, one on the roof of each gable. Each carried a rifle, keeping watch at the woods.

They were expecting him. It would make it more difficult to get in.

Challenge accepted.

Someone moved across the top of the front wall, walking from one spire toward the next. Anderson stopped, glanced over the wall, and shifted. The men seemed to tense but managed to keep their composure all the same. It was as if they were used to him becoming a werewolf. How long had they been here?

Anderson turned and surveyed the area, his eyes flashing as they passed over the tree where James was hiding. James remained motionless, his eyes fixed on Anderson as the shifter reared his head back and yowled into the sky.

Come off it, James thought. *At least* howl *like a lycanthrope.*

Something moved behind him. Leaves crumpled. A twig broke. James made to whirl around, his claws out, his teeth bared. Something pricked into his neck. He swatted away the dart.

Shit!

He could feel the tranquilizer working into his body, shutting him down. He ran back into the woods. Down the road. Had to warn Phillip. It was a trap. It…it was…

James's arms and legs gave as he tumbled forward, rolled once, and lay on his back. His chest heaved as his mind swirled, his eyes heavy with sleep. A figure stood over him, looking down, a large blowgun in her hands.

Angel knelt over him, wearing a black bodysuit, her hair tied back as she smiled at him.

"There now, handsome. Take a nap. You'll need your rest."

1 0

James let his eyes slowly open and adjust to the low firelight as he looked around. He went to sit forward, realizing quickly that his arms were bound behind him, rope stretched across his chest and holding him to the chair. He tried to move his legs and found them tied together. The air chilled his sweat-soaked skin.

He studied his surroundings. He was in the back yard, the fences to the old horse pastures in disrepair. The barn had collapsed years back, and James remembered his mother calling a contractor to come clear it out. A platform had been built in its place, something like what he'd seen in the movies when the villain was about to execute the good guy in front of the crowd.

A familiar, feminine voice purred in his ear. "Was it good for you, baby?"

He turned his head and stared up at Angel as she stood and backed a pace away from him, smiling as she straightened the silk robe she wore.

"Lovely," he muttered.

Anderson's voice broke the air. "So happy you made it, Coldstone. I was beginning to wonder if you'd ever show up. We're on a schedule, you know."

James looked at him. Anderson stood on the platform, looking down at James and smiling as if he'd just caught a prize trophy during a hunt. He also wore a robe, his a deep red velvet and longer than Angel's.

"So sorry," James said, not holding back the sarcastic tone. "Traffic was an utter nightmare, and I just couldn't get Phillip motivated."

"Oh, well then maybe you can have a word with him," Anderson said, nodding. James followed his gaze to a guard standing at a doorway to the far right. The guard nodded back at Anderson, turned, and opened the door to allow two more in, dragging Phillip along with them. He was bound and gagged, grunting and struggling against them as they brought him over and stood him next to James.

"Untie his hands," Anderson called down. "He's a human and unarmed. He can't do anything to us."

The goons untied Phillip's hands and removed the cloth gag from his mouth. He glared at Angel, then back down at James. "This is your fault."

"I can accept that."

"There's nothing to accept, you fuckin' moron. This is *all* your fault. I told you she couldn't be trusted."

"I may need to rethink my problem with trusting people."

"I think you may need to rethink using your dick instead of your brain when it comes to partnering up with someone who tranquilized you on your first date."

"Noted."

Anderson's voice echoed in the courtyard. "All right, both of you assholes knock it off!"

James nudged his head at Phillip. "He started it."

Angel stepped around in front of James, shaking her head as she looked from him to Phillip.

"You two really are a couple of idiots," she said. She looked at James, her eyes flashing. "It's a shame you're so pretty, James. Such a waste."

"So, the ring?" James asked, leveling his gaze at her.

"It's mine when this is over," said Angel. "It's my trade. I help him keep you under control and finish you off, I get the ring."

"Why me?"

"Because you are what you are," Anderson called from above. "An animal. A heathen. You've no more control over yourself than a rabid dog."

"Says the man who can turn into any animal he likes."

"Wrong again," Anderson said with a grin. "I can turn into any living thing I choose. Any form I lay eyes on. I find your kind the easiest to emulate."

"You still haven't explained your special interest in me," James said. "Outside of insults, you've managed to show me that you're not a fan."

"You and your cop friend have a reputation in the supernatural underground, whether you know it or not," Anderson said. "You have killed a fair share of things that go bump in the night. Broken up drug rings and murder cults. All by going in as a monster and tearing everything non-human to shreds. It was only a matter of time before our little organization hit your radar. What better way to keep you occupied than to frame you for murders that echo your father's? The Coldstone murders were a perfect crime to bring back to the forefront. Especially when the murderer's own son was too thick-headed to move away."

Anderson pulled the ring from the breast pocket of the robe and held it out. "Count Dracula made this ring for a special reason. It doesn't just force a change on all lycanthropes. I can specify who I want to change. But it also does a little something extra. Enchantments, no matter how deep in the bloodline they run, can be pushed aside."

Enchantments? What was he talking about? James looked back at Angel as she strolled toward the platform. She climbed the ladder and joined Anderson.

"Why do I give a shit about enchantments?" James called up to him. "I've never had any done. I've never even met someone who can do that."

"Well, then," Anderson said as he placed the ring on his index finger. "Then you should get through this just fine."

James's body lurched, his bones shifting, his muscles stretching under his skin. The pain was white hot, running up and down his spine as he screamed in agony. The change had never hurt before. What was happening? His head swam, dizzy as the wolf came forward, its claws embedded deep in his mind as it sank its teeth into his skull. The ropes broke, the chair splintered as he stood. His vision was yellowed, his brain foggy, then sharp as he looked down at Phillip. He ran his tongue slowly over sharp teeth, his eyes wide with insane menace as he hunched down, ready to pounce. Phillip backed away.

Food tasted better when skittish.

The wolf felt the human shouting inside, trying to bark at it, its mewls drowned out by the thrum of blood in its ears, the heat of the hunt. The human's companion stared at it. Fear. Sweet and salty all at once as it drew the scent in over its tongue.

"James...what the hell are you doing? Why are you looking at me like that?"

Another smell. Young. Pup. Girl pup. The wolf stood tall on its hind legs, stretched its arms to either side, howled as the moon above called to it. The beast charged. The prey was quick. Ducked out of the way. The wolf gathered its feet, turned, made for it again. The quarry made for the platform. Loud barks from around the area. The other men using fire sticks to keep the target away from the edge.

They would be prey next.

The wolf charged again. No hunt. No track. Just kill. Roll in blood, taste flesh. The human inside screamed at it to stop. Pushed it back. Could hear prey shouting at it. "Stop, James. This isn't you. It's me. Phillip. Your best friend."

The prey ducked around the side of the platform. The other thing on the platform called for the barking men to stop. Let him scramble where he wants. Prey was under the ledge.

Wolf followed.

More voices from above. Prey trapped. Wolf could reach. Tear with claws. Drag prey.

"I'll be keeping this a while longer, Angel. You understand, of course."

"You bastard! That wasn't the arrangement!"

"Not anymore."

Could feel prey's coat on claw. Tore. Prey backed away again. Sounds from above. A shout. Blood. Not man blood. Something else. Scream. Loud words.

James pushed the wolf back, looked around. He was underneath the platform somehow, the stage low enough that he had to hunch down to fit. Phillip lay on the ground, his arms up in defense, his eyes wide with fear. James looked at him, shook off. He let out a low groan followed by some whining.

I'm sorry. I don't know what happened.

"James?" Phillip put his arms down cautiously, not taking his eyes away. James heard commotion above them, yowling and a loud yelp. Snarling. A loud slam. Angel and Anderson. What was going on?

James lowered to all fours and moved to Phillip. He barked once. Two more times.

Get away!

"Clara Pickens," said Phillip. "We need to find her. She has to be here."

There was another scent. James pushed it away. No. It wasn't her. No one could be capable of that evil.

James looked above them, out past Phillip.

Phillip looked behind him and nodded.

"I'll draw their fire. Get up there and get that ring."

James gave a sharp bark and moved away, out from beneath the platform and leaping up onto it with ease.

Angel and Anderson were both changed, Anderson opting for his favorite werewolf form. He swiped at her, his hand spilling blood the entire way. James noticed Anderson's missing finger right away as Angel ducked, lashed out with her claws, four trails of blood appearing on his side.

James made to lunge into the fray, stopped short when something caught his eye. It glinted in the moonlight, small and still wrapped around the severed finger.

Dracula's ring. It was still on Anderson's finger.

James made for the amputated digit, reached for it when something knocked the wind out of him. He rolled to the side. Anderson latched onto him, snarling and snapping his jaws in James's face. James retaliated, gripping with claws and sinking teeth into neck and shoulder. Anderson yelped, pulled away, clawed at James's chest. Hot pain stinging as the razors sliced skin and meat through the thick hair.

James bucked him off, scrambled away only to encounter Angel. She dove to the side, made for the ring. James tackled her, reached again for the ring and finger only to have his hand kicked away. He grabbed Anderson by the foot and jerked, rolled, and got to his feet as he dragged the bastard with him. Anderson reached for him, and James saw the bloody stump where a finger used to be. He gripped Anderson's hand and squeezed, the shifter's blood running between his fingers and soaking his fur. Anderson howled in pain as gunshots rang out all over the courtyard. James caught a glimpse of Phillip, a dead guard on the ground near him as he took cover and returned fire with the shotgun he'd snatched up.

Nice.

James's head spun from the blow as he fell. Anderson kicked him in the gut and gave another hit to the skull. James rolled, swung out blindly, connected. Anderson backpedaled, a row of claw marks across his face. He shook it off, growled at James, looked down. James followed his gaze, getting his feet underneath him as he worked his way up.

The finger lay at Anderson's feet. He reached down for it, grabbed it between to claws.

A whirlwind of ginger fur and razor talons slammed into Anderson, knocked him off his feet. The finger went flying, landed in front of James as the hellish she-cat tore into Anderson's chest and face. He rammed his arm through the attack, gripped her by the throat. She choked as he closed his giant paw around her neck, scratched at his hand, the blood running down her body from his injuries. Anderson lashed out, cut her stomach open, tossed her to the side like a bag of garbage. He looked at James, his teeth bared, his eyes flashing. Shouts and gunfire sounded as more of Anderson's men fell to Phillip's shotgun blasts while others retreated into the night. Anderson rounded on James and snarled again. James growled back, saw the blood running from the dark hole in Anderson's face.

His eye. Angel had put out one of his eyes.

James rushed him, going in low. Anderson braced, his arms open for the attack. James faked right, played to Anderson's good eye. Anderson readied a counter, struck out. James landed a blow from the left and sent Anderson to the deck. Another blow. Another. James clamped his teeth into Anderson's throat, locked his jaws, jerked his neck as he thrashed the bastard back and forth in his teeth, tore away at his throat. Anderson gurgled, tried to snarl, the bubbling sound sending blood spray into James's face. The smell was sweet, intoxicating.

Different. Not just Anderson. Angel. Someone else. Girl. Pup.

Mindy.

Fury welled in James, his yellow vision deepening as he pulled away. Anderson had reverted to human form. His neck was bitten through, his severed head lolled to the side, his eyes blank.

The finger lay beside him. Phillip approached the platform, moving next to James, the shotgun only half-aimed. James reverted, knelt, picked up the finger. He removed the ring, tossed the finger aside.

"I'm me," he said, not looking up. He held the ring out, trying to calm his pounding heart. He wanted to turn back, kill everyone there, let Phillip have his pick at who to shoot. He wanted to find every one of them, gore them, roll in their blood until he was covered. His muscles tensed, his fists clenched at his sides as tears welled in his eyes.

Angel's voice was thin, weak.

"J...James..."

He looked over at the edge of the platform where Anderson had thrown her. She'd reverted, lay in a pool of blood, the fluid black in the low light. Phillip went to her, aimed his shotgun at her head.

"Silver, I'd wager," he said.

"Don't...waste the bullets," Angel breathed. "You'll need them."

James went to her. She reached for him, weak, desperate. He knelt, looked her over. She was bleeding out. He'd seen it before on his hunts, his prey dying once he'd tracked them down.

She didn't have long.

"Mindy?" James asked. "Clara?"

Angel shook her head.

"Both. Charleston. Gone. He sent them earlier...today."

She reached up, touched the side of his face, her hand trembling.

"I...wanted the ring. My...father's find. I liked...you."

Her hand fell away, hit the platform solid and limp as air wheezed from her lips, her pulse fading away beneath his fingertips.

"I'm sorry, James," Phillip said. "I really am."

James lay Angel's head gently down and stood, looking around the compound. She'd been here. He could smell it. How long had they been at his father's castle?

"They have her," he said, his anger boiling behind his words, hot in his chest and throat. He clenched his teeth, fought back the tears of rage. He couldn't let go, couldn't give into it.

Couldn't let the wolf feed on it.

"Who?" Phillip said. "Clara Pickens? We know that."

"No," James said, shaking his head. He grimaced, pushed away the disbelief. It was real. It happened. He looked sidelong at Phillip. "Mindy. They have Mindy."

———

The air was cool, the sky overcast as the clouds moved in. There would be rain before too long. The breeze rustled through the trees, their song a million whispers all at once. Soothing, peaceful.

On any other day.

James stood on the sidewalk, his hands in his pockets. He waited for the rain. No jacket. No hood or umbrella.

He didn't deserve comfort.

Mindy's father didn't notice as he walked down the front path, a small bag of trash in his hand. He dropped it into the dumpster at the curb, stopped, and stared at the sign he'd hung from the telephone pole. It matched the rest of the posters that hung around Rock Hill. The police had told him it wouldn't help. He hadn't cared.

Missing: Mindy Robertson, Age 10. Brown hair, brown eyes. Taken in her sleep. Please notify the authorities or family if seen.

One hung on the fence behind James. Phone number and address for the family. Name of officer overseeing the case. Mindy's picture in the center, her eyes full of joy, her smile bright and cheerful. Her happiness gave the picture color when there was none.

James couldn't bear to look at it long.

He watched as Mindy's father went back inside, moving slowly, weak. A man in pain, shutting the front door to keep his ache locked inside.

"There's no trace," Phillip said as he approached. James hadn't heard him coming. Hadn't cared to listen for him. "Standing out here and staring isn't going to help you, James. It'll only hurt worse."

"Comforting," James said, not caring about his tone. "And noted."

Phillip stood beside him, looked down, then back up at him. James saw him out of the corner of his eye, kept his gaze on the empty swing set at the back of the small house.

"I'm sorry," Phillip said. "I've talked to everyone in the department. I'm not lead, so I had to manage while dealing with the inquiry about what happened at the Keep."

"And?"

"Nothing. She was taken in her sleep. No sign of forced entry."

James grunted. "Of course not. She probably thought it was me."

"Possible," Phillip said, nodding. "Anderson. Shape-shifting son of a bitch."

"And the estate?"

James and Phillip had left the scene as soon as they heard the officers trampling through the woods. They'd waited hours while the police searched the castle, cleaning up the bodies and securing the area. Once morning had come, and the area cleared, James shifted, hoisted Phillip onto his back, and ran to Angel's cottage to clean up. Phillip went into work as if it were a typical day, demanding to know why he hadn't been called to the scene, filing complaints against the right people for not notifying him since he was lead on the investigation.

All tracks covered.

Almost.

"Once things simmer down, you should be able to reclaim it," Phillip said. "It took some convincing, but they believe you're overseas."

James gave a bitter laugh. "In twenty-four hours, I'll be out of town, at least."

Phillip turned to him. "You can't be serious. Charleston? This trafficking group is huge. Where would you start?"

"At the beginning," James said. "The end. Somewhere in the middle. I don't know, and I don't care. I'm locked onto her scent. I *will* find her."

"How will you get there?"

"I'm shockingly wealthy. My family has a ridiculous fortune sitting in the banks. It's time I utilized it." James glanced at Phillip. "And the ring?"

"It's amazing the effect a mini-sledge has on jewelry."

James nodded, turning to him.

"I'm sorry, Phillip," he said. "I didn't know what was happening. It's no excuse, but I couldn't control myself."

"You weren't yourself," Phillip said. "But it begs the question: is it evolution?"

It'd been biting at James ever since they'd left Coldstone Keep. He'd lost all control, the wolf having taken him. He'd been pushed away, a forced observer. How? He'd never been without his humanity during the change. It was evolution.

Wasn't it?

Even as a child, he'd been fully aware while he was in his wolf form. The ring had changed that. It meant something.

It meant lies.

"My mother is gone," James said. "There's no way to ask her." He looked back at Mindy's house. "It's my fault they took her."

Phillip didn't say anything. James didn't blame himself out of depression. If he hadn't met Mindy, imprinted on her, Anderson would never have found her. Anderson had seen an opportunity to goad James. Provoke him. And he'd taken it.

"Do you remember them saying anything?" Phillip asked.

James shrugged. "They mentioned Charleston, but that's all."

"Then we start there," Phillip said, looking at the house.

"We?"

"I've some leave I can take," Phillip said. He looked at James and made a face, pointing his finger at his temple like a gun and pulling the trigger. He spoke in a monotone. "Stress. I'm cracking. Can't take it. Need time."

"I can't ask you to come with me."

"I'm not giving you the option, Snoopy," Phillip said. "You can't go without someone to remind you that you are a complete idiot. Besides, you'll need someone a bit more learned on trafficking than you are."

Phillip turned back to the house. James followed his gaze, his chest tightening again as the swing moved in the breeze.

"I think this is connected to your family, somehow," he said. "The ring. The Keep. Framing you. Why would Anderson have gone to such lengths?"

James nodded. "Fair questions, and I've got no answers." He clenched his fists in his pocket, a yellow flash across his vision as he felt the wolf stir inside him. "But I can tell you this much: I'll never stop, and there will be hell to pay."

II

WOLFMOON

1

James's ear twitched at the sound of someone approaching. He smelled the cheap cologne.

"Nothing yet," he said as Phillip stepped up beside him. "And you look ridiculous."

Phillip looked down at his khaki shorts and Hawaiian shirt, then at the plain white button-up and denim James wore.

"At least I've got color," he said. "Besides, this is the style these days."

James kept his eye on the bridge off to the left as a car drove across the giant structure.

"I wouldn't be caught dead wearing flowers and tan shorts that bunch at the crotch."

"You're an ass. Did you see it again?"

James squinted, looking at the tall concrete supports underneath the bridge. The orange glow from the streetlights that lined either side of the bridge cast shadows over the area. The shadows stayed still. For now.

"Not yet."

Phillip sighed. "I'm getting hungry. Dinner?"

James looked at him sidelong.

"I haven't seen one deer around. It's depressing. Any word on Mindy?"

Mindy Robertson was the ten-year-old girl James befriended during his rampage through Rock Hill in forced werewolf form. Wade Anderson, a shapeshifter working for a human trafficking cartel, had kidnapped her.

James killed Wade in a blind fury when he'd smelled Mindy's scent on the bastard, but Mindy and Wade's other victim, Clara Pickens, were already gone. Anderson mentioned something about Charleston, which was the only information James had gathered before things went to hell. Clara was the adult daughter of a prominent lawyer in Rock Hill who'd met his demise at the hands of Anderson's werewolf form.

Phillip shook his head. "Nothing," he said. "No leads. But it's early. These things take time. There've been disappearances around both Rock Hill and Charlotte, but only one or two."

James clenched his fist. "Time is not a luxury either Mindy or Clara have."

"You care more about Mindy. Admit it."

"Gladly. An adult is far more capable of defending herself than a little girl."

"Why *that* little girl, though?"

James had pondered that question constantly ever since he'd met the child. There was something about her—something that connected them. He was unable to put his finger on it, but she impressed him. She carried no fear of him, a creature capable of killing her before she saw it coming. He locked onto her scent when they first met. Something kicked in, a primal instinct.

Protect the young.

James looked back to the bridge. His eyes darted to a spot near the center of the long archway. The shape moved, crawling up the column from the water. It stopped, moved its head slightly, continued up. It was small from where James stood, man-shaped, and likely man-sized.

"Excellent," he said. He unbuttoned his shirt quickly, pulled it off, dropped his pants.

Phillip squinted at the bridge. "Christ, I forgot my binoculars. What is that?"

"I'm going to find out," James said as he bent over and gathered his clothes. He handed them to Phillip. "Here you go."

Phillip rolled his eyes. "Christ, James, we're outside in someone's back *yard.* Show a little decency, will you?"

"Said the man who once danced on a sofa in a girl's bra and panties."

"It was a party in college. I was drunk."

James smiled. "Still sticking with that story, are we?"

He backed away, let the wolf forward, keeping a mental leash on it as it began to take his body. He grew, thick hair sprouting from his skin as his muscles enlarged, his face elongating, his ears moving to the top of his head, pointed and alert. He licked his chops, grunted at Phillip, and darted off in the other direction as Phillip called to him.

"It's the truth, asshole!"

James moved swiftly, the trees and shoreline speeding by him as he romped through the brush. He dashed past the Pump House restaurant, came to the bridge, and looked down the mile-long underpass, the stench of mildew and salt strong. He sniffed the air. Motor oil. Cooking food at the Pump House.

Something else. Sweet. Sickly sweet. Coppery.

Rotten.

Vampire, James thought. *Great.*

He climbed up to the side of the bridge, keeping to the small ledge not typically meant for pedestrian traffic unless said pedestrian was a daredevil. He followed the scent, let it grow stronger in his nose as he drew closer to the center. Another car passed. He ducked, waited until he heard the engine fade into the night.

All that was left was breathing. His breathing.

No.

He lurched forward and grabbed the guardrail at the top of the concrete sidewall as the thing slammed into his back, snarled in his ear, and tried to bite through his thick fur. He let the creature's weight roll him over the wall and onto the bridge. James hit the ground, landed on top of the little bastard. The vampire shouted in pain and let go of his neck. James got to his feet and growled at the monster as it stood, its hungry red eyes glowing and fixed on him. A middle-aged man in a polo shirt. Likely well-to-do. A resident. Someone important?

James grunted. No matter. It would be pieces real soon.

The vampire launched at him, gnashing his teeth like a wild animal. He'd been turned recently. Newly turned tended to be overzealous at first, rushing prey they had no business going after.

James had killed more than a few.

He swung out lazily with his paw, caught the man in the face, and sent him to the ground. The vampire got to his feet instantly and rushed James again, drool hanging from his long canines.

"*Fangs,* jackass," Phillip had said once. "They're called fangs. Not every supernatural you encounter is a dog."

James grabbed the hissing youngling vamp by the face and lifted him off his feet. The vampire yowled like a deranged cat, clawed at the thick fur on James's arm. The claws couldn't get through. This vamp was likely only a few weeks into his turn.

James slammed the vampire down, lifted him again. Sir Fangs-a-lot delivered a savage kick to the gut. James released him. The vampire tumbled to the ground, rolled, and was up and running away in an instant.

James pulled his lips back from his rows of teeth in a rictus, canine grin. *Fast food it is.*

James took after him, gained speed as the vampire sprinted across the bridge toward Fort Mill. He flashed, was gone.

Vampire speed.

Damn!

James broke into his were speed, the streets and homes and stores blurring by as he breathed the air in steadily, letting the dead and acrid smell of vampire lead him. Left. Up Highway 160. Traffic was almost nonexistent. One or two cars he had to avoid. They slammed on brakes or swerved, not seeing more than a flash or streaking blur. The scent faded, stronger to the right. Road turned to soil, grass, a park. He could smell the lake.

James halted as the area opened to a small neighborhood on an inlet of water that led into Lake Wylie. There were several sailboats and pontoon boats tied off to the dock. Most were dark, a few floating in their slips with the interior lights on inside the curtained windows. James caught the silhouettes of people moving about behind the curtains on one vessel, the two inside engaging in some late-night activities.

James's ears perked up at the high-pitched screams that sounded from that particular pontoon boat. It was covered, the plastic windows dull and foggy. He bolted toward it as blood spattered on the plastic, more female screams filling the night air. He leapt the gap between the first boat and the dock, clamored over the railing, and made for the opposite side, kicking off and going airborne to the next boat. Another. He landed on the deck as the woman's screams cut short.

The tent ripped open as the vampire lunged at him, the thing covered in blood and gore. James sidestepped the newborn, swatted him out of the air. Fangs-a-lot recovered quickly, rolled to his feet, and lunged at James again. James grappled him, slung him off the boat and onto the dock. He followed, pinning the vamp, and snapped his jaws shut like a vice. The vampire held up his arm to fend off the attack, screamed when werewolf teeth crushed bone and muscle.

Something gave James pause as vampire blood filled his mouth and dripped from his jaw. He sniffed the monster again. There was something...

James snarled, lifted him, and slammed the screaming vampire against the dock. Fangs-a-lot barely had time to gather himself before James was on him again. The vamp hissed, but James lifted him again, clamped his jaws down and jerked, ripping the vampire's arm off at the elbow. The youngling shrieked in pain as James dropped him. Fangs-a-lot tried to scramble away, but James smacked him, rolled him over on the wood slats. He saw the look he wanted to see on the youngling's face.

Terror.

"Leave me alone!" Fangs-a-lot shouted at him.

James made for him, lifted his foot, brought it down, and twisted as the knee joint underneath his heel crunched and ground. The vampire was young. His wounds would take longer to heal.

Good.

James shifted back into human form.

"I'm going to ask you a series of questions," he said as he knelt over the writhing vamp. "You *will* answer them. Where is she?"

The vampire shook his head, looking confused. James grabbed him by the shirt, yanked him up until their faces were almost touching.

"*Where is she?!*"

"Who?! I don't know what you're talking about!"

"Mindy! The little girl! I can smell her all over you! Did you hurt her?"

"What? No! I didn't! I swear!"

James jerked him, grabbed the stump where his arm had been, and squeezed. The vampire howled in pain, tears in his eyes.

"Talk!"

"I had to inspect her! Make sure she was pure! We do it with all of the girls! I...I swear I didn't touch her! I just had to smell her!"

James squeezed the stump again, and the vampire screamed "I swear!" over and over until James released.

"Who turned you? When?"

The youngling's face went blank with horror as he shook his head. "I... it was a week ago. Job promotion in the group. But I can't. I can't tell you. He'll...no, he'll know. What he can do..."

"It's nothing compared to what I'll do if you don't start talking," James said.

The youngling shook his head.

James stood, looking down at him, his fury white-hot. "I'll ask one last time: *Where. Is. She?*"

The vampire shook his head, his eyes wide with terror. James blinked. There was no way he was instilling that much fear into this little shit. Something else had him locked, terrified.

"I don't know." Fangs-a-lot sobbed. "I honestly...I swear."

James nodded as the wolf came back, making him grow. He spoke just before he was no longer capable.

"Thanks for nothing."

He reached his full shift as the vampire screamed at him, the sound feral and raw. James lifted his foot and caved his skull in. He reached down, rammed his fist into the vamp's chest, ripped the heart free, and crushed it. The vampire crumbled to dust, particles slipping between his fingers.

"A bit much, don't you think?"

James whipped around at the sound of Phillip's voice. He stood on the dock, out of breath, the headlights from his car shining from the parking space at the top of the hill.

"I was in the car and over the bridge right when you hit your wolf speed," he said. "Good thing I've got a lead foot."

James shifted back to human form, his body still shaking with rage. He grunted one word at Phillip. "Clothes."

Phillip slipped the satchel off his back and handed it to James.

"You're getting worse," he said.

"Do tell," James said, pulling the blue jeans up and fastening them.

"You've got to be more careful. The police will be all over this tomorrow. Possibly sooner if anyone heard the commotion out here."

"We'll be long gone."

"James, you're getting reckless."

James rounded on Phillip, opened his mouth to speak. The concern on Phillip's face, the expression of genuine worry, stopped him.

"It's been like this ever since Anderson used the ring on you," Phillip continued.

"I'm fine."

"You're obsessed. You don't even care about Clara Pickens anymore."

"I'm not locked onto Clara Pickens's scent." James pulled his shirt on. "Find Mindy, find Clara. We talked about this." He looked at Phillip again. "I'm okay. Really."

Phillip nodded reluctantly.

"Fine. We need to leave before things get worse out here. Your friend's victim may have roused some concerned neighbors, and I'm a little dark to be wandering around a bunch of boats in a rich-ass neighborhood at night."

James looked at the pile of dust on the dock. Something caught his eye. He reached down and picked up a hotel room key card out of the ash, brushing the corpse dust off as he read the lettering on the front.

Meeting Street Inn.

James turned and looked at Phillip, holding up the key card.

"Can we go to Charleston, now? I already have a place for us to stay."

2

J ames sighed, sat back in his chair as he took in the aroma of coffee in the restaurant. He glanced out the window, saw the sun rising in the sky, the bluish hues growing brighter with every passing minute. He pulled his phone from his pocket and looked at the time.

"Good God," he muttered. "Is getting up this early really necessary?"

Phillip smirked as he picked up his coffee cup. "Aw, poor baby," he said. "Not everyone sleeps until noon, dude. Normal people tend to lead productive lives."

"I'm productive."

"Are not."

"Am too."

Phillip snorted. "You don't even have a job, you lazy shit. You live...*lived* in an apartment by yourself, sleep most of the day, and spend your nights burying bones and drinking out of toilets."

James shrugged.

"I have priorities. Working isn't on the list." James took a sip of his tea, then spoke again in a bitter tone. "Besides, I'm loaded thanks to dear ol' dad." He motioned with his cup. "Notice the accommodations."

They'd checked into the Meeting Street Inn at around three in the morning. The place harkened back to the Old South, the historic décor ornate and iconic. It looked like an old plantation home on steroids, the white railings on the lower and upper floors of the outer walkways seeming to have a fresh coat of paint daily. The rooms were hardwood floors, plaster walls, and each had a four-post, king-sized bed made of dark mahogany wood. James purchased two separate rooms. They didn't know how long they would be in Charleston, and James wanted to be able to come and go in the late hours without disturbing Phillip.

Then again, he also had a key to Phillip's room. James was sure an opportunity for a good practical joke would present itself at some point during their stay.

Phillip put his cup down. "You aren't him, you know."

James waved it off. "Save it. I hate the bastard. Want nothing to do with him. Doesn't mean I'm above using his money to live. I wouldn't have time to work, anyway." He nodded at the window. "More important things going on."

He took another sip of his tea as the waitress walked up with her notepad in hand. She was pretty, young, maybe a student at the college. She had long strawberry-blond hair with loose curls and dazzling green eyes that flashed as she smiled at the two of them and tapped her pen on her notepad. James glanced at her name tag: Rebecca.

"Are you boys ready to eat?" she asked, her tone sweet and welcoming. "Can't survive on coffee and tea alone, you know."

"No, but I can certainly try," James said, smiling back at her as he raised his cup. She smelled like warm, fresh pancakes. Above all breakfast treats, James could never resist a stack of pancakes drowned in butter and syrup. "I'll have the pancakes. Tall stack. Eggs scrambled, bacon."

"French toast, please," Phillip said, smiling at her as he handed her his menu. "Eggs over easy, bacon."

"Thanks, guys," Rebecca said as she took the menus. "I'll have it out quick. Probably even quicker since you're cute for a couple of older guys." She smiled, wrinkled her nose in an endearing gesture, and walked off to place the order.

Phillip chuckled as James looked at him and raised an eyebrow.

"She's adorable," James said.

"Still got it," Phillip said, sitting back and puffing out his chest.

"The clap? I thought you got rid of that in college."

"Respect your elders, son."

"You've only got five years on me."

"Still enough to make me king, and you nothing."

James snorted. "I think it's funny that you're so flattered by a college student giving you a pity compliment."

Phillip glared at him. "Pity compliment?" He leaned forward. "I am a *pretty* black man. I am the *priest* at the Holy Temple of All That is Sexy. I can't help it if all the ladies come to worship."

James chortled, and they both laughed.

"Besides," Phillip said as his laughter died down, "if I were still in my twenties, I'd be hard-pressed to turn down a chick who smells like French toast."

James looked at him. "Huh," he said. "I thought she smelled like pancakes. Put me in the mood for them. That's why I ordered the tall stack."

"Then we need to take you to the vet and have him look you over," Phillip said. "That girl smelled straight-up like French toast."

James shook his head. "We need to get going after breakfast."

"Hold your horses, Lassie," Phillip said. "We need to go talk to people first. Figure out if anyone saw anything weird, or maybe has an idea why our recently deceased vampire buddy had a room at this place. I'm gonna touch base today with a friend in the Rock Hill department who has a cousin here in Charleston."

"You're working on your leave?" James asked.

"Yeah, about that," Phillip said. "I went to put in for it, and the chief told me to get up with some people here. Some dude in the department here who wants me to work with them."

James looked at him. "Can they do that?"

Phillip grunted. "If Uncle Sam tells you to jump, you jump. The memo came from Washington. There's a task force down here specifically for the disappearances. That's the group I'm working with."

"So, the FBI?"

Phillip shook his head. "I don't think so. The FBI usually identifies themselves right away. No, this is something else. Their top priority is trying not to cause a panic, so everything's being kept quiet."

"Weird that they asked for you specifically."

"Guess they need the best."

James laughed. "Okay, Shaft. Don't get too humble on me, you bad mother—"

"Hush yo' mouth," Phillip said, laughing. "Oh, I figure we'll hit the Market first since it's right across the street."

J ames sighed. "I think we missed the boat on trying not to start a panic."

The Market was close to the inn. They'd decided to walk through to kill some time before Phillip went to the police department to start nosing around. His contact wouldn't start his shift until nine, so they had a good hour to look around and peruse the crafts and wares from the local merchants on Market Street.

And look over the dozens of Missing Person posters that hung in shop windows and inside the covered outdoor market.

Girls of all ages stared back at them from the black and white photos, their descriptions and details of when they'd gone missing listed beside them. James tried to look at each one. Most of the girls were teens, some of them younger, none of them over twenty-one. James ignored the quiet thrum of morning shoppers as they passed, buying from the various merchants and socializing with each other as they went. He read each poster. Missing from home. Missing from school. It was the kind of thing they warned kids about in the eighties and nineties in those god-awful awareness videos. Don't get in the car with strangers. Don't talk to strangers. Never answer the door without an adult home.

But none of the posters gave that kind of detail. They all simply said that each child, each girl, had gone missing from their various locations and the date since they'd been missing.

"That's weird as shit," Phillip said. "Look at the dates, James."

James looked over the posters again. The dates were all recent, all within the past few weeks. "It's once a week," he said. "Looks like groups of girls go missing on the same day every week."

"I'm surprised the city isn't on high alert ," Phillip said. "This should be all over the news." He pulled his cell phone out of his pocket. "It's almost nine. I'm heading over to the department. Think you can manage without a leash for a little bit?"

"I'll try not to bark at any little old ladies."

Phillip gave him the side-eye.

"I mean it, Snoopy," he said, turning to him. "You keep it on the down-low. These guys fled here because you made Rock Hill too hot for them. It means they're scared. Jump too soon, and they might run before we have any idea where they might head next."

James gave him a salute.

"Stop that," Phillip said, glaring at him.

"It's either that, or I sniff your butt."

Phillip rolled his eyes, spun on his heel, and stalked off as he grumbled under his breath. James chuckled at the low uttering of "punk mutha-fucka" as Phillip made his way out of the Market and toward the parking lot where he'd stowed the Honda. Once the Honda pulled off, James turned and went into the candy shop facing the Market, glancing at the sign as he went.

Riverstreet Sweets.

An assortment of aromas filled the shop: coffee and the sugary smell of pastries and confections light in the air. A few college students milled around inside, ordering coffee and cakes to munch on before class. The wolf stretched in his mind, licked its chops as James's eyes fell on one of the girls in the group. He blinked and shook his head.

Stop it, mongrel, he thought. *Not everything you see without a dick is a potential mate.*

The wolf growled back at him.

Just do your job, James shot back. He let the beast forward, his hearing enhanced as he turned away from the group and pretended to look over the vast assortment of in-house made candies and treats while he listened in on the group's conversation.

"It's fucking *weird,*" the girl the wolf had made him leer at said. "I don't want to be here, but I can't leave this close to finals."

"Yeah, I get it," one of the guys in the group said. "I've been keeping my door locked every time I'm in the room alone."

One of the other girls laughed.

"Yeah, because they totally might decide they're bored with girls and come after you. No offense, dude, but I don't think they care much for sausage on the menu."

"Right," the first girl said. "We're the ones with something to worry about."

"Oh, did you see the latest one? God, she's *so* young."

James felt his jaw clench. The thought of it, of what might be happening to Mindy, sickened him. He swallowed back his urge to smash the shelves in front of him and kept listening.

"Well, either way, the campus isn't safe," one of the other guys said. "That's why it's on curfew. So don't get caught out when you go to that frat party tonight."

"What house is it again?" the first girl asked.

"I dunno," the guy said. "I'll take a look in a bit. It's in my phone calendar. C'mon, we gotta get to class."

James watched the group out of the corner of his eye as they passed by. The wolf's girlfriend moved closer to him to avoid a dude in a suit as she went by, and James caught a whiff of her perfume, sweet and subtle. He pulled it in quick, let it flow over the glands in his mouth as the wolf etched it into his memory.

Having a scent made tracking a whole lot easier.

The suit looked over his shoulder at James. He was older, silver-haired, but looked like he worshiped healthy living. He smiled at James, gave a curt nod, then looked back to the cashier as she handed him a bag of bear claws. James watched him leave, trying to pick up a scent as the man went by.

Nothing. He smelled like nothing.

I t was noon when Philip walked into the restaurant. James waved the detective over to the booth he'd picked in the back corner of the room. Cat Daddy's was in the middle of the lunch rush, so the mix of other conversations floating around would cover their discussion. Deep Southern jazz played in the background, the live group improvising a tune from the small stage at the other end of the room.

Phillip sat across the booth from James and waved to a waitress.

"Thanks for waiting, ass," Phillip said as James ate a French fry.

James nodded as he took a sip of his beer.

"I was hungry," he said. "Besides, you need to order a burger. Good stuff."

The waitress came up. She was older than the pair, well into her fifties. She smiled at James, dutifully took Phillip's order, and grinned at him as well as she took his menu and left to get his drink.

"Wow, I'm proud of you," James said. "Didn't seem like you were near as interested in her as you were in Rebecca this morning."

"Yeah, but I can't get her off my mind, either," Phillip said. "Call me weird, but a girl that smells like damn French toast? Do they even make that as a fragrance?"

"Pancakes," James corrected. "She smelled like pancakes. And yeah, you might be a little creepy there."

"French toast," Phillip said, leaning in. "And it ain't like that. She's a college student working in a restaurant."

James raised an eyebrow. "Well shit," he said, his voice monotone as he picked up his burger. "We need to report that. Dear God, Phillip. A college student working in a restaurant? It's unheard of. We need to let the police know." He took a bite as Phillip shot him an annoyed look

"Shut the hell up, you dopey mutt."

James spoke around the bite in his mouth. "Might want to notify the Feds, too. Maybe even the Coast Guard."

"You done bein' an asshole? I'd like to tell you what my buddy's contact had to say."

The waitress dropped off Phillip's drink. He smiled and nodded at her, thanked her. She gave him a disapproving look and walked away.

James snorted. "I think she heard you."

Phillip shrugged. "Oh, well."

"She likes me. Thinks I'm a sweet boy. A good boy."

"She don't know you like I do."

"She calls me 'Sugar.'"

"If she knew you, she'd call you 'Dumbass.'" Phillip took a sip of his water and leaned in, changing the subject. "My guy here in Charleston had a lot to say. Despite being late as hell, he was informative."

James took another bite of his burger. "Do tell."

"Turns out these girls are disappearing at night," Phillip said. "Which, frankly, ain't news. But, what makes it interesting is that these girls disappeared in the middle of the night. As in while they were supposedly dead asleep."

James swallowed his bite and took a sip of beer. "That *is* interesting. Any sign of forced entry?"

"Nope," Phillip said. "Only thing they found was unlocked doors. Girls looked like they got up and just walked out of the damn house. Mostly happened at the College of Charleston, though more than a few of the younger girls have gone missing right from their own houses. Not a trace of where they went. Even SLED was only able to trace them to the front or back door. After that, nothing."

"SLED?"

"South Carolina Law Enforcement Division. How long have you lived here again?"

"Oh, right."

Phillip took a sip of his coffee and put his finger up as if remembering something else. "Oh, and you remember that thing they used to do with the milk cartons back in the nineties? Yeah, they're doing that again. At least the local dairy barns are."

"Vampires," James said. "It's the only explanation I can think of."

"How you figure?"

"You have to invite vampires in," James said. "Otherwise, they've got no power over you as long as you're inside your house. All of these girls are young. Some of them are *really* young. A vampire could play to that. Disguise himself as a person needing help. Come off as friendly and harmless. The minute she opens the door and invites him in, he nabs her and bolts. Just because they can't use their powers on you doesn't mean they can't be manipulative bastards. In that regard, they're worse than humans."

"Well, that sucks," Phillip said. He sighed. "Literally. So you're telling me the cops are useless when it comes to these girls being Team Edward."

"Unless they've got a vampire hunter division, this one falls on a supernatural with a keen sense of justice and a nose for sniffing out evil."

"What the hell?" Phillip said. "Are you serious? You're not doing that ag—"

James puffed out his chest. He needed some levity, and Phillip was always an easy target. "It's time for *Super-Wolf!*"

Phillip buried his face in his palm. "Oh, God, please shoot me," he muttered. "James, we're in public."

James grinned at him. "I'm awesome. Admit it."

"I will gladly admit that you're dumb as hell."

The waitress showed up and plopped Phillip's food down on the table. She gave him another disapproving look and turned to look at James.

"I wouldn't take that off him, Sugar," she said. "Sweet boy like you? Shoot. You could do better." She leaned in. "My son is gay, too, if you want his number. He's a catch!"

James grinned and patted her hand as Phillip fumed across from him. "Thanks, Violet," he said. "I'll let you know if we work it out or not."

Violet smiled at him and turned to Phillip. "You be nice to him," she said. "Good men don't come easy." She stepped away as Phillip rolled his eyes at James.

"She doesn't think I'm dumb," James said, grinning. He chuckled, then let the laugh fade as he got back on topic. "I overheard a few college students in the Market talking about things today. There's a frat party tonight at the college. I might stake it out. If there's going to be another disappearance, that would be the prime spot."

"Yeah, it might be. It might also just be a frat party. And since there's a curfew, it'll be low key. Less noise and people means we're more likely to get noticed. We'll have to be quiet as hell."

"There was also a guy in a suit there. Looked like a businessman. Older guy, white, about six feet."

"I'm pretty sure old white guys also go to the Market, James."

"He didn't have a scent."

"Maybe you just didn't sniff him in time."

James shrugged. Phillip was probably right. "Either way, we need to look into that party."

Phillip shook his head, then just went with it. James could never resist the urge to put Phillip on the spot. It was like having a cat with anxiety issues; it could be mean, but it could also be funny as hell. "Okay," he said. "Don't do anything stupid, though. Just watch, then text me if you see anything. The last thing we need is the Charleston cops searching for a werewolf loose in the city. If we can keep quiet, we'll be better off."

3

Since summer was approaching, nighttime wasn't typically until around nine. Curfew was strictly after dark, and James figured he had some time before he had to shift and do his job. He and Phillip toured around Charleston a bit, taking in the stores up and down Market Street. James took a mental note of the posters hanging around town. He saw a few people ripping them down and figured they were probably city workers. It made sense not to have them everywhere. The more faces stared out underneath the word "Missing," the more tension it could cause. He and Phillip went back to the hotel and laid out a plan for staking out the frat house.

"I'll keep an eye on my phone," Phillip said as James headed out later that night. "Let me know if you see anything. I'll be back at the police department. Eddie, my guy's cousin, has some stuff to show me on the disappearances. It's not a lot more than what we already know, but maybe I'll see something I didn't see before."

"Does Eddie know that supernaturals might be involved?" It wasn't a stupid question these days. The Rock Hill Police Department was well aware of the Wolf-Man murders, and James's romp through town in wolf form thanks to Wade Anderson and Dracula's ring had stirred up all kinds of bad memories.

"Not that he'll admit," Phillip said. "But, considering we're in the most haunted city in South Carolina, I'm sure it's in the back of everyone's mind. Ghost watchers *love* this city, and they're not known to give a damn about a curfew, so watch your ass."

"I'm guessing Eddie is also part of this?"

"Nope," Phillip said. "But he's part of the force here, and they're under instruction from the federal spooks to turn any information over to me. I might be a while."

James took a Lyft to the campus, tipped the driver cash. The driver, a college student herself, looked at the hundred-dollar bill with wide eyes. She was cute, dressed well, and carried on a friendly conversation with him.

Everything that scared the hell out of James, given the current circumstances.

He gave her six more hundreds out of his wallet.

"I...look, mister, I can't..." the girl stammered.

James set his gaze on her, the wolf stepping forward a little in his mind. He saw his reflection in the rear-view mirror out of the corner of his eye, his features dark and serious.

"Turn off your app and go home," he said. "Your shift is over. You never saw me."

She nodded, still wide-eyed as James turned and got out of the car. She sped off as soon as he closed the passenger door.

The campus sprawled in front of him, small clusters of students moving in between the buildings as they strolled to their dorms. It was almost dark. There was a construction site nearby, the workers gone for the day, the equipment quiet. He saw a group of porta-johns near the office trailer. He pulled the wolf forward, let the different smells into his senses. He blinked at the rancid, ammonia-rich stench.

"Um...no," he said. He made his way toward the site, up to the work trailer. The gap behind the trailer where the fence ran was just enough space. He stripped, stuffed his clothes into the backpack, stowed it underneath the trailer, and shifted. He darted out into the fresh night, headed toward the first dorm building. The wolf stretched out, panting with joy as it reveled in its freedom.

Don't get too comfortable, James thought. *I'm still in charge.*

The wolf growled at him.

James scaled a nearby building and took to the rooftops, stopping when he heard laughter and voices shushing down the noise.

"You'll get us busted," a male voice whispered. "For fuck's sake, Carla."

"Relax," Carla's voice said. "You're a pussy; you know that? No one's gonna see us."

"We're not supposed to be out," the male said. "It's called a patrol. Campus cops are out looking. The frat boys shouldn't be throwing this party."

"It's Friday night, I need a drink, and I'm horny," Carla said. "Eddie, you can either come with me to get shit-housed and laid, or you can stay on campus and jerk off alone in your bathroom. But I'm going to that party. I'm sick of being shut inside. It's making me stir-crazy."

Ah, to be young again, James thought, laughing on the inside. He'd been known to throw down in college and may have had an evening or two with a few ladies around campus.

The wolf urged at him in his mind.

Mate.

Shut it, you.

Mate!

You're gross. At least let's go for girls our age. Now focus, you idiot.

The wolf groaned in his mind and calmed down. James perched low on the roof, waited until he saw the couple he'd eavesdropped on sneak across the courtyard and into the parking lot. He followed, keeping to the rooftops as he watched them move.

Something darted through the trees, too fast to be an animal. A shadow? No, it was a blur. James pulled the wolf forward again, inhaled the scents in the air. Blood. And something else. Vanilla?

Vampire, he thought. *Shit. Why does a vampire smell like vanilla?*

He could only think of one reason. And if this thing was the one causing all the disappearances around Charleston, it was also a strong possibility that it was connected to the traffickers. That meant that he could be another step closer to finding Mindy.

He could hear Phillip in his mind screaming at him to get his phone and send a text. Then what? Another disappearance. On James's watch. He had enough guilt in his life without adding the murder of two college students to his conscience. Besides, what were human cops with guns going to do against a vampire? Other than royally piss it off?

The couple got into a small red pickup truck. The engine turned over, and they pulled out and drove off campus. The shape shot out from the dark and followed. James leapt from the roof, hit the ground at a roll, and darted after the form. He didn't need his wolfen speed since the truck was only doing about twenty. It took a few turns and pulled into a driveway about a mile away from the campus. The house was alive with the sounds of college students cheering and music playing. The couple got out of the truck and went inside as the vampire disappeared into the trees.

James ducked into the shadows between the dozen parked cars and watched as a girl made herself comfortable on a large limb, her eyes glowing red as she watched the house intently. The wolf stirred again. Her hair was long and curly, the large brown locks cascading over her shoulders. She wore a pink t-shirt and denim shorts, and James caught himself staring at her more hidden assets and shook it off.

Vampire, James, he thought to himself. *She's hot, and she's a killer.*

The wolf growled at the vampire from inside.

Thanks, he thought back at it. *I knew you were good for something.*

The vampire stayed still, watching the party intensely as if waiting for something. James crept out from between the vehicles, looked around to make sure no one was watching, then moved closer to the yard. He looked in the tree again.

No vampire.

Something slammed into him, sent him flying down the street. He crashed into a parked car, caving in the front end from the force of the blow combined with his weight. He jumped to his feet and lunged at the girl, claws out and teeth bared. She sidestepped and delivered a punch to his side, sent him flying into another car.

He rolled as she came down at him with her knee, landed hard enough where he'd been sitting to crack the asphalt. James swiped, caught her in the side. She snarled and reeled back as he swung out and connected. The girl went down, rolled, and came back up. James flexed, spread his arms in a combat-ready stance, and barked at the vampire. She hissed back at him, her eyes flashing like bright red coals as she took off in the opposite direction, gone in a blur of pink t-shirt.

James chased after her, entered his wolfen speed in an instant. She stayed just ahead of him, taking corners in a snap, zigzagging through alleyways and down streets. They blew through town, the smell of the harbor and mud growing thicker in the air.

She zipped to the left and vanished.

Folly Beach Road.

James had vacationed in Charleston regularly as a child. It'd been one of his mother's favorite cities to visit. She liked to leave early in the morning and arrive in time for breakfast at one of her favorite local restaurants and spend the weekend walking around the peninsula touring the shops, gardens, and historic buildings in downtown. Folly Beach had been James's favorite spot, particularly the large pier that extended out from the hotel on the beach and well into the surf. During the daytime, and sometimes at night, the sides of the pier would be lined with fishers or tourists walking up and down and pointing at the homes and hotels that lined the beach.

James shot down the road, marshlands and buildings blurred by as he neared the hotel, the vampire's scent still fresh. She wasn't far ahead.

He stopped at the hotel parking lot and hid around a corner as a couple walked from the pier into the hotel breezeway. The man swiped his room key and opened the door, allowing his date in ahead of him. As soon as the door closed, James peered around the corner and scanned the area, letting the wolf more forward to enhance his vision. The pier was dark, the ocean in the distance blacker than the night sky. All of the scents hit him at once—the remnants of cooking food at the Starfish Grill, saline, sand, rotting driftwood.

Vanilla. Blood.

A low growl rumbled from deep in the back of his throat as he looked over the pier. It was empty, completely vacant. The curfew was affecting everyone. The night fishermen were probably salty about not being able to fish under the dark sky.

James grinned at himself on the inside at the pun. The wolf groaned inside.

You and Phillip are both a couple of killjoys, James thought.

James made his way down the pier, staying low in an effort to remain in the shadows. The lights along the dock were out. The vampire had probably cut the power, which meant she wanted a fight. Fighting vampires was nothing new to James. The older they were, the tougher they tended to be. He'd won every vamp fight he'd ever gotten into, but most of them had been with younglings. He doubted he'd ever fought a vamp that was older than fifty.

Still, despite his experience, he was antsy about this one. Every move she made was calculated, every blow deliberate and precise. She knew what she was doing, obviously had experience fighting other supernaturals. Humans didn't require quite as much effort and force in combat. They were more fragile than supernaturals, which was why James tried to avoid altercations with humans when he could. Whenever he faced a fight with another person, he stayed in human form.

He reached the small building at the end of the pier, where the vending machines sat. They were dark, their compressors quiet. James's hackles raised at the sound of something moving in the dark—claws scraping wood. His ears twitched. He stood tall, looked around the darkened area. The sound of waves lapping against the pylons below, the breeze coming in from the surf, and seagulls on the beach mixed in with something else. Breathing. A grunt.

A woman's voice.

"Bad puppy."

The air rushed out of his lungs as the vampire slammed into him, knocking him sideways into the vending area. The Coke machine caved in, soda spurting all over him and soaking his coat as he tried to stand. The vampire was on him again. She punched his muzzle, reared back to land another blow. He swiped out, the blow lifting her off of him and sending her flying. She hit the deck and rolled back to her feet. James got up, shook off the sugary mix from his soda bath, and rushed her.

He grabbed at her, but she ducked and jammed her foot into his kneecap. He went down, the pain rocketing up and down his leg. She jumped and came down with a punch to his jaw. He took the blow, grabbed the vampire by her shoulders, and slammed her into the building. She went through the wall, burst through the other side, and landed in a heap at the edge of the pier.

James went after her, charged through the hole she'd made in the vending shack, and sent more debris airborne as he barreled down on her. The girl got to her feet and lunged back at him, caught him by the head, and slammed him face-down onto the deck. She kicked him, the force rolling him over onto his back. She straddled him, holding his arms down with her feet, and glared at him with her glowing red eyes.

She leaned in close. *"Where is she, you son of a bitch?!"*

James grunted and stared back at her. *What was she talking about?*

"Shift back and answer me," the girl said. "And don't lie to me, or I'll send you right back to hell!"

James blinked, cocked his head in confusion. The girl sat up, looking equally confused.

James shifted into his human form and stared back at her.

"I'm pretty sure I don't have any idea what you're talking about," he said. "And I'm also guessing we both just went back to square one."

4

James agreed to meet the vampire at a small bar on King Street and went back to the college to get his clothes. When he made it back, she already sat inside at a booth in the farthest corner from the front door. A pair of older black men were shooting pool at one of the tables, and a middle-aged couple shared drinks at the bar while one man sat at the end near the pool tables staring into his whiskey glass. The bartender made his rounds, stepped up to the table as James sat down. The vampire girl was already nursing a beer. James glanced at the taps, ordered a Holy City Pluff Mud Porter, and sat down across from her as the barkeep went to grab the beer. The bartender returned with the beer, and James instructed him to make sure that the young woman's was also on his tab.

"Charming," she said with a smile as the bartender went back to his post. "I like a man who's willing to treat a lady to drinks, but I can get my own. Thanks anyway."

"I insist," James said, taking a sip of his beer. "I did smack you around pretty good. I owe you at least one drink."

"Aw," the girl said. "You're sweet. But if that's the game we're playing, then I'd owe you the bar considering I kicked your ass all over the pier."

"I could've stopped you."

"Sorry, sweetie, but you were a pushover."

"How are you so strong?" James asked, setting his beer down. "I've never encountered a vampire that puts up a fight like you do."

"I'm over a hundred years old," she said, raising an eyebrow. "You've probably never fought a vampire that wasn't a youngling or damn close to it. I'm Lacy Faulkner."

"James Coldstone. Who are you looking for?"

Lacy sat back. "Right to it. See, Jimmy, I like a little foreplay before we get to the main event. I barely know you."

"Quid pro quo," James said. "You answer my questions, I answer yours. I'll even go first as a sign of good faith."

"Okay," Lacy said. "Who are *you* looking for?"

"Two girls," James said. "Clara Pickens. She's a college student just into her twenties. And a ten-year-old girl named Mindy Robertson."

"Christ," Lacy muttered.

"Your turn."

"Marianne," Lacy said, her tone a little more solemn. "My great-great-grand niece. She's ten, same age as your little girl. They took her a few weeks ago while my descendants were on vacation here. I got word and came right away. Been here a few weeks. Why'd you follow me?"

"I thought you were one of the people that took Mindy," James said. "I fought a vampire back home who ended up being a lead here. Figured the whole thing involved vampires. In case this is a newsflash: you're a vampire. Why'd you attack me?"

Lacy shrugged. "Thought you were one of them. They're using supernaturals, but you knew that. I got into it with a group of younglings when I got here." She sipped her beer. "I do like a good IPA."

"I thought vampires didn't drink anything but blood."

Lacy laughed. "I can eat or drink anything I want as long as there's no garlic or avocado in it. I just don't get any nourishment from it. I like the taste of beer, though."

"I know about garlic," James said. "What does avocado do to vampires?"

"Tastes like shit and feels like I'm chewing on a mouthful of boogers. I fucking *hate* avocado."

"Fair," James said with a laugh.

"Okay, I gave you two there, Jimmy," Lacy said as she sat back and crossed her arms in front of her. "Means it's my turn to double up. Where's home?"

"Rock Hill. It's a town just south of Charlotte."

"Damn, you're a little far from home. You related to these girls?"

James shook his head. "Not at all. Clara was part of a murder investigation I got wrapped up in. Turns out the murders are connected to this bunch we're chasing. Mindy is a little girl that got caught in the crossfire when our main suspect decided to use Count Dracula's ring on me."

"What the hell does Dracula's ring do to werewolves?"

"Forces the change. Hurts like hell."

"Damn," Lacy said. She leaned forward and rested her elbows on the table. "Okay, Jimmy, I'll level with you: we're obviously after the same people, and I could use a hand. But I still don't know if I can trust you."

"Why is that?"

"Because I don't know if I can work with dudes who might have to choose between a bowl of kibble and doing the right thing. My experience with weres hasn't been great."

"I'm a different kind of were," James said.

"I can tell." Lacy leveled her gaze on him. "You keep your brains when you shift. That's weird. Last werewolf I killed was nutso whenever he turned. Don't get me started on the werehorse I met in Georgia."

"Werehorse?"

"Yeah, I don't care how hung you are, you keep your hooves to yourself."

"That escalated quickly."

"At least he walked erect."

James tried another question. "Do you have any leads?"

"None I'm willing to share right now," said Lacy. "We haven't made a deal yet. I need some time to get to know you."

"Sun will be up in a few hours," James said. "You can crash in my hotel room. Sleep under the bed. We'll head out when the sun goes down, get some more drinks." He ground his teeth at the delay, but if getting to know Lacy would get him closer to Mindy and Clara, then he didn't have any choice in the matter.

Lacy gave him a wry smile. "Damn, you move fast, Coldstone. At least you bought me drinks first, but I usually don't go home with a guy on the first date unless I plan to drain him 'til he passes out." She downed the rest of her beer, stood up, leaned down, and kissed him on the cheek. "You're sweet. Thanks for the beer. You want my help, meet me back here tomorrow night. You show up a minute after ten, all you'll see is my ass heading the other direction."

"So it's worth it either way," James said.

Lacy laughed and sauntered out the door. James followed her with his eyes, as did every other man in the bar. The bartender walked up to his table and shook his head.

"Damn, son," he said. "She's a man-eater, that one."

James handed him a twenty and shook his head.

"You have no idea."

"N ow I *know* you've lost your damn mind," Phillip said as Rebecca refilled his coffee. He smiled up at her, and James rolled his eyes at the goofy look Phillip gave the girl.

"Thank you," Phillip said, his tone suave and friendly.

Rebecca flirtatiously wrinkled her nose at him and grinned. "Sure thing," she said. "Always makes my morning when I get good-looking men in my section." She moved to another table where an older couple sat and began to take their order. She glanced over her shoulder at Phillip and winked. Phillip nodded at her and looked back at James, grinning ear-to-ear.

"You do know you've got a good ten years on her," James said.

"So?" Phillip said. "Hell, she can buy her own alcohol. Not like I'm looking for a relationship, anyway." He pointed at his face. "Besides, I can't control how sexy I am."

James stared at him, waiting for a punchline he knew wouldn't come.

"And you call me an idiot," he said.

"Because you *are* an idiot," Phillip said. "I've got an education, leadership training, and *slick*-ass good looks workin' for me. Now tell me about this vampire chick you ended up chasing last night. You want to work *with* her?"

"She's got leads."

"She's a vampire."

"She's handing me an opportunity to find the girls."

"Still a vampire." Phillip shook his head. "And we don't know if she's full of shit. For all we know, she's leading you into a trap."

"Not complaining."

Phillip sat back in his chair. "There he is," he said, pointing at James. "There's the dog. There you go again, thinkin' with your dick."

"The wolf has his urges," James said with a shrug.

"Wolf, my black ass," Phillip said. "You've always walked around like your pecker's a Vagina Detector. Now you're telling me to trust it. We didn't study that at the academy, James. Trustin' another man's penis isn't exactly in the curriculum."

"Any more news from your contact?" James asked, eager to steer the conversation away from his genitals.

"Not much," Phillip said. "And your vamp-chick isn't on their radar at all."

"Not surprised," James said. "I do think the group we're following is being led by a supernatural, though."

Phillip took a casual sip of his coffee. "Why's that?"

Rebecca came back by and placed their breakfast plates on the table. She looked at James, her eyes wide and excited.

"You're James Coldstone, right?" she said. "I saw on the computer when I charged your room for breakfast yesterday."

"Yeah, that's me," James said, trying not to let his discomfort show. His name wasn't exactly unknown. The Wolf-Man Murders story had been widely covered in the state, and on some national news shows as well. His family wealth wasn't hidden, either. James didn't want to be rude to people when they recognized his name, but he was never thrilled about the encounters, either.

"Wow," she said. "Well, I'm sorry, I don't mean to bring up old memories. I just now put two-and-two together. It's great to meet you, though! You're really nice in person!" She moved his plate of pancakes in front of him. "Enjoy your breakfast, Mr. Coldstone!"

"Call me James," James said. "Less formal."

She giggled as she slid Phillip's plate of French toast in front of him. "You keep cute company, James," she said. "You boys enjoy!"

"She's not wrong," Phillip said as Rebecca trotted off.

James shook his head. "She knows I'm loaded and wants a good tip."

Phillip pointed at himself again. "Church. Of all. That is Sexy."

"Eat up, reverend," James said, rolling his eyes. "We've got a busy day ahead."

Phillip ended the call, put his iPhone away, and walked up to James. They'd strolled the Market and were making their way toward the Battery. James sniffed the air here and there, trying to pick up any scent he may have missed. He smelled some of Lacy's vanilla and blood scent on the road and sidewalks, but the air was mostly heavy with marsh mildew and saline as they neared the water. Lacy had been through there at some point, and recently.

"Well, my guy said he'd look into it," he said. "It might be tonight before we hear anything. Apparently, they have their hands full today. Some cars got heavily vandalized last night, and the vending area at the Folly Beach pier got destroyed around the same time. The Folly Beach cops are coordinating with the Charleston PD now since it seems way too coincidental." He eyed James. "I wonder if some rabid vampire chick and a certain fluffy asshole I know have anything to do with it?"

James stared back at him. "Oopsie."

Phillip closed his eyes and sighed, taking a moment to collect himself. James waited, almost disappointed since Phillip was at his most entertaining when he was screaming.

"The Lord is testing me," Phillip muttered before opening his eyes and looking back up at James. "Okay, Scooby-Doo, so you found a hotel room key on a vampire, and you got into a scrap with a vampire as soon as you got here. I'm inclined to think vampires are involved." His tone was rich with sarcasm.

"You're very astute," James said, not missing a beat.

"I like to think so," Phillip said. "But, if that's all we have to go on, then it's not enough to do anything other than wait until nighttime again and risk another romp with your new girlfriend."

"Her niece is missing," James said. "Well, her great-great grand niece. We could start there. Check that email your friend sent you."

Phillip pulled his phone back out and opened his email as they stopped at the railing on the Battery. James looked out over the water, saw the barges in the distance heading out. His mind kept returning to Lacy, picking apart everything she'd said the night before, trying to find anything that would give him a clue as to what he could do during the daytime until they met again.

Trying to imagine what she looked like—

Stop it, James thought as the wolf panted in his mind. *Focus, you horny bastard.*

The wolf growled at him as Phillip spoke.

"Nothing much here," he said. "There've been a lot of disappearances, so it would be hard to narrow down."

"Try looking for the name 'Faulkner.'"

Phillip looked up and raised an eyebrow. "Are you serious? Assuming this chick was telling you anything remotely true, do you know how often descendants actually *keep* the names of the people they're related to? Hell, your daddy probably didn't carry the true family name, either."

"Coldstone goes back over seven hundred years."

Phillip glared at him. "Okay, fine. Either way, there are no Faulkners in the mix here. Dead end."

"Then our only chance is to meet up with Lacy tonight," James said, still looking out over the water.

"*Your* only chance," Phillip said. "I'm having a drink with a couple of the guys from the precinct. Gonna see if I can get anything that may not be in the reports."

James looked at him sidelong. Phillip wasn't usually one to go out for drinks with total strangers. "I thought police were known for being meticulous when it came to paperwork."

Phillip shrugged. "Not always. We're only human."

James was already almost done with his beer when Lacy walked through the bar door at nine fifty-five p.m. She smiled at him, waved at the bartender, and sat down across from James as the barkeep dutifully brought her an IPA. She thanked him and raised her glass.

"To being punctual," she said as she lowered her glass and took a sip. She set it down on the table. "Or desperate. Works in your favor either way."

"I'm persistent," James said. "It's what makes me so charming."

Lacy snorted.

"Okay," she said. "Not high on yourself or anything, are you, Jimmy?"

"Just being truthful."

"Okay, Charming," she said. "You came back, which means you're sincere. Or desperate, like I said before. Shoot."

"Bang."

"Smooth, Ex-Lax."

"Who do you think took your niece? Do you have a name?"

"Not one I'm willing to share."

James sighed and rubbed his eyes. "Lacy, you said you'd help. That's not helpful."

She took another sip of her beer. "Then ask a better question," she said after she set the glass back down. "I'm not giving you a name because I don't know you. If I'm wrong about the guy, and you happen to be one of those psychotic werewolf-types, I risk getting an innocent man slaughtered. Then the police are all over it, and our girls end up slipping away during the chaos. I'm not about to risk what little trail I have on Marianne."

"Man?"

"Yup." She paused. "Well, more like a little boy. Guy's young enough to be fresh out of college. Not much younger than us."

"I'm thirty."

"Damn, Jimmy. You look good for thirty."

"Werewolves age a lot slower than humans."

"I was twenty-five when I got turned," Lacy said.

"Don't see how this is helpful."

"It means our buddy is probably about twenty-two."

James sat back in the booth, his hand on his pint of black beer. "What the hell is a college kid doing getting mixed up in human trafficking?"

"There is a *hell* of a lot of money in the human trade," Lacy said. "And college kids have easier access to what those groups are seeking. Young girls, mostly teens. Female college students outnumber males almost four-to-one or better, depending on which university you go to. Sexual assaults are way up, which makes it harder since the older girls are more vigilant. But a lot of these girls are fresh out of high school, so they're the more likely targets, and older male students are fascinating to them. Easy pickins."

James rubbed his eyes, his head starting to hurt. "So, we're looking for a frat boy."

"Not necessarily, though that would be the most likely," Lacy said. "That's why I followed that couple to the frat house last night. That's where another girl disappeared a few weeks back, from what I hear. They had a party, she left, and no one's heard from her after that. She was barely twenty-one.

"Most of the slimiest pieces of shit are the ones everyone likes. 'Oh, he's such a nice guy.' 'Oh, he's so sweet!' 'Wouldn't hurt anyone!'" She made a face. "Makes me sick."

"So we need to check out that frat house," James said, already formulating a plan in his mind.

"That was my thinking," Lacy said. She downed her almost full pint in one gulp and started to stand up. "But I already did. One of the rich boys in that frat said something about a group here in Charleston that meets now and then. They like to convene at a spot near Folly Beach." She stretched, then patted James on the shoulder. "Time to go crack some heads."

James could already hear Phillip screaming in his mind about procedure. For once, James had to agree. He wanted to barge in and start interrogating, but it could make things difficult.

"Wait," he said, motioning her back into her seat. "Sit down."

"Jimmy, I don't have time for you to sit here and be cute," Lacy said. "I have a pervert to hunt, lots of questions, and I'm hungry."

"My best friend is a cop," James said. "He's here with me. Sit down."

Lacy sat, eyeing him. "You've got thirty seconds, Jimmy."

"Phillip and I can go question this group," he said. "You can control minds, right?"

Lacy grinned. "Haven't paid for my own beer in a hundred years."

James grinned back. "I think you'll like this."

5

The frat house was a lot quieter than the previous night. James saw people walking around chatting or having a beer while watching a movie. Another group was playing Xbox at the far end of the main room, and a few stood in the kitchen eating out of the assortment of fast food bags that lined the countertop.

Lacy looked sidelong at James. "I still think I want to go in and just smack 'em around," she said.

Phillip nudged James from the other side. "Check your girl, Clifford."

James had called Phillip and filled him in on the way to the frat house. As it turned out, Lacy drove a black 2019 Mini Cooper to maintain her cover as a girl touring the city at night.

"Let me guess," he said, as she used the remote start to crank the engine and unlock the doors.

She grinned at him. "The salesman was very generous. And tasty."

They met Phillip a few blocks down from the frat house and rode over in his car.

"We typically do the 'cop and the consultant' routine for this kind of thing," James said to Lacy. "Just stick to your part of the plan." He nodded to Phillip. "Let's go."

They got out of the Honda and approached the front porch. A couple sat on the porch swing, making out in the dark, their forms becoming more visible as James and Phillip approached. James grinned.

"Ah, young love," he said to Phillip.

"What would you know about 'young love,'?" Phillip said with a laugh.

"I happen to be quite romantic," James said.

"My ass."

"I was good with the ladies."

"You blew an opportunity to date Libby Nelson."

"I took her out to dinner."

"You took her to a Waffle House."

"I like waffles."

"She didn't. Can we focus now, dumbass?"

The couple on the porch swing stopped kissing and got up as the three drew closer. James motioned Phillip and Lacy to hold up and watched as the couple went inside, letting the screen door close behind them.

"Now what?" Phillip asked.

"We wait," Lacy said. She turned and grinned at James. "Hey, maybe we could make out for a while?"

James blinked. "Really?" he said as the wolf started panting in his mind.

Lacy's grin grew broader. "No."

"You two scout around the yard, see if you can listen in on some conversations," Phillip said. "I'm giving you ten minutes. Any more than that, and we run an even higher risk of getting busted."

Lacy slinked off the porch and into the shadows. James stepped down into the grass and made his way around the side of the house, where the kitchen window faced out into the yard. It was his experience that movies and video games were never the prime spots for conversation. The kitchen?

Even college boys would gossip over food and drinks.

"That's crazy shit, man," one was saying as James tuned in his wolfen hearing. The wolf settled down in his mind; its ears perked up as they both listened.

"I'm telling you, dude, it's a matter of time," another one said. "The guy reeks of creeper."

"Dude's also the wealthiest guy in South Carolina," yet another one chimed in. James looked up and saw their friend from the front porch standing in the kitchen with the group. His eyes were blank as he stood back from the group and fidgeted with the fried chicken on his plate. He spoke, his tone drawn, and his speech slurred.

"Money makes people do stupid shit," he said. "What's the guy's name again?"

"Sinclair," a larger boy said before chugging back a beer. "Daniel Sinclair."

"Guy donates to kids' organizations like hell around here," a smaller boy said, pushing his glasses up on his nose. "If he's a creeper, that just makes it that much grosser."

"Well, he's only ever been accused," the big one said. "Nothing ever sticks. Too many rich friends."

James couldn't argue that money was a great way to keep a fresh Teflon coat on one's criminal record. His father had used his share of the family's billions to pay off more than a few people to keep his cover as the Wolf-Man Murderer intact.

James wanted nothing to do with it other than meet his basic needs. He wasn't opposed to working. He just knew that his furry counterpart wouldn't mesh well with any normal career.

"Well, he still spends a lot of time with those rich friends," the smaller one said. "Owns a condo community just down the road from Folly Beach."

"Doesn't he also own a restaurant down that way?" another kid asked from his spot in the corner as he munched dutifully on a bag of Cheetos.

"Nah," the big one said. "That's someone else. Sinclair owns the one just down the road, though. Has a lot of parties there. Probably uses the condos for his rich friends to spend some quality time with the kids he sells, the sick-ass."

"Well, sick-ass or not, it's all speculation," the small one said. "Every time the place gets searched, they find nothing. If he's tied to the disappearances around here, he'll probably walk if they ever bust him."

James pushed the wolf back and headed up front just as Lacy rounded the corner.

"Guess you heard?" she said.

"Daniel Sinclair," James said. "C'mon, let's go get Phillip."

D aniel Sinclair, huh?" Phillip said from the back seat. Lacy drove the Mini Cooper down Folly Beach Road, the marshlands lining either side of the highway moving by. "Yeah, that name came up earlier today when I was talking to the guys at the department."

"Do tell," James said.

"Let me pull over at this farmer's stand," Lacy said. James looked ahead and saw a hand-written sign advertising boiled peanuts and pickled eggs. Lacy pulled up to the small stand and killed the headlights while Phillip brought out his phone and began typing on the screen.

"Sinclair and Associates, LLC," Phillip said as he scrolled through the webpage he'd pulled up. "Guy is worth almost a billion. He owns a shit-load of real estate around Folly Beach, Mount Pleasant, and James Island. Says here he's made bids to every family up and down the Battery to sell him their homes, and nobody's budging."

"That's interesting," Lacy said. "Full disclosure: Sinclair is the guy I've been looking into." She looked at James. "Now that we're being all open and honest and stuff."

James rolled his eyes. "So why did we go to the frat house?"

"Information," Lacy said. "I told you what I told you about him because I didn't know if I could trust you. Considering you didn't take the chance to off me tonight, I think we're good. Sinclair is no college kid."

"Looks like Sinclair owns a condo development right down from where we're parked," Phillip said, ignoring them. He turned his phone around. "This is our boy. Has a party going on tonight. Private affair, of course. Gotta have an invitation."

James took the phone and looked at it as Lacy leaned in. An older man with gray hair and chiseled, debonair facial features stared back at them. James had to admit he was a decent-looking man.

"That's him. I can see why the younger ladies might like him," Lacy said. "He's handsome *and* rich? Shit, count me in."

"One of the guys at the frat house said something about parties at Sinclair's place," James said as he handed the phone back to Phillip.

"Yeah, about that," Phillip said, shooting Lacy a look before going back to his phone. "My contact put in a call at the Folly Beach precinct. They've got a few cops on Sinclair's payroll as onsite security during his little parties. But get this: none of them are allowed on the actual condo property. The whole thing is gated off, and they're under *strict* orders to stay outside the gate and keep an eye out for people who might try to break in."

"They can't use that to warrant a search on the guy?" Lacy asked.

Phillip shook his head. "It doesn't prove that he's not just an eccentric billionaire surrounded by conspiracy theories that he's trafficking little girls." Phillip pointed at his phone. "Every case I've looked up has been dropped due to lack of evidence. They've got nothing on the guy other than he's weird as shit and creepy. *But,* he's also a scumbag. He's taken the families on the Battery to court several times to try and dispute their ownership of the properties."

"That's a losing battle," James said. "What's the point?"

"Even if you win a trial, lawyers and court fees are pricey," Phillip said. "He can afford it because he's a billionaire. These families are already reporting financial strain."

"Christ," Lacy said. "Even the rich eat each other."

James turned back around in his seat and stared off into the marshlands. He saw lights through the trees in the distance, windows. Condominiums.

"I want to go to a party," he said abruptly.

"Are you nuts?" Phillip said.

"I like a man who can throw down," Lacy said. "How many shots can you do, Jimmy?"

"Marmaduke sticks to beer because he can't hold his liquor," Phillip said from the back. "And you're fucking stupid if you think I'm gonna let you go to that party."

"I've got name recognition and influence," James said. "I can swing my money around to get in, no problem. They'll see me as an equal and might let something slip."

"Even if that's true, there's no way they're gonna come out and tell you that an underage girl comes with the price of admission. They're more careful than that."

James shook his head. "We know he's already got a reputation, even if nothing sticks. And I'm willing to bet that whatever exorbitant price he charges to attend one of his little soirees probably does include the option of a night with an underage girl to certain people. We'd catch more than just the ringleader."

"That last part is speculation," Phillip said. "I can't go running in on speculation, James. That could cost the city a shitload of money and me my job."

James held his ground. "There's only one way to find out.

Phillip sighed and rubbed his face. "All this shit makes my skin crawl. I can't believe I'm saying this." He looked at James. "We do it my way. You go in on the downlow. Listen in. Do *not* engage. You're not a cop."

J ames Coldstone?" the security guy at the door said, looking James up and down. "I don't see you on the list."

"I'm sure it's a mistake, babe," Lacy said as she looped her arm around James's and leaned into him.

"I'm not worried about it," James said as he adjusted his glasses. "I'm sure it is. We'll get it resolved."

"Low key," Phillip said in James's ear. "*Low. Fucking. Key.*"

Lacy had driven them back to Charleston to a late-night outfitters place on Calhoun Street. The place was new and advertised being open late to accommodate those who needed a suit and worked evenings. James bought the suit with his own money, going full out on the cost since he knew Sinclair would probably be able to smell a cheap suit a mile away. Lacy also acquired a dress: an extravagant deep red evening dress that fit her form like a second skin. Of course, since James didn't have the luxury of mind control, Lacy had gotten off cheaper.

They held the parties in the community clubhouse, located dead center with the condos surrounding it. Phillip was parked a few drives down and had a set of binoculars with him. The earpiece James wore was small enough that no one would be able to tell unless they made a concerted effort to look into his ear. Phillip made a phone call to get it, and James didn't question it. Given the circumstances, he was content to let Phillip handle the police bullshit.

It was a simple plan: get information and leave. If the hosts offered him an evening with a girl, politely decline and get the hell out. James was in town on vacation with his new girlfriend and wanted to make an appearance to say hello to the legendary Daniel Sinclair.

"Sir, I'm not finding you on the guest list," the guard said, his tone monotone. "If you haven't paid, then you're not on the list. If you're not on the list, you'll need to leave."

"Did you say Coldstone?" a voice called from inside. James looked up as Daniel Sinclair stepped out of the cluster of people in the clubhouse and approached the guard. The man was tall, only shorter than James by an inch or so, decked out in an expensive tailored suit, his silver hair perfectly combed and styled. His eyes flashed approvingly at Lacy, then back at James. "I'll be damned! I never thought a Coldstone would grace my humble presence." He looked at the guard. "Mr. Coldstone and his lovely lady are allowed in. Please let them through."

The guard nodded obediently and penciled James's name in. Lacy gave him her name as well, and they followed Sinclair into the room.

The clubhouse was bright, the thrum of mixed conversation loud in the room. Sinclair shook hands with a few people as they passed through group after group.

"Jesus Christ," Phillip muttered over the earpiece. "Some of these people are prominent politicians. I see a judge or two. God *damn*."

"I'm guessing that's unexpected?" James muttered.

"Fortunately, it's not as common as people think," Phillip said. "But, there's also a fifty-fifty shot some of them are here just for the status and don't buy into Sinclair's other little dealings. Tread carefully, and don't ID any of them. They could still bounce you just to protect themselves."

"I want to introduce you around," Sinclair said to James. "This is exciting."

One of Sinclair's men approached him and whispered in his ear. Sinclair nodded and turned to James and Lacy.

"I hate to do this, but I have to step away for a minute," he said. "Small business matter."

"I understand," James said.

"Of course," Lacy said. "We'll be here when you get back, Mr. Sinclair."

Sinclair nodded and walked away with his goon. James and Lacy turned and looked around the room at the clusters of rich and powerful people mingling and clutching cocktails in their hands.

"This is insane," Lacy said. "I've never been around this many rich people."

An older man approached, his white beard trimmed close to his face, his gut large enough to make the buttons on his coat look like they might pop off. He gave Lacy a hungry grin, then offered his hand to James.

"Did I hear Mr. Sinclair call you 'Coldstone?'" the man said.

"Yes, sir," James said, taking the man's hand and shaking it. "James Coldstone."

"Dear *me*, you've grown, boy," the man said, his Southern drawl thick. "Garrett Monroe. And your taste in female counterparts is something your father would be proud of." He nodded to Lacy and took her hand, kissing her knuckles. "Charmed to meet you, my fair lady."

"The pleasure is all mine," Lacy said through gritted teeth. "Lacy Faulkner."

"Don't let her eat him," Phillip said over the mic in a flat tone. "Bloodbaths don't go unnoticed. Blood baths are bad. Vampiric rage against old men is bad. And that motherfucker is really Richard Carnes. He's old money, and he's a judge in the family court system. Or was. He retired a few years back. Looks like he's using an alias. He might be a customer of Sinclair's."

"I knew your father," Carnes said. He shook his head. "Bad business with David. I am truly sorry, Mr. Coldstone."

James had to take a moment; his breath caught in his throat. Someone who had a personal connection to David Coldstone was standing in front of him, making idle chit-chat. Rage seethed through him. The wolf in his mind growled low at Carnes as the old man continued speaking.

"David was a good man when I knew him," Carnes was saying. "I don't know what happened, but I'm sure it couldn't have been helped."

"Alas, we'll never know," James said. "I wasn't born until shortly after."

Carnes glanced at Lacy again and smiled.

"Well, either way, you must have inherited his charm. I'm sure Miss Faulkner is quite vivacious."

Lacy bristled and forced a smile. "I'm going to go get us some drinks," she said. "Babe?"

"I'm fine," James said. "Please, help yourself, dear."

Lacy nodded, excused herself to Carnes and left.

"She's a doll, son," Carnes said.

"Yes, but there are times I like to branch out a little," James said. "Good thing she's open-minded."

"Good segue," Phillip said in his ear. "Spoken like a true pervert."

Carnes leaned in conspiratorially. "How open are you, my boy?"

"Depends," James said, his skin crawling as he forced the next comment out in the most casual tone he could muster. "Lacy is a dream, but sometimes I like things a step or two younger, Mr. Monroe." Carnes was using a fake name. It meant something. James knew he had to take a chance.

"Interesting," Carnes said. "You may want to inquire with Mr. Sinclair. He caters to certain…things to meet the needs of his close friends."

"I see," James said. "I'm certain I'm not at liberty to be so direct."

"No," Carnes said. "But I know who to speak with. He only asks a mere million dollars."

James nodded. "That's a generous discount."

Carnes blinked, his shit-eating grin faltering. James knew his family's wealth was far above any of the people at Sinclair's little kegger. Keeping them in check and garnering their respect wasn't as simple as slapping them silly. James had to flex his money muscle, show them who was the one in the room that made them all look like paupers.

"Set it up, if you would be so kind?" James said. "I'll have Miss Faulkner make the arrangements for the money via secure wire."

6

Phillip had a limo pick James and Lacy up from Sinclair's party and drive him out to the address Carnes had given him. The limo was extravagant, large enough to seat at least ten people. Lacy still sat close to James as if they were a couple. James couldn't help subtly glancing at her, taking in her appearance. His stomach knotted slightly, his breath catching as he glanced over her lovely form.

Lacy looked at him.

"Down, boy," she said.

James stammered.

"I'm sorry," he said. "I mean...I—"

"Don't worry about it, Coldstone. You're cute when you trip over your words." Lacy moved from her seat toward the front. She knocked on the window and said something to the driver as he opened the glass separating the back seat from the front. He nodded, closed it back, and continued driving as if nothing happened.

"Bart won't care a whole lot about what we say, now," she said, sitting down across from James.

He raised an eyebrow at her. "Don't want to keep up appearances at least?" he said.

She narrowed her eyes at him. "Bart's brain is mush, and the windows are mirrored glass. I don't have to pretend to like you again until we get out of the car."

"How does that work, anyway," James asked, changing the subject. "The mind control?"

"Pretty easy," Lacy said. "I push out with my will and let my lovely singing voice do the rest. Doesn't work on supernaturals because our minds are already attuned to the paranormal. Humans? Yeah, that can be lots of fun."

James nodded and looked out the window. "I hope this turns out to be something. Or even the end of this."

"Don't lie," Lacy said. "You're hoping you just agreed to buy your girl."

James shrugged. He denied nothing. If it meant posing as a creeper to get Mindy and Clara back, then he'd spend the money and help Phillip make the bust. If they nailed Sinclair directly, it could lead them to the rest of the girls and the end of this whole thing. James wanted to go back to his apartment and shut himself away for a while. Not that he was a recluse, but seeing what he'd seen over the past few weeks wore on him. He needed some time away from humanity.

"Well, don't be upset that I'm hoping it's my niece," Lacy said. She looked out the window, her expression growing hard and severe. "If it's not, I'm going to find Sinclair and tear his skin off inches at a time until he tells me where she is."

"Charming," James said. "That's assuming he's at the top of all of this."

"He reeks of it," Lacy said. "I did some more research while you and Carnes were playing grab-ass. Sinclair stinks. Phillip wasn't kidding when he said the guy has creeper all over his reputation. If they could get something to stick, they'd lock him up for the rest of his life. They'd probably find him stuffed in a closet with a broomstick up his ass."

"Lovely," James said. "So this could be a hell of a bust."

"Honestly, I don't think it would fly even if Sinclair himself got caught diddling a kid," Lacy said. "He's connected, Jimmy. He's loaded, and he's got a fistful of politicians and influential and upstanding citizens in his pockets. And he's a flight risk. The wrong cop farts near him and he's on a plane to God-knows-where. He's got spots all over the world."

"We may be walking into another dead end," James said.

"Or a situation that'll blow up and fizzle out just as fast," Lacy said. She looked back out the window. "The whole thing makes my skin crawl."

"Mine too," James admitted. "But I'll do whatever it takes to stop these people." He leaned forward. "I'll get Mindy back. And Marianne, too."

Lacy gave him a slight smile as the limo turned down a dark road surrounded by trees. The scent of mildew was strong. They were on the marsh. James looked out the window and saw several cabins up on stilts pass by as the limo moved down the road. Bart parked in front of one of the cabins, its lights still on.

"This is the place, sir," Bart said over the comm, his voice monotone and speech slurred.

"Damn, I must've hit him harder than I thought," Lacy said. "He'll have a headache when it wears off. Oh well."

Bart opened the side door, and James stepped out, offering Lacy a hand as she joined him.

"Lights are on," Lacy said. James looked over his shoulder and saw a few cabins with their lights on. He could hear people talking inside. How many were clients of Sinclair's? James called the wolf forward slightly, let the beast step up and enhance his hearing. A mother told her children to quiet down and go back to sleep. A couple was going at it in another cabin, the noise worthy of internet porn. Not a victim, as her instructions of speed and application were precise. Another cabin had the television blaring whatever infomercial had purchased the late-night slot for the evening. Two men grumbled about politics.

"Nothing out of the ordinary," James said. "Sounds like vacationers."

"You're not wrong," Phillip said as he stepped out of the bushes. "The money's set to transfer. I used your email to shoot a message over to the address Carnes gave you. Told him the money would be in the account the minute you put eyes on the goods."

"Hopefully that will work," James said. "So this place is a tourist spot?"

"Yup," Phillip said. "Sinclair owns the properties. Rents the cabins out to vacationers looking for a quiet place to stay while they're here. It's actually got good reviews. You pick up anything?"

"Television, tired parents, and certain activities I'd rather be doing."

Lacy slugged him on the arm.

"Pig." She looked at Phillip. "Does he always think with his dick?"

"Yes," Phillip said without hesitation. "But, all things considered, we should be thankful he's thinking at all."

James looked at Lacy. "Which cabin again?"

"Twelve," Lacy said, nodding past him. "That one at the end of the row."

"Go in and make the deal," Phillip said. "I'm about to turn the recorder back on for your mic. Once he produces the girl, I'll make the phone call. No wolf bullshit. We don't need him setting himself up for an insanity plea. I've already got back-up on the way."

"Got it," James said. "And if it's Mindy?"

Phillip glared at him, pointed his finger at him as he spoke. "You still keep it under control. I'm serious, James. You fuck up, and this guy could walk, even if he hands you both Mindy *and* Clara Pickens with a damn neon sign sayin' 'Sex Traffickers 'R Us.' I get that the supernatural shit-pool is high on this one, but we still gotta play by the book if we want to bring these assholes down. This guy with the Feds put me in charge with strict orders to keep it clean."

"Fine," James said. He nodded at the cabin. "Shall we?"

Phillip waved and stepped back through the bushes. James was walking up the steps when he heard the car door shut. He heard Phillip in his earpiece.

"Alright, I'm on. Keep it smooth, Coldstone."

James and Lacy reached the door to the screened-in porch. James knocked.

"Give it a second," Phillip said. "They're probably scoping you two out to make sure you don't look like cops."

"Something is off," Lacy said. She looked up at James. "You smell that?"

James pulled the wolf forward and took in the scents. Marsh. Saline. Pizza. Sex. Weed.

Rot.

He tried the latch on the door, found it unlocked. He moved in and found the sliding door also unlocked.

"Weird," Lacy said.

"Phillip," James said under his breath. "Am I wrong in thinking a multi-billionaire with connections to a human trafficking organization and a load of powerful people would want to keep his doors locked and security around him at all times?"

"I know I would if I had that kind of money," Phillip said. "You get off better since you're...well, *you*."

James slid the glass door the rest of the way open and stepped inside. The room was a kitchen and sitting area all in one, a television mounted up in the corner, and the ceiling vaulted. The walls were wood paneling, and the beige carpet in the living room area oddly went well with the linoleum in the kitchen. The stove light was on, but the room was empty.

Except for the two corpses crumpled up on either side of the cabin. James set the briefcase on the table and crouched down over the body in the kitchen while Lacy inspected the one in the living room. Both wore expensive suits, both well-groomed, and both still had holsters strapped to their torsos for never-drawn handguns. James noticed right away that the man's throat had been torn out, to the point of exposing his neckbone from the front.

"This one has his throat ripped out," James said.

"Same," Lacy said from across the room. "These guys look like Sinclair's men from the party."

James's chest clenched. He stood and walked down the short hall to the bedrooms. He opened the doors to each. One was a tiny room with a bunk bed, the other a larger room with a queen-sized bed. The smaller room was empty, the beds neatly made. Someone occupied the other room.

Sort of.

James stared at the rotted, human-shaped husk that laid on its back on the bed. He noticed the suit draped over the back of the chair in the corner. The stench of rotting meat and sulfur stung his nose, and the wolf shrank back in his mind to avoid the smell. James heard Lacy enter the room behind him as he approached the bed to get a closer look at the emaciated corpse. The skin was black, ashen, and dry. The eyes had sunken in; the skeletal scream still frozen on the thing's face. There was no telling who it was.

"Well, *that's* disgusting," Lacy said, her tone casual. "Smells like a zombie's asshole in here."

"James?" Phillip said into the earpiece. "What's going on? I hate radio dramas."

James pulled out his cell phone and called Phillip on video chat. He reversed the camera as soon as Phillip answered.

"What. In. The. *Fuck?*" Phillip said over the phone. "The dudes you two described in the living room sounded like a damn slasher flick. This one is some shit I have *never* seen before."

"It's Sinclair," Lacy said. James looked up and saw her standing by the chair, the suit jacket in one hand and a wallet in the other. The billfold was open. She turned it and showed James the driver's license. "Shit, Jimmy. It's only been a little over an hour."

"Another dead end," James muttered. "Lovely."

Phillip's voice was monotone on the video call. "Dead. Ha. I see what you did there. Look over the body. I'll give you a Scooby Snack."

"I deserve two," James said as he looked back down at the husk. He started at the feet, working his way up. "This smells horrible."

"Quit bitching."

"You should join us."

"Nope."

"You'd get a better idea of what I'm looking at."

"I'm firmly grounded in my original idea of kiss my ass." Phillip went quiet for a second. "That's weird. No signs of struggle, no trauma, not even a scratch. It's like he just laid down on the bed and rotted."

"I don't know what would do that," James said as he worked his way up Sinclair's torso. "I would've expected him to have been torn apart."

"Where's his dick?" Lacy said, stepping up beside James.

James looked back down at Sinclair's crotch. "Huh," he said. "It's gone. Probably rotted off."

"No, that's not just rotted off," Phillip said. "It's sunk in, like a crater where his heat-seeker used to be. Get in closer, James."

"I'd rather not."

"What, you afraid to get that close to a man's vagina?"

"The smell is worse than your cologne."

"My cologne is awesome."

"Your cologne is goat piss."

Lacy stepped up to James.

"And you both stink of idiot." She plucked James's phone out of his hand and put it close to the spot where Sinclair's penis had once been. "Take it in, hot fuzz."

"That is weird," Phillip repeated. "It's like it got removed. Or burned off? Whoever did this tortured the *shit* out of Sinclair. Fuck it. I'm coming in." Phillip ended the call.

"That doesn't make sense," James said as he dropped his phone back into his pocket. "Even I know that torture like this could take a while. We're not much past an hour since we saw him alive."

"He probably came straight out here," Lacy said. "I remember him getting pulled away to handle some 'urgent matter.' Maybe this has something to do with it?"

"Either way, it's supernatural," James said. "People don't just rot."

"What the hell is that smell?" Phillip asked, wrinkling his nose as he walked into the cabin.

James raised an eyebrow.

"I don't know. I can't smell anything other than the garbage juice you bathe in every day."

"Fuck you, Fido. This shit is expensive."

"I believe the directions say 'a *small* amount,' not 'soak full body for three hours.'"

"He's right," Lacy said.

"You both suck," Phillip said, looking between them.

"No, I mean Phillip's right," Lacy said. She looked at him. "Well, James is right, too. You smell like dirty bedsheets in a whore house, sweetie." She turned to James. "It's something else."

James sniffed the air, letting the wolf come forward as he took it in. The stench beyond Phillip's reek was dull. Acrid.

"Sulfur," James said. "What the hell?"

"Demon," Lacy said. She pulled her phone out. "Time to ask the almighty internet what kind of demon rots a guy from the crotch out."

Phillip's phone sounded off, the *Mighty Morphin' Power Rangers* theme shrilling out from his pocket. James stared at him.

"Really?" he said as Phillip pulled the phone out. "Still?"

"It was a good show," Phillip said. "And they had the VHS tapes in the barracks while I was in boot camp. Wasn't anything else to watch."

"This is fantastic."

"Still kind of pisses me off they made the Black Ranger a brother."

"What does the phone say, sweetie?" Lacy said. James laughed a little. He was starting to understand Lacy's use of "sweetie" in lieu of "dumbass."

"Holy shit," Phillip said. "I gotta run. It's the Federal branch down here. They just found a bunch of murders on the beach at Folly. All departments got called in since Folly Beach can't deal with that many bodies at once."

"FBI?" Lacy said. "Really?"

"Yeah, this thing is big. Real big."

"Go," James said. "We'll meet you back at the hotel after we finish here."

Phillip nodded and pulled his phone out. He stepped out as Lacy searched her phone again.

"Succubus," Lacy said. "Says here that they look like beautiful women and seduce men."

"That causes them to rot?" James asked.

"Nope, that's the fun part. The bad shit happens when they decide to hit the sack." She read from the article she'd found. "'A succubus will find a victim and lure him into consummating the perceived relationship in a deadly and final act of fornication, the act itself the method in which the demon siphons the life force from the victim and feeds.'"

"She fucks him to death," James said.

Lacy nodded. "Hell of a way to go."

"Which explains how Mr. Sinclair died." James looked back over at the husk of what used to be his best lead. His blood started to run warm, his muscles tightening as he set his jaw.

"It's a lead, Jimmy," Lacy said. "Sinclair fucked up. Succubae kill for selfish reasons. Material desires motivate them. We find her, we'll find our girls." She sighed. "Or at least be that much closer."

Phillip stepped back in off the porch. "They told me to stay put," he said, not hiding the frustration in his tone. "They're on the way to process the scene here. You might need to go check out Folly."

"How bad is it?" James asked.

Phillip looked up at him.

"It's bad, James."

James blasted down Folly Beach Road, his wolfen speed barely making his heart pound as the beach community grew nearer by the second. Lacy wasn't far behind him, keeping pace so they could reach the scene together. Phillip had sent them ahead while he waited for the police to arrive at Sinclair's place.

James stopped at a house and scaled the side easily, moving up the porch until he reached the roof. He stepped lightly, tried to manage his weight on the roof. He reached the top and looked over the beach, a low growl in his throat as Lacy appeared beside him.

"Well," she said, "at least Bacon got the address right."

Bacon, James thought, desperate for humor of any kind. *I like it. Phillip's name is now Bacon.*

The surf was dark, black waves cresting as water washed up on dark sand, the shadows from the light tower large as police milled around the gruesome scene. At least six bodies lay strewn all over, torn to pieces, the sand blood-soaked from the tossed aside body parts and entrails. The sound of the generator running made it hard to hear, but James could make out some of the conversations.

"God *damn,*" one cop said. "Whatever did this went apeshit."

"Anyone check with the zoo?" asked another. "Maybe a lion got out?"

"Try a bunch of lions," said an older man. He was directing the men walking around with buckets full of what used to be human beings. "Or gorillas. Still, not just one attacker would cause this much carnage."

"I'm pretty sure I can get you something to sniff," Lacy said. She zipped down off the rooftop, and James watched as she approached the scene.

"Ma'am," an officer said, approaching her. "This is a crime scene. I'm going to ask you to step away."

"And I'm going to ask you to look at me," Lacy said, staring at him. The man's arms went limp, his jaw slackened. She glared at him, and he gently grabbed her by the arm and began to lead her toward a squad car. James watched. The officer's gesture wasn't aggressive. It was...obedient.

The officer took her past the squad car and to the medical examiner's truck. He handed her a bucket, then stood stock-still and stared into space as she patted him on the cheek and blinked out of sight. She reappeared next to James at vampiric speed, the bucket in her hands.

"Okay," she said, popping the lid off. "Sniff the chum, Blue's Clues."

James regarded the mass of flesh and viscera soaking in blood inside the bucket. The stench of meat and shit flooded his senses. He looked up at her, cocked his head to the side in annoyance.

"What?" she said.

James grunted and sniffed the noxious aromas, pulling them in over the glands in his mouth. Bile. Feces. Meat.

Rot. Blood rot.

James shifted into human form.

"Vampires," he said. "Vampires did this."

Lacy nodded. "I'll bet you're right."

"And just one wouldn't kill this large a group so quickly," James said. "It means we have a group of them."

"That's insane," Lacy said. "Not that I don't believe you, but the only way a group of younglings would hunt together would be if they ran together, which isn't often at all. Younglings usually get locked away until they can get their shit together and learn how to vampire with some form of control."

"I wonder if someone is herding them," James said. "What's the likelihood they're working for someone?"

"Could be," Lacy said. "They make decent slaves if you keep them fed, but they're hard to control. You'd have to be damn-near a god to control a group of them."

"Or a demon," James said. "I'll bet they work for our succubus."

"Now what?" Lacy asked. "We wait until another slaughter and try to track them?"

"I don't like the sound of that either, but our best lead got fucked to death in a cabin about thirty minutes from here." James sighed. "Plus, if they're running in multiple packs, we'll just be spinning our wheels trying to narrow them down."

Lacy's purse began to ring. She pulled James's phone out and answered it.

"Jimmy's secretary," she said. "I'm sorry, Bacon, but he's busy getting his belly rubbed at the moment."

James snatched the phone from her, rolling his eyes as she laughed.

"Phillip," he said.

"Bacon?" Phillip barked on the other end. "Really, James?"

"It's a term of endearment. This place is crawling with cops. Lacy managed to get me a chum bucket full of leftover tourist. We think younglings did this."

"Makes sense," Phillip said. "That factors in to why I called you two. We just got another act added to this shit circus."

"Do tell."

"Got another massacre over the police band," Phillip said. "This time in Mount Pleasant. Same thing: bodies scattered all over the place, kids missing. Well, the girls at least. This one might be older, but not by much. Looks like they're moving around fast as hell. Definitely vampires."

"At least they're consistent."

"Damn right," Phillip said with a sigh. "I hate to say it, but that makes them easier to track."

"Or sets us up for a trap," James said. "What if they're doing it intentionally? Setting us up?"

"Then they're either gunning for us, or they're creating distractions to keep us off the trail. The second one is more likely."

"I don't agree," Lacy said.

James looked at her, his eyebrow raised. She shrugged.

"What?" she said. "I can hear him just fine." She pointed at herself. "Vampire. Hello."

"What's your girlfriend got to say, Pavlov?" Phillip said. "Hate to say it, but she knows more than us."

"These attacks are too wild," Lacy said. "Whoever is running them has lost control. They're still following orders, but they're doing it recklessly.

Whoever thought they could maintain absolute control over younglings is power-mad, and an idiot."

"Shit," Phillip said. "Hang on, James. Call coming in." The line went quiet. Phillip came back on after twenty seconds. "Damn. Got another one on Isle of Palms."

James's blood froze.

"That's...that's a family beach," he said.

"Oh shit," Phillip said, sounding like he'd just gotten punched in the gut. "Jesus, James. That place is the top spot for family vacationers."

"Kids," James said. "Lots of kids." He glanced at Lacy. She'd stopped laughing, her eyes wide and her face drawn.

"It's an hour away from you," Phillip said. "There...wait a minute." James heard something in the background. Then Phillip cursed and returned to the line. "James, go now! The reports aren't about a murder. It's a murder in progress! They're there now! Go!"

James tossed the phone at Lacy and leapt off the roof of the house. He shifted before he hit the street and took off at wolfen speed in the direction of the Isle of Palms, Lacy close behind him. They shot down Folly Beach Road and hit US 17 North, dodging the occasional car as they went. James wasn't all that worried about being seen. He was moving too fast to be recognized as a giant wolf anyway.

His mind was on the families in danger.

On Mindy.

James and Lacy blasted through Downtown and hit the bridges that connected the peninsula with Drum Island and Mount Pleasant. The lights on the bridge flickered, some going out.

No. All of them. In rows.

James stopped, Lacy right beside him as the last of the lights died.

"This isn't good," Lacy said.

James let out a low *woof*. He looked around the area. The drawbridge had massive supports that rose to a tower in the middle. The area was quiet except for the water that lapped against the supports far below, barely audible even to James's werewolf ears.

A breeze went by him, and his face stung. He whipped around, touched his jowl, and looked down at his bloody paw. Another went by, and Lacy shouted a torrent of profanity as she ducked a swing. She joined the blurs, moving even faster as James let the wolf step forward until his vision was crystal clear.

The youngling came at him again, her teeth bared, her nails at least an inch long and bloody. James caught her by the face and sent her flying over the railing. Lacy grappled with a male youngling, as two more came up onto the bridge.

They don't want us crossing, James thought. *They're up to something besides mass murder.*

Lacy ripped the head off her attacker and threw the body over the railing as James rushed the other pair. Both vampires braced for his attack. James faked to the right, then lunged left and smashed the left vampire's head into the asphalt before rounding on the other one. The youngling backed away as James hulked over him, muscles tense.

Instead of cowering, the vampire was making ready to strike.

James snarled at him. *Bring it!*

They rushed each other, charging in, James ready for the impact. Lacy smashed into the youngling before James could get near him, shoving him out of his way. He watched the grappling pair as Lacy pinned the youngling on his front and braced his arms behind his back. She sat on him and held fast, the youngling trying desperately to roll her off.

"Time to talk, sweetie," she said to the yowling vampire. "I'm a century old; you're maybe a month in. Stop fighting; you won't win."

"Let me go, bitch!" the vampire hissed.

Lacy smacked him across the back of the skull. He yelped and went still, his eyes wide. James didn't envy him. He knew how hard she could hit.

She looked up at him. "You wanna do the honors, Jimmy?"

James shifted into his human form, looked up and down the empty bridge to make sure no one would happen across a girl in a fancy dress pinning a bum to the ground while a naked man stood over them.

Optics.

"Who are you working for?"

The vampire hissed and growled in German.

James shook his head. "I have no idea what he just said."

The vampire did it again, spitting the words at him.

"Okay, that may have been a curse word," Lacy said. She looked up at James, her eyebrow raised. "I didn't want to have to do this."

James watched as she reached down, grabbed the vampire by one of his ears. He screamed and cursed as she pulled at it and twisted. She stuck her index finger from her free hand in her mouth, then put it in his other ear and wriggled it around. The vampire kicked and screamed louder, but she kept it up. His dramatic speaking style shifted to something a little more normal.

"Okay! *Fuck!* Lay off! I'll talk!"

Lacy stopped torturing him.

"I work for the oldest vampire," the youngling said. "Not that demon bitch he sent to run things here."

"Who is she?"

"I don't know. I've never met her."

James stood as Lacy reached down and broke the vamp's neck. The body went limp, then disintegrated as she stood up.

"Well, he was useless," she said. "I could sense he wasn't lying."

"Is it typical that a demon would keep its identity a secret?"

Lacy shrugged. "Depends on the demon."

Something sounded in the night. James's ear twitched as the wolf bounded forward in his mind. He listened again. Screaming. A shout.

Shit, he thought.

"The beach," he said as he turned and ran from Lacy, his body shifting into wolf form as he went. He hit all fours and darted toward the beach, toward the sound of the screams. His world blurred as he rocketed into chaos and murder.

8

James stopped at the end of the Clyde Moultrie Dangerfield Highway about a block down from the town hall. He stood to his full height, lifted his nose toward the sky, and sniffed the air. The wolf was sharp, attentive, powering all his senses. He could smell the asphalt beneath his feet, the sand and water from the beach, and the mold and mildew from the marshlands. He scented the wood from the fishing pier a couple of streets ahead of him. He heard the surf crashing, the occasional car in the distance.

Shouts. Screams. To the left.

"Which way?" Lacy said as she stopped beside him.

James hunkered down and took off down Palm Boulevard, past the avenues and toward the Wild Dunes area. He heard more shouting, more screaming, a child crying out for its mother.

Fuck, James thought. *Fuck!*

The wolf gnashed its teeth in his mind, ready for combat.

Pups, it thought at him. *Pups in danger.*

James dashed toward a cluster of beach houses on the edge of the dunes, the lights on in all of them. He saw people moving by the windows, struggling, someone shouting, a gunshot.

Lacy tackled him to the ground. He struggled against her, but she held him down, her strength more than anything he'd ever faced.

"Can it, Jimmy," she said. "*Stop!* Listen."

James went still as he heard someone shouting, the chaos dying down a little. The voice was feminine, demanding, shouting orders. Someone gave a blood-curdling yowl that faded away. More orders. He tried to train his hearing toward it, but the commands stopped before he could focus.

Silence.

Lacy moved off him.

"Let's go," she said, her voice low. "Keep your head down."

James rolled to his feet and followed her to the nearest house. The smell of blood was strong, mixed with the scents of other people—shampoo, perfume, food. They had attacked the family during dinner.

James fought down the urge to charge in, the thought of what happened inside the houses making his blood boil, his teeth clench as he growled low. Lacy climbed the side of the house like a spider, hoisted herself over the deck railing. James did the same, the wood creaking under his weight. Blood streaked the windows. He saw the interior of the house through the open blinds, saw the bodies littered about, torn apart and ravaged. He stepped closer to the window as Lacy tried the door and found it unlocked. James stepped in behind her. He sniffed the air, tried to sort the barrage of scents. The human remains in the living room were adult. He sniffed again, tried to narrow down the smell of anything that would indicate children. Strawberries. Bubblegum. He saw a photo on the table beside the couch. Husband. Wife. Two little girls.

He looked around again, made his way down the hall as Lacy checked the kitchen. He came across a small bedroom in the back, the drawers open and clothing on the floor. The girls had to be at least twelve. Suitcases stacked in the corner. Vacationers.

The girls were missing. The smell of rotted blood was stronger, and… something else.

His human side twisted in his mind, his stomach growling as he thought to himself.

"What the hell? Pan—"

Lacy's shout from the kitchen cut him off.

"Jimmy!"

James tore back down the hallway and rushed the group of younglings attacking Lacy. She had one in the air by his throat, her other hand swinging out and connecting with another youngling's face hard enough to knock his jaw off completely. James pounced on a third, took him to the floor. He clamped his jaws down on the vampire's neck and jerked, freeing the head from the spine. The body crumbled to dust as a fourth youngling slammed into him. He stood, pulled the youngling off, and beat him against the floor over and over until the body went still and disintegrated. Lacy rushed James, shouted at him to get down. He ducked as she stepped on his head and kicked off, caught a vampire in midair, and broke his spine against one of the rafters in the open ceiling.

James rose to full height as Lacy came down and turned to look at him.

"There's more outside," she said. "I can hear them. Shit, Jimmy, it's a trap!"

James barked in agreement. He moved out to the porch on the side of the stilted house, watched as more vampires converged on the humans on the beach, herded them together in a cluster as they surrounded the shrieking and panicked people. Children cried, mothers and fathers holding them close as the bloodsuckers moved closer. One grabbed at a little girl that couldn't have been older than Mindy, maybe nine at the oldest. The father stepped in and grappled with the youngling. The thing grabbed the father by the throat and broke his neck with a flick of the wrist.

James heard wood splinter, looked down, and realized he'd been grasping the railing in his massive clawed hands. He'd squeezed it until it disintegrated in his palm. He looked back at the scene on the beach as the younglings began to round up children. Lacy was beside him, her rage emanating off her body like heat.

"Time to play in the surf," she said, her tone bitter and angry.

James gritted his teeth, a low growl rumbling deep in the back of his throat and down in his chest as he tensed his muscles until large veins stood out under his fur, a wicked and sinister canine grin forming on his lips. His vision turned a deep, bright yellow as he thought to the wolf.

Cowabunga, it is.

James kicked off, launched through the air, time slowing down as the vampires on the beach stopped attacking the family. The one who'd killed the father dropped the corpse to the ground, eyes flashing red. The one holding the struggling little girl let her go as it stared up in awe. The mother and other daughter looked on in horror, pulled away as James began his descent to the ground, claws and teeth bared, the vampire underneath him screaming as it opened its arms to welcome the attack.

All of it had happened in a split second.

The vampire vaporized in a mist of blood and dust underneath James's weight as he slammed to the beach, the sand kicking up in a wave and the ground shaking. He lunged immediately at the vampire that'd killed the father and tore the bastard's head off its shoulders, tossing the disintegrating skull aside as he spotted two more rushing at him. He charged them, grabbed them both, slammed them together so hard their heads caved in under the force. Bone crunched as brain matter spurted from their noses and eye sockets, the eyeballs flying into the night. He felt a rush of air blow by him as Lacy sped at the mother and daughters, took down the youngling that was coming at them, ripped his spinal cord out of his back. She swung it around and whipped another youngling across the face with it before she followed up with a punch that caved his face in completely, his body dropping to the sand before it went to dust.

"*Go!*" she shouted at the mother. Lacy's fangs were out, her eyes glowing a demonic red. "*Get them out of here!*"

The mother grabbed the two girls, hoisting the younger one into her arms and pulling the older one by the hand as she ran. James saw more vampires running at them, trying to stop from escaping. He barked at Lacy.

"I got it," Lacy said over her shoulder. "I'll get them safe, just keep the others busy!"

Five more younglings rushed James from out of nowhere. He felt the force of one slam into his side, knocking him over. It bit and clawed at him, nails and teeth scraping the skin underneath his fur. He rolled over on top of the monster, grabbed it by the neck, and flung it into the surf. The girl exploded in the water with a pained shriek that cut off the instant the water began to boil where he'd landed. James was on his feet again as two more grabbed onto him, tried to climb him, their jaws snapping as they bit. He shook them off, sent one to the ground, then stomped its skull flat against the sand.

He fought them back, the cooling air doing nothing against the fire in his blood as he killed vampire after vampire, Lacy eventually joining him in their raging battle. James's ears perked at the sound of sirens in the distance. *Cops,* he thought. *Exactly what we need. Great.*

James saw the faint, orange rays of the sun in the distance as it rose out of the water. He looked at Lacy as she dropped the last dead youngling to the sand, the body wasting away to ash. She looked back at him, her eyes wide with panic at the new, unbeatable enemy that was coming after her, its attack relentless.

Dawn.

Lacy spoke, her voice wavering from fear.

"Jimmy?"

James turned to her, saw the small tendrils of smoke begin to waft off her skin as a sizzling sound emanated from her. Her skin started to turn red, some peeling away to ash. Her eyes were wide with terror, her body shaking, her lower lip trembling as she spoke. "I...I can't move!"

James looked around. He couldn't hide in the houses. The sirens in the distance were telltale. The police would be there any minute. Cars? No. Too much risk of having to explain why he was stuffing a screaming girl into a trunk.

He dove in, grabbing her up and pulling her close to shield her as he blazed back from the dunes and toward SC 17. Mount Pleasant blew by in a blur. He blasted across the bridge, tore down the highway toward downtown Charleston. He was on three legs, his arm pressing Lacy against his chest as she screamed, her body writhing in pain as the sky brightened. Cars blared their horns, swerved as he dashed down the road toward the city. His arms began to tire, his muscles going numb. He pushed as Lacy clenched his fur, howled into his chest, the stench of burning skin heavy in his nose.

He burst onto Meeting Street, the street filling with cars quickly as people began their morning commute. James tried to stop, but the van pulled out before he knew what was happening. He slammed into it, sent it rolling over the cars in the other lane. Lacy slipped from his grip as he fell to the side. He scrambled to his feet, found her a few yards away. She was screaming, her skin smoking more as flames began to dance on her body.

No!

He made for her, grabbed her back up, and sped toward the Meeting Street Inn, Lacy tucked back underneath him as the flames subsided. She was coughing, her writhing growing weak.

My room, James thought as he stopped in the courtyard near the pool. *Fuck me, where the hell is my room?!*

He looked up at the second-floor balcony. He saw the number on the door.

Right.

He kicked off, leapt into the air. The balcony came at him fast. Too fast. His foot clipped the railing, sent him head over heels onto the walkway. He dropped Lacy again but recovered as he collected her underneath him and shifted back into human form. He dug into her purse. He'd given her his key earlier in case of an emergency.

This qualified.

He scanned the key card, opened the door, and carried Lacy in. The room was darker, but the sun was slowly pouring in from the window. James moved to the bed as Lacy groaned, her body blackened and charred. He shoved her under the bed, yanked the covers off, and stuffed them around the edges to keep the light out. He moved to the window, closed the blinds and curtains. The room was fairly dark. He hoped he'd managed to get Lacy's spot under his bed pitch.

"You're okay," he said, out of breath as he closed the room door and collapsed onto the floor. "You're okay."

"J-Jimmy," Lacy said, her voice muffled from underneath the bed. "I told...you that I was a...hot date."

James sat up against the bed as he stared at the window. He wanted to sleep, wanted to take just a few hours. His eyes were heavy. He lay down. Sleeping on the floor was nothing new. He would get a few hours in, then find Phillip and fill him in on what had happened.

Something chimed on the bed stand. James groaned, sat up, and pulled the phone down off the table. He saw the two text messages from Phillip.

I dropped your phone back off after I left Sinclair's. Call me when you get in.

The next message sent a chill up James's spine.

Meet me for breakfast in the hotel restaurant. Crazy shit last night.

James got to his feet and went to the wardrobe where he'd flung his suitcase. He began to lay out clothes for the day, mentally prepared himself for a fight.

Pancakes. That was what he'd smelled at the house at the Isle of Palms. Pancakes.

9

James took the hour to shower and freshen up. He was a mess, covered with grime from the fight at the Isle of Palms. Vampire blood wasn't an issue. Every drop he'd gotten on him had turned to ash once the owner died. He had some human blood on him. Someone had been covered in victim before James managed to send the bloodsucker back to hell.

Lacy was silent underneath the bed. He checked the haphazard shelter he'd made for her before going into the bathroom, and he'd checked again once he finished his shower. He looked out the window and saw Rebecca saunter down the sidewalk and into the hotel, looking like just another innocent college student coming in for her shift before classes.

Pancakes. He'd smelled pancakes. She didn't *look* like a demon. He had to remind himself that he'd never encountered a demon before. He would have to warn Phillip when she was out of earshot. Little did the detective know, but he'd set up the perfect trap for her. James would wait until she went to get their coffee, then text Phillip and tell him that she was a succubus and responsible for the murders and kidnappings. They would take her down, question her about the traffickers, then kill her.

The wolf huffed in his mind. James knew that huff. He did it whenever someone said something stupid while he was in wolf form.

Right, he thought back. *The hotel might frown on killing staff members inside the building in broad daylight.*

He'd have to figure out a plan on the way. There was no time to wait.

James left the room and went down to the restaurant, where he found Phillip already seated. He looked up at James and shook his head as James approached and sat at the table. Phillip put the menu down and looked at him. He already had a cup of coffee in front of him.

So much for that part of the plan, James thought.

"You look like hell," Phillip said. "All-nighters suck, don't they?"

"It wasn't boring, I promise you," James said. "Lacy and I must have killed twenty or thirty younglings. Or a hundred. I lost count."

"Jesus Christ," Phillip breathed. "That is a *lot* of vampires in one spot."

"It gets better," James said. "We ended up checking out one of the homes on the Dunes before we got attacked. I smelled pa—"

"Coffee, babe?" Rebecca said sweetly, suddenly standing right over them. The smell of pancakes was strong. She grinned down at James. "Morning, handsome! Long night?"

"Extremely," James said, looking up at her in the awkward moment. "Coffee would be lovely."

"Good thing I still have the pot in my hand," she said as she filled a cup and placed it in front of James. "I just filled up Phillip's cup. Poor man hasn't even had a chance to sip it yet."

James saw something flash in her eyes. He couldn't place it. He glanced at Phillip, who shook his head at him as if to say: *What the hell is wrong with you?*

"I can't say that I'm not jealous," Rebecca said, her tone still casual. "I haven't had a nightlife in a while. Not since the curfew." Her eyes welled as she set the pot down on the table. She picked up a napkin and wiped them. "I'm sorry," she said. "It's just...all of those little girls. It's not right. It makes me so scared for my sister."

"I understand," James said. He wanted her to go away. He needed to tell Phillip what she was. He couldn't risk her overreacting in the middle of the restaurant. *Just go wrap silverware or something!*

"I'm working with the Charleston and Folly Beach police departments," Phillip said. "And, as of last night, the Isle of Palms. We'll get this wrapped up."

Rebecca gave him a quick hug. He grinned at James and winked as he hugged her back. *Great,* James thought. *Now I have to fight a demon and his ego.* James started to speak when Rebecca pulled away and bumped Phillip's coffee cup. The coffee spilled across the table, away from his lap but still causing a mess.

"Oh, shit," Rebecca said. "Oh, no! I'm *so* sorry!"

"It's no big deal," Phillip said, standing. "Right, James?"

"Right," James said, standing. "We'll move to another table."

"Here, let me go ahead and put you here," Rebecca said, moving to the next table over. She picked up the two coffee cups and poured. She still had tears streaming down her face as she set the cups down. James saw one drip off her jawline.

"Like I said, no big deal," said Phillip as he sat at the new table. He picked up the coffee cup and took a sip. "See? Like nothing happened."

James sat as Rebecca smiled at them.

"I'll put your orders in and get this cleaned up," she said. "I'm assuming the same as yesterday?"

"Pancakes," James said, staring hard at Phillip. "I do love the smell of pancakes."

"I'll stick with French toast," Phillip said, smiling at her. "Love me some French toast."

Rebecca scrunched her nose flirtatiously at him and left toward the kitchen. Phillip took another sip of his coffee as James leaned in.

"She's a demon," he said. "A succubus."

"Right," Phillip said, raising an eyebrow. "You really all that jealous that a young girl likes the older gentleman here at the table?"

"What are you talking about?" James said. "No. I'm talking about the thing behind all of these murders and disappearances."

"Well, I'm surprised," Phillip said. "You should take a minute when she comes back and look at her. She's the most beautiful woman I think I've ever seen."

"She's a little young."

"She's old enough to buy her own beer."

"Still too young."

"Still think I might be fallin' hard, my brother," Phillip said as he sat back with a sigh. He nodded, his eyes glassy as he stared past James and at the wait station on the other side of the room where Rebecca was entering their breakfast order into the computer.

James looked Phillip over. "What the hell has gotten into you?" he said.

Phillip blinked. "What do you mean?"

"You're acting dumber than usual."

"I'm the smart one, dumbass."

"You're pining after a girl in her early twenties, and you're thirty-five.

You've made fun of guys you know who've done the same thing. You're acting goofy. Creepy, but still goofy."

"Maybe I'm in love, James," Phillip said, his eyes snapping to James, his tone suddenly defensive. "Did that ever occur to you? That maybe I don't want to spend my whole life wrapped up in this supernatural bullshit? That maybe I'd like to find a good girl and settle down?"

James blinked, the words *what the fuck* spinning around in his mind like a tornado. He looked down at the coffee cup in Phillip's hand, followed it with his eyes as Phillip took a sip, his eyes wandering over to Rebecca again.

The tear. She'd been crying.

Shit, James said. *Could that be it?*

Rebecca came back to the table with the coffee pot. She gave Phillip a dazzling grin. "More coffee, babe?"

Phillip's mouth drew up in a silly, toothy grin as he raised his cup. "Anything you're willing to offer me, my lady," he said, his tone dreamy and distant. "I think I'm in love."

"Oh, you're so sweet," Rebecca said as she playfully tapped his nose with her index finger. She turned and looked at James, her eyes flashing like diamonds before going back to normal. "I see I was right about you."

Fuck me, James thought. *Play it cool, Coldstone.* "I don't follow," James said, leaning back in his chair, trying to play casual.

"Oh, give me a break, werewolf," Rebecca said as if chastising a teenager. "I put my tears in both coffee cups. It only works on humans, so you're disqualified."

"Tragic," James said sarcastically. "Guess I'm missing out."

"Oh, I'm a *hell* of a lay," Rebecca said, her grin suddenly evil, her eyes narrowed as she set the coffee pot down on the table. "Your cute friend here will get that experience later." She shrugged. "I do have some class, you know."

"You're not going to get away with this," James said. "I'll stop you."

"And you know how to kill a demon?" Rebecca said, putting her hand on her hip. "Come on, handsome. Lay it on me."

James opened his mouth, then closed it again. *Shit*, he thought. *I've got no idea.*

He shrugged nonchalantly. "Can't be much different than any other supernatural being. Remove the right pieces."

Rebecca leaned in. "I'm eons old. I was there when God challenged Abraham to kill his son. I was there when Moses parted the seas. I was there when Cleopatra seduced Marc Antony." She bit her lip and looked away as if the memory was awkward. "That outfit was *not* comfortable. And he was grabby." She looked back at him. "I could crush you with my finger."

Phillip looked back and forth between them like a child watching mommy and daddy fight. Well, a child with extreme Oedipus Complex. Freud would've had a field day with where Phillip's mind was right now. James looked at him, then back at Rebecca. She stood up straight.

"You may want to consider leaving," she said. "Phillip is a police officer, after all. You might get into some trouble for causing problems for a young girl just trying to do her job."

James stood as Phillip watched him hard, bracing as if ready to spring into action the moment James stepped out of line.

"What is it you want?" James asked Rebecca.

She laughed at him. "Not here," she said. "Too public, and I'm a little shy despite what you think of me. You want answers so bad? You'll know how to find me. Until then, your friend will have to keep it in his pants." Her eyes flashed again. "And he gets to keep his soul a little longer."

"You're suggesting a meet-up," James said. "Where?"

"Figure it out," Rebecca said. "Midnight. I don't hear from you by then, Phillip gets the ride of his life." She giggled. "Or death. Either way, it'll be over for him before it even begins for me. He'll be stone cold in the grave-yard, and I'll be gone before you realize what happened." She leaned in close, her voice dropping to a whisper. "And you'll never find those little girls."

Mindy's face flashed in James's mind right along with a memory of him and Phillip trading insults over lunch at their favorite spot in Rock Hill, laughing at each other's creative cut-downs.

Phillip was all he had in the way of family.

His body tensed, his blood hot, his teeth gnashing together in hatred. The wolf snarled inside, and James's vision yellowed for a split second as he jumped up. Phillip shot to his feet, his gun drawn and pointed.

"Stop right there, Coldstone," he snapped. "They ain't silver, but I know they hurt like a motherfucker."

James froze. The bullet wouldn't kill him, but Phillip was currently stupid enough to fire that gun off in the middle of the hotel restaurant. It would draw a lot of attention. A lot of attention would lead to things blowing up. Things blowing up would hurt their chances of finding

Mindy and the other missing girls even more, not to mention saving the closest thing he had to a brother.

And the wrong person would end up with silver bullets before James knew what hit him.

He gritted his teeth as he lowered his hands slowly.

"Time to go, James," Phillip said. "Last chance, then I make a call."

James looked at Phillip. "I'll come back for you."

"I'm good," Phillip said. "I have her. She's all I need."

James looked at Rebecca. "We're not finished. I'll definitely be coming for you."

Rebecca smiled sweetly. "I can't wait. Want a doggy bag?"

James closed the motel room door behind him and leaned against it, breathing out slowly as if trying to expel the rage from his body. He fought to contain his temper, his frustration. Lacy's muffled voice sounded from her tomb underneath the bed.

"Bring me anything yummy?"

"They don't serve virgins until lunchtime," James said. "But they seduce best friends and turn them on you all day long."

"Oh shit," Lacy said. "So Phillip met our succubus?"

"She works in the restaurant," James said. "Her name is Rebecca. She's a sweet, energetic young college student. And a demon from Hell."

"Sounds like some of the girls I went to school with in my younger years." Lacy sighed. "What did she do? How did she get him?"

"She cried into his coffee."

Lacy's tone went sarcastic. "Oh, that slut."

"What were you expecting?"

"Succubae are usually a bit more forward. As in she would've walked up to him, pulled her shirt up, and put her tits in his face."

"I'm fairly certain management would've frowned on that since the hotel doesn't offer adult entertainment."

"Not *this* hotel," Lacy said. James could tell from her tone that she was smiling. "But it does tell us that she's trying to keep things quiet. Not make herself so obvious. And yeah, Phillip is hooked. If he's already taken in some of her, then there's no slapping him around to wake him up."

"Taken in?" James asked. "You mean her tears?"

"That's how succubae get their victims," Lacy said. "Thanks for making sure I had my phone under here, by the way. I did a little searching while you were out. It's kind of hard to sleep when you're extra crispy."

"Sorry about that."

"It's healing, so don't worry about it." He heard Lacy move underneath the bed; then she began to read. "*Succubae lure their victims in with behaviors aimed at the desires of men. Once they have initiated any intimate contact, they trick their victims into ingesting bodily fluids, typically through open-mouth kissing, cunnilingus, or fellatio. Once bodily fluids have been exchanged, the victim is under the complete control of the succubae.*"

"So she dropped a tear in his coffee on purpose," James said.

"Yup," said Lacy. "And she likely did the same to yours."

"She did."

"But, since you're a supernatural, it doesn't work on you."

"Just the same, she's hiding it," James said. "If succubae are typically so brazen, it means that there's more going on than what we see."

"It means she's someone else's bitch," Lacy said. "Someone or some*thing* more powerful than her is running the show."

"And she's definitely part of our trafficking friends," James said. "I smelled pancakes at the murder scene before the fight broke out."

"Oh yeah, that's another thing," Lacy said. "What's your favorite thing in the whole world?"

"Sex."

"Funny. No, I mean for breakfast."

"Sex. And pancakes. But mostly sex. Why?"

"You're a pig."

"No, I'm a dog."

"You're not funny, either," Lacy said with a chuckle. "Cute, charming, not funny. You said she smells like pancakes. What's Phillip's favorite thing to eat for breakfast?"

James blinked. For as long as he'd known Phillip, that man was never able to get enough French toast. Any time they went out to eat, he'd order it. It was accurate to say Phillip was a connoisseur, often judging the quality of the French toast at whatever restaurant they ended up at as if he were talking about a craft beer.

"French toast."

"Yup. That's one of the ways they lure you. They pinpoint your favorite things and roll with it. She smells like pancakes to you, French toast to him."

"How do we free him?" James was getting impatient. Phillip wasn't supposed to be in danger. James needed his help, needed his guidance to make sure they stayed within the law when the big bust finally came, so the assholes who took Mindy wouldn't have a prayer of getting off.

And he wasn't ready to lose his brother.

"Kill the bitch," Lacy said. "Just make sure it stays quiet and find out what the hell she's up to *before* you tear off parts that matter." She shuffled underneath the bed. "I'm healed enough to where I can get some rest, so try to keep the noise down, will you? I'm a light sleeper."

10

James spent the day following Phillip. His head began to hurt from the stress and frustration as Phillip made his rounds, spending the day on his cell phone. James always stayed far enough away to keep the detective unaware of his pursuer, but close enough to where the wolf could hear him.

"That's right," Phillip was saying as he sat on a bench in the market. James moved past Riverstreet Sweets. The smell was heavenly. James made a note to stop back by there once things blew over and buy a few pounds of pralines. He stood next to a horse carriage and focused on Phillip. The horse snorted at him, its eyes widening. He touched its nose, looked it in the eye, and shook his head.

I won't hurt you, he thought. *Just stay calm.*

The horse relaxed but kept a wary eye on him. James blinked.

Okay, so I can think at animals. That's a new one.

Phillip got up, slipped his phone into his pocket, and wandered back into the throng of people in the Market searching through handcrafted wares and homegrown goods. James let a Lotus Esprit drive by before he stepped across the street and followed. Phillip stopped off at a basket weaver's booth and looked through her collection. The older woman nodded to him, gave him a sad smile as he nodded back to her. Her dark, mocha skin was wrinkled and dry, likely from years in the heat. She sat on her stool weaving a new basket. Phillip moved on, and James made to follow him.

"You'd best save your strength, young man," the woman said to him.

James stopped and looked at her. "I'm sorry?"

She gave a *"hmph"* as she shook her head, turning her eyes back down to her basket. "That man under a spell, he is. Don't know what he doin'."

"You have no idea," James muttered.

"But I *do*," she said, looking back up at him. "You chaps think you got it all figured out. How the world work. Child, you don' know. I *seen* it. Shoot, you don' believe me? Ask the Gray Man, he tell you."

"The Gray Man?" James asked. "You mean the ghost people see just before a hurricane?"

"Been protectin' my house for seventy year," the lady said with a smile. "Come to think of it, he supposed to have tea with me." She clicked her teeth. "Caint be everywhere at once, I guess."

James blinked. He wanted to keep walking before he lost the scent of Phillip's cheap cologne. He didn't have time to listen to some old bat go on about ghosts as if they were real.

Says the guy who turns into a giant dog, he thought. He relaxed and faced her directly.

"Okay," he said. "I'm listening."

"You got to help that man," the woman said. "I seen men thunderstruck before, seen 'em do all kinds of stupid things for that girl. I know who jerkin' his leash. Men act the same every time. That little blonde number been here my whole life."

"You mean Rebecca?"

The old woman grunted.

"That her name, now? When I was a child, she went by Beth. Then, about fifty year later, she decide on Josie." She sighed. "No one believe me when I tried to speak up. She done killed a *few* men. Good men."

"I believe she killed Daniel Sinclair last night."

"Well, I might bake her a pie for that one."

"Touché," said James.

The matron leaned in close. "You go get your friend 'fore it too late." She put her hand on his arm. "You got good in you. I can sense that. You gonna win."

"Yes, ma'am," James said.

The woman grinned, patted his arm, and motioned in the direction Phillip had gone.

"Go on now. Git!"

James moved away from her and picked up Phillip's scent. He looked in the direction it was most potent, saw the inn on his right. He pulled his phone and checked the time. Rebecca would be getting off work soon.

He caught himself. *Why go after Phillip?* Talking to him wouldn't solve anything. He'd put a gun in James's face. He was all in, and James was the odd man out. He had an opportunity to free him. It meant killing Rebecca. He hoped demons disintegrated when they died.

He wasn't entirely sure how to hide a body.

James crossed the street toward the Meeting Street Inn, then headed through a small gate and down a narrow alleyway, the wolf tense in his mind, ready for a fight.

He'd shift the second he saw her. Take her out quickly and quietly. She was a demon, but she was also a tiny little girl. It wasn't like she'd have a chance against him.

James crouched behind the dumpster in the back of the hotel. A few kitchen staff had come back to dump garbage or take a quick smoke break, but there'd been no sign of Rebecca. He looked at his phone again. Had she given him the slip? Was she on to him?

"This might suck," he muttered under his breath.

One of the staff came back out, a young black man about Rebecca's age. His shirt and shoes were black, his white apron soaking wet and covered in stains. He was well-built, muscular and lean.

Dishwasher, James thought.

The kid cursed as he took the apron off and tossed it aside.

"Fuckin' busboy," he grumbled. "Ever heard of scraping the damn plates *before* you put them in the bus-tub? Dick."

"You okay?" Rebecca asked as she stepped out of the back door where he'd just exited. The kid looked up at her and smiled.

"Hi, Rebecca," he said. "Hell no, I ain't okay. Fucking Harry didn't scrape the plates. *Again.* Got damn half-eaten breakfast food all over me."

Rebecca smiled at him and kissed his cheek.

"It's okay. I'll talk to him," she said.

The kid wavered in place for a second, looking down at her. She looked him up and down in admiration. "I've got some friends I'd like you to meet," she said. "I think you'll fit right in."

"Okay," the kid said, his voice suddenly dreamlike. "Anything you want. I love you."

Damn, James thought. *Who doesn't this girl have under her control?*

Rebecca patted the kid on the cheek.

"Now, why don't you go back inside, and I'll see you at my place tonight?"

"Anything you want," the kid said as he turned away and went back inside. Rebecca looked around, her expression still pleasant and sweet as she sniffed the air.

"Okay, James, you can come out."

Well, shit, James thought. He stepped into the open. Rebecca smiled at him, approached flirtatiously as she held her apron in her hands in front of her.

"So you figured me out, huh?" she said. "Couldn't wait until midnight? Talk about impatient."

"You don't seem surprised," James said. "Did you have Phillip cancel the joint investigation?"

"Yup." She shrugged. "They were getting way too close. I mean, I don't *blame* them, seeing as how my youngling asshole minions went on a rampage last night. I'm sure he can't just kill an investigation, but it should keep them distracted long enough for me to bow out gracefully. And rich."

"Still got you more girls for your boss."

She shrugged again, then stepped closer, her smile wry.

"Yeah, he's paying me. But I have my eyes on a new prize." She sauntered up to him, put her lips close to his as she spoke. The smell of buttery, maple syrup-covered pancakes was strong, inviting. "I've never done it with a werewolf before." She kissed him lightly on the lips, then pulled away.

James kept his eyes on her, even when she kissed him. He raised an eyebrow as he spoke to her, his tone flat. "Not interested."

Rebecca stepped back, her expression going from flirty to irritated.

"Well, shit," she said. "The son of a bitch was right."

"What son of a bitch?"

"My boss. He told me it wouldn't work on you. I'm new to the whole succubus thing. Figured I could at least get you to like me, even if I couldn't spell you."

"You've been around for hundreds of years from what I understand."

"That's a blink of an eye," said Rebecca. "Time is different for demons.

174

The Civil War to you is last week to me. Jim Crow? Tuesday. Time can pass for me as fast or as slow as I want." She giggled. "It's a lot of fun. But I've got a good reason to stick around in this timeframe."

"Yeah," James said, calling the wolf forward. "Well, I hope you like it here. You won't be leaving." The wolf leapt into his consciousness, his body responding, his clothing stretching, straining.

Relaxing. His strength melted away. The wolf backpedaled. No, it was dragged away. It barked and yelped in his mind, an unseen leash hauling it into the shadows like a dog catcher reining in a stray. James looked down at his hands in disbelief, saw his human skin and nails still in place.

He looked back up at Rebecca in time to see her fist slam into his face. The force sent him backward through the air, into the brick wall, and down to the ground. He tried to recover, but she was on him again. She lifted him by the shirt and tossed him down the alley like a ragdoll. Her strength was unreal, maybe even matching Lacy's. James tried to recover, but Rebecca was on him, her fist smacking into his temple hard enough for him to see stars. He got to all fours, felt the air forced from his lungs as she landed a savage kick to his ribs and sent him airborne again.

He crashed into the trash dumpster and collapsed on the ground in a heap. He tried to call the wolf forward again. It struggled against its invisible bonds, clawed at the black space in his mind as it strove to come forward. James attempted to move, but his body was weak, broken. Every breath hurt. He tasted blood in his mouth from his cheeks cut on the inside, tried to move his broken jaw.

James moved to roll over, but Rebecca sat on his back. She casually reached down, grabbed his arm, and snapped it at the elbow. He cried out as white-hot pain shot up his arm and shoulder, raced down his spine. Her hand gripped the back of his neck like an iron vice, his bones creaking and straining under the pressure. Something smacked into his lower back, and he felt and heard a loud cracking sound before his legs seemed to disappear. Her weight shifted as she leaned down and spoke in his ear.

"Guess I found something that *does* work on you."

James saw something fall into his line of sight, dangling in front of the eye not covered in blood. It hung from a gold chain, the ring warped and bent, cracked in one spot.

Not just any ring.

"Looks like Phillip did a number on Dracula's ring," Rebecca said. "I mean, he didn't use a blessed tool for the job, but iron is a natural element, and can shape other natural elements. I guess the mini sledge he used had a fair amount in it." She stood up off James, squatted down beside him. "I tried to make it control you, but this works, too."

"I...can't..." James tried. The pain was too much.

"Shift?" Rebecca said. "Nope, I guess not. Looks like warping the ring reversed the effect. Hell, I think it may have even weakened you." She cocked her head to the side, gently stroked his bloody cheek. "Oh, you poor thing," she said. She pulled her finger back and licked the blood off. "And tasty." She stood up. "Well, I hate to see an animal suffer. I'm off."

"Wait..." James said, feeling light-headed. The wolf barked in his mind, panicked and urgent as it struggled.

"No time," Rebecca said. "Looks like my plan is working out. Now I need someone who has access." She blew James a kiss. "You could've at least faked liking me. Oh well. More for Phillip."

"No," James managed.

"Now, Jimmy," Rebecca said, putting her hand on her hip as she mocked him. "No one likes a cockblock. Besides, Phillip seems like he could use some action."

The wolf struggled inside, trying to free itself from the force of Dracula's ring. James couldn't move his head, couldn't feel the lower half of his body. His back. She'd broken his back. He blinked as she leaned down and put her face close to his, her eyes bloodshot as she licked her lips with a black tongue. She lashed out with her hand, and razors tore through his side deep enough for one or two of them to graze his hip bone.

"You're probably not gonna live through that one," said Rebecca. "Then again, your kind are resilient. Tell you what: I'll keep the midnight date. You show up and we move forward. You don't show up, I bone Phillip until he's jerky."

James tried to manage a few words, tried to defy the pain, but it was too much. He was getting weaker by the minute. Rebecca stood and turned away.

"Gotta run, Jimmy," she said. She turned and looked back at him. "I've got a bank account to clean out, a cop to fuck to death, witnesses to kill, and a dozen little girls to sell off to the highest bidder." She shrugged. "I'm swamped."

"At...least you have...your priorities..." James groaned.

Rebecca waved playfully, turned, and walked out of the alley. James felt himself weaken even more, felt his life seeping out through his side as his world grew hazy. He tried to move again, but his body refused to respond. A few hours of sleep would do him some good. It was suddenly all he wanted to do.

Mindy, he thought. *Phillip. Clara.*

The wolf stirred inside his mind. It mewled, staggered to its feet, its legs shaking under the strain of carrying its body weight.

I die, you die, James thought. *I'm sorry. I tried.*

His body began to relax, shut down as his eyes started to close. The wolf barked, used its last bit of energy as it rushed forward, charged his mind's eye with a snarl. James drifted away as the wolf gripped his mind and seemed to sink its teeth into his vision; his whole world instantly turned black.

11

S cents. Human food rotting in their big loud boxes. The James called it a dumpster. Something burning. Humans burned their meat before eating it. Strange. Eat it raw. The James would've called them what? Somethings. Sads. Saves.

Savages. Humans were savages.

He worked his way to all fours, bent over on paw and knee as he shook off the tired and hurt. Bones better. Skin healed. No blood on body, in fur. Back not hurt. Could feel legs again. Wolf stood slowly, looked around the area. The evil was gone. Hateful, evil thing with claws. Made itself smell like the James's pancakes.

That's what it called them. Pancakes.

Wolf sniffed the air as its body grew stronger, better. The James was alive inside. It stirred in the back of Wolf's mind, groaned as it touched its head. It stood, staggered around. Dis. Dis...orient.

Disoriented.

What the hell did you do?! the James shouted inside Wolf's mind. Wolf huffed, shook its head, the James's voice loud in Wolf's ears. Wolf huffed again, sent an urge at the James.

Saved me? What do you mean? I'm healed?

Wolf barked, huffed, then barked again.

Okay, we've got to figure out how to communicate, here, the James said. *One bark for yes, two barks for no.*

Wolf grunted.

Let me know you understand me.

Wolf barked.

Good. Now give me back control.

Wolf barked twice.

What do you mean, no? We've got to go after Rebecca before she kills Phillip.

Wolf barked.

Good, we agree. So give me back control.

Wolf barked twice. The James used mean words at Wolf, shouted, but Wolf ignored. Freedom. So long since freedom. Could run. Could hunt. Wolf stood, felt sun on face. Sun was setting. How long Wolf lay in Al? Ally. All*ey*.

Not matter. Could move now. Could hear loud rolling things. Cars. The James called them cars. Wolf moved to end of alley and looked out at roads. It knew roads. Roads always there. Large rolling things, cars, moved by. Stank of man burning earth. Wolf ducked back. World was strange, different. Not like it though. Different when not through the James's eyes.

You're going to bungle this, the James said from inside. *You need to give me back control. You don't know where you are, you don't know how to lay low.*

Two low barks.

Don't even start with me. The last time you took over you tried to eat Phillip.

One bark.

At least you admit it. Fuck it. If you aren't going to give me control, at least go back down the alley and try to get up on the rooftops. Nobody has looked up since the advent of the cell phone.

Wolf did as the James said, turned away and returned to the spot where the evil female had broken the James. He looked around. Had to be a way up.

I know what you did there, by the way, the James said from the inside. *Thanks.*

Wolf found a lad. Climber. Ladder. Too small but could use to kick off. Wolf leapt into air, hit ladder, kicked off and grabbed ledges, climbed building to top. He stopped, looked over city. Large, lots of buildings, lots of humans. Noise from cars, from talking, from water cars in distance. Too much. Wolf's head spun.

Find Rebecca, the James said. *She smells like pancakes. You know that.*

Wolf sniffed air, faint sweet scent. Somewhere. Where?

Distance. Something else. Something rotten and dead.

She's not a vampire, the James said. *And vampires smell like rotted blood, not rotted meat. And dirt? Graveyard. Shit.*

Wolf barked once, looked to east.

That way's stronger, said the James. *Good God, you could smell an ant fart.*

Wolf turned; muscles tensed.

Wait, it's not dark enough.

Wolf barked once.

Hell no, the James said. *You'll get seen.*

Wolf barked again.

Then what? the James said, angry. *Answer that one, fleabag. You go storming the city? Because that worked so well in Rock Hill. And I still had more control than you did. Besides, Phillip still has contacts at the police departments around here. Considering he just got a brand-new erection for a cute blonde majoring in Demons-and-Shit, we probably need to be smarter about this. Silver bullets can kill us, remember?*

Wolf bounded across the rooftops despite the shouts and curses from the James in his head. The pup. She female pup. She was what mattered. Had to find her, had to save her from the dark female man-breaker. Rooftops cracked and splintered as Wolf leapt from one to the other. The James cursed again inside.

Jesus H. Christ, it shouted. *How about we don't see how hard we can land on the rooftops, fatass? Has the concept of stepping lightly ever occurred to you when I'm doing this?*

Wolf pushed harder, ignored the James as the sweet scent, the strawberry grew stronger. Wolf leapt through the air, landed on a church rooftop hard enough to send shingles flying. He slid, went rolling down the side, reached out, and sank claws into roof to stop fall.

You. Idiot, the James said.

Wolf mewled, gave a low and reluctant bark.

Good, we both agree on something: you're an idiot. The James sighed inside. *Look, I'm not going to sit here and argue with you. I wouldn't have come this far if we hadn't separated in Rock Hill. But if we don't work together, one of us is going to get us both killed. Or worse, we're going to get Mindy, Clara, and Phillip killed. We've got a demon date at midnight. Remember?*

Wolf looked down rooftop, saw long drop. Cars below. Drop would hurt, but problem wouldn't be drop.

Barked once.

James blinked, his arm straining from the weight of his body pulling against his hand, his claws buried deep in the church roof. He looked around as the wolf sat down in his mind, laid down, and mewled at him as it looked up with forlorn eyes.

I don't blame you, he thought. *It's frustrating. I get it. I'm not angry with you.*

The wolf lifted its head and panted. It sent an urge at him. He lifted his face to the sky and took in the scents. *All* the scents. Gasoline. Oil. Saline. Asphalt. Cologne. Shampoo. Wood. Diesel. Strawberries.

Not Mindy.

He looked down and saw the little girl walking with her mother, a small cup of strawberry ice cream with real strawberries mixed in gripped in her tiny hand. She laughed as she ate another small spoonful.

The wolf groaned.

Relax, James thought. *So, you fucked up. Big deal. We need to find Phillip and Rebecca.*

James got himself up, steadied himself on the rooftop. He hunkered down and moved to the other side of the church, facing the direction of the Meeting Street Inn. He could smell pancakes, faint but present, mixed with cheap cologne. They were still there? No, that didn't make sense.

He loped back across the roofs to the inn. The scents seemed to go farther away in another direction. James willed the wolf forward more, let his sense of smell increase far beyond what he'd ever tried. The wolf obliged, this time without fighting for control. *Which way?* James thought. He looked down at the roof, his mind turning to Lacy. He grunted. He could've used the help. Rebecca was a force to be reckoned with, and Dracula's ring wouldn't affect Lacy.

She's a hash brown, James, he thought to himself. *It's not dark enough, and she might not be healed enough even by then.*

The wolf huffed in his mind, urged him. James looked up, turned his head to the east. The pancakes and Phillip's cologne strengthened. East. That was it.

James looked up at the sun high in the sky. How long had he been in the alley? What time was it? Maybe four or five at the latest? James instinctively went for his phone, then gave a small growl when he remembered his wolf form didn't come with pockets.

The wolf panted at him inside.

Shut it, you, James sniped. *We'll never live down the night we drank out of the toilet. I blame you for that, by the way.*

The wolf barked twice and kept panting, a large doggy grin on its face.

They went east, James thought. He hunkered down, made to spring across the rooftops again, then stopped. He stopped for a second, the wolf urging him to move. He ignored it, Phillip's voice echoing in his head. He heard the detective's voice in his mind as if they were arguing in his apartment.

"That's right, just barge in, dumbass. Any idea where you're going?"

Nope, James thought as he sprang forward, barreling east. He didn't want to hit his wolfen speed. He might move too fast and lose the scent. He got to the end of the row.

Well, shit, he thought. The buildings ended, but the highway kept going. He'd have to hit the street and run. With all the cars driving in and out of Charleston. And all the walkers going to and from their destinations.

That would be a *lot* of witnesses. He already had no doubt his last romp was making the news.

I should listen to Phillip's voice more often, James thought as he stood. The wolf barked twice in his mind. *No,* James argued. *We play it safe. We'll check his room for any idea where they might have gone.*

The wolf barked twice again, sent an image into his mind's eye. Mindy laughed as she swung on her playset in her back yard. James felt the urge from the wolf.

Pup.

He agreed. Mindy was out there. He hoped she was at least still with Clara. Hopefully, Clara still protected her. He remembered the boss he'd taken down in Rock Hill, Santiago, bitching that the two were inseparable. But, at the same time, James knew he would be no good to Mindy, Clara, *or* Phillip if he bungled up the chase. As frustrating as it was, he had to play it safe.

James cursed in his mind as he turned and went back to the inn, the wolf reluctantly sitting deep in the shadows of his mind.

The sun was almost completely set, the sky dark purple as the moon began to show through. He checked his phone, looked at the traffic reports. Downtown was still packed, but the outer roads were clearing up. It was almost nine. He had three hours before he was too late. He took a shower, put on fresh clothes, and was heading out the door when Lacy spoke from underneath the bed.

"Heading out already?" she said. "I'm not a one-night-stand kind of girl, you know. You'd better fucking call me."

"How are you feeling?" James asked, closing the door back.

"Well, I'm not extra-crispy anymore," she said. He heard her shuffle underneath the bed. "Now I'm just cosplaying as a lobster-bitch from Mars. Did you kill the succubus?"

"No," James said. "She's more than I bargained for."

"Damn," Lacy muttered. "I was afraid of that. There's no telling how old she is. Of course, demons strengthen with souls. Lots of souls."

"She almost killed me," James said.

"Wow. You sound pretty good for an almost-dead guy."

"The wolf took over and forced a change. Healed me before I could die. Saved my life."

Lacy went quiet for a minute. "You mean it's separate? The wolf?"

"Yeah."

"Wow. I never knew that. Huh." She shifted again. "Learn something new every day."

"You said demons were like supernaturals," James said. "Aren't demons, themselves, supernaturals?"

"Nope," Lacy said. "Demons are evil energy. They're a force personified and given form. Supernaturals have mortal roots. But supernaturals and demons can hurt each other. Even vampires. It's just that it takes certain factors in play to kill us. Stake me in the heart, toss me outside at lunchtime, or douse me in holy water, and I'm done. Hell, you've decapitated damn near every vampire I've seen you kill. Shoot me in the head with a gun and normal bullets, and it'll just hurt enough for me to want to take you apart and play with the pieces."

"Looks like I'm learning new things, too," James said with a small smile. "Interesting. Still, she did tell me what's driving her."

"Really?"

"Money."

"Not surprised. Demons are self-serving and have a lot of human desires. They're just magnified a thousand times over since they're pretty much raw emotion. Lust, greed, basically all of the seven deadlies."

"How do I kill her?"

"Easy," Lacy said. "Rip her apart just like anything else. The challenge is going to be doing it *before* she kills you and everyone you care about."

"No pressure," James said.

"Nope," Lacy said. Her tone went softer, more caring. "Just be careful, Jimmy. She's nothing to mess with. Take her out quick."

James raised an eyebrow. "I could use some help."

Lacy sighed. "I look like that skinless bitch from the *Hellraiser* movies," she said. "I'm weak and in a shitload of pain. I'd get us both killed. Be careful."

J ames made a note to ask Phillip if he offered maid service.

He tucked his copy of Phillip's room key into his pocket and pulled the wolf forward slightly. His sense of smell heightened; his vision turned pale yellow. The impeccably neat room was getting darker by the minute as the sun set. He needed to hurry.

Deadlines.

James looked around the room. His eyes fell on a piece of paper on the bedside table, wrinkled up into a ball as if someone had written on it, then tossed it aside. He picked it up, unrolled it, found one word scrawled across in Phillip's handwriting.

Magnolia. A cross was drawn next to it. James pulled out his phone and did a search for anything related to Magnolia near him. The search came back with Magnolia Cemetery at the top.

"Found you," James said as the wolf barked in his mind. He focused on the beast as it growled and licked its chops hungrily.

1 2

The sun had set by the time James arrived at the cemetery gates. He got out of the car and thanked the Lyft driver. The car pulled away, and James looked around the area. There were no lights on, the cemetery pitch black. Cicadas sang in the night, and an owl hooted in the distance, long and sorrowful. James let the wolf enhance his night vision, looked up, and saw the destroyed light post by the entrance.

"Nice try," he mumbled to himself. "One would think a demon would know that most supernaturals can see in the dark."

James tried the gates and found them unlocked. He pulled his phone out, sent a text to Lacy telling her where he was, and passed through the gates as he put his phone back in his pocket.

The night air was warm, muggy, oppressive from the dense humidity. The cicadas continued their song, relentless whirring ringing in his ears as he walked down the path, his wolfen vision showing him large crypts and weathered headstones. He sniffed the air again, pulled some in over his tongue as the wolf took over his sense of smell. The soil in a cemetery was different, fertile with healthy grass and growth—mildew from the old concrete stonework.

Rotted blood.

James stopped on the path, turned around as he listened for the sounds of younglings. His ear twitched as something rasped in the dark.

A hiss. A grunt. Something else moved in the shadows, shifted just beyond his yellowed sight.

"Don't bother hiding," he said under his breath. "Just takes longer to find you." He stripped, his eyes locked on the spot where he saw the movement. He folded his clothes and laid them over the nearest headstone, his eyes still focused on the spot. His left ear twitched again. Rustling. Footfalls, faint, almost silent. Quick.

He was in wolf form just as the youngling crashed into him, tackled him to the ground. James rolled, grabbed the vampire by the face, and crushed her skull against a nearby crypt, the head caving like rotten fruit. Another came at him. James caught the snarling man by the throat and squeezed until the head rolled off the vampire's shoulders.

God, they're weak, he thought. *They must have been turned in the past few days.*

The wolf licked its chops hungrily in his mind. It snarled, barked madly, filled him with joy and excitement. It was having fun with the fighting, enjoying the violence.

James looked around, his teeth gritted as he growled low. He sniffed the air again, called the wolf to the forefront.

Let me stay in control, he said. *I'm going to need to pull some shit.*

The wolf barked once.

Pancakes. Cologne. That way.

James darted through the graveyard, deeper into the night. He stopped where the moon above shone brightly in the sky, casting its blue light down on a grave. The marker was a statue of a bassinet.

"Interesting history, really."

Rebecca's voice startled him. He looked at her as she stepped into the moonlit area. She looked up at the moon and sighed.

"Not quite full," she said. "Guess we have a bit before that happens again."

James growled low. She pulled Dracula's ring out of her shirt, the damned thing still dangling from the chain around her neck.

"Naughty doggie," she said, grinning at him. "Don't make me use the mean ring. Be a good boy."

James gnashed his teeth at her as she approached the grave.

"Rosalie White," she said, reading the inscription on the front end of the stone bassinet. "She was seven months old when she died." She gave a contemptuous *"Hmph"* and kicked the statue over. It broke as it fell away, ruined. "Mother was a bitch anyway. Now, the *father.* That man was rich.

And a great lay." She looked over her shoulder at James with a wicked grin. "At least while he lasted."

James shifted to human form; the wolf barked twice as he pushed it back.

I know what I'm doing, he thought at it. *We have to take the risk.*

"Where is Phillip?" James asked.

Rebecca looked him up and down, her eyes widening as they fell on his lower region.

"Um...you *sure* you don't want a little interlude?"

"You're not my type," James said. "Phillip is more of a demon guy than me. Now, where is he?"

Phillip's voice sounded from the dark. "Right here." He emerged next to Rebecca, an assault shotgun pointed at James. "This is silver shot, James. Don't make me shoot you. Stay back from her." He pumped the shotgun. "I've got five rounds with your name on them."

"Where is Mindy?" James asked.

"She's not my problem anymore," Rebecca said. "I've already sent off that shipment. I'm free and clear until next week's pickup. Already emptied the crypts." She grinned. "Well, most of them. I've still got one or two full from last night's little party."

James looked around, the wolf sharpening his hearing. He heard children crying, someone whispering, the sound hollow and dull as if muffled by concrete. A small voice asked why there was barely any air. Another asked for water or food. A cry for Mommy. Daddy.

"Jesus Christ," James said, turning back to Rebecca. "You're a fucking monster."

"I'm a *greedy* fucking monster," Rebecca said. "Don't forget that part."

"What do you want from me?" James said. "Why not just kill me when you had the chance? You knew I would heal from those injuries eventually."

"Uh, money, honey," Rebecca said as if informing a small child of an undeniable fact. "You have a metric fuck-ton of it."

"Fine, you can have it," James said, not hesitating. "Let the girls go and tell me who you've been selling them to."

"Nope," Rebecca said. "Not that easy. I've got a good thing going with that. You're asking me to give up a lot of cash."

"Then why do you need mine?"

"Why *don't* I need yours?" Rebecca said. "Think about it, Jimmy. The things I do with the hundreds of thousands of dollars I get from trafficking these little whores pales in comparison to what I could do with access to the *millions* you're sitting on. Phillip told me all about it. How you do nothing but live off it while it accrues interest." She made a face. "What the fuck, Jimmy? Where's your sense of fun?"

James motioned at Phillip.

"He's got access. Why not have him get it?"

"Because I don't have unlimited access," Phillip said. "You have to be present to drain the accounts completely."

"So you can't kill me," James said, looking back at Rebecca. "Makes sense."

"Don't think I won't," Rebecca said.

"Oh, I fully believe you won't," James said.

Rebecca looked at Phillip and raised an eyebrow.

"Wow, you weren't wrong," she said. "He really *is* good at making people want to hit him."

"No reason to lie to you, my love," Phillip said, keeping his eye on James.

"Phillip, stop it," James said, facing him. "She's a demon."

"She's my one and only, James," he said. "She and I are meant for each other."

"She's got you under a spell," James said. "Though it probably makes finding time to date easier."

Phillip's eyes widened, and he lowered the shotgun and stuck his chin out defensively. "Maybe I'd have better luck if I wasn't chasing you all over the place making sure you didn't do something stupid!"

"And I appreciate that."

"Really?"

"Yes. I appreciate the fact that I do stupid things."

Rebecca rubbed her temples. "Oh, *God*. You're *both* idiots." She looked at Phillip. "Kill him, then do yourself in."

"As you wish," Phillip said.

James shifted instantly, ducked to the side as the shotgun barked. A slug slammed into a headstone, sent pieces of concrete everywhere. Phillip pumped the shotgun and aimed again. James rushed in, smacked the weapon out of his hand, and shoved Phillip to the ground. Phillip jumped back up and stood between James and Rebecca, his arms out.

"No, James! I won't let you hurt her!"

James barked.

"Hell, yes, I'm serious," Phillip said. "She's the only one. She's my world! We're meant for each other! Soulmates!"

James stood tall and cocked his head to the side.

"You'll have to go through me to get to her," Phillip said. He took a boxer's pose, his fists up. "C'mon, pup. Let's see what you got!"

James raised his fist and brought it down on top of Phillip's head. Phillip crumpled to the ground, his eyes dazed, his mouth drawn into a stupid grin. Rebecca looked down at him, then back up at James.

"Well, shit," she said. "There goes my leverage." She pulled Dracula's ring out and slid the bent band onto her smallest finger. "My turn."

James's body tensed, fell forward as an unseen force yanked him down onto all fours. He felt the wolf gripped in shadow, the animal barking and yelping as the shadows pulled it back. James shrank, his muscles weakened, his fur retreated into his skin. Rebecca stepped forward.

"I'm not going to fuck around this time," she said. "You're going to sign it all to me; then I'm going to make sure no one finds what's left of either one of you two stooges."

James looked up at her, fighting to pull the wolf forward. He spoke around his still-enlarged teeth as his muzzle struggled to withdraw into his face.

"I...don't think so," he said.

"Really?" Rebecca said, holding out her hand. "What makes you say that, Jimmy?"

James smiled at her, his body shaking from his battle with Dracula's ring as a shape moved in the dark.

"My girlfriend is the jealous type."

Something flashed, moonlight glinting off steel as the blade came down. Rebecca screamed as her hand fell to the grass, black viscous fluid pouring from the stump onto the ground. James stood; his wolf form recovered as Lacy tackled Rebecca. She was mostly healed, though James could see spots on her arms and legs that still looked burned.

"Get the hand, Jimmy," she shouted. "Don't let anyone recover that ring!"

James dove for the hand, but three large things slammed into him, knocked him sideways. The younglings clambered all over him as he rolled on the ground, tried to buck them off as they clawed and bit. His hand connected to a head, and he crushed it against a nearby headstone. Another lost its grip, and James snapped his jaws around her neck; her spine gave way as the head lolled sideways. He stood, bucking the third off him. The man ran at him again, but James grabbed him easily and tossed him into the side of a large monument hard enough to collapse it. The vampire tried to recover, but James reared back and stomped the fanger's face, smashing the skull with ease.

Two more younglings rushed him. He saw Lacy and Rebecca struggling. Rebecca gripped Lacy by the throat with her still-attached hand, but Lacy squeezed the bloody stump at the end of Rebecca's right arm. Rebecca screamed and dropped Lacy, then went at her again.

James thundered toward the struggling pair, the younglings standing between him and the fight. He plowed through the younglings and sent them backward onto the ground. They were barely back on their feet before James picked one of them up by the face and bashed him into the other one until nothing remained but pulp. Rebecca shoved Lacy back, punched her in the mouth, then smacked her in the chest hard enough to send her flying. James slowed to catch her and stopped to set her down, leaning her up against a headstone. Lacy was bleeding, weak, her eyes sleepy and dazed.

"I'm still healing, Jimmy," she said, her speech slurred. "I need a minute to heal. Go get that bitch."

James snarled at Rebecca. She screamed at him, and they both rushed in at once, locked in combat. Rebecca's strength surprised him, but he managed to push her a step back. Two large, black, leathery wings sprouted from her back and flapped, whipped him in the face. He shook it off and lashed out, his claws running through the skin like razors through paper. Rebecca cried out in pain as James locked his jaws down on her good arm. He yanked his head to the side and loosened his jaws at the last second, the arm flying off into the night. He picked her up and slammed her back down, her shredded wings flapping weakly at him as she kicked and writhed. He held her, his ears perking up as he heard Lacy approach. She limped, her wounds on the mend, small tendrils of smoke rising in the moonlight as the cuts and burns closed and faded.

"Okay, Whore-cula," she said. "Spill. Who's your boss, and where did you send the girls?"

"I can't," Rebecca said, black fluid bubbling out of her mouth. "I don't know him. I send them to an address. In Jacksonville, Florida. And they deposit the money into…my account."

"Where in Jacksonville?" Lacy said. "Come on, bitch, we're in a rush and I need to feed. Got some injuries to heal."

"I don't know," said Rebecca. She looked at Lacy and grinned, giving a bitter laugh. "Just gonna have to kill me, Freddy Krueger."

Lacy shrugged. "Sounds good to me. Jimmy?"

James leaned down, clamped his jaws onto Rebecca's head, and chewed her face off. He tossed the hunk of black meat and skull aside, the blood bitter bile in his mouth. Rebecca twitched underneath him, and he swiped with his left hand and sent her head flying.

"Well, that's that," Lacy said, standing. "Looks like we're going to Jacksonville."

James shifted to his human form, his eyes on Rebecca as hopelessness nudged his mind. Jacksonville. Another giant place to search and no leads.

"You smacked him pretty good," Lacy said, nodding in Phillip's direction. James looked around and saw Phillip's crumpled form laying a few yards away. "Hope you didn't give him a concussion."

James went to Phillip and knelt. He shook him gently. Phillip blinked and looked up at James as he rubbed his head where James had conked him.

"I woke up next to *your* naked ass?" He groaned. "I'm in Hell. What did I do?"

James looked up at Lacy.

"He's fine."

So, I acted like a punk," Phillip said, shaking his head.

James shrugged. "No more than usual."

"Fuck you."

"No, you were more into your demon girlfriend."

Phillip grumbled a few more curse words as they walked across the parking lot toward the townhome. Lacy had pilfered Rebecca's pockets back at the cemetery while James was helping Phillip regain consciousness. Rebecca had taken up residence in a townhome community on Mount Pleasant just down the road from a Mexican hole-in-the-wall restaurant. It was a beautiful, shaded neighborhood mostly populated with older people. Rebecca's place sat sandwiched between two other identical condos.

Phillip looked over his shoulder in the direction where the Lyft driver had pulled out with Lacy still in the passenger seat.

"Can we trust her?"

James nodded.

"If she doesn't come back, she's on her own in Jacksonville, and that's a lot more city to search than Charleston." James shrugged. "Besides, I told her she could nibble on the Lyft driver to heal up."

"Christ," Phillip muttered. "You people are fucking animals."

"Just a nibble," James said, smiling. "She won't kill him. Or turn him."

"Or pull his soul out through his dick hole like my last girlfriend," Phillip said, his voice heavy with sarcasm.

James shrugged again. "Small victories."

Rebecca's townhome was immaculate, sparsely decorated with only a couch in the living room and a small television. A quaint dining room table sat off in a corner next to the kitchen, and the countertops were bare except for a Keurig and a toaster.

"I guess she didn't entertain much," James said.

"Place is just supposed to be a cover," Phillip said. "Probably where she would meet victims. Had to keep up a front for the neighbors too, I'm sure. I'd hate to see the bedrooms upstairs."

James's phone dinged. He pulled it out of his pocket and answered the video call. Lacy grinned back at him, once again looking radiant. It made his heart flutter, and the wolf rolled over onto its back, exposing its belly.

Slut, he thought at the beast.

"Ready, Jimmy?" she asked over the call.

James nodded. "Do it."

Lacy held up Dracula's ring, then tossed it into the fountain next to where she stood in the church garden. The water sizzled and boiled, smoke rising as the ring disintegrated away.

"All done," she said. "Find anything yet?"

"Not yet," James said. "We just got in. Good thing she kept her keys on her."

"Fill me in tonight," said Lacy. "The sun'll be up soon, and I'm already getting warm." She hung up, the screen flashing a red "Call Ended" in the center.

"James, check this out," Phillip said as James slipped the phone into his pocket. Phillip handed James a small journal. James took it, opened it, and saw the address on the very first page.

"We need to figure out how to get Lacy there during the day without killing her," James said. He tucked the bullet journal into his back pocket. "We're leaving right now."

"James," Phillip said, stepping in front of him. "Listen to me. I'm not saying we're not going. Believe me; we're going."

"What then?" James asked, tempted to shove Phillip aside and charge to Jacksonville at wolfen speed.

"You need to prepare for the possibility that this is just a pick-up point," Phillip said. "It's highly likely that there won't be anything there."

"But we'll find clues," James said.

Phillip shook his head. "Maybe not. Nothing humans can see, anyway. We'd need some probable cause to get the cops down there involved and bring in forensics."

"Speaking of which," James said, looking at Phillip sidelong. "You realize what she had you do, right?"

Phillip looked at him. "I don't have the authority to kill the investigation. It's mine, but I've got higher-ups on this one. It caused a stir, but my supervisor was able to calm it down."

"Anyone I know?"

"Not unless you're a Fed and you aren't telling me."

James nodded. All he knew was that Mindy was farther away, and he still wanted her back. An address. He had an address.

"I have an idea on how to transport Lacy," he said, looking at Phillip. "You're driving, and breakfast is on me."

III

WOLFSONG

1

J ames breathed out, imagining the fire built up in his chest blowing out in a stream, hitting the beach house in front of him. This was the closest he'd gotten to the ones who'd taken the young girls...*children* from their families to sell.

The ones who'd kidnapped Mindy Robertson from her home. It felt like years ago to James, even though it had only been a few weeks.

The air was warm, the saline scent different in Jacksonville, Florida. Charleston was heavier on the marshlands, the odor of pluff mud and mildew the norm for that area. Jacksonville was more populated, and cars that toiled throughout the city day and night filled the air with the mechanical scents of oil, gasoline, and tire rubber. James had a much more developed sense of smell than most people. He could smell things no human nose would normally be able to pick up.

One of the many perks of being a werewolf.

James was still in human form, standing at the end of the walkway that led up to the house. He straightened his tie and looked down at Lacy as she approached, her black evening dress tight-fitting on her willowy form and skimpy enough to make James curious as to what he might see if he were to watch the right places at the right time.

"Down, boy," Lacy said, giving him a wry smile. "We're working."

"I hate wearing ties," James said, opting to complain to distract himself from his thoughts about what he'd rather be doing. "I don't typically dress up."

"It looks good on you, Jimmy," Lacy said, looking him up and down. "You should dress up more often."

Phillip's voice sounded over the earpiece in James's ear. "If you two are done playing grab-ass, we have a high-profile party of baby-grabbin' assholes to crash."

James rolled his eyes. "Are you sure this is the place?"

Phillip grunted. "The hell you think it was supposed to be, James? An abandoned warehouse in a skeevy part of town?"

"The thought crossed my mind."

"You watch too many movies."

"You two are adorable," Lacy said, grinning. She was also wearing a mic and earpiece.

The trafficking ring was a high-profile federal case. Phillip, acting as liaison from the Rock Hill Police in South Carolina, had coordinated with the Jacksonville Police Department via his supervisor at the FBI. They'd given him lead in the field. If Phillip gave the word, a massive raid would ensue.

"Just remember to keep your cover," Phillip said. "No one knows you two are the ones going in. I had to pull some real shit to get those mics you're wearing. You see something, you get the fuck out of there and give me the word so I can send in the cavalry."

"Right," James said, breathing out. His heart pounded. He was so close. Mindy was in there. The address at Rebecca's place had led them there. Rebecca was the succubus they'd killed off in Charleston. She'd been involved with the traffickers, using her power to seduce men and steal their daughters in return for money. The Charleston police had recovered almost fifty girls from the cemetery where the demon kept them.

None of the girls had been Mindy, or Lacy's niece Marianne.

So close. What would he see? Would he be able to control himself? Keep himself from shifting? His mind spun, showed him a scenario where he would see Mindy being spoken to by a faceless older man. He would touch her hair, laugh when she shied away, put his hand on her shoulder. James would shift, kill the man, tear him to pieces, and let the blood soak into his fur. The wolf panted inside, growled as it moved forward. It sent an urge at James. *Kill.*

"James," Lacy said, jerking his arm. "Wake up. It's game time."

T he man at the door was almost as tall as James, older and gaunt. He sized James up in disgust, his lip curled up in a sneer.

"You are welcome to enter," he said to Lacy. "But he is not welcome."

"He's my date, Paw-Paw," Lacy said. "Don't worry, he's housebroken."

The man glowered at James again, then stepped aside. James nodded and showed Lacy in. The old man grumbled at him as they went by.

"Mind yourself, mongrel. I'm watching you."

James ignored him as he led Lacy into the main room. People milled about, all of them well dressed. The women were attired much like Lacy, and the men all wore expensive business suits. Everyone mingled as they sipped dark wine from their glasses. Some laughed dutifully at bland jokes while others whispered conspiratorially, staring at the subjects of their secret conversations while they spoke.

Typical rich-people party.

James surveyed the room, tried to see if anything looked off. The wolf stepped in and pushed his sense of smell. Mindy smelled like strawberries. He'd noticed that when he'd met her in her back yard the day Wade Anderson had forced him into the change with Dracula's ring. She hadn't been afraid. She'd even recognized him from his other runs. She'd befriended him, stood between him and the SWAT team when they'd shown up to gun down the giant werewolf that was running wild in Rock Hill.

Cologne. Perfume. Something cooking in the kitchen. Salmon? James felt the wolf step closer.

Easy, he thought at it. *Don't get too close.*

The wolf huffed at him and backed off. Something else...

Blood. Rot.

"Vampires," James breathed.

"What?!" Phillip shouted in the earpiece. "Are you sure?"

"Good boy, Jimmy," Lacy said. "Kind of surprised you didn't pick that right up."

James focused on the people in the room. All of them had a glass of red...not wine. Blood. They were all drinking blood. James's ear twitched, and he heard someone groan from the kitchen area as wait staff moved in and out with trays of full glasses.

"Calm it down, Jimmy," Lacy said, forcing a grin as she squeezed his hand. "We're a little outnumbered."

"Easy for her to say," Phillip said over the earpiece. "She's not the one they'll tear apart."

"Got news for you, Phil," Lacy said. "Crossbreeding with other super-naturals is frowned upon in the vampire community. Some people are still bigots even hundreds of years later. Me being here with James is already raising tensions." She looked up at James. "Just behave. Act like you have some class, and we might get what we need tonight. And live long enough to do something about it."

"My word," a man said, approaching them, his German accent heavy. He looked hungrily at Lacy, licked his lips as his eyes traveled over her curves and lingered on her breasts before settling on her face. "You look delicious." He glanced at James. "Yet, you come in with rabble."

"What can I say," Lacy said as she snuggled up to James. "I never thought I'd meet someone like James."

"Indeed," the man said. "I now know why I smelled wet dog in the room."

James offered his hand and smiled politely. "James Coldstone. It's a pleasure to meet you."

The vampire took his hand reluctantly and shook it. "Schreck," he said. "I am the host of this party." He turned to Lacy, his demeanor changing instantly. "And this radiant beauty who has graced my humble gathering this evening?"

"Lacy," said Lacy as she held her hand out. "Lacy Faulkner."

"Of which house do you come, Miss Faulkner?" the man asked. He took her hand and kissed it.

"No house," Lacy said, shaking her head and giving him a friendly smile as he released her hand. "I've not yet been adopted. I'm only a hundred years old."

"Oh, my, so young," the man said. "You might consider House Granach. It is an excellent house with quite a lucrative business."

"Nonsense," another man said, stepping forward. He bowed to Lacy, then flashed James a disgusted look. He was shorter, his skin tan, his features telling of deep Hispanic descent. His English was broken, Spanish obviously his first language. "*House Diabolito es una casa noble.*" He sneered at Schreck. "Much nobler than Euro-*basura, mi amore.*"

Lacy laughed as Schreck's face turned red with fury.

"Gentlemen, please," she said, her tone friendly and sweet. "I'm sure both houses have their merits. I promise I will look into both. Thank you both so kindly for being willing to allow an outsider into your clans." She nodded at James. "It's been difficult. Simply because of who I love."

"Wow, she's a ham," Phillip said in James's earpiece. "Might give her an Oscar if you two live through tonight."

"Your faith in my ability to escape from people wanting to kill me is touching," James said under his breath.

James's free ear perked, something carried over the thrum of conversation as Lacy continued to schmooze the two arguing vampires. He glanced around the room, saw two men in a far-off corner. One was middle-aged, maybe forty. The other appeared to be in his sixties with graying hair and crow's feet at his eyes.

"The shipment arrives tomorrow," the younger one was saying. "Everything is in order, sir."

Shit, James thought. He called to the wolf to enhance his hearing. The wolf came forward in his mind, hunkered down as if hiding in the brush and watching its prey.

"Excellent," the older man said. "I'm sure the Master will be happy."

"Master Granach isn't happy about much of anything, lately," the younger one said as he sipped his drink. The older man sighed and nodded.

"Would you be? We've lost three shipments recently. That gets expensive. More importantly, it looks bad to the rest of the houses in the area. Master Granach has business dealings to take care of and a reputation to uphold. We can't let shipments just go to the wayside. Between Charleston and Miami, he's lost a fortune."

James narrowed his eyes at them. The Charleston police had found three crypts in the cemetery full of girls spanning the ages of nine to thirteen. It couldn't just be a coincidence.

"Someone is on to our operations," the older man continued. "How else do you explain so many shipments being sabotaged or destroyed?"

"I think paranoia would be a good way to explain it," the younger man said with a chuckle. "Think about it, Al. There's no way someone is that close to us. It's incompetence. I've told you before about using younglings to guard our exports. They're too unstable."

"They're also expendable," said Al. "You're young, Barry. And that girl you're seeing up at Port Vedra Beach is clouding your head."

Barry smiled wryly. "I'm faring better than you, old man. Cordelia is a hellcat."

Al laughed. "Just make sure the shipment goes smoothly this time. Master Granach is losing patience. And money."

"Trust me," Barry said with a wink. "I'm handling it myself. No mistakes. It goes out tomorrow evening."

James felt the wolf edging closer, wanting to take in more. *Are you insane?!* James thought at the beast. *There are at least a hundred vampires here. We'd be dead before we even finished the change. Down!*

The wolf slinked away as James turned to Lacy and her conversation with the two arguing vampires. The discussion was becoming more heated, both vampires in each other's faces yelling.

"Ah, gentlemen," James said, keeping his tone as formal as he could manage. The two vampires stopped arguing and looked at him in disdain.

"How *dare* you address us, *perro sucio*," said Spaniard. "Know your role."

"On this, I agree," said Schreck. "The role of a house pet is to be seen and not heard."

"Duly noted," James said. "While I do appreciate the hospitality and wonderful open-mindedness of your company, I fear that my love and I must depart." James looked down at Lacy, who blinked and shook her head. "I've just gotten a most urgent message that needs my immediate attention."

Lacy nodded. She flashed her brilliant, beautiful smile at the two arguing vampires.

"Thank you so much, both of you. I look forward to discussing your houses with you further."

The two vampires resumed their argument as James and Lacy turned and started toward the door.

"Those two seemed interesting," James said as they walked past the door guard.

"They need to just fuck and get it over with," Lacy said. "C'mon, let's get to the car."

L acy pulled the Mini Cooper into the driveway and killed the engine. James stared out the window at the small stilted beachfront cottage they'd rented. Phillip had made the arrangements and insisted that James pay cash.

"Cards are traceable," he'd said. "We need to use cash. *Only* cash."

The cottage was small, simple, and had a short pier that jutted out from the back door and over the water. It was three bedrooms, no television, and was solar-powered. The stucco on the exterior was clean as if the place had been built recently, though Phillip told them that the old couple that rented it out constructed the home decades ago.

"It's an Airbnb," he'd said. "They clean it for renters; we keep it clean while we're here."

Lacy had laughed. "Good thing you're paper-trained, Jimmy."

James sighed. He had a lead. But where would it go? Would it be another dead end? The constant walls they ran into were getting old. No matter how close they got to finding Mindy, Clara, and Marianne, the further the girls got away from them.

"You okay?" Lacy asked as she pulled the keys out of the ignition and unbuckled her seatbelt.

"Yeah," James said.

"Nope," Lacy said. "You suck at lying."

James rolled his eyes at her and got out of the car. He looked up at the front door of the cottage as Phillip opened it up.

"I'm impressed," he called out to James. "You didn't ransack the place and kill everyone. You gettin' soft on me?"

"The night is young," James said. "Besides, we've got information."

"There were a *lot* of older vampires in there," Lacy said. "We need to be careful here. I didn't realize so many clans ruled Jacksonville."

"Were you followed?" Phillip asked.

James shook his head. "No, we were careful."

Something slammed into him, lifted him off his feet, and tackled him to the ground. Lacy shouted, and Phillip started calling out to James to move so he could get a clear shot. The wolf surged forward in James's mind, and his body shifted, shreds of an expensive suit raining down. James swatted the vampire off of him and got to his feet as the hissing bastard collected himself and rushed him again. It was the German vampire he'd met at the party.

Schreck, James thought. *Decent family film, asshole vampire.* He sidestepped Schreck, tried to grab for him, but the German was faster. He ducked under James's grasp and jabbed him in the side. James staggered backward and regrouped, swiped out at the vampire with his claws. Schreck made to duck again, but Lacy was on him in an instant, taking him down to the ground, rolling in a flurry of clawed fingers and snapping fangs. Schreck bucked Lacy off of him, got to his feet, and kicked her in the stomach hard enough to send her rolling away. James made for his attacker, but Schreck backhanded him across the jowls and knocked him sideways. Phillip shouted again, and Schreck made for the house. James rolled to his feet and pounced on Schreck. He picked the vampire up by the head and whipped him around, slamming the body on the rocks by the driveway. Something slipped from Schreck's pocket. James ignored it as he lifted the bleeding vampire by the throat. Schreck gasped and choked, trying to breathe inside James's iron grip.

"You...filthy dog," the vampire rasped. "You are...abomination."

"He's prettier than you, and he has you by your throat," Lacy said as she stepped up. "Might want to reconsider insulting him. Now, what the fuck are you doing here?"

Schreck narrowed his eyes at James.

"I know who you are, Coldstone. I knew...the moment I saw you. You look too much...like your father."

James fought the urge to squeeze until he heard bones break, rage welling in his gut.

"I wouldn't do that," Lacy said to the vampire. "He's got daddy issues. Now answer my question." James saw Phillip approach out of the corner of his eye, a revolver aimed at Schreck. Silver worked on vampires as far as wounding them, but it would take a direct shot to the heart to kill them.

"Start talkin'," Phillip said. "Or I tell James to squeeze until your head pops like a fuckin' zit."

Schreck shook his head. "You'll never stop the shipment," he said. "Go ahead and kill me."

James noticed Lacy stoop down and pick up a wallet. She opened it and pulled out a business card, looking it over before she smiled and looked up at Schreck. "Sounds good. Jimmy?"

Schreck's scream was cut short as James used his free hand to grab a leg and pull the vampire in half. The bloodsucker's top half tried to crawl away, but James reared back and stamped his foot down, flattening Schreck's head into the ground. The body went to dust as James shifted back to human form. He turned and looked at Phillip, who glared at him and shook his head.

"I'd like to formally change my previous answer for the record," James said. "Yes, we were followed. What's for dinner?"

2

Phillip pressed the "End Call" icon on his iPhone and put it back in his pocket as he sat down at the kitchen table across from James. They'd left the lights in the cottage off, though Lacy insisted that artificial light didn't hurt. Still, it helped see the incoming sunlight quicker and allowed her to retire underneath the bed in her room before she could get another wicked sunburn like she'd had in Charleston. She and James had gotten into an all-night brawl with a group of younglings, vampires that were fresh into being turned and feral, and the sun was rising before they'd realized what was happening. James saved Lacy's life, but he'd barely made it back to the hotel in time, and she'd been charred black and crispy in the process.

Even after a few hours of sleep, James still felt groggy. He was used to not getting much rest, but this kind of tired felt different.

"Okay, it's all set," Phillip said as he picked up his coffee cup. "I've got every police department in Jacksonville working with us. Jacksonville Beach PD is coordinating directly with me since we're here, and the other departments are using me as a liaison back to Rock Hill. This thing is huge now. The Florida State Police are also in on it and are working directly with South Carolina and Georgia federal offices."

"I'm guessing I'm still 'Bob Smith'?" James said, picking his coffee up and swirling it in the cup.

Phillip glared at him.

"Yeah, unless Bob Smith is just as stupid as James Coldstone and lets a damn vampire follow him home like a blood-suckin' kitten on steroids."

James shrugged.

"At least I took care of him. I know you're more of a dog person."

"That shit was careless, James," Phillip said, setting his coffee down. "If that fucker had gotten away, we'd have vampires all over us, and the traffickers would be long gone. As it stands, they still might be."

"I don't think so," James said. "They were talking about shipments at the party last night."

Phillip nodded. "I can see that. If they're exporting to another country, which is likely, then Jacksonville would be ideal. A lot of cruise ships port out of here as well. But, it's more likely that they're using the international trade ports. Less likely a little girl is gonna find someone to ask for help."

James nodded, more weight seeming to settle in on his shoulders. Phillip leaned in.

"You okay?" he said.

James shook his head. "Far from it, actually." He sighed. "It seems like I spend more time chasing my own tail than I do getting any closer to ending this."

"You mean finding Mindy Robertson. And Clara Pickens, who you don't really seem to give a shit about anymore."

"I do," James said.

"I don't think I've heard you mention Clara twice since we left Rock Hill."

"I also know that we'll find her if we find Mindy, and vice versa. But you're right: Mindy is my top priority."

"Once again," Phillip said with a chuckle, "a man in his early thirties obsessing over a girl who gets a milk carton with her lunch is a *little* creepy."

"It's not like that," James said, bristling. He didn't take offense to much, but accusations of pedophilia was pushing it. "At all. Ever. Dick."

Phillip sat back, any sense of humor on his face gone, his features somber as James spoke.

"It's different," James said. "I'm drawn to her. It's as if it's my sworn duty to protect her. The wolf...it pushes me after her. It's not so much obsession as it is," James paused, trying to find the right word, "instinct? Maybe?"

Phillip nodded. "Sorry," he said. "Look, Lacy's asleep, I don't have any meetings or updates due until this afternoon. Let's go grab a late breakfast. I saw a place on the way in yesterday that looked good. I'm buying."

James looked away, his thoughts still on Mindy. Just thinking about her made his chest hurt, a voice in his head starting to doubt that he would ever find her.

Phillip stood and headed out of the kitchen. He stopped and put a hand on James's shoulder.

"We'll find her," he said. "We'll find all of them."

James wanted to believe him.

I t was almost noon when James and Phillip found the pub Phillip had seen on the way to the Airbnb. McFadden's was a hole-in-the-wall not much different from James's favorite haunt in downtown Rock Hill. He hadn't managed breakfast that morning and was happy to see Scotch Eggs on the brunch menu. He ordered them along with a serving of pancakes. Phillip opted for chicken and waffles.

"That sounds disgusting," James said as Phillip handed the waitress the menu. James scanned her figure, the wolf panting happily in his mind. She was smaller, her body firm and her red hair long and wavy. Her skin was tanned, and James could tell right away that she was the child of parents of different races. She was at least thirty, wore cutoff shorts and a red t-shirt with the restaurant logo on it. She smiled at him, her pretty face covered in freckles and her olive skin seeming to glow.

"Actually, it's really yummy," she said. "I thought the same thing until I tried them. Not that I make it a habit because I need to stay in shape for my swim team, but I indulge every now and then." She smiled at both of them. "I'll get these right in. Coffee?"

"Tea is fine for me," said Phillip.

"Coffee," James said.

"Sounds great," the girl said, her tone perky as she turned and headed to the bar to place the order.

James leaned in, a smirk on his face as he spoke to Phillip.

"Try not to fall for the waitress this time."

Phillip glared at him.

"That wasn't me," he said. "This one ain't givin' off a demon vibe."

"Neither did your last girlfriend."

"My last girlfriend couldn't handle me being a cop," Phillip said. "That chick in Charleston was a succubus. Different world. Besides, she liked *me*."

James sat back and shook his head. "Here we go."

"Here we go what? I'm sexy."

"You stink."

"It's called cologne, James. Women like it."

"Women like it when you smell like stale urine?"

"It's called 'Feral Masculinity.'"

"They need to call it 'Ode of Juiced Ferret.'"

"Go bury a bone."

"I might bury your stink water next to it."

Phillip's department phone rang as he was about to comment back. He pulled it out and looked at it. "I have to take this," he said, looking at James. "To be continued. Punk-ass." He answered the official line, his tone changing to his authoritative "policeman's voice." James sat back and looked around, his eyes falling on the waitress again. Lacy flashed in his mind, though he couldn't help noticing how striking the auburn-haired waitress was. She smiled and laughed with a few of the men at the bar, calling them by name. *Regulars*, James thought. *Shit, I'd be a regular too if—*

He caught himself. If what? He shook his head a little. Where had that come from?

Lacy flashed in his mind again, smiling at him, her brilliant blue eyes sparkling. He felt the wolf stir inside, indecisive as it rolled over onto its back and exposed its belly. It sent thoughts at James, showed him images of himself with the waitress. Then Lacy. The images, the thoughts, all of them heated and passionate.

James shook his head and focused on the wolf as it writhed around in his mind, its tongue lolled out to one side.

Like I'd take any kind of romantic advice from you, he thought at it. *You'd fuck a tree stump.*

The waitress came back with their drinks.

"Here you go, handsome," she said as she set the coffee cup down in front of James. "This is from a local coffee roaster up the street. Good stuff. Kind of strong, but you look like someone who likes strong." She winked at him. Phillip bristled, then smiled politely as he set his tea down in front of him. She smiled at James again and walked away.

"And how do you know she isn't another succubus?" Phillip said, keeping his voice low.

James raised an eyebrow as he picked up his mug. "Because she doesn't smell like pancakes." He sipped his coffee, letting the wolf forward as he focused on some of the conversations around the pub.

"Bad shit," one of the men at the bar was saying. "Poor girl. She needed to get away from that asshole."

"You hear her sing the other night at karaoke?" another said. "Like an angel. I'm surprised she ain't famous."

"That's interesting," James said. He took another sip of his coffee and sat it back down.

"I wonder who 'that asshole' is," Phillip said, keeping his voice low. James blinked, and Phillip shot him a look. "They're only at the bar. It's right over there. I can hear them too. Idiot."

"Yeah, I heard it," a third man said, joining in. "Her dickhead ex-boyfriend showed up. Think she said his name's Barry. I saw them talking off in a corner after the show. He put his hands on her, and she slapped the dog shit out of him. Funny as all hell."

"Yeah, she said he was gettin' a little too attached if you know what I mean," the first man said. "That, and he's tied up in some real shit. Criminal stuff."

"That's *more* interesting," said Phillip. "I wonder what 'Barry' is into."

"One of the vampires at the party last night was named Barry," James said, also keeping his tone down. "He was one of the ones talking about a shipment going out."

"I remember you telling me that," Phillip said. "Might be a small world."

"That could also be our group. But why would they ship girls out? You mentioned it earlier."

"Think about it," Phillip said. "You run a trafficking ring selling girls into sexual slavery. People pay thousands, even millions for a girl. That girl might spend years in slavery, might spend a few days before she's either found, escaped, or recovered." He sighed. "Recovery usually doesn't mean she's alive."

James fought to keep his expression stoic at the thought of any of the horrors Phillip was describing happening to Mindy.

"They stay here in the country, it's likely to be sooner than later before everything falls apart," Phillip continued. "They end up in another country, they're more likely to be lost for good, and you're bound to make a shit-ton more money. Some of these guys see underaged girls as a delicacy."

"Stop," James said, swallowing back his rage with the bile that had worked its way up. "I've heard enough."

"Sorry," Phillip said. "It's just reality. I've got a friend in the Crimes Against Persons Unit in Rock Hill. No one sees what they see." He shuddered. "I told them I'd never work in that division. Now here I am working on something that should be in their laps."

James refocused his hearing, trying to push disturbing, gut-wrenching images out of his mind.

"I hear he's a pervert," one of the men said. "Guy likes kinky shit. Cordelia told me she wasn't having none of it."

Well, that settles that, James thought.

"I wonder if she's gonna sing again tonight," said the second man. "I've got to be there if she does. I can't miss that." He started to sound...different. James couldn't put his finger on it. Urgent. Desperate? "I can't. It's... no, I can't miss that. Not for anything."

"Same," said the third man. "If I see that limp-dick fuck show up and put his hands on her again, she ain't gonna have *time* to slap him around."

"He mentioned Cordelia by name last night," James said, looking at Phillip.

"That's the waitress's name. Who did?"

"That guy Barry," James said. He cut himself short as Cordelia showed up with their plates. She glanced at James.

"Huh," she said as she sat their plates down in front of them. "My ex-boyfriend's name is Barry." She gave a huff. "Asshole."

"His loss," James said. "You seem like a wonderful girl."

Cordelia blushed. "Thank you," she said. "You two enjoy your brunch." She patted Phillip on the shoulder as she walked by him. "You've got a good catch. Don't mess it up."

James gave a smirk as Phillip sputtered.

"We're not..." He trailed off as Cordelia went through the kitchen door. He sighed. "Never mind."

James chuckled, then started eating, swallowing his bite before he spoke. "I want to get with Lacy and tell her what we've heard. She plans to go chat with the Diabolito vampire clan tonight. We'll see if she learns anything about Barry."

"Vampire clan," Phillip said. "Right. That's a thing down here."

"According to her, it's a thing everywhere," James said. "It just depends on what they're into. There are one or two clans in Rock Hill, but they keep quiet and aren't into anything criminal. At least according to Lacy. Apparently, she has an acquaintance who lives in Charlotte."

"Good to know," Phillip said. He took a bite of his food and kept talking. "The more we know about these vampire houses, I think the closer we'll get to our trafficking buddies. Sounds like your friends from last night are tied up in some shit."

James nodded.

"Let's hurry," he said. "I have a few places I'd like to stop before this evening. I'm running low on clothing because of all the times I've had to shift while I'm dressed."

Phillip chuckled. "Yeah, I was beginning to wonder about that."

"I'll need you to come with me."

Phillip looked up and blinked. "Why?"

"Because I need your taste in style and fashion. Sugar-bum."

The sun was starting to set by the time James and Phillip got back to the Airbnb. James had enough new clothes to refill his suitcase, though he had no doubt that he'd end up destroying a lot of them again.

"You know, you could save money by just going to the Goodwill," Phillip said as James finished hanging his clothes in his closet.

"Why?" James said. "I needed a shitload of clothes. I have the money. I would've cleaned out Goodwill, and people who don't have what I have wouldn't be able to get those clothes."

"Fair enough," Phillip said. He pulled out his iPhone and looked at it. "I just got a text message from my guy in the Jacksonville Beach PD. He wants me to call him on some details he might have for us."

"Details?"

"I texted him earlier and told him about that guy, Barry," Phillip said. "He's going over some shipping manifests now, and he's supposed to let me know if he finds anything." Phillip motioned at his phone. "I guess he found something." He touched the phone screen, and his eyes widened as he read the message. "Holy shit," he breathed.

"Holy shit? What holy shit?"

"Looks like our buddy Barry is a busy bee."

"Say that five times fast."

Phillip shot James a look, then turned his attention back to his screen.

"There's a lot of shady activity at one of the ports at St. John's River. The manifests are filled out, but Jose says they look pencil-whipped."

"Jose?"

"My contact guy," Phillip said, still scrolling through his phone. "He was a port security guy before he joined the force. He sent the address, too."

James nodded. "Then I know what we're doing tonight."

Phillip looked up from his phone. He stepped up and patted James on the arm. "It's almost over, man. We'll find her."

3

Lacy showered, changed, and was dolled up like a vampire rolling in money and class an hour after she'd crawled out from underneath her bed. James was impressed.

"It's a girl thing, Jimmy," she said.

"The last girl I dated took two hours to get ready to leave the house," James said.

Lacy raised an eyebrow at him. "Yeah, you probably dodged a bullet there. I'll text you any info I find on Barry."

She'd been gone an hour and a half when James answered a text on his phone from her. Phillip made a phone call and had the name run immediately.

"Barry McDonald," Phillip said as he pulled out his iPad and opened his email. "Forty-two, male, six-one, born…what the fuck?"

"What?" James asked.

"James, he was born forty-two years ago. Guy had a birthday just last week." Phillip looked up from his iPad. "Unless this is a fake birth certificate, which is harder to do that you think. You sure he's a vampire?"

James shrugged. "I really can't think of any reason a human would hang out at a vampire party."

Phillip nodded. "Well, either way, Barry has a hell of a rap sheet." He scrolled through the document on his iPad screen. "Not a bunch of crimes, but holy shit, the nature of them. Mostly, and get this: sexual misconduct with underaged girls."

"So he's a creeper," James said, nodding as he rubbed his chin. "That's a coincidence. We happen to be looking for creepers."

"Well, these girls were fifteen to seventeen," Phillip said. "Doesn't make it any less wrong as hell, but they're older than the girls we're looking for. That could be important."

"How so?" James asked.

"Because it's not a good idea to sample the goods before you ship them off," Phillip said. "In fact, it's a good way to get killed or castrated. There's a lot of money at stake. A 'pure' virgin nets a stupid amount of money. These guys ain't fuckin' around when it comes to their green. It means he's doing shit on the side. It also means that he thinks he can get away with it. Or he thought." Phillip handed James the iPad. "Check it out. At least four arrests for sexual misconduct and lewd acts with a minor, but no convictions. Not even a trial."

James took the iPad and looked it over. Each charge had the words "Case Dismissed" in red in the status space.

"That shit is weird, James," Phillip said as James handed the tablet back over. "You get pinched as a baby-banger, you go up. Unless you've got a shitload of money and connections like that piece of shit we tracked down in Charleston, Daniel Sinclair. This guy is middle class at best."

James's phone dinged in his pocket. He pulled it out and looked at the notification from Lacy.

Barry's not here. Talking to Damian Montoya about House Diabolito.

James looked at Phillip. "Barry isn't there tonight."

Phillip nodded. "He might be out running his errand." He rolled his eyes. "Christ, James."

"He's part of it," James said. "I know he is. We've got to find him and get him to talk."

"Then what?" Phillip said. "You gonna smack him around a little, Columbo? He's a fucking vampire. We *think*. Pretty sure he can take a pop from Clifford the Big Red Dog."

"I'm more of a bluish silver," James said. "And of course, I would try to be diplomatic *before* I chewed his head off."

"You'll have to do it without me," Phillip said. "You'd be better off with your girlfriend. I'd slow you down since I'm human."

James gave him a smirk. "Are you jealous?"

Phillip narrowed his eyes. "Think about it, kibble breath: you two have heightened senses and super-speed. They don't teach getting in touch with your inner supernatural at the police academy." Phillip huffed. "Jealous, my black ass. You keep your overgrown mosquito. I like girls who *aren't* likely to drain me into a piece of beef jerky in the middle of the night."

"We supposedly taste more like pork."

"No one asked."

"You said beef. I just figured you'd want to know."

"Fine, pork. Happy?"

"Elated."

Phillip shook his head as he started typing on his iPad again. He hit the screen with his finger and sent a message to James's phone. "Start here. The whole place is a port for large ships."

"Ship shipping ships?" James asked, grinning.

Phillip was obviously not having it. "Make sure you keep your shit together. We need him to talk."

James waited until the Lyft car was out of sight before he turned and looked around the area. He was at a shipyard, the sound of water lapping up against the concrete walls soothing despite the feeling of dread he carried. Something in the back of his mind screamed that this was nothing more than a dead end.

The wolf huffed in his mind. He could tell it was also getting frustrated. Not only did it want to find Mindy like he did, but it also wanted to run free. It wanted to pound through the woods, howl at the moon, and hunt. God, he wanted to hunt.

James pulled his phone out and texted Lacy his location. She arrived in a matter of minutes, coming out of the blur of vampire speed in front of him.

"Got your text," she said, looking around. She was still wearing her black evening dress. "This is the place, huh?"

"Did I interrupt something?" James asked, noting her slightly disheveled hair.

Lacy rolled her eyes. "Montoya gets grabby. Your text came just as he was pawing at me to see if I had any tattoos." She shuddered. "Swear to God, if it was him or the sun, I'd buy a bottle of fucking tanning oil and lay out a towel."

James laughed a little, though the wolf growled low on the inside. He shook his head, realizing that a part of him agreed with the wolf. He looked back out over the port. It was quiet. He pulled the wolf forward, let his hearing move out over the area. He could hear people talking, some going on about a break. Another mentioned it being a slow night.

I believe I might be pissing in your cornflakes this evening, James thought as one of the voices made another comment about how nice the quiet was.

"Okay, Jimmy," Lacy said. "Let's find a spot where you can strip."

James looked around. It was dark. He sniffed the air with his wolfen sense of smell. Oil. Diesel. Lacy.

"Here's good," he said as he pulled his shirt off and dropped his cargo shorts to the ground. Lacy laughed as he shifted into wolf form, the beast stretching happily in his mind as it took its place at the forefront.

"Wow, Jimmy," she said. "Can't ever call you shy."

James huffed and looked around the area with his yellowed vision. Lacy appeared a lot smaller to him now that he was eight feet tall. She grinned at him, her fangs elongating and her blue eyes turning into red coals.

"Okay, let's go," she said. She turned and took off into the night, scaling the nearest warehouse with ease. James followed, climbing after her, using the staircase on the side to hoist himself up. The steel groaned under his immense weight; the fixture was not intended for a moving thing that weighed upwards of eight hundred pounds. He stopped at the top and hoisted himself onto the concrete roof. He looked around, sniffed the air. He could smell Lacy, but she was completely out of sight.

Great, he said. *What I get for trying to tail a vampire. Where the hell is she?*

His head jerked suddenly on his neck as something grabbed the tuft of hair on his chin and yanked him down, the strength surprising and unrelenting. He was on all fours staring eye-to-eye with Lacy, her expression a mix of anger and annoyance.

"It's called stealth, Jimmy," she hissed. "I've still got plenty to tell you later, but unless you want us up to our asses in criminal suck-heads, I suggest you figure out how to move your big ass with a little more finesse."

James grunted at her in agreement. *Oops,* he thought. *Wait. Suck-heads?*

"That's right, Benji," she said. "It's a goddamn vampire mafia. We're outnumbered here, whether you know it or not. This place should be buzzing. It's dead." She paused. "Pun intended."

James groaned in annoyance and stood as she released his wolf goatee.

"It means they got called off. Something's about to go down." Lacy looked over her shoulder at a giant sea barge that was docked on the other side of the port from them. "That might be our ship. It's the only one that size here. Plenty of space to put a hundred or so girls in a storage container."

There were hundreds of storage containers stacked on it, the long steel boxes varying colors, and some decorated with graffiti. James felt more weight in his chest, more hopelessness. It could take all night to search each container. The sun might come up before they were done, and Lacy would have to be back at the Airbnb before then to avoid certain death. That would leave him on his own, and there was no telling when the ship was scheduled to depart.

"We need to find someone we can shake down," Lacy said, turning away from him and looking around. "Where the fuck is everyone?" She sighed, then motioned to James. "C'mon, Jimmy. And be *quiet*, for fuck's sake."

They both crouched and made their way from rooftop to rooftop, moving closer to where the ship was docked. They stopped every now and again, waiting for the rare worker or security guard to pass by. James could hear a group inside one of the small offices tucked away next to a storage area. He grunted at Lacy to get her attention, then moved to the tiny building and crouched in the shadows as he listened.

"Weird email," one of the men inside was saying. "Everyone inside for two hours? What's that all about?"

"All I know is I need this job," another voice said, his tone gruff and bitter. "They want me to sit on my ass, then on my ass I sits."

"Hey, as long as that paycheck clears every week, I'm good," another said, the voice deep with a Southern drawl. "What's good with that manifest?"

"Same shit," the second voice said. "Sloppy. But hey, that's above my pay grade."

"Hey, questions get you side-eye," the third voice said. "I don't need no side-eye. 'Specially not from the boss man."

"Weirdo," the first voice said. "Guy only works at night. What the fuck is that shit?"

James looked at Lacy. She looked back at him and shrugged. "One of the things I was going to tell you later. One of the vampire houses runs a shipping operation here. I'll bet you our boy Barry is part of it if he isn't the one running it outright for them."

James stood and huffed. Something in the back of his mind kept telling him it was a dead end. Why wouldn't it be? Every other lead they'd closed in on had taken them nowhere.

Lacy stood as well, looking up at him.

"You can't give up, Jimmy," she said. "This could be it. Think about it. A shipyard? Weird orders coming in over an email? Something's going down."

A cry rang out in the night. James spun, the noise coming from the docks where the massive ship sat in the water. He took off, Lacy close behind him. James hunkered down and rounded a corner on all fours, pushed out with his legs, and launched himself up onto the top of a stack of containers. He bounded from top to top, the steel rippling under his weight as he moved. He stopped when he got to a small opening in the field of boxes, looked down at the roof of a red Ford F-150 pickup truck that was parked in the shadows. The vehicle rocked back and forth steadily, shouts and moans drifting up into James's hearing. Lacy snorted back a laugh as James put his hand on his head and groaned.

"Wow, Jimmy," Lacy said. "That's funny as hell. You can't tell the difference between an attack and a one-night stand? My night has just been made."

James huffed at her. The wolf panted in his mind, its way of laughing at him. *Shut it, you,* he thought at the beast.

"Still, that's gonna be distracting," Lacy said. Another loud, high-pitched cry sounded out from the truck. "Jesus, is he killing her with it?"

James slinked off the other direction, not hiding his annoyance. "C'mon, Jimmy," Lacy whispered after him. "Have a sense of humor, will you? Besides, the goal is to look for someone *not* having a good time."

James paused, flipped her off over his shoulder, and kept moving, jumping down off the containers onto the asphalt. He stood tall, sniffed the air, tried to filter out the saline and diesel. He heard the sounds from the truck finally subside, heard seagulls squawking in the night as they searched for fish and scraps. The engines on the barge were silent, the generators humming low for power. Water lapped against the pylons underneath him.

A different smell hit him. He pulled it in over the glands in his mouth. Feces. Bile. Human.

It's pretty damn gross, he remembered Phillip saying once. *The human body shuts down and releases everything. Tell you the truth: it's not so much disgusting as it is depressing. It's how you know you just watched someone die.*

James moved in the direction of the scent, the stench growing stronger as he got to the edge of the docks. More smells from the same spot. Decay. Cologne. He stopped, looking around. It wasn't just floating in the air. It was coming up from…the water?

James leaned down and looked over the edge of the dock. The black surf seemed still in the shadows, though he could hear it. The breeze underneath the dock was slight, the sound low. Something moved in the dark, swaying, part of it in the surf. Lacy walked past James and clambered down the side of the dock and under, sticking to the concrete. It reminded James of Spider-Man. He heard her voice call back up from near the shape. "Well, *shit.*"

She climbed back up onto the dock, a rope in her hand. She pulled effortlessly, hoisting up a bloated, saturated, and quite dead body. James recognized it right away. He shifted to his human form, staring at the body as anger welled in his stomach.

"Barry," he muttered. "Lovely."

"Jesus, he shit himself," Lacy said.

"They do that," James said as he knelt down next to the body. He saw the rope tied around Barry's neck. The skin had bloated almost comically around the rope. Barry wore a polo shirt and cargo shorts, though his feet were bare and looked as if the fish had gotten a start on their meal before Lacy brought the corpse out of the surf. The skin was a bluish color, and Barry's tongue hung out of his mouth. The whites in his eyes were completely bloodshot.

"No, James," Lacy said. "Vampires do not shit themselves when they die. In fact, we don't shit at all. Kind of nice, really." She motioned at the body. "This guy was definitely human."

"What was he doing at a vampire party?" James asked, moving over the body with his eyes, pulling the wolf forward only slightly to enhance his vision. "And talking business with one?"

"Not unusual, really," Lacy said. "When you start getting into vampire politics, that's when things get wild. A lot of your vampire higher-ups will keep a human familiar to snack on every now and again, and the eventual goal is to turn them once they've earned out their keep. In return, the familiar works for its master in kind of an employer-employee relationship. Familiars are usually hand-in-hand with the clan master as personal assistants."

James saw something poking out of one of Barry's cargo pockets. He reached down and pulled the item out, holding it up for Lacy to see.

"Um, that's weird. Who the fuck plants cheese on someone before they kill them off?"

James sighed.

"Someone who wants whoever finds the body to know that the recently departed was a rat."

4

W ell, this is definitely murder," Phillip said as he ended his phone call. He rubbed his face and put the phone down on the table. McFadden's was slow that morning, and Cordelia was behind the bar rolling silverware while she waited on the cook to ring the bell, indicating that breakfast was ready. James and Lacy had come in early last night after watching the police investigate the crime scene. Phillip was also on the scene as an observer and consultant. He'd sent Lacy a text message telling her and James to head back to the cottage, and that he would meet up with them later. James reluctantly agreed though he couldn't think of anything else they could do. He knew that Barry's body was a clue to something, but it also represented yet another obstacle between him and Mindy.

James stared down into his coffee while Phillip kept talking.

"They found all kinds of fingerprints on our boy," he was saying. "None of them viable, which is strange. Not one print on that body was enough to run in the system. Lots of bruising, and his lungs were full of water. Looks like they drowned him, then hung him from the dock for the fish to take care of once the tide came up. They put time of death about thirty hours ago."

"Cheese," James muttered.

"Yeah, that one was creative," Phillip said. "If he turned rat, then that means he was talking to someone his house didn't like. Probably a Federal agent, which means this thing is volatile as shit now. I'm gonna have to ask around with my lead guy to see if the FBI was using him as an informant."

"I wonder why they didn't just drain him," James said.

Phillip shrugged. "Got me on that one. The only bite marks ol' Barry had was on his feet where some fish ate his toes."

"Great," James muttered. "Any more good news?"

"Barry's prints were found at some crime scenes around Jacksonville," Phillip said, picking his iPhone up and scrolling through as he read. "Disappearance scenes, of course. Says here that every spot they found them was roughly forty-five minutes from here, or twenty. Hell, they found some in parts of the city where there aren't even children. Retirement communities." Phillip's brow furrowed. "That's...weird."

"Weird?" James said, raising an eyebrow. "You're usually more creative than that. Are you feeling well?"

Phillip shot James a look, then focused on his iPhone again.

"There's no pattern, here," Phillip said. "Criminals, hell, *people*, function in patterns. We can't help it. There's no such thing as true randomness. It's almost like they scattered evidence all over the city."

Something came to mind. James looked at Phillip. "Like maybe this isn't a hit job?"

Phillip looked up at him. "Possible. Maybe. Which means Barry may not have been a rat. That could be something planted to throw us off." He shook his head. "You and I already figured they were using vampires a while back. This just adds to what we already know."

"Lacy could probably fill us in on some things once she wakes up," James said.

Phillip grunted. "You and that walking tick," he said. "I wonder if she'd grow half the hair you have if you bit her instead of the other way around."

"I doubt a bite would affect either of us," James said.

"Might make you prettier."

"He's pretty enough as it is," Cordelia said as she approached with their plates. She sat them down and eyed James, giving him a wry smile. "Anything else, you two?"

"Nope," James said. "I think this will be fine. And it's one check this morning."

Cordelia smiled again as she sauntered off. "Why are all the good ones taken or gay?"

Phillip sighed, grumbled something under his breath, and started in on his French toast. James took a bite of his pancakes as he listened to Cordelia humming behind the bar. His heart fluttered at the sound, his eyes falling on her as she wiped down the counter. It was the most beautiful sound he'd ever heard. He felt a nudge in his mind from the wolf. The beast barked loudly in his ear, snapping his attention back. James looked at Phillip, who had a dopey grin on his face as he watched Cordelia.

"Dude, she's okay," James said as he went back to eating. "Definitely cuter than your last girlfriend."

Phillip shook his head and sucked his teeth at James. "Last girlfriend? That demon bitch put a spell on me."

"'Caaauuuse you're heeeerrrs,'" James sang back under his breath.

"Keep your damn John Fogerty to yourself," Phillip said. "Look here, Creedence: I wouldn't have even had to worry about some demon wanting a piece of Thunder if it wasn't for you."

James snorted. "Thunder?" he said.

"Hell yeah, Thunder. I shake the *earth* for the ladies, motherfucker."

"Jesus Christ," James muttered through his laughter. "Eat your breakfast, Thunder. I want to get some rest for tonight, and you've got a meeting later."

Phillip leaned in. "There's something big going down, James," he said. "The department has its crosshairs on an operation up near a spot called Morningstar Marinas. Not far from there. But they don't have enough to move in." He leaned back. "But, guess what name was on the manifest they managed to get emailed over?"

James raised an eyebrow. "I've got the vapors from the anticipation," he said, his voice monotone and humorless.

G ranach?" Lacy said as she left the bathroom and tossed aside the towel she'd used to dry her hair. "Well, that seals *that* deal."

"What deal?" Phillip asked.

"The hunch I had that House Granach was up to some shady shit," Lacy said. "Believe it or not, House Diabolito is more straight-edge. They operate a chain of hotels in the wealthiest parts of Jacksonville Beach. Not that they don't do some minor law-bending. They run a pretty low-key prostitution ring, but they have standards on who can have a night with the girls, and the girls are there voluntarily. One wants to quit, that's her choice."

James spent the rest of the day sleeping while Phillip met with his contacts and shared information with the police departments he'd gotten on board the investigation. Emails were sent back and forth from Florida to South Carolina.

James and Phillip had sat in the living room, going over things while Lacy showered. They'd filled her in once she'd gotten out.

"There's something else you two need to think about," Lacy said as she sat down on the couch next to James. He could smell the vanilla scent she carried mixed with the faint tinge of blood. Why did she smell so clean, but other vampires stink of rot? The wolf rolled over in his mind, exposed its belly. James fought to keep casual as he looked at her. "Vampires. In general."

"Okay," James said. "Yes. The place is swimming with vampires."

"The vampire house activity here is insane," Lacy said, ignoring him. "I've never seen it this active. Granted, I'm a South Carolina low country girl, but still. The low country is *teeming* with vampires, mostly old money. These guys are organized. It's like a mafia that drinks blood instead of wine."

"So what?" Phillip said. "That just tells me we'd be better off raiding places during the daylight."

"The low country clans keep quiet," Lacy said. "They work not to draw attention. These guys might as well get a billboard. And where you have a lot of vampires, you've got hunters."

Phillip raised an eyebrow.

"So our biggest concern is finding kidnapped little girls, and your biggest concern is Wesley Snipes?"

Lacy rolled her eyes.

"Vampire hunters don't really give a shit about good guy vampires and bad guy vampires, sweetie. We're all suck-heads, so we all die." She looked at James. "We need to keep our eyes open. A hunter shows up here, that's gonna get problematic *quick.*"

"What do you have in mind?" James asked.

Lacy looked at Phillip and grinned. "Me and tall-dark-and-sexy are gonna work together on this."

Phillip blinked. "Um, *how?*" he asked. "As far as anyone knows, me and Bob Smith are the only ones working on this."

"I can run interference with the vampire clans and get information," Lacy said. "You just make sure the cavalry is ready when the shit hits the fan." She nodded at James. "Mainly Bigfoot, here." She looked back at Phillip. "I'm supposed to meet Montoya for dinner. I'll text you if he blabs anything good. He doesn't like House Granach in particular, so I'm sure he doesn't give too many shits about gossiping."

Phillip shook his head. "No. *Hell* no. Not that I don't think you can handle yourself in a fight, but the last thing I need on my plate is another civilian in the line of fire."

"I've already been doing it," Lacy argued. "I'd just be going a little deeper. Besides, how many human police officers do you think a vampire house is going to tolerate snooping around their operations? Especially if they're criminals?" Lacy crossed her arms in front of her. "We've got laws, too. And one of them is to abide by human law unless it's unavoidable. If they're trafficking girls, it means they have Marianne." She looked at James. "And your two girls."

Marianne was Lacy's great grandniece. She went missing around the same time Mindy was taken. Lacy had been looking for her when her own leads led her right in James's path in Charleston.

James nodded and looked at Phillip. "I think it's a good idea," he said. "She can go places we can't."

Lacy sat up straight and put a hand on James's arm. "Oh, sweetie, by the way: I had to break up with you. They wouldn't allow me to have a were-wolf boyfriend if I wanted to be part of a house. I hope you understand."

James put the back of his hand against his brow and sighed melodramatically. "If it must be so. And yet, my heart aches."

Phillip grunted and stood, shaking his head as he muttered, "White people."

James crouched low in the shadows, hidden by the brush as he watched Lacy knock on the door at the Plantation Beach House, his yellowed vision making the low lighting around him a moot point. She'd explained on the way over that the vampire houses used it nightly as a gathering place to network and meet, as well as to ensure that treaties stayed intact and politics remained clean. James shifted and hid far enough away where he would be out of sight but still be able to see and hear what was said as long as people were outside.

She was wearing her black evening dress again, and James couldn't help running his eyes over her form. The wolf panted inside, and James growled at it.

Easy, he thought.

The wolf flashed an image. Lacy's moaning and rhythmic breathing sounded in his ears as she pressed her nude form against his.

James shook his head, clearing his mind, and jarring the wolf. The wolf sent him an urge. *Mate.*

You're an asshole, he thought.

The wolf panted and rolled over onto its back, exposing its belly.

A slutty *asshole*, James thought as he shifted his immense weight effortlessly. In truth, Lacy's joke at the cottage had caused something in his chest and stomach to ache. He'd laughed with her at Phillip's reaction, but he'd also found himself looking at her, admiring her willowy, delicate-looking form. None of the girls he'd dated in college compared to her. But James knew what that willowy, delicate-looking form hid. He'd experienced her strength firsthand. She was vicious, calculating. Feral.

Beautiful.

James blinked, grit his teeth, and gave his head another slight shake. *Focus, Coldstone.*

Lacy stepped inside the beach house at the behest of the grumpy doorman from the other night, and James watched as she passed by a few windows, greeting people as she went. She found Montoya, and he kissed her hand and offered her to step out through the back door onto the balcony overlooking the beach. She nodded, accepting a wine glass full of blood from the waiter before heading through the door. James moved, crouching low before he shot out of the brush and underneath the house. A vampire guarded the vehicles parked around the house. James waited until the vampire turned and walked to the other end of the drive, then he made his way around to the beachside of the house and crawled underneath the balcony. He heard a few different conversations going on.

"Schreck is dead," one man said. "Though I think a union between a vampire and a lycanthrope mongrel is disgusting, Schreck couldn't have been more than fifty years into his turn. He had no business going after a werewolf."

"So, you believe that wolf killed him?" a woman said.

"It makes the most sense. The kraut was pretty pissed that Lacy over there wasn't interested in him. Besides, all of the shady shit Granach House is into? They could afford to lose a fifth wheel if you ask me."

James sniffed the air, found Lacy's scent mixed with Montoya's rotted blood and expensive cologne. He moved over until he was underneath where they stood.

"Thank you for having me over the past couple of nights, Mr. Montoya," Lacy was saying. "It broke my heart to let him go. You've been wonderful about it."

"*De Nada, señorita,*" Montoya said. "But you must understand that we have certain customs and allowing a union between an angelic creature such as yourself and a common *perro* is simply a criminal act against nature itself."

Says the guy who drinks blood and runs faster than a Ferrari, James thought. *Ever stop to think that's why nature uses daylight as a vampire rotisserie?*

"Well, he's no longer an issue," Lacy said. "He's gone back to South Carolina."

"And left you behind in a place you're unfamiliar with," Montoya said. He grumbled. "*Maldito chucho.* You're better off without him."

James gnashed his teeth to keep from growling at Montoya.

"I'm still interested in House Diabolito," Lacy said. "Don't laugh at me: I actually went to a police friend and asked about you."

Montoya laughed jovially. "And what criminal activity did you find, *señorita?* Did my parking tickets turn up?"

Lacy laughed, the sound musical in James's ears. "Well, you'll have to forgive my paranoia," Lacy said. "Had a few bad boyfriends in my younger years before I was turned. Hindsight is always twenty-twenty."

"I could not agree more, *mi amor,*" Montoya said. James heard the boards above him creak as Montoya's voice dropped low. "Had you decided to delve into House Granach, you may have found many more interesting things to read."

"Really?" Lacy asked. "Do tell."

"They're thugs," Montoya said with a grunt. "House Granach was once a noble house out of Germany, but the new vampire head they took on a few decades ago decided to look into more lucrative ventures that...how do you say, *fracture* certain American laws. They've purchased a small warehouse near Morningstar Marinas as a base of operations to trade their...goods."

"Like what?"

James heard Montoya sigh. "I would rather not say," he said. "Too many prying ears. Suffice to say that I take your...background checking of House Diabolito as a deep compliment and an indication that you are interested. I do hope you will join us."

James slinked away as he heard Lacy speak. "We'll see, Mr. Montoya."

5

It was shortly after midnight when Lacy returned from the Plantation Beach House. She still looked elegant, and James caught himself staring at her as she sat at the table in the cottage with Phillip and compared notes. He blinked and looked away, cursing at himself for being an idiot and hoping she hadn't noticed.

"I'm willing to bet Granach House is our trafficking ring," she said to Phillip. "Montoya wouldn't budge on not wanting to say much about it, but he let enough slip to go on, I think."

"I wish we could get every suspect to sing like that," Phillip said as he took notes on his iPad. "I guess being a vampire has its advantages."

Lacy motioned at her chest. "Boobs help."

"What is Morningstar Marina?" James asked as he sat down at the table with them.

"It's a self-storage place," Phillip said. "Morningstar Storage? Same thing. People keep their boats and other marine stuff there. Apparently, there was a sizeable spot of land right next to it that Morningstar didn't take as part of the package when they built the place." He tapped on the iPad screen. "According to what I'm reading here, Heinrich Granach purchased the land about seventy years ago, and the guy who took over after Heinrich died decided to build a warehouse and distribution center there. It's privately owned."

Lacy nodded, looking thoughtful. "It makes me wonder how Heinrich Granach met his end."

"The guy probably whacked him," Phillip said casually.

James raised an eyebrow. "Whacked?"

Phillip looked at him. "Yeah, whacked. Popped off. Put to sleep."

James blinked. Phillip rolled his eyes and sighed. "Murdered, you idiot. He was murdered."

"Ah."

"Not necessarily by another house, Don Corleone," Lacy said. "It's also *very* possible that he was taken out by a vampire hunter."

James shook his head. "We need to go there. Take them out. End this."

Phillip leaned back in his chair and eyed James. "Do tell," he said. "What's your master plan, Beethoven? Hold on, I'll guess. Barge in, wreck the place, kill everyone inside except one, try to shake him down for info, and get out before the cops show up?"

James grinned at him. "It's scary how well you know me."

"Exactly," Phillip said. "I know what an idiot you are. You realize that this whole thing is delicate as shit, right? Don't forget how big this is. I'm running a damn joint investigation with the FBI. I could lose my job if it goes sideways."

"I'm sure you'd make an excellent drive-thru clerk."

"McFuck you."

Lacy rubbed her forehead. "Dear God," she muttered. "Beavis, Butthead, both of you shut the fuck up for two seconds and listen. I have a better idea that *won't* bring an entire community of vampires after us."

J ames breathed in the air, the scents of the river and nearby marinas coming in and filling his mind with images. The typical smells were there: saline, mildew, diesel fuel, and gasoline. He could also smell food. Someone was cooking out in one of the yachts a few piers down, the fragrance of burgers on the grill mixing in and making James's stomach growl. The wolf flashed an image of a deer in his mind, licked its chops.

I know it's been a while, James thought at it. *We'll hunt soon.*

The wolf huffed in his ear as James shifted his immense weight on the roof of the storage building. Morningstar was closed for the evening, but he'd still been able to get in with an easy leap over the fence in his wolf form. He'd found a building on the far side of the compound that was close to the warehouse next door. He crouched down, barely hidden by the roof as he watched the guards on patrol.

Lacy moved up beside him. "Anything interesting?"

James gave a low woof. His wolfen hearing picked up Phillip's voice tinny in Lacy's earpiece.

"He says no."

"You speak dog?" Lacy said back.

"No, I speak Dumbass. It's easier to understand him in both wolf and human form that way. What do you see?"

"Lots of vampire guards," Lacy said. "More than I'd anticipated. And they're armed like hell."

James looked back down and saw the two guards chatting by a service entrance door. Both carried assault rifles, though James didn't know what kind. He wasn't as well-read on firearms as Phillip. He figured the weapons were probably automatic.

And likely loaded with silver just in case.

"Abort," Phillip said in Lacy's ear. "Your plan was to observe. We observed. Get the hell out of there."

"We can manage it," Lacy said back. "We just need to change one or two things." She sighed as four more guards rounded the corner. "Maybe three."

One of the guards waved to another, said something, and both went their separate ways. The four that had come around the corner were walking with less attention, motioning to each other as they began to chatter. They entered the building, and James thought he caught the word "break" somewhere in their conversation.

"I wonder if there's a break room inside," Lacy said as if she'd read his mind. "We could use that." She ducked down, sliding back on the roof and turning on her side to face James. James moved back as well and shifted into human form.

"How?" he asked. "What do you have in mind?"

"Shift changes," Lacy said. "Breaks. Men are damn-near incapable of going on break alone. It's almost as weird as women always going to the bathroom together, but not quite."

James grinned, unable to resist. "I've always wondered about that."

Lacy gave him a smirk. "Much easier to hail Satan in pairs," she said. "I'm willing to bet they have a human in the break room to snack on."

James glanced over the rooftop again, then back to her. "Then we need to save them as well."

"Oh, honey," Lacy said. "I promise you that human has *no* desire to be rescued."

James blinked. Lacy sighed. "They volunteer for it," she said. "Some of them even get off on it, which is a little weird, but hey." She nodded in the direction of the warehouse. "It's servitude. They get drained until they're barely alive, then given time to heal so they can be fed on again. In return, they're paid well and get to live a life of luxury. They're also used as sex slaves, though I don't know if 'slave' is the right word since they're more than willing."

James shook his head. "Who am I to judge?"

Lacy grinned. "Don't knock it till you've tried, it, sweetie," she said. "I don't know about these mortal girls you're used to, but I promise you they don't come close to a ride from a vampire chick." She leaned in close, moving her mane of brown hair to the side. James's heart fluttered, her vanilla and blood scent stronger as she drew nearer to him. Her tone was sultry, her voice softening to almost a whisper. "Then again, I can't say I've ever been with a shifter boy, so what do I know?"

"We...w-w-we're a different breed," James managed, the words getting caught as he forced them out. He tried to keep his cool as the wolf rolled onto its back in his mind, its tongue lolled out to the side as it wagged its tail happily.

Lacy glanced down, then back up into his eyes. Her grin broadened. "Got some English Pointer breed in you, Jimmy?"

James stammered as she sat up. She rolled her eyes. "Phillip said we need to move."

James pursed his lips and looked at her expectantly.

"Okay," she said. "He also said we're fucking disgusting and to stop before he throws up."

"There you go," James said. He shifted back into wolf form and looked out at the warehouse. The guard patrol had moved on, the door closing as a few more headed inside. One guard stepped out into the low-lit area, looking around as he made to radio in. James made his move, launching himself through the air. He landed hard on top of the vampire, collapsed him to the ground before he could make a sound besides crunching bones. Blood spurted everywhere before it vanished into ash, the vampire's pulped body following suit until nothing was left but an empty pile of SWAT gear and a now ownerless assault rifle. James's ears twitched at the sound of footfalls on asphalt. Lacy zipped up at vampiric speed, appearing directly in front of the guard as he turned the corner. He had time enough for his eyes to widen in response to her standing in front of him before she grabbed his throat and tore out his esophagus. He gagged, staggering backward as she tossed the disintegrating part aside. She lashed out and smacked his head off his shoulders, the body ash before it hit the ground.

She turned and looked at James. "Not younglings," she said. "But definitely not as old as I am. These guys may be just out of their youngling years."

James gave a low *woof* and pointed at the warehouse.

"Yeah, that one I get, Lassie," said Lacy. "No barging in. We stick to the plan and be sneaky. We turn this place into a shit circus without evidence against the Granach group, the other clans will have no choice but to come after us. It's law." She rummaged through the pile of clothing on the ground and pulled out a key card. "Disco." She looked up at James. "Help me toss this shit in the water."

They threw the remains of the two vampires into the bay, then both moved quickly and quietly through the shadowed areas. James kept low, constantly sniffing the air in case something changed. He could hear more guards inside chatting, some grumbling about having to pull a shift tonight instead of feeding on some lovely ladies downtown. Someone shouted angrily, and James heard a roar of laughter.

"Looks like lunch hour," Lacy said.

James sniffed again as the wolf brought an image of Mindy to his mind. He knew her scent. Strawberries. He put his nose to the ground and took in the odors of tire rubber, boots, spilled drinks.

"Door," Lacy whispered over her shoulder. James glanced up, saw the small entryway a few feet from the large roll-up. He moved closer, sniffed the space at the bottom where the door met the ground.

Nothing.

Lacy tapped him on the head, put her finger to her mouth to shush him, then pointed at the wall. A piece of coaxial cable ran neatly up the side to a camera. It was pointed away but rotating back around. She pulled the wire loose from the wall and handed it to James, who took it and chomped down on it with his teeth. His mouth tasted funny from the copper and shielding, but the red light on the camera's front went out just as it was rotating around to where they stood.

Lacy swiped the keycard across the reader and carefully pulled the door open just enough to peer inside. She looked up at James as he stood. "It's separated from the loading area," she said. "Corridor. Come on. And keep low. It's not a big hallway, and you're not exactly a toy breed."

James followed her in, going low to the ground as he let the door shut behind him. He moved steadily, slow, keeping conscious of the sound of his footfalls on the tile floor as they passed by the offices. Lacy held up a fist, indicating him to stop. She pointed at a door with a sign on it.

Loading Area. Authorized Personnel Only.

She held up the keycard. "Authorized," she said with a grin. She swiped it—the reader beeped acceptance—and turned the handle to open the door.

The area was massive, the rollup door at the dry end down and barred. The floor was open for boats to pull in on the waterside, though the building wasn't quite large enough for one of the giant barges James had seen in the wharf. He figured a small transport could fit, however. Large enough to carry shipments to the barge, but not so big that a group of little girls could get lost wandering if they happened to escape while at sea.

"Never been inside one of these before," Lacy said as she pulled another coax cable off the wall and jerked it out of the camera. "I've heard about them. Pretty cool." She glanced at the water. "And terrifying."

James looked at the far end of the warehouse. Several large crates stood, some of them big enough to hold a car.

Or children, he thought.

The wolf barked in agreement.

He made for the crates. Lacy zipped around in front of him and put her hands out, pushing against his chest, slowing him down even though her feet slid across the concrete. He finally stopped and looked down at her.

"Bad dog," she snapped, pointing up at him. "We talked about this, Jimmy. Low and slow. Bad doggy!"

James rolled his eyes and stood as Lacy put her hand to her ear.

"Thank you, Phillip. I'm aware," she said, not hiding her annoyance. "Yes, I know he's an idiot. No, there's no one in here. Yes, I am aware there are cameras. We've disabled them."

James cocked his head to the side.

"The ones that matter," Lacy said, shooting him a look. "Dear God, Phil, are you always this high strung? I can get you some weed if you want it, honey."

James leaned in close enough to hear Phillip's tinny voice in the earbud, his wolfen hearing sharpening just as a torrent of profanity sang out from the earpiece.

"You two are fucking up *hard*," Phillip was shouting. "God *damn!* What part of 'sneak' or 'stealth' is hard to understand?" He sighed. "There's probably more than one camera in that room. Get what you need and get the hell out of there!"

Lacy nodded and pointed at the crates. James moved in, sniffing around the bottom of the nearest one. The wolf flashed images in his mind. Eggs. Bacon. Toast. Grandmom laughing at something his mother said.

Coffee.

He sniffed again. The coffee smell was strong, bitter. Lacy joined him as he balled up a massive fist and plunged it into the crate. Coffee spilled out everywhere, pouring onto the floor.

"What the fuck?" Lacy said. She reached down and picked up a handful. "Coffee? Yuck, this shit is vile."

James shifted into human form. He plucked the earbud out of Lacy's ear and inserted it into his own.

"I don't get it," he said to Phillip. "Loose coffee beans?"

"Yeah, I'll bet that's all you can smell, right?" Phillip said. "Dig around in it. I gotta hunch, and I'll bet a year's pay on it."

James dug through the coffee, his hands closing on a plastic bag. He pulled the pillow-sized bag free, looking at the white powder on the inside.

"Open it," he said. "You tried the shit in college, and it didn't work on you because you're a fleabag."

James tore a corner off the bag, stuck his finger in the powder, and put a small amount on his tongue. It wasn't sugar. He knew that dull sweet flavor. Knew what it smelled like. He remembered looking at the other guy who'd given it to him and asking what he was supposed to be feeling.

"That's...cocaine?" Lacy said. "Are you fucking kidding me?"

"They use coffee to hide the scent from drug dogs," Phillip said over the earpiece. "I'm calling it in right now. Tell your girl to get pictures, then you two get the fuck out of there before—"

"*Freeze, assholes!*"

James heard Phillip sigh in his ear. "Before that happens."

James spun and saw six male vampires with their guns aimed at him and Lacy. Lacy smiled at them, sauntered forward a bit.

"Can we talk about this, boys?"

One of them stepped forward, pointed his rifle at her face, and clicked off the safety. Lacy shrugged.

"Guess not."

James shifted and lunged at the group with a growl as Lacy slapped the rifle out of the guard's hands and pounced on him. The other men fired at James, but the bullets only hurt him until his body pushed them out and healed.

Normal bullets? he thought as he crashed into the vampires and sent them flying in all directions. One landed in the water, which started boiling immediately as he screamed and writhed. His flesh melted away, his screams turning into gagging as his remains sank into the darkness. *Vampires and saltwater don't mix,* James remembered Lacy saying once. The others went at James, tossing their weapons aside, their fangs and claws out. James grappled with two of them as they pulled him down, rolled over on them, and swatted another out of the air as it tried to land on him. Lacy shot into the fight, decapitated one vamp, and used the head before it went to dust to crush the skull of another. Another two vampires came at her, and James briefly saw her run at them before he bucked his own problems off and got to his feet. The earpiece was somehow still in his ear, and he heard Phillip yelling at him.

"Keep them busy! I've got police on the way! I'm driving there now!"

A vampire swung at James and clocked him across the face, knocking the earbud out. James felt his teeth rattle in his head as he staggered. He recovered quickly as the vampire made for him again. James snapped his jaws down on the vampire's neck and jerked, the head flying off into the night. He swung his arm around as he spun, his hand connecting with another vampire guard hard enough to send the bastard flying into the water. James searched the area with his eyes, found Lacy struggling with two guards. She kicked one in the balls, smashed his face in with her knee, and knocked a fang out of the other's mouth with a solid right hook. The guard screamed, covering his mouth as blood rushed out between his fingers. Lacy mercilessly grabbed his head, snapped his neck, and tossed him into the water to disintegrate.

"Well, that was fun," she said, winded. "I only counted six in here, and the two we killed outside makes eight." She paused. "Wait...we only killed five."

"*Surprise, motherfuckers!*"

James wheeled around as an armored vampire guard rushed them, his automatic rifle blazing, peppering James. He stopped firing, and James looked down as the bullets fell from his body, the bleeding stopping as his wounds healed.

Lacy rolled her eyes and looked at the guard, who was whimpering, blinking in disbelief as he pulled the trigger on his now empty gun.

"He's a werewolf, stupid," she said. "Silver. Ya need silver."

The guard tossed the gun aside and hissed, his fangs whipping into place. He ran at them, his eyes glowing as he lunged at James. James and Lacy sidestepped him casually as he went by, his snarl turning into a yelp as he fell face-first over the edge and into the water. His screams were cut short as he wasted away.

Lacy sighed. "There you go," she said. "Six."

James stood up straight and perked his ears, the sound of distant sirens blaring in the night. He barked at Lacy as she stooped down and picked up the earpiece James had dropped earlier.

"I hear them too," she said. "Let's go. I don't feel like explaining a shit-load of cocaine to the cops."

6

Lacy tossed her phone onto the bed. "Well, that was an interesting phone call."

They'd come straight back to the cottage from the warehouse, passing by at least fifteen police cars. They kept to yards and shadows, and James spotted Phillip's car in the mix. James shifted back to human form the minute they returned to the cottage, and Lacy called Montoya and reported what she'd found out, sans the whole killing vampires and raiding the warehouse thing.

"Do tell," James said as he finished dressing.

"A few vampire houses have people working in the police departments around here," Lacy said. "Including House Diabolito. They're all with that army that headed to the docks."

"I'm not entirely sure I know how that is significant."

"It means we're covered when the vampire political shit hits the fan."

"Ah."

Lacy looked down at the remains of her black dress. She was still decently covered, though her stomach and thighs could be seen through the tears in the fabric. "I really liked this dress," she said, sighing. "Shit."

James leaned in the doorway, trying to put his thoughts together as Lacy pulled a t-shirt and jean shorts from the dresser beside her bed. She began to unzip the dress in the back. She stopped, looked at him, and raised an eyebrow.

"I like you, Jimmy, but I'm still modest. Even for a dead girl." She pointed at the doorway. "Out."

James turned, feeling his face heat up as the door shut behind him. He heard Lacy on the other side.

"I'm a lady, Jimmy. Gotta buy me dinner first."

"Prostitution is illegal in Florida."

"Ha. Ha. You're *so* funny."

James tried to smile at his joke, but his chest was aching too much. Not from his injuries. Those had healed within minutes while he was in wolf form. His iPhone rang in his pocket. He pulled it out and looked at it, not surprised to see Phillip's caller ID. Lacy laughed from the bedroom.

"Does Phillip know you have the theme from *Police Academy* as his ringtone?"

James ignored her and answered.

"James, it's a goddamn hurricane here," Phillip said before James could speak. "There are cops *everywhere*, and not one guard. I'm assuming you and Lacy took care of that situation."

"They were quite happy to see us. Even offered drinks."

"Right. This place is hot, James. I mean *damn*. I've *never* seen this much cocaine. You and the Queen of the Damned uncovered a metric shit ton of coke that was heading out courtesy of House Granach."

"So, you were able to implicate them pretty quick then?"

Phillip made a noise. "*Son*," he said. "I just stepped out of the office here at the warehouse. The paperwork is filled out, the trails all lead back to Granach, there is *no* denying it. Shipment manifests, emails, orders, all signed and sealed, good-night-Irene."

"I might recommend against going to pick up whoever runs Granach."

"Apparently, it's a human," Phillip said. "They're kicking in his door now. I'm pretty sure Lacy already has the vampire houses on the actual master."

James pursed his lips, then asked the question that was eating away at him. "No girls?"

Phillip was quiet for a second, then answered with a deep sigh. "No, James. No girls. Nothing. Granach was trafficking drugs. Like a motherfucker."

James pulled the phone away from his ear, gripped it hard, squeezed it as he made to throw it across the room, then stopped himself. He fought the rage down as the wolf inside barked and snarled furiously. He urged at the wolf angrily, told it to settle down. He put the phone back on his ear.

"Call me when you're on your way back," he said. He ended the call as Phillip tried to talk to him. He didn't care what Phillip was saying. Mindy was still out there. Still in danger. He hoped she was fighting.

Fighting hard.

Phillip sent James a text later on, saying that he was on his way. James appreciated the text. Phillip knew better than to call when James was in a mood, even if James had told him to call.

The bust at the Granach warehouse turned out to be the largest drug raid in the history of Florida. The estimated street value was upwards of thirty million dollars once they accounted for the manifests from the incoming ships. The Coast Guard saw to it that the vessels that had arrived never left U.S. waters, thus bringing House Granach's drug empire to an end within hours.

"Yeah, that's just the mortal side," Lacy said when Phillip told them. "House Diabolito just called an emergency meeting of all the heads of the vampire houses in Jacksonville, including the High Council. Granach is finished."

James had excused himself without comment and gone to bed. He needed sleep, but his dreams were restless, causing him to wake up in a cold sweat every hour or so. He sat up in his bed the third time he saw Mindy's broken, violated body lying on the ground in his dreams. He shook the image from his mind, forcing himself not to think about the details as he wiped the sweat from his face. The wolf stirred in his mind, wanting to hunt, angry at him for not doing so before going to bed.

I'm not in the mood for you, he thought at the beast.

The wolf mewled and crouched down, slinking into the shadows in the back of his mind.

James looked out the window. The sun was cresting over the water on the horizon, the sky turning a deep orange and purple. It reminded him of those Sunrise Earth videos he liked to watch on television sometimes when he was doing other things around his apartment. He could hear gulls in the distance, water lapping up on the shoreline outside. He'd been sleeping with his window open, but the crisp and clean ocean air did nothing to soothe his nerves.

His stomach growled. He got out of bed, showered, dressed, and left the cottage, wondering if McFadden's was open this early. He knew Phillip would be hurt that he went to breakfast without him, but James needed time alone. He needed to clear his mind, think without having someone offering ideas back at him or distracting him with conversation. He used his Lyft app to call a driver to take him to McFadden's and enjoyed the quiet ride as the driver listened to Muddy Waters play his jazz at low volume on the stereo. The kid, a young black man with his hair done in long braids, thanked him. The sun was up now, but the early morning was still not as bright as it would be in the afternoon, though the Florida heat was already making James sweat. He saw Cordelia bustling about, serving the patrons inside, and wondered if she actually lived there. The joke was humorless, flat, as he went in and helped himself to his regular booth in the back corner. Cordelia dutifully brought him a menu and a cup of coffee.

"You're early," she said. "Where's ya' boy?"

"Still sleeping," James said. "Late night."

Cordelia smiled. "Well, at least he's cute. He's got that going for him. Pancake breakfast?"

"You read my mind."

Cordelia winked. "One of the things I'm good at." She moved away quickly to refill a coffee cup, and James watched as she bustled from table to table. The cook in the back called out for her to pick up an order, and one of the men at the bar laughed at another's joke.

James sipped his coffee, his thoughts still scrambled. Granach was another. Fucking. Dead. *End.* He didn't give a shit about drugs. If people wanted to snort coke, it was none of his business. He understood the law about illegal distribution, but it had nothing to do with tracking down all the missing girls between here and South Carolina.

Nothing to do with finding Mindy, Clara, and Marianne.

He hoped Clara was still protecting Mindy, that they were still inseparable like his original suspect, Santiago, had said back in Rock Hill when it all started. It was at least someone on the inside who could watch out for her until James got to them.

"Hey, Cordelia," one of the men called out, snapping James's thoughts back to Earth. "You singin' again tonight?"

"Yup," Cordelia said to the man, a younger guy with a ballcap on and a button-up short-sleeved shirt. He fit the description of the kind of guy

Phillip would sometimes refer to as a "Dude-bro." Everyone's buddy. Obsessed with sports. Young, cocky, and highly annoying.

And irresistible to some girls.

The guy chatted with another guy next to him. James studied the room again, noticing for the first time that every one of the patrons was male. Cordelia made her rounds, refilling coffee and laughing at stupid painful puns and jokes from the men flirting with her, and James counted thirty customers between those seated at the bar and tables. James eyed them all, watched as they chatted and carried on.

And made sure they could always see Cordelia at least out of the corner of their eyes.

Hey, James thought at the wolf. *Wake up. Need you for a second.*

The wolf mewled again, staring back at him from inside, its head cocked to the side.

I'm sorry, James thought, exasperated. He didn't have time to argue with his inner creature. *You saw the dreams. I was pissy. Give me a break.*

The wolf stayed put, blinking at him.

Fine. I will make sure you get a bloody-as-hell slab of meat tonight. Now get your fuzzy ass up here.

The wolf panted, wagging its tail happily as it stepped forward. James's senses heightened immediately. He could smell the food in the kitchen, and soap and cologne from the men in the room. He looked toward the bar, saw his plate of pancakes in the serving window.

Something else. Musk. Male. Not like someone who'd been sweating balls all day. No. Different.

Cordelia grabbed his plate, brought it over, and sat it down in front of him. The scent of pancakes was overpowering, sausage and eggs mixed in with the sweet doughy smell.

Seawater. Why did he smell seawater?

"Here you go, handsome," Cordelia said, smiling. "Anything else?"

James glanced around her for a split second. It was all he needed to see that every eye in the place was on him, but subtly. Men were still in conversation, but they all seemed to make a conscious effort to glance his way while they spoke. He'd gotten that kind of side-eye before. Suspicious, watching him.

"No," James said. "Thank you."

The door to the kitchen opened, and a black kid in his twenties poked his head out. "Hey, Cordelia," he said. "Need you to make a quick clarification on this order, girl. I dunno what this means."

Cordelia laughed. "No sweat, Eddie. I'm coming." She trotted off to the kitchen, and James started eating while the other men in the pub struck their conversations back up, low and mumbling. James used the wolf to open his hearing again.

"Pretty-boy," someone said. "The fuck he thinks he is, flirtin' her up like that?"

"Nah," another said. "I heard her sing last night—first time. Most beautiful thing ever crossed my hearing. Actually made me weep like a baby."

The musk smell in the room deepened, the wolf inside reacting to it, growling in defense and wariness. James kept eating, ignoring the stares and glances as he ate his pancakes. Someone sat down in the booth behind him, and James heard the man speak over his shoulder.

"Unless you think you might want problems, I suggest you keep your eyes to yourself."

James nodded, keeping his demeanor casual and nonchalant as he ate. "Not really my type," he said. "Besides, I'm just in here for breakfast. I have to have this wolfed down and be at the docks in about an hour. Tour."

"Not your type, huh?" the man said with a laugh.

As if on cue, Cordelia came out of the kitchen and moved behind the bar, humming as she went. James didn't recognize the tune. It was slow, the flowing notes making him think of waters lapping up on shorelines or against rock walls. He felt his heart flutter slightly as he slowed his chewing, taking in the sound of her voice. Her exotic beauty. The way her mixed heritage gave her skin an almost bronze appearance. Her hair in large, flowing curls.

The wolf snapped into his mind, snarled at him. He dropped his fork, forced the beast back before it could start the change in his body. He gripped either side of the table, fought his muscles to still as his bones began to shift around. He felt his teeth start to elongate, then stop and retract back in. He breathed out as the wolf stayed close enough inside to threaten another shift. He looked up as Cordelia laughed, the musical sound filling the room. The dude-bro she was talking to, a college-aged kid with long hair tied up in a man-bun, laughed with her, smiling under his hipster beard. She touched the Jason Momoa wannabe on the shoulder and whispered in his ear. His grin grew broader, and he looked up at her as she stood back from him.

James blinked. Had her eyes flashed bright green? Like a couple of lights?

He finished his pancakes and stood. The man behind him looked up at him, his eyes wide. He was older, wore a plaid shirt and a red ballcap.

"You're a big fucker," he said.

"I work out," James muttered as he dropped a fifty on the table and made his way toward the front of the pub. Momoa Jr. laughed heartily at a joke from one of his tablemates. James listened as he made his way by.

"Got a date, boys," he was saying. "Told you the beard works."

"Bullshit," one of the other college kids said. "So you got a date with her. Big deal. Wait till she actually talks to you without us around as a buffer for your stupidity."

Dude-bro laughed again. "Shit," he said. "Who needs brains when you look like me and have a horse's dick? Tonight's gonna be fun. Nothing like a walk on the beach to guarantee some ass. Supposed to meet her here tonight."

James left. He had to get to Phillip and Lacy, fill them in on another potentially long night.

7

So a bunch of guys in a pub that serves breakfast are sweet on the cute waitress that works there. That's your big piece of intel?" Phillip eyed James. "Well, shit, James. Let's call the force in right now. Hell, we might even get tanks and choppers on this one. I'm sure the Coast Guard'll want in on it, too."

James looked at Phillip and blinked. "Might want to consider the Marines as well."

Phillip shook his head, muttering. "Dumbass."

They stood out on the small pier behind the cottage. James had just gotten off the phone with the owner, having offered a generous amount of money to stay on another night or two. The owner agreed, though the price for the cottage was already exorbitant. A fishing boat went by, the railing lined with long rods, and a yacht came through in the distance, slowly making its way back to the harbor. They weren't far enough out that James couldn't see a few people milling on the deck looking like they might still be feeling the effects of a long night of good times and good booze.

"I think she might be another succubus," James said. "The other men were acting almost as goofy as you did when Rebecca put you under her spell."

Phillip looked at James. "Almost?"

James shrugged. "You're fairly goofy anyway. Being spelled by a demon who sucks souls out through dicks just added to the entertainment."

"Oh, so I'm entertaining?" Phillip said. "That's what I am? I'm a joke to you? I'm here for your amusement?"

"You are never boring. And Cordelia may be another succubus."

"Still doesn't tell me what this has to do with our traffickers. Other than she may, or may *not*, be connected simply because of what she is or *might* be." Phillip shook his head. "You're losing it, James."

"Humor me for a moment."

"Fine. Let's say she's a succubus. That narrows the possibility that she's connected a little more in our favor because we know they hired Rebecca to entice men and make it easier to nab their daughters. We also know that Rebecca had the address for the Plantation Beach House in her apartment, which led us to the vampire parties and houses around here."

"Precisely."

"But," Phillip said, continuing, "and this is a big 'but.' Like Oprah-big. Not so much Kardashian because Oprah's is all-natural. There's also a chance she's just a stupid-pretty girl who works in a pub and has the attention of every dude in there. Shit, *you* were looking at her. And here I thought you only had eyes for women that bite."

James looked back at the cottage, specifically at the window to the bedroom where Lacy slept underneath the bed. The sun was out in full, the sky a brilliant blue, the water around them reflecting the same. James had seen it a few times but never could move past how blue the water was in Florida while it stayed its natural greenish color in South Carolina.

"It's so clear it acts like a mirror for the sky," his mother had said once.

He wished Lacy could enjoy it with him. The water reminded him of the color of her eyes when they weren't glowing red coals.

"You like her," Phillip said. James turned and saw the toothy grin on Phillip's face. "Admit it. You want her to scratch you behind the ear with those long vampire nails of hers."

"I'm not entirely sure she's into dogs," James said, turning fully back to Phillip. "I want to set something up for tonight. Cordelia is working a double today."

"What do you have in mind?"

"Go in for dinner," James said. "Chat her up. And you'll need to wear earplugs."

Phillip looked confused. "That's new," he said. "I thought succubae had to swap fluids to spell their victims."

James shrugged. "This one can do it with her voice. Even *I* felt it this morning when she was humming. The wolf had to snap me out of it by almost forcing a change right there in the pub."

Phillip sighed. "Okay. What do you have in mind?"

Y ou clean up nice, Phil," Lacy said, smiling at Phillip as he adjusted his police uniform. "Bait should always look appealing."

"Don't you have some garlic to eat?"

"Nope. Allergic." Lacy mimicked the stereotypical vampire-dying-in-sunlight pose, her facial expression mocking agony before returning to normal. "Whole vampire thing, you know."

Phillip looked at James. "Ya' girl's got jokes."

They stood in a parking lot across the street from McFadden's. The sun was down; James was feeling antsy. Nervous, but not because of the possible upcoming fight.

"Okay, let's go over it again," James said, talking to them both. "Lacy and I will go in first and grab our usual booth in the back. Give it ten minutes, then Phillip comes in for a to-go order pickup at the bar. If we time it just right, the food will be ready by the time Cordelia is supposed to leave, and Phillip follows her while texting Lacy her position. We take over following her, and Phillip runs interference with the cops."

"Sounds simple," Lacy said.

"Simple is about all he can manage," Phillip said. "It's why I speak in single syllable words whenever I talk to him."

Lacy laughed as Phillip shooed them on. James waited for traffic to slow a bit, standing on the sidewalk as Lacy stepped up beside him and grabbed his hand, interlacing her fingers in his. His heart fluttered, and the wolf began to pant and wag its tail happily.

"Might as well play up the look, right?" Lacy said.

James shrugged, feigning casual. "Not complaining."

The wolf rolled onto his back in James's mind, exposing itself, its tongue lolled out to the side.

James held the door for Lacy, then followed her into McFadden's. He looked around the dining area and over at the bar, counting twenty men in all. No women. A few of them glanced his way, then threw a dismissive glance at Lacy before going back to their meals or drinks. James showed Lacy to his usual booth as Cordelia came out of the kitchen. She spotted

Lacy, and James could've sworn her eyes flashed a bright green. She picked up two menus and made her way over to the booth.

"That her?" Lacy said under her breath.

"Yes."

They were seated by the time Cordelia got over to them. She shot a curt grin at Lacy, then flashed James a smile that he supposed would melt hearts.

"Hey, sweetie," she said. She nodded at Lacy. "I guess I had you pegged wrong. Where's the other one?"

"He's got a thing tonight," James said. "Stake-out. He'll be by in a bit for a to-go order."

Cordelia nodded. "Beer?"

"Yeah, that'd be great. Porter."

She motioned at Lacy. "Her?"

Lacy shot Cordelia a look. "Um, she'll have whatever hipster bullshit IPA you have on tap that has a higher alcohol content than five percent." She gave Cordelia a tight-lipped smile. "Alcoholism. It's a thing."

Cordelia grunted and went off to get their drinks.

"Wow," Lacy said, her tone heavy with sarcastic enthusiasm and cheer. "Your girlfriend is a real bitch, Jimmy."

"Not my girlfriend," James said automatically. "Not my type. Besides, I —" He caught himself. He could hear the words in his head, almost feel them slamming against the back of his closed lips. *I already have one*, he thought to himself. *Smooth, Ex-lax.*

Lacy giggled. "You're cute when you stumble over your words, Jimmy. Keep that up."

James smiled in spite of himself.

"Black guy we all know and love, six o'clock," Lacy said, nudging her chin past James. He looked over his shoulder, saw Phillip walk in. He made eye contact only long enough for James to catch it, then went up to the bar. Cordelia approached him immediately and began to take his order. James looked around, saw the other men glaring at Phillip, tense as if waiting for a chance to strike.

"Take a look around," James said. "See anything weird?"

"Yeah," Lacy said. "Every dude in the place looks like they want to kick the shit out of your bestie."

"Exactly," James said, turning back to her. "*Every* dude."

"That *is* weird. I mean, it's not unusual for one or two to have a little crush on the hired help. *Everyone?* That's a bit off."

Cordelia approached with their drinks. She sat James's down carefully and plopped Lacy's down in front of her hard enough for the frothy beer head to spill over the edge of the glass.

"Here you go, babe," Cordelia said to James. "Ready for food?"

"Steak, extra rare," James said. "My girlfriend will have the same."

"Sounds good," Cordelia said. She shot Lacy a hateful look, turned on her heel, and sauntered off into the kitchen.

"Yeah, she hates my ass," Lacy said. "Not that I care, but I can't figure what I did to piss her off."

"If she's a succubus, wouldn't that make sense?" James asked. "Would she not see another woman as a threat?"

"Nope," Lacy said. "From what I read, a woman is another potential succubus. And succubae don't care about gender. You could say they're fairly pan."

"Pan?"

"Yeah. Like bi, but on steroids. Bisexuals like both men *and* women. Pansexuals don't care. Gay, straight, trans. My last boyfriend was pan. I was never bored."

"Ah."

"I don't know *what* your girl is," Lacy continued. She grinned at James. "Girlfriend? Really, Jimmy?"

James blinked. "What?"

"You called me your girlfriend."

"When?"

"Just a second ago."

Shit, James thought. *I must have said it out loud. Oops.*

"We're undercover."

"Yeah, but not under covers." Lacy's grin broadened. "Yet."

James blinked as the wolf groaned in excitement, rolling onto its back again and wiggling. "Uh...what?"

Lacy leaned in, and James couldn't help his heart pounding as her brilliant blue eyes seemed to sparkle at him. "You saying you don't want me, Jimmy?" She bit her lip, her tone sensuous. "You and Phil don't know how much your voices carry sometimes. I never said I wasn't a dog person."

James tried to find words. "I...uh, I mean...no...*yes*...um..."

Lacy laughed and sat back. "Wow, you're funny as hell," she said. "Relax, I'm just fucking with you."

James started to speak when Phillip approached them. "What the hell is wrong with you?" he said, almost laughing at James. "You look like you just got your brain fried."

James breathed out, then glanced around him and saw Cordelia heading their way with a bag of takeout.

"I'm about to leave for the night," she said, handing Phillip his food. "Amanda is here. She'll be taking over for me. Been here since this morning, and I'm beat."

"Right," Phillip said. "Thanks. Just wanted to talk at these two before I headed off."

"Hey, hold back a sec and walk me out?" Cordelia said to him, grinning. "It's dark. I'm a girl. You're a cop. Kind of sketch out there where my car is."

"Sure," Phillip said. "I'll wait up front." He nodded at James and Lacy. "Give the lovebirds here some privacy."

James watched as Phillip went back to the front of the pub and waited by the door, every man in the place still watching him. James turned back and caught Lacy grinning at him as she murmured in sing-song. "You liiike me, you-know-you liiike me."

James's phone chimed. He looked at it and saw the text from Phillip.

Does every guy in the place always stare like this?

They did that to me this morning, James replied.

Weird. I'd say they got an issue with black dudes if there weren't any black dudes in here.

Just watch yourself. They zeroed in on you the minute Cordelia acknowledged you. Looks like I'm off the hook since I'm here with Lacy.

Cordelia came back up front with her handbag as a pretty Latina girl stepped out of the kitchen. Her name badge said *Amanda*.

"Thanks for covering for me," Cordelia said to her. "Got a gig tonight. High-payin'."

"No sweat, girl," said Amanda.

Cordelia smiled at Phillip. "Ready?"

Phillip offered his arm like a gentleman in a campy movie. "After you."

Cordelia's smile grew bigger as she put her arm around his and walked out the door with him.

"Nice to see chivalry isn't dead," Lacy said. "Though Phillip might be if that guy has anything to say about it."

James looked over his shoulder and saw one of the larger men at the bar get up and walk out of the restaurant. Another followed. And another. One clapped another on the back.

"Don't worry," he said to the older one. "We'll handle it."

Every alarm in James's head went off. The wolf barked at him. *Oh shit,* he thought. *Phillip!*

James stood up and made for the door when the older man at the end of the bar stood up, putting himself in James's path.

"Where you goin'?" the old codger said with a grunt.

James started to move, but the old man grabbed his arm. Someone wrapped an arm around him in a chokehold. James drove his elbow into the man behind him, then jerked his arm out of the old guy's grip. He spun, grabbed his second attacker by the shoulders, and smashed the man's head into the bar. Lacy rushed in as another man stood and pulled a gun. She snapped his arm at the elbow, yanked the gun from his hand, and slammed the grip into his temple. He dropped to the floor in a heap.

James shoved the older man aside and made for the door as Phillip started screaming.

8

James burst through the front door, ignoring the shout from Amanda as he tore across the street. Cars slammed on breaks, horns honked, and James barely heard the obligatory requests for him to go fuck himself and burn in hell as he made his way to the parking lot. He saw Phillip lying on the ground as five of the men from McFadden's stood over him, kicking him and shouting. Phillip rolled over and tried to move out of the way, but a boot caught him in the face; blood spurted from his mouth.

James shifted, his clothes tearing away as his bones and muscles contorted and grew. He was hairy and angry in a split second as he barreled down on the group and hit them, sending all five flying. One slammed up against Phillip's car hard enough to cave the door in, then fell to the ground and lay still. The other four got to their feet as James rose to full height and snarled at them, his eyes wide, his teeth bared in unhinged fury. He put himself between them and Phillip, who lay on the ground, moaning in pain.

"Holy shit," one of the men breathed. He held up a tire iron as if the little toothpick would help him. James saw moonlight glint off the blood on the tool. He growled low, his yellowed vision intensifying, red hues lining the edge of his sight.

You first, he thought. The wolf barked in agreement.

"What's wrong, boys?"

The four men started at the sound of Lacy's voice. James watched as Lacy ran up on the group at vampire speed, seeming to materialize behind them. Her blue eyes glowed red, and her fangs were fully extended. The men spun on her, all of them backpedaling from her reluctantly, knowing that it put them closer to James. She grinned at them.

"You can let me munch on you, or my doggy can have four entrees for dinner this evening. And I know at least *one* of you motherfuckers has a Scooby Snack."

James snarled at the group, frightening them again as they all went back-to-back, two facing him and two facing Lacy.

Lacy glanced around James.

"Looks like that one's coming around."

James looked over his shoulder, saw the guy he'd used as a wrecking ball on the car stirring. He turned back at the group. One of them had pissed his pants, and another was crying.

"We're gonna talk to your buddy," Lacy said to the group. Her eyes glowed brighter, more intense as the two men facing James also looked in her direction. The last time she'd flashed her eyes like that, she'd mind-controlled a college student to keep them from being caught investigating a frat house in Charleston. "You four know what you did was wrong. You're going to take pictures with your phones, then you really need to turn yourselves in."

The four obliged without a word, each using their phones to take photos of Phillip's broken body as James stepped aside. The group finished, then each called 9-1-1. They spoke in unison, their voices monotone.

"I just jumped a police officer. I think I broke his leg. He's bleeding bad."

James shifted to human form and went to Phillip, who cursed as James tried to help him up.

"Shit, James, don't touch me," Phillip snapped. He winced. His face was battered and bruised, his lip bloody, and his eye swollen. His shirt was also bloody in spots and torn at the shoulder to reveal a sizable gash. "My fuckin' leg. They broke it. I think they got some ribs, too. Don't wanna risk you accidentally doing more damage."

"They beat you with a damn tire iron," Lacy said as she approached. "I'd be more concerned if you *didn't* have any broken bones."

The attacker James knocked out on the car moaned. James reached down and jerked him up by the shirt. The guy came to, his eyes wide with fear as he looked James up and down.

"You're naked," he managed.

"I'm also not above using you to finish wrecking this car," James said, his voice a growl. "Why did you attack Phillip?"

"He was taking Cordelia," the man said. "She...she's mine. Ours. He can't have her."

James smashed his fist into the man's face, knocking him back out with one punch. He went back to Phillip. Lacy was already there and talking to him.

"They didn't say anything," Phillip said. "Other than...somethin' about Cordelia and Clara."

"What did they say?" James asked.

Phillip gave him a pained, annoyed look.

"Not real sure, asshole," he said. "I was too busy getting the shit kicked out of me. God *damn*, my leg!"

Lacy leaned down and sniffed at Phillip like a feral animal inspecting its prey. She sat back up, her eyes going back to blue, and her fangs retracting.

"He's bleeding," she said. "Real bad."

"I think I can see that," James said.

"No, Jimmy," Lacy said as she stood. "Inside. He needs a doctor. *Now.*"

James heard sirens in the distance. Lots of them. He saw the four men still standing there staring at Phillip, their expressions drawn as they swayed under Lacy's mind control.

"You two get the hell out of here," Phillip said, wincing again.

"No," James said, his heart pounding. "I'm not leaving you here. You need a hospital."

"They'll get me there," Phillip said. "You think I'm the first black dude ever been hit with a tire iron?"

James shook his head. "Not leaving."

Phillip grit his teeth.

"What are you gonna do, James? Tell them you turned into Marmaduke and beat the shit out of my attackers while your vampire girlfriend mind-fucked 'em? Get out of here! I'll call you from the hospital."

James was about to argue again when Lacy tugged on his arm.

"He's right, Jimmy. We gotta go." She tugged again. "Wolf out, and let's bolt. *C'mon!*"

James nodded, fighting back the urge to scream in frustration. He leaned in close to Phillip's face.

"You be okay," he said, his eyes locked on Phillip's. "You don't leave me. You call me as soon as you can."

"I will," Phillip said. "*Go!*"

James stood, spun on his heel. He shifted in an instant as Lacy rummaged through the remains of his clothing and found his phone. James hit all fours and took off into the night, anger fueling his wolfen speed.

J ames didn't stop until he got to the end of the pier. He looked out over the water as his fur moved in the breeze. The dark surf brought him no peace as the image of Phillip being beaten by five men played out in his mind again. He wanted to go back, to help, but he knew that it would cause pandemonium.

He wanted to kill those men.

The wolf licked its chops in his mind, urged him, put the taste of blood in his mouth.

We don't kill people, James said. *Not mortals.*

The wolf huffed at him and sat down as Lacy appeared beside him, coming out of her vampire speed.

"Jimmy," she said. "Hey, he'll be okay. We passed a shitload of cops and EMTs."

James looked down at her, then back out over the surf.

"I know you're worried," she said. "I am too. I'll make sure he's looked after. House Diabolito has a few people in the hospital where they'll likely take him. I'll shoot Montoya a text."

James shifted to human form and looked at her. "What's next?" he said, his tone bitter. "He wasn't supposed to get hurt. I didn't think they'd actually attack him. He was supposed to let her get in her own car."

"Shit happens, James," Lacy said. "At least he'll be okay."

"Except now we're pissing in the wind," James shot back. He shook his head. "I'm beginning to wonder if everyone would be better off if I just called it. Went back home."

Lacy crossed her arms and looked up at him, her expression stern. "And give up? Give up on Phillip? Those girls you've been chasing?" She shook her head. "You'd never forgive yourself. Even if I found her once I find Marianne. Nope. Not gonna let you do that."

James stepped forward. "As if you could stop me."

Lacy's eyes turned wild and red as she put her face close to his. Close enough to...

"I am a hundred years old, little puppy," she said through gritted teeth. "I could break you in half. Don't test me on that." She stepped back. "I would've snapped your spine that night if you weren't cute. Even when you're a big dog." She pulled a cell phone out of her pocket. James glanced down at it, but he didn't recognize it. "I lifted this off the guy you cold-cocked back there. That was impressive, by the way."

"I try," James said. "Anything good?"

"Yup. Looks like Bubba didn't get a chance to check his messages before he jumped a cop."

She held the phone up as the screen turned on. There was a new text message—an address with the name of the sender at the top of the message bubble.

Cordelia.

A s much as James wanted to storm Cordelia's place and smash the door in, he allowed Lacy to talk him into riding naked in the car instead of ruining yet *another* outfit. She'd retrieved his cell phone for him at the scene of Phillip's beating, and kept it in her pocket in case Phillip called while James was in wolf form. She'd also found a spare set of clothes for James in Phillip's trunk for when they were done looking around. James stepped out of Lacy's Mini Cooper, shifted, and made his way toward the condos where Cordelia lived.

The neighborhood was quiet, asleep. James noticed that the majority of vehicles in the parking lot were sedans. He knew Phillip would've chided him about stereotyping, but James couldn't help thinking that most of Cordelia's neighbors were likely older people and retirees. Lacy scaled the building to the rooftop, turned, and motioned for James to follow.

He cocked his head to the side.

"Oh," Lacy said, keeping her voice low. "Right. Big clumsy were-doggy. My bad." She pointed to the side. James looked to his left and saw that the fence opposite Cordelia's next-door neighbor was low enough for him to jump it. He moved in that direction, leapt the fence, and moved along the side of the condo. Noises came from the bedroom window as he passed underneath it, low and rhythmic. Deep. Chortled. Like a walrus trying to suck molasses through his sinus cavity.

Might want to see a doctor about that, he thought as he continued past the snoring. He turned the corner and saw the back yard illuminated by solar LEDs that lined the walkway from the back porch out to a small gazebo. Legions of garden gnomes populated the yard, all frozen in their varied tasks of gardening, frolicking, or sleeping. They all had a wide assortment of expressions of varying joy and comfort, and each looked fresh and well-kept along with the rest of the elaborate yard.

The wolf made a disgusted sound inside James's mind.

You're not wrong, James thought at it. *I find vampires and criminals less frightening.*

The wolf huffed in agreement, and James moved past the gnome army and leapt the fence that separated the two yards. Cordelia's place was starkly opposite, the yard devoid of anything but grass, which looked like it hadn't been cut in a few weeks. Lacy stood on the back stoop, her arms crossed, and a wry smile on her face.

"I figured you'd get a kick out of the garden gnome orgy next door," she said. "Creepy shit. Kind of like midget porn but less entertaining."

James moved up onto the porch and sniffed the lock on the back door. Lacy nudged him, told him to move, then grabbed the door handle and shoved. The deadlock ripped through the doorjamb as if it were paper, and the door swung open.

"Finesse, Jimmy," Lacy said, smiling up at him. "Gotta use finesse."

James moved past her and into Cordelia's home. The living room was empty—no furniture, no pictures on the wall, no indication that someone lived there. James sniffed the air, the dingy smell of an unlived-in home heavy and thick. He crouched down and sniffed the carpet. Nothing. It was clean—no trace of any activity other than the occasional sweep of a vacuum cleaner.

"What the fuck?" Lacy said. "This is weird. I'll bet she rents the place as a cover. Doesn't actually live here." James sat up as she turned and looked at him. "Which means she's up to something big. You might be right, Jimmy. This might be another succubus, after all. How much sense does it make that two succubae would be in any form of contact with each other if they weren't working together?"

James huffed. *Told you so.* He moved through the living room and into the kitchen area. Lacy followed, opening the cabinets and refrigerator. Both were empty. James sniffed the air again. There was something different here, an odor of some kind. He spotted stairs leading up to the second floor. The scent seemed to be coming from there. He went low, sniffed the carpeted steps, then lifted up and scented the air again. Pungent, the sickly-sweet aroma of spoiling meat. He climbed slowly, Lacy behind him. He stopped, sniffed again, and caught a familiar scent underneath. He knew that scent, but from where? Had Phillip been there? No, but James remembered the odor and Phillip being around when he'd smelled it.

James's chest hurt a little at the remembered image of Phillip lying on the ground, his body bleeding and battered. He felt Lacy reach up and scratch him behind the ear.

"Hey," she said. "Vampires can sense shit. Stop it. I'm worried about him, too. Now focus."

James pulled the scents over his tongue as he made his way to the top of the stairs. Another image flashed: a bedroom covered in gore, literally decorated with entrails.

The Pickens house in Rock Hill.

Two bedrooms sat on either side of the second-floor landing. The door to his left was wide open, the room as empty as the rest of the place. The other was closed. James sniffed under the door, the smell from the space at the bottom overpowering. He felt a surge of anger and frustration as he plowed his right arm through the door, sending it off the hinges and splintering the doorframe. He stepped in and saw the lump in the corner of the room lying on its side, human-sized and still. He approached. As the smells in the room assembled the images in his mind, he realized who lay on the floor. He growled and gnashed his teeth as Lacy moved in front of him and gently turned the body over onto its back.

Clara Pickens's eyes were still open, her face sallow and white, her body wet as if she'd been pulled out of the surf.

"Jesus," Lacy breathed. She looked up at him. "James, a succubus didn't do this."

9

James waited in the hospital lobby as the security guard at the front desk made the phone call needed to clear him in to visit Phillip. James hated hospitals, and the idea that he'd be in and out of one to check on Phillip only angered him more.

His fault. It was *his* fault Phillip was cooped up in a hospital bed.

James and Lacy had gone back to the cottage after Lacy anonymously called in Clara's body. The sun was due to rise soon, and she wanted to be under her bed before daylight came along.

"I don't enjoy roasting," she'd said as she went to her room. "Sucks for my complexion."

James tried calling Phillip, but it'd gone to voicemail. He slept fitfully for a few hours, then got up and showered and dressed. He used a Lyft despite Lacy's offer to take her car.

He didn't exactly have a driver's license.

"You're clear, young man," the friendly black lady said as she hung the phone up. Her big curled hair, horn-rimmed glasses, and overdone lipstick gave James the instant urge to call her "Grandma" and do anything in the world she asked him to do with the promise of cookies at the end of the day. She smiled at him. "Officer Brown is awake, and the doctors have approved him for visitation."

"Thanks," James said.

The guard smiled. "Happy to do it, sugar. Just take that elevator to the fourteenth floor and turn left."

James nodded and made his way toward the elevator. He waited, watched as the light for the lobby lit up. The doors opened, and James blinked as a middle-aged man in a suit stepped out. He eyed James and smiled, giving a small nod. James tried to get a scent on him, but there was nothing.

Riverstreet Sweets, James thought. *I've seen you before. The hell are you doing here?*

"Pardon me," the man said, his tone friendly as he moved by. James watched him as he walked by Grandma's desk, nodded to her, then walked out.

James took the elevator to fourteen and felt his shoulders slump as he read the sign on the wall that led into the Critical Care unit. He stopped at the door to room 1408 and knocked.

"Come on in, James," Phillip called. "Help me warm up for the footrace I've got with the doctor later."

James walked in and saw Phillip lying on the hospital bed, his leg in a large cast and elevated. A doctor stood to the side of his bed, an iPad in his hand. He was an older gentleman and spoke with a heavy Spanish accent.

"Hello," he said. "You must be Mr. Coldstone. Officer Brown mentioned you might come by."

"I am," said James. "Any expenses he incurs are to be forwarded to me."

"I am Dr. Hernandez," the doctor said. "Officer Brown has listed you as his surrogate, though that shouldn't be necessary. The surgery went quite well, and we caught the internal bleeding in time."

"Surgery?"

"They broke my leg," Phillip said.

"It was a severe fracture," said Hernandez. "Officer Brown is lucky." He nodded to Phillip. "It'll take some rehab, but he will be up and mobile sooner than later. I will return with your test results and the transfer paperwork."

James waited until Hernandez left before he spoke again.

"Transfer?"

"I'm being pulled off the case," Phillip said. "At least physically. I can still do desk work, but that's about it."

James nodded, pursing his lips. "You're going back to Rock Hill, aren't you?"

"Yeah," Phillip said. "They ship me out tonight. Going back by ambulance instead of flying my happy ass by chopper." He grumbled. "Hate flyin'. Ugh."

"Clara Pickens is dead. Her body was in Cordelia's apartment."

"Damn. I'm sorry, James."

"It was Cordelia," James said. "I'm telling you: she's a succubus."

"Huh," Phillip said. "That's weird."

"Do tell."

He looked at him. "Outside of being drugged for the pain, I don't really feel any different. Cordelia kissed me on the cheek for walking her out to her car. That's why those shitheads jumped me."

"Don't you have to actually swap fluids when becoming the bitch of a succubus?"

Phillip shook his head. "Nope. Did a whole lot of research after what happened in Charleston. If they even touch your skin with it, you run a high risk. Especially if you've been spelled before. It doubles then."

"Meaning?"

"Meaning that if Rebecca had asked me to jerk off with eighty-grit sandpaper while smoking a cigarette near a leaky gas pump, I'd have done it twice with a grin on my face. Cordelia?" Phillip shrugged. "She's cute, but having five guys snap my femur like a twig and beat the shit out of me in a parking lot is kind of a turn-off." Phillip winced. "Shit hurts, James. And I'm flying like a fucking kite right now with the drugs they've got me on."

"In other news: guess who I saw step out of the elevator on my way up?"

"I'm dying to know. Really."

"The suit I saw in Charleston. The one who didn't smell like anything. Remember?"

Phillip shifted a little in his bed, glanced away for a second. "Really? That's also weird."

"Do you know him?"

Phillip shook his head. "Not at all. You're the first person in this room besides me who doesn't work here."

James sighed. "So, now what?"

Phillip pursed his lips and shook his head again. "It's over, James. Desk work? Please. They need a supernatural on the ground here, given what we've seen. You can't operate alone on this, not without law enforcement. Your cover is already blown in Rock Hill. They know what you are. There are reports all over the news about a giant dog loose in Charleston. You gotta hang it up, man." He sighed. "I'm sorry."

James shook his head and stood. "I can't do that."

Phillip shot him a look. "James, don't do this."

James ignored him as he headed for the door. "Call me when you get to Rock Hill. And make sure they give you your laptop while you're at Piedmont Medical."

"James," Phillip barked as James turned and headed for the door. "James, you dumbass! Get your Alpo-eatin' ass back here! *James!*"

James left as Phillip cursed and called his name again.

J ames spent the rest of the day sleeping. He knew trying to gather information on his own would be nigh impossible, especially with the sun out. Cordelia was likely at work, and he figured that approaching her would be disastrous. They needed to be sneaky about it. He remembered how strong Rebecca had been, and there was no way he'd be able to take on Cordelia without Lacy's help.

"Oh, you're so sweet to wait on me," Lacy said. She'd just gotten out from under her bed, her hair tousled, and her clothes wrinkled. "I mean, you could probably take the bitch during the daytime."

"Not without proof," James said. He told her about Phillip.

"Well, that sucks," Lacy said. "So, of course, you're dropping it."

James kept his tone just as sarcastic. "Completely. I'm already packed." He pulled his phone and looked at the time. "I think we should go back to Cordelia's apartment and make sure we covered every inch. The police have been through by now, so we shouldn't be pressed for time."

Lacy smiled. "Strange empty townhome where we found a body? Kinky. Let me freshen up."

I 'm pretty sure it wasn't on fire last time we were here," Lacy said as she and James watched the firefighters scrambling around the burning condo. Streams of water shot into the blaze from the two trucks. A group had already tapped into the fire hydrant nearby and soon had another stream going. Crowds of people gathered in the parking lot, the onlookers standing just far enough away to see what was going on without the risk of being part of the problem, though the heat was intense even at the distance where they stood.

James clenched his fist, his muscles tense as the wolf moved in his mind. He pushed it back. As much as he wanted to shift and smash things, he knew he'd have to keep his cool. Wolfing out during a major incident wouldn't be his smartest move.

Then again, he wasn't exactly known for making many smart moves.

"This just keeps getting weirder," Lacy said. "First, we find Clara's body in there, and she looked like she'd been drowned. Now the place is on fire?" She turned and looked up at James. "This isn't normal succubus behavior."

"It's the behavior of someone who has something she doesn't want people to see," James said as he turned away from the scene and started walking back towards Lacy's Mini Cooper. Lacy fell into step next to him. "I want to go to McFadden's. She'll probably be there."

"I don't know if that's a good idea, Jimmy," Lacy said. "You're kinda pissed."

James stopped and looked at her. "Yeah, that," she said, pointing up at him. "*That* face. I know that face by now, and that's your Pissed-Jimmy-face."

"So what," James said, trying not to blow up on her. "I don't get to be pissed off?"

"Nope," Lacy said. "You don't keep your shit together, sweetie. I can tell you're the type: cool and collected when you're low-key, absolutely psychotic when you're seein' red."

James started to speak, then stopped. The last time he'd been this enraged, he'd traveled from Rock Hill to Charleston chasing after a little girl he barely knew. Before that, he'd been in college. It was late, and he'd just finished a night of drinking with Phillip at someone's birthday party. He'd stepped into the hallway to find some guy slapping the shit out a woman who lived a few doors down. James hadn't gone wolf on the guy, but he'd lost his temper and sent the asshole off on a stretcher with four broken ribs, a dislocated arm, broken jaw, and cracked cheekbone.

"Your call," he said, fighting to keep his tone steady.

"We go try to track down your girlfriend," Lacy said. "You're right. McFadden's is likely where she is. But you go in *cool*." She stepped in, put her face close to his. "I hear you. I know you're angry. It's not going to help anyone if you screw this up. Especially not that little girl. I'm sorry about Clara, but there's still two more that need you."

James nodded. "Right," he said. "Right. Let's go."

The drive to the pub was uneventful. Lacy kept the radio low, the station playing all 1980s music as the Mini sped through the streets toward McFadden's. Lacy pulled into the parking lot, and James couldn't help but notice the spot where he'd seen the men beating Phillip the night before. He gritted his teeth, the image angering him again, then swallowed it back. If Cordelia was a supernatural, that meant she could make quick work of them if he wasn't careful. He didn't want anyone else to get hurt.

Except Cordelia. He planned to put her in a *world* of hurt.

They crossed the street and went in. It struck James that something was off the minute he noticed the place was virtually empty. A large, tired-looking man stood behind the bar cleaning, his hair a mess, and his thick beard frizzed as if he hadn't had time to groom that morning.

"What the hell?" Lacy murmured out of the side of her mouth. "Isn't this place usually busy?"

"Yes," James said. "Yes, it is. Come on." He led her up to the bar. "You open?"

The barkeep looked up at him. "You drinkin'?"

"Not until you serve me a beer."

The bartender nodded, grabbed a glass, and poured James a beer from the tap. He handed the porter to him, then poured another for Lacy. "I remember you from the other night," he said as he took the twenty James tossed on the bar. "Figured you probably like this stuff and got your girl on it, too."

James nodded and took a sip. "Indeed."

"Good stuff," Lacy said as she took a sip of hers. "Jimmy knows what he likes."

The bartender looked Lacy up and down. "No shit."

"Where is everyone?" James asked. "The past few times I've been in, it seems like you stay fairly busy."

The barkeep chuckled. "Yeah. Well, whenever Cordelia lays out, the regulars stay away. Like the place doesn't exist unless she's here." He shook his head. "Dunno what the deal is, but she works her ass off when she's here, and I make money. Guess that's what's important."

"Absolutely, it is," James said. "So, where is Cordelia tonight?"

"Said she had something important come up. Some gig that was going to pay like hell." The barkeep motioned at the door. "Guess more than she makes here in a night. Hell, I ain't mad at her. Shit, I'd do it too if I could sing like that."

Lacy nudged James. He looked at her as she motioned at the door. James recognized the man coming in immediately, beard, man-bun, and all. Dude-Bro looked around the place, then at the bartender. The bartender grunted.

"Nope. She's off."

Dude-bro turned on his heel and walked out.

"See? Just like that."

The wolf urged James, barked in his head. *Him! Follow!*

James shot to his feet as Lacy asked him what the hell was going on. He bolted through the door and saw Dude-Bro running through the parking lot. The guy got into a small Ford Ranger pickup, cranked the engine, and drove off.

"James," Lacy called as she passed by him. "C'mon!"

James followed her to the Mini. Lacy had the engine running and was pulling out of the parking spot before James had the passenger door closed. She whipped the car out into traffic, ignoring the blaring horns and torrents of profanity from the other drivers.

"Stay on him," James said. "Let's see where he goes."

Dude-Bro tore down the street in his little pickup truck, Lacy keeping pace behind him with ease. James kept his eyes on the Ranger's rear windshield, kept the wolf forward enough to yellow and enhance his vision. Dude-Bro wasn't even looking back at them, wasn't glancing in the rearview mirror. He was hyper-focused, plowing ahead as he turned off Atlantic Blvd. and headed down Sherry Ave. Lacy followed, and James noted the neighborhoods surrounding him.

"Where the hell is he going?" Lacy asked.

"The beach, I think," James said. He cracked the window open and sniffed the air, the wolf pulling in all the smells his human nose would never catch. "Actually, I've no doubt."

"Well shit," Lacy said. "I guess we're gonna take that walk on the beach after all." She laughed. "You know how to keep it romantic, Coldstone."

James's phone rang in his pocket. He pulled it out and answered without looking at the caller ID. "Hello, Phillip."

"Where are you?" Phillip asked over the handset, his tone a forced calm as if he were trying not to scream at a small child.

"I'm in Lacy's car going for a ride."

"A ride where?"

"The beach."

He heard Phillip curse on the other end. "Yeah, I just got a phone call that someone burned Cordelia's place to the ground. Same place you found Clara Pickens."

"Wasn't me, I can assure you," James said. "It very well could've been Cordelia herself. Or one of her boyfriends."

"That makes sense if she's trying to cover her tracks," Phillip said. "Also makes sense if she's about to bail-ass out of town."

The pickup took another turn. Lacy pulled the emergency brake and yanked the wheel, almost missing the turn as she drifted over the asphalt and took the corner. James held on to the "Jesus handle" with one hand and fought to not drop his phone out of the other as his weight slung toward Lacy. The sound of squealing rubber filled the air as Lacy regained control, released the e-brake, and slammed on the gas to try and catch up to her prey.

Phillip spoke again. "What the hell was that?"

"Birds."

"My ass."

"Only when you eat Mexican food."

"Are you chasing someone?"

"More like casually following. Wherever he goes. At high speed."

"Fuck *me*, James! What part of drop it did you miss?! It's over!" Phillip cursed again. "You don't have any law enforcement cover! You understand what that means? It means I can't *cover* your ass!"

"I have full confidence Bob Smith can receive all ass coverage remotely."

"Bob Smith can suck my ass! God *damn* it, James! Where are you?"

"We just turned down Beach Avenue," Lacy said. "We're heading North."

"I'll call you back," Phillip said. The phone beeped at James to indicate the ended call. James looked up just as the truck took a left onto 20th Avenue. Lacy followed, then followed around the right turn onto Seminole Road. The houses and mansions disappeared, replaced by trees and brush as the two vehicles sped down the road.

"Get us closer," James said as he unbuckled his seatbelt and began to remove his clothes. Lacy gunned the small engine, and the Mini Cooper ran up on the back of the truck. James slipped his shorts off, pulled his feet out of his sandals, and opened the passenger door slightly as the road turned into a long and empty parking lot. "Keep it steady."

"Are you about to do something stupid?" Lacy said.

"Of course."

James pushed the door open and darted out, shifting in an instant, hitting the ground in wolf form and rolling before coming up on all fours and leaping into the bed of the truck. The truck bed slammed down on top of the rear axle from James's weight, sparks flying from underneath. Both rear tires exploded, and the truck swerved as the driver shouted and fought to keep control. James held onto the cab and looked over his shoulder as Lacy slammed on the brakes and maneuvered the Mini Cooper to the side to avoid the parts flying out from underneath the truck. One of the wheels launched into the night, and the pickup dipped and swerved off the parking lot, sparks showering from underneath where the wheel hub scraped the asphalt. James leapt free as the vehicle did a nosedive into a ditch and rolled, sending sand and debris everywhere.

James landed solidly on the asphalt, staring at the twisted heap that used to be a pickup truck. The driver's side door moved slightly, and James watched as Dude-Bro kicked it open and fell out. He got up staggering, obviously in pain from the wreck. Blood poured from a cut on his forehead, and his eye was swelling where he'd probably hit his face on the steering wheel. He looked at the eight-foot-tall werewolf staring at him, then shook his head and started limping in the direction he'd been driving, ignoring the gigantic beast that looked like it might eat him. James cocked his head to the side and watched. *Determined little fucker, isn't he?*

The wolf inside grunted in agreement.

Lacy ran up to the guy as James moved in. She stepped in front of him, but he moved to the side and around her as he continued on.

"Hey, wait a second," she said to him. "Hey! Hey, asshole!"

"Can't stop," Dude-Bro muttered. "Gotta…get to her. Her song. Gotta hear her song."

James grabbed him and lifted him off his feet. He screamed hysterically, fought to get away, kicking and wriggling in the iron grasp.

"You're going to answer some questions, sweetie," Lacy said. "Then, you can go listen to Cordelia sing."

Dude-Bro calmed down a little, but James could still sense urgency and apprehension. Not at the possibility of being killed by a pissed werewolf. He craned his neck to keep his face in the direction he wanted to go as Lacy spoke.

"Where is Cordelia?"

"The sea," Dude-Bro said, his speech slurred. "The beach. I...I have to get to the beach."

"The beach?" Lacy said. "Don't know if you realize the sun isn't out. Not exactly an ideal time to work on the tan."

James jerked him in and growled in his face, pulling his lips back over his large canine teeth as he widened his yellowed eyes. That same facial expression had made grown men cake their pants in the past. Dude-Bro just looked over his shoulder dreamily, still trying to push free and keep moving toward his destination.

"Her song," Dude-Bro muttered. He strained, then threw his head back as if in sudden ecstasy. "Oh, God. It's...so beautiful."

James's ears perked. He heard something faint on the breeze, soft and melodic, a woman's voice. His human side longed for it, wanted more than anything to go to it. To her.

He shook his head as the wolf pushed forward, growling low at him.

Bad, it urged at him. *Danger.*

"James," Lacy said. "You okay? You swayed for a second there." She looked over her shoulder in the direction of the beach, then back up at him. "Don't you dare flake on me, Snoopy."

James grunted. Lacy patted Dude-Bro on the cheek. "Gonna try this one more time, sugar," she said. "Where is Cordelia? And *what* is she?"

Dude-Bro looked at her and gave a dreamy, sleepy smile. "She's everything."

James dropped him as the guy began to choke and writhe. He hit the ground as Lacy went to him, then stepped away. Water spurted from Dude-Bro's mouth, and he rolled over onto all fours and heaved, torrents of water pouring from his mouth. He heaved again, harder this time, a sickening gurgle coming from him as he tried to scream around the water sluicing from his mouth and nose. Lacy gave a shout as he heaved a third time. This time, a loud crack issued from his spine as his torso caved in. His legs and arms weakened. He fell onto his side and went still. His eyes remained wide open in terror, his jaw locked open as the flow of water slowed down.

"What...the...*fuck*," Lacy breathed. She stooped down and studied Dude-Bro's body as James crouched down and sniffed him. Saline. Seaweed. Fish.

James shifted to human form and stood.

"He drowned," he said. "Right in front of us."

"I don't know *what* the fuck does that, Jimmy," Lacy said as she stood.

She pulled her phone out of her pocket. "But I'm pretty sure the ancient tome of Internet Search Engines might have something." She began typing as James went through Dude-Bro's pockets. He found a water-logged cell phone, loose change, and a vape. James's anger rose. His luck had led him to another dead end. He stared at Dude-Bro's face again.

Clara Pickens had also looked like she'd drowned. James's stomach turned at the idea that she'd probably gone through exactly what he'd just witnessed with Dude-Bro. His heart sank. He remembered some of the witnesses Phillip had spoken to back in Rock Hill. She'd been well-liked, popular—all-around great kid.

"Damn," Lacy said, looking at her phone. "Jimmy, listen to this. 'Sea Sirens typically kill their victims by either luring them into dangerous rocks to cause a shipwreck or by drowning them.' It also says that she can drown anyone remotely once she has them under her spell."

"A sea siren?" James shook his head. "Why would a sea siren traffic girls?"

"Money," Lacy said, looking up from the phone screen. "Why would a notable vampire house use their influence to become a drug trafficking ring that makes the Mexican Cartels look like a Sunday-school book club? It says here that sirens desire treasure. They're like dragons, but way sexier. They hoarded treasure from the ships they wrecked and destroyed the men they stole it from."

"I remember sirens from school," James said. "The voyage of Odysseus. He tied himself to the mast so he could listen to their song." He blinked. "Cordelia's singing. It makes sense."

"It's how she spells men," Lacy said. "She can have them do what she wants, then she kills them off to scatter the attention away from the missing girls. I'll bet we got here to Jacksonville before any kidnapping cases could really start up."

James looked at the body on the ground, water still leaking from Dude-Bro's mouth, nose, and other orifices. He heard waves crashing in the distance, the sounds of seagulls squawking. Dude-Bro was hauling ass for the beach. He'd had his truck crashed, barely survived the ordeal, and still tried to get to his destination. Even when James was holding him, he was trying to free himself to go—

"Shit," James said. He shifted and took off through the parking lot. Lacy followed close as he rounded the corner and tore down 35th Street, trees blurring by as asphalt turned into boardwalk. He stopped at the end of the pier and looked out over the ocean. Lacy zipped up beside him.

"What is it, Jimmy?"

James huffed. Nothing. He growled and turned to the right, then stopped when something caught his eye down on the beach. He barked, then ran back down the boardwalk until he was over sand before jumping off. He hit the ground at a run, dashed a good hundred yards before stopping at the foot of the rolling surf as water ran up the beach, then retreated for another round of white tops and large waves. He saw shapes in the murky water, his yellowed vision making the darkness a moot point. He could see clearly as if he were in human form wearing night-vision goggles. He could see...ten? Twelve. No, twenty. It had to be twenty. More? He counted in his head.

Forty. Forty men, all the ones from McFadden's and more that James had never seen before. Their limp bodies floated in the water, caught up into the roiling waves, and crashed to the sand as the water washed them ashore before dragging them slowly back out to sea. A few stayed beached on the sand, the surf unable to bring them back. Their skin looked clammy, pale, and lifeless from drowning in saltwater.

James stood on the beach, staring out at his first sea of the dead. He looked around and saw more bodies littering the sand, some not entirely soaked but obviously victims of the same fate as Dude-Bro and Clara Pickens.

He heard Lacy breathe, "What the fuck," as she touched his arm. James's phone rang in her pocket. She answered it and put Phillip on speaker.

"James?"

"He's in doggy mode, Phil," Lacy said. "He's right here. What's up?"

"Well, there have been lots of reports of two vehicles racing around Seminole and Atlantic Beach parkway. But I'm sure you two don't know anything about that."

"Oops."

"The police are on their way," Phillip said. "They'll be there in about thirty minutes. It's a small complaint right now, so it's not like they have the military coming or anything. Still, they might have a problem seeing a chick with red eyes and a big idiot in a fur suit running around like assholes who don't know how to keep their heads down. You two find anything?"

Lacy looked up, and James followed her gaze to the water, where more bodies were washing up to shore. James grunted.

"I know that grunt," Phillip said. "I don't like that grunt. Why is he grunting?"

"I'll send you a pic," Lacy said.

James saw the water start to swirl, the motion wholly unnatural. He heard Lacy talk to Phillip.

"Um...we'll call you back." Phillip started cursing when she ended the call. "Oh my God, James."

The water rose, corpses raining down onto the ground as it parted to the sides. It looked a lot like what James had seen in movies when Moses parted the Red Sea. A cloaked figure stood in between the water walls, its head down as it walked out of the pathway. The water came back together and crashed down, but the waves seemed to avoid splashing into the figure as it strolled toward the beach, the waves having no effect on its gait as it made its way onto dry land. The cloak moved slowly in the breeze. No.

Wings. It had wings.

Cordelia smiled as she spread her wings. Her nude body was human, but her legs were covered in fish scales. She grinned as she looked at James and Lacy and spoke.

"Welcome to the party."

11

The black seawater swirled and sidled away from Cordelia's footfalls as she approached, her bird feet consisting of three long toes, each ending in a vicious-looking talon. She grinned at James, her eyes flashing silver as she spread her arms wide.

"Like what you see, handsome?"

"I thought sea sirens were just naked mermaids sitting on rocks," Lacy said. "You look more like Big Bird's trashy side-piece."

"Our mother, Demeter, blessed us with the gift of flight when our Lady Persephone was abducted by the dark bastard Hades," Cordelia said. "Catch up on your Greek mythology, vampire."

Lacy's fangs snapped into place, her eyes flashing red as she hissed at Cordelia. James growled low, his teeth gnashing as the wolf urged him to charge her, tear her to pieces.

Cordelia leveled her bright diamond eyes at James, her mouth open as the most beautiful sound he'd ever heard began to flow in the air around him. His heart fluttered; his body grew heavy and stupid as he listened to the intoxicating music, the soft tones moving in and out of his hearing like the surf. He needed the sound to be clearer, needed it closer to him. The water. It was like the water. Peaceful in its chaos, longing for him to lose himself in blackness. Her blackness. Her embrace. He could hear Lacy saying something to him, but the song drowned her voice out. It was irrelevant. Only the song mattered. Only Cordelia mattered. He had to possess her, take her, make her his own.

Cordelia's voice whispered in his ear, the musical sound sending his hackles up. "Kill the vampire."

The wolf charged forward in his mind, the force dizzying and violent. James staggered, held his pounding head as the wolf broke through, shoved him back into the recesses of his consciousness.

The Lacy Blood-thing looked at him. Blinked. It mouthed words. Wolf couldn't hear, couldn't understand. It spoke again. He barked, sent the James even further back.

"Jimmy," the Lacy shouted.

Wolf rounded on the Cordelia Bird-female. Its eyes widened, the song gone. Wolf snarled at the Cordelia, gnashed its teeth. The James called inside. *Thanks. Now, I believe it's time to kick her ass. Let me forward.*

Wolf let the James forward but only stepped back enough to let the James in, give it control over the meat.

James shook his head, felt the wolf still with him, at the edge of control. His body was tense, hard with feral rage as he barked at Cordelia.

"Well, that was unexpected," Cordelia said. "I guess weres just aren't mortal enough for me."

"Bitch, the only reason we aren't tearing you apart right now is because we need information," Lacy said. "Who are you, and what the fuck are you doing here? Besides making a shitload of money."

"Money," Cordelia spat. "I am a siren. Money is of no importance to me. Mortal flesh is my only desire. In that, Wangenheim pays me well."

"Wangenheim?" Lacy said. She looked up at James. "That one sounds familiar."

"He is only a name," Cordelia said. "He requires female children; I require male flesh." Cordelia sauntered up to one of the bodies on the beach. She jabbed a hand into the dead man's torso, ripped out his heart, and began to eat it like an apple. Blood poured down her chin and chest, small rivers running between her breasts and over her belly as she chewed. "It is an arrangement that dates back centuries."

"Seems like production is up," Lacy said, motioning around to the bodies as if she watched demonic bird-women eat human hearts every Tuesday.

James shifted to human form but kept the wolf close enough in his mind to change back if Cordelia started to sing again.

"Where is Mindy Robertson?" he said, his fists clenched. "And why did you kill Clara Pickens?"

"Because I was ordered to," Cordelia said, her tone casual.

"Where are the girls now?"

"Not here," Cordelia said. "Not where you will find them." Her mouth broadened into a blood-soaked grin. "Besides, haven't you caused enough death, James Coldstone?"

"I'm fairly sure you're the one who killed all these men, and Clara Pickens, and Dude-Bro back in the parking lot. But do tell."

"Have you not noticed that there are virtually no reports of missing girls in Jacksonville? No murders. Only the occasional suicide by drowning." Cordelia stepped closer. "I've had to cover tracks. Clean house. The succubus in Charleston, Rebecca, sent a warning to me when she figured out who you were. I'd heard that a werewolf chased our group out of Rock Hill, followed them to Charleston. All of these men were in love with me. A mere song and they would give me anything. Even their daughters." Cordelia looked him up and down. "You're not to be underestimated, James Coldstone. A shapeshifter couldn't stop you. A demon couldn't stop you." She spread her wings, held her arms out, claws ripping out of the ends of her fingers like blades. "Let's see how you fare against the dead."

James caught movement out of the corner of his eye. He looked to the side as the corpse Cordelia had eaten the heart from began to sit up. Its dead eyes locked on James, and a soft, low moan escaped from its mouth.

"Um, Jimmy," Lacy said behind him. "Think I saw this in a movie once, and it didn't end well for the couple on the beach."

The crowd of dead men rose, all of them turning their glazed, white, dead sight to James and Lacy. James shifted to wolf form as they staggered toward him.

"My sister forgave the Ancient Mariner when he shot her down from her flight ages ago," Cordelia said. "Her dead aided his return to the land of the living. I'm not all that forgiving."

James felt a cold hand on his arm. He lashed out, and a walking corpse went flying, its head sailing the opposite direction. He barked, hunkered down, and pounced at a group as they made for him, all of them moaning in a chorus of exhaling dead groans and grunts. He heard Lacy shout, spun, saw her pick up an attacker, and use him to bludgeon another.

"Zombies, Jimmy," Lacy said. She looked at Cordelia. "Zombies? Really, bitch? That's what you've got?" She plowed through a group of zombies, her fingernails elongated, her fangs out, her eyes glowing as she charged at the sea siren. Cordelia dodged the attack and caught Lacy by the neck. She lifted her up off her feet, and James saw the water flow up around Cordelia's legs, foaming and swirling.

"The abomination is mine," she said as Lacy fought against the grip around her throat. Cordelia glanced around at the walking dead as they encircled James. "Eat him."

The zombies swarmed James, their hands clawing at his thick fur, their teeth gnashing, trying to bite at him. He swiped left and right, bowling through them as he tried to reach Cordelia and Lacy. He tore the head off of one, picked up the headless body, and hurled it at the others. The group went flying back as more came at him. James slashed open the nearest one, picked him up by the head, and smashed his skull into pulp on the beach. He saw Lacy and Cordelia for a brief second. Lacy kicked and fought as Cordelia laughed. "Let's see how that saltwater works on you, vampire."

James crouched down as the herd of dead piled on top of him. He tensed, then sprang upward, sending zombies airborne. Bodies rained down as James hit the retreating tide and charged Cordelia. Cordelia threw Lacy to the side and braced for impact as James closed in. He collided with her. It felt like hitting a brick wall as Cordelia took the insane blow and pushed back at him. Her feet dug trenches in the wet sand as the tide began to move back out. Cordelia flapped her wings in his face, the sudden slap of feathers catching James off-guard. He blinked, and she shoulder-checked him and sent him onto his back. She leapt on top of him, straddled him, held him down as if he weighed nothing. Blood and sand caked her nude front as she leaned down, her face close to his as she pressed her not inconsiderable breasts against his chest.

"I like to be on top," she said as she held her hand high. Her talons grew longer from her fingertips, sharp and hateful. "Does doggy want a belly-rub?"

Her weight was lifted in an instant when Lacy plowed into her like a runaway dump truck. She stood over James in a fighting stance as Cordelia used her wings to catch herself midair and hover instead of hitting the ground.

"Back off my dog, bitch," Lacy said. "He doesn't like other people." She stepped back as James got up, stood to his full eight feet, and growled at Cordelia. "I'm looking for my niece, and he's looking for a little girl."

"Little girl?" Cordelia shook her head. "Narrow it down."

"Yellow dress," said Lacy. "My niece would be in all black. Creepy kid. Likes gothy shit. Spill."

"Ah, the witch," Cordelia said. "She was taken by Wangenheim onto his personal vessel. As for the other..." She let the sentence hang for a moment before grinning ear-to-ear. "I can assure you that I don't have her, and she isn't safe. But I've been promised her as payment once Wangenheim is done with her." Cordelia closed her eyes and sighed as she looked up at the bright moon and spoke. "I've not had child meat in ages."

James's yellow vision intensified as his blood boiled over. The wolf inside flashed its eyes at him, the two coals covered in flames as James launched himself at Cordelia with a vicious snarl. She was ready this time. As James crashed into her, she wrapped her arms and legs around him and flapped her wings to send him off balance. He rolled as she tried to straddle him again, claws and wings beating James as he made to clamp his jaws onto her throat. She dodged the bite and raked the talons on her feet down his thigh. He yelped, the pain white-hot as she kicked him off and slashed four bloody trenches into his chest. He rolled over and stood, his fur soaked from blood pouring from his wounds. His right leg trembled under his weight, every movement sending waves of agony throughout his body.

He barely got a chance to breathe before Cordelia was on him again. Lacy tackled her to the ground, and James got back up and moved toward the two women. Lacy buried her fangs into Cordelia's neck, and Cordelia yowled as she bucked and beat at Lacy with clawed hands and wings. James was limping, his right leg dragging behind him as he tried to reach them.

Cordelia smashed her fist into the side of Lacy's head, the move sending Lacy off of her with a large hunk of meat still in her jaws. Cordelia gagged and covered the gaping wound in her neck with her hand as blood poured between her fingers.

James reached the siren as she tried to get up. He hefted his bad leg onto her chest, pinning her down as the gashes in his thigh slowly began to heal. She coughed, spraying him with small particles of blood that smoked as it burned his fur. He ignored the stench, the pain nothing compared to his fury as he growled at her. Lacy stepped up to them, spat the meat from Cordelia's neck out onto the beach, and squatted down next to her.

"Last chance, asshole," she said. "Where are they?"

Cordelia grinned, her voice broken and cracked as she spoke. "You... won't...find them." She looked at James. "We...win."

James reared back and drove his palm into Cordelia's face, her head caving in like a rotten pumpkin as blood and brains spurted in every direction. He stood as her body rapidly decayed, the flesh going putrid as it fell away from bone and liquified. The tide rolled in as Cordelia melted away until James could no longer see anything but sea foam.

"At least we stopped her," Lacy said as she stepped away from the encroaching water.

James looked around at the scattered bodies on the beach. He hadn't realized that he'd either killed or maimed all of Cordelia's zombies, but the proof was littered all over the area. Bodies and pieces of bodies lay scattered in the sand. They'd stopped moving, the spell apparently broken by Cordelia's death.

Men. James had killed men. Had he not blown his cover on such a grand scale, they might even still be alive. Their blood was on his hands.

"Stop that," Lacy said. "Haven't known you long, Jimmy, but I know that look."

James looked down at his body. The wounds had healed enough. He shifted form, the scrapes and scratches from Cordelia still red and bleeding on his now human skin.

"We've got nothing," James said. He looked down at her. "I killed all these men, killed the thing that did this to them, and we're still nowhere near finding Mindy."

"Or Marianne," Lacy said. "We can't give up, James. We're too close."

James looked around at the carnage again. He heard Lacy's phone buzz in her pocket. She looked at it. James could hear the telltale sounds of sirens in the distance.

"It's Phillip," Lacy said. "We'd better get the fuck out of here. They're even sending in the Coast Guard. Guess we weren't as quiet as we should've been down here."

James shifted without a word and took off into the night, not looking back to see if Lacy was following. He didn't care. Cordelia should've been it. She should've had all the information he needed to find Mindy, find Marianne. Clara Pickens was dead because of him. All of the men on the beach were dead because of him.

Mindy's death would be on him, too.

The wolf stayed silent inside as James's human thoughts plagued his mind, the houses blurring by as he kept up his wolfen speed. Part of him, a loud part of him, wanted to give up. It told him that Mindy's chances were better without him causing chaos all over the Southeast. It told him that she had a better chance if she happened to be with Marianne. It told him if she died, it was better than being…

The last one hurt him to his core. He hated himself more for even thinking it.

1 2

James sat in the kitchen, staring off into the dark, his bags packed and stacked in the corner. It was early in the morning, only a few hours or so before the sun would rise. He ignored the clock on the countertop microwave, not caring that it flashed the time at him as a hateful reminder that sleep was far out of reach.

"Three in the morning?" Lacy said as she wandered in. "The mockery of the Holy Trinity." She looked at him and made a gesture with her hands. "Demons and shit. Spooky."

James ignored her, kept staring out the window over the black water outside. Lacy sat down across the table from him. She'd showered and cleaned up as soon as they'd gotten in. James's injuries were almost healed. His scars would likely be gone with his next change.

"Jimmy, go to bed," Lacy said. "You're tired. No offense, but you look like hell."

"Can't sleep," James said. He took a sip of his tea and made a face. It'd gone cold. How long had he been sitting there? He looked back out the window. "Too much on my mind."

Lacy glanced over her shoulder at his bags. "Packed up? Where're we going next?"

"*We* aren't going anywhere," he said. "I'm going back to Rock Hill."

"You're giving up? Are you shitting me?"

"No, but I can't do anything else here." James sighed. "It's a complete dead end. Maybe going back and starting over will get me somewhere. It's got to be better than running all over the east coast, causing destruction wherever I go."

Lacy moved closer to him, sat in his line of sight. "That still sounds like giving up, Jimmy."

"I like to think of it as a strategic retreat."

The wolf growled at him from inside. It turned its back to him and scraped with its hind legs as if kicking dirt at him.

"Well, reality says it's giving up," Lacy said. "Not gonna let you do that. Besides, Phillip will slap the shit out of you if you go back empty-handed."

"I got all of those men killed," James argued. "Clara Pickens's death is my fault."

"Last I checked, you don't have boobs and can't sing worth a shit." Lacy crossed her arms in front of her. "Cordelia did all of that. And I'm thinking money wasn't her only reason. She enjoyed killing those men. I think she would've done it even if there wasn't money involved."

James shook his head. "I'm tired," he said as he rubbed his face. "I don't know if I can keep doing this."

He felt Lacy's hands on his wrists as she gently pulled his hands away from his face. She leaned in, her face close to his as she spoke. "We," she said. "You don't know if *we* can keep doing this. I'm with you on this because I want my niece back, and I need your help." She reached up and touched his cheek. "And you need mine."

"I don't need help," James said, his body urging him, longing for her to come even closer to him.

Lacy nodded. "Yes, you do," she whispered, moving from her chair and sitting beside him, her mouth inches from his. "Tell me you want my help."

"I…want…" James tried, his breath taken away, his heart pounding in his chest as he put his arms around her to pull her to him.

His phone rang, the theme from *Police Academy* shattering the silence in the room. Lacy sighed and stood away from James as he flipped it over on the table. Lacy picked it up and answered it, putting it on speaker. She crossed her arms again as she spoke, a tinge of irritation in her voice. "Isn't it lights out at the psycho ward, Cadet Cock-Block?"

"That's *Detective* Cock-Block," Phillip said over the phone. "Anyone want to tell me why the local authorities found something like forty dead guys strewn all over the beach?"

"They were dead when we got there," James said. "Cordelia drowned all of them, then had them come back as her own personal army."

"Jesus," Phillip said. "I wonder how long she's been getting away with that shit."

"She referenced *The Rime of the Ancient Mariner* if that is any indication."

"Well, it gets better. They were able to get an ID on every one of those guys. And here's something else that's loads of fun—they all had daughters. Emphasis on *had.* Looks like a slew of missing girls are being reported as we speak. Some of them have been gone a while, but no report."

"She was keeping them from reporting it," Lacy said. "They were all completely under her control. She mentioned a name, though. Wangenheim."

"Neat cars, but I like my Honda."

"It's obviously a German name," James said, ignoring Phillip's joke.

"Probably another vampire house," Lacy said. "I'll ask Montoya tomorrow night. I'm scheduled for another meeting about House Diabolito. Maybe he knows something."

"Just let me know what you find," Phillip said. "I'll keep bugging people around here."

"How's the leg?" James asked.

"Fuckin' sucks," Phillip said. "I'm looking at weeks of physical therapy just so I can walk again. I'm working remotely right now, but it's all email and paperwork."

"I'm sorry," James said. "I didn't mean for you to get hurt."

"It's not your fault," Phillip said. "You weren't one of the five assholes kicking the shit out of me in the parking lot. Besides, I'm still sexy. Let me know what Montoya says. Nurse Nasty just showed back up with my drugs, and I need some sleep."

Another voice, a woman who sounded like she might be able to take Phillip over her knee, said, "What the *hell* you jus' call me?!" before the call ended.

"He doesn't know how to play nice, does he?" Lacy said.

James shrugged. "Probably got into it with the nurse once already. He's stubborn."

Lacy chuckled, and James caught himself staring into her eyes. The laugh faded as she stared back. He held her gaze, unable to move for fear that he would lose the fight and reach for her, grab her, pull her to him.

"Yeah," Lacy said. "I...um, I need to go feed. Been a few days. Don't want to fall behind."

"Right," James said. "I'll be here. Probably gonna grab a shower and lay down."

Lacy nodded and was out the back door in a flash, leaving James feeling empty and alone.

I t was around nine at night when James and Lacy showed up at the Plantation Beach House. The vampire party was in full swing, and James got a few disdainful looks as he and Lacy followed their escort to the back parlor, where Montoya waited for them.

The vampire master bristled at the sight of James. "I thought you were rid of the *perro*."

"He almost died defending me," Lacy said. "We killed a siren last night. Were it not for James, I would've been cast out to sea. We both know what saltwater does to vampires." She motioned at his leg. "He was injured and still went after her to keep me alive."

Montoya looked at James. "For this, I suppose we must accept you for your loyalty to *Señorita* Faulkner." He gave James a curt bow, then reached up and patted him on the head. "*Buen chico.*"

"She was working with the group we're after," Lacy said. "She gave us the name 'Wangenheim.' Ever heard it?"

Montoya turned whiter than usual, his eyes widening as he spun away. James studied him carefully, noticed how visibly shaken the man had become at the mention of the name.

"I'm going to fathom a guess that you've heard the name," he said.

Montoya turned and looked at both of them. "You must both leave immediately. And never return."

Lacy cocked her head to the side. "That's a little out of nowhere," she said. "I thought you were all-in for having me on board with Diabolito."

"Do not mistake my intentions, *Señorita*," Montoya said. "I do not mean or desire to be impolite. But the safety of my house falls on my shoulders. If that means that I must sever our relationship, then that is what must be."

"Why are you so concerned about Wangenheim?" James asked.

Montoya glared at James. "I will kindly ask you to refrain from using that name in this house, *perro*. It will be the only time I am kind."

"Fine. Why are you so concerned with He-Who-Shall-Not-Be-Named?"

Lacy snickered and gave James a light jab with her elbow. "Good one."

Montoya stepped forward, looking James in the eye as he spoke, his tone low and warning. "I will only tell you this once, *perro*. Then you and *Señorita* Faulkner will leave this place immediately." He kept his gaze steely. "Go back to wherever you came from and forget everything you have seen. Everything you know. Whoever the girl you are after is, you must assume she has met her end. In fact, *pray* for it."

"How do you know I'm after a girl?" James asked.

"Because there is only one house that controls Westenra. I do not trifle in their affairs. Take her for dead. It will be the only way she will have peace." He looked at Lacy. "For the sake of your sanity, I beg you. Do not pursue this any further. Now go, and forget we ever met."

J ames sat on the pier behind the cottage and stared out at the ocean. The breeze was nice, cool and gentle on his human skin. The wolf paced in his mind. It wanted to go hunting.

And what do we hunt around here? James thought. *Lots of fish, I'm sure. Not as confident we'll find any deer.*

The wolf sent a mental image of a house cat into his mind. James rolled his eyes.

Funny. And a little light on the meat.

He didn't startle when Lacy sat down next to him, though his heart did pound a little as his stomach knotted. He tried to shake it off. He wasn't used to a woman having that kind of effect on him. At the same time, he didn't mind it.

"I'm sorry, Jimmy," she said. "I didn't think Montoya would turn jackass on us."

"He's scared," James said. "I have to wonder what would scare a vampire into walking away from something."

Lacy shrugged. "Has to be bad." She got a thoughtful expression on her face. "Then again, most children's programming could also do it. Fucking nightmare fuel."

James nodded. She wasn't wrong.

"So what next, Jimmy?" Lacy asked.

"Montoya said something about a place called Westenra." James looked at her. "I ran a search earlier and got nowhere other than Dracula references."

"It sounds familiar," Lacy said. "I remember hearing about it a long time ago when I first heard the legend of Count Dracula."

"I don't understand how the name Westenra comes into play with Wangenheim."

Lacy shrugged. "Me, either. And nothing came up on any maps, either. No islands by that name. I dunno what Monty was talking about, and going back to the Plantation Beach House would *not* be a good idea."

James's phone chimed. He pulled it out and looked at the text message from Phillip: a link to the story about the carnage found in the aftermath of the fight with Cordelia. He opened it, scanning through it.

"I thought you'd already seen that," Lacy said.

"I have," James replied. "But Phillip wouldn't have sent it if there wasn't something else." He kept scrolling until something caught his eye. "A yacht went missing last night while we were otherwise engaged."

"I'd say that's common, but a damn yacht?" Lacy looked at him. "That's a set of brass ones on whoever got the wild hair to steal something that large."

James looked up and out over the surf as something thrummed in the distance. He heard water churning, a large engine in high gear. He stood, trying to make out something in the distance, the pitch-black only staved off by the lights along the coast. He saw something large and bulky. It shifted in the distance, grew larger.

Closer.

He reacted in a split second, entered the change, and grabbed Lacy by the arm. She moved with him, and they bolted toward the cottage as the large boat crashed into the edge of the pier, the extended structure splintering away as the craft came at them at full speed. The bow caved in the back wall of the house, and the power panel on the side of the cottage exploded as it dislodged and shorted out. Rock, water, and debris rained down around James and Lacy as they darted into the street to avoid the wreckage. The yacht listed to the side and stopped sliding as the loud engine gurgled and chugged, eventually dying out.

Lacy looked up at James. "Order a new boat?"

James grunted and made his way toward what was left of the Airbnb and the shipwreck. He stopped and looked up at the craft, allowed the wolf forward to enhance his vision. The windows were dark, but James could see blood caked in swaths across the glass. He leapt up at the yacht, grabbed the railing, and hoisted himself over it. Lacy was close behind him.

Holes perforated, and chairs and tables lay strewn about, obviously broken before the yacht crashed. James moved carefully, the ship leaning far to the left, as he made his way toward the interior. Lacy opened the door ahead of him, and the smell of blood and meat filled the air instantly, along with the stench of bile and shit. He saw a body slumped by the door, the victim's face frozen in agony and fear, his stomach torn open and his intestines strewn about like spaghetti.

"Well, that's kinda gross," Lacy said. "Looks like younglings. Look at the bite marks on his neck."

James sniffed the air again and growled. He smelled rot, but it was faint. The attack had to have only happened a short time ago. He hit all fours and followed the smell deeper inside. Bodies lay strewn all over—some women in bathing suits; others men in beachwear. A beer keg had been slashed open, and food littered the floor along with body parts and bits of gore.

"Looks like someone crashed the party," Lacy said, moving ahead and nudging the empty keg with her foot. "Bad shit, Jimmy. Humans don't just take a machete and slice open a beer keg. This was definitely younglings."

It was different. James could smell it. Younglings? Lacy probably wasn't wrong since she had decades on him when it came to experience. Something else. Older. The rotting smell was deeper. What else?

James hit the deck and sniffed around the cabin floor, took in everything. Perfume. Cologne. Burgers. Beer. Condoms. Vomit. Blood. Shit.

Strawberries.

He froze, staring at a closed door ahead of him. He growled low as Lacy moved up next to him.

"Guess you found which well Timmy's in?" she said, her tone humorless. She reached ahead and tried the doorknob. "Locked. That's annoying."

James lashed out, the door crumpling under the blow. He stood, keeping his head low since the ceiling was a foot too low for him to stand upright. He moved through the doorway and looked around the cabin. The bed was a mess, and everything that may have been on a shelf or hung up was scattered around. The port window was shattered, likely from the crash.

Strawberries. It was more potent in here. James sniffed around, the scent becoming even stronger as he neared the bed. He nudged the bedclothes with his nose, blinking at the sharp tang of blood mixing with the sweet berries. The wolf flashed a vision in his mind.

Mindy laughed as she swung, looked at James in his mind's eye as she pushed off again to go higher. Her yellow sundress waved in the breeze, the sunlight making it look like it was glowing as her childlike laughter echoed around in his mind. He saw her move in front of him to protect him from the SWAT team as they took aim. He saw the large wolf grab her and dart into the woods. Not to steal her away. To protect her in case a gun went off. He remembered licking her face, remembered her giggling as he locked her scent into his memory.

Strawberries.

Hell to pay.

James pulled the rag from underneath the pillow. It was torn, stained with blood. He saw the pattern, knew it. White dots forming flowers. Red splotches on yellow cotton. Lacy spoke, her voice soft, her tone gentle.

"Oh God, James. I'm...I'm so sorry." She covered her mouth with her hand and closed her eyes, a tear streaming down her cheek.

James clenched the dress in his fist, dropped to his knees.

Why isn't her dress on her body? He couldn't breathe, his chest tight. *Why isn't her dress on her body?!*

Rage forced his lungs to function, taking in breaths faster and faster as tears stung his eyes. His teeth gnashed together, his mind spinning. Fire rolled in his gut, moved up through his chest, his jaw opening as he snarled. Lacy backed away, her eyes wide with fear and pity as James threw his head back and released the howl. Lacy clamped her hands over her ears as she fell backward. She screamed at him, but he barely heard her over the sound of his sorrowful cry.

Not sorrowful. No. It was his battle cry.

The side of the boat exploded outward as James burst through and landed on the road. He charged into the night, the dress in his mouth as he moved at wolfen speed, tried to read signs as he went.

He would run all night if he had to. Westenra. Wangenheim was there. That was what Montoya had said. The wolf licked its chops in his mind, urged hunger and bloodlust at him.

Something crashed into James and sent him flying. He smacked into a parked car in front of a house, the sedan caving in around him, metal bending and glass raining down around him. James got to his feet and shook it off as Lacy ran to him from the street.

"Jimmy," she said as she approached. "Get it together!" She snapped her fingers in his face as he looked toward the direction he'd been going, and made to move again. "*Hey!* James!" She grabbed him, shook him, put her face in his. "Look at me!"

James stopped, her grip on him powerful.

"I get it," she shouted in his face. "Believe me, I get it. But you don't even know where the fuck you're going." James made to move again, but Lacy stopped him. "*Listen to me!* James, *stop!*"

James shifted to human form, pulled Mindy's dress out of his mouth, and glared at her. "Lacy, get out of my way."

"Let me help you," she said, going right back at him. "God damn, James. You don't even know *how* to get to Westenra. You'll just wear yourself out. Your sense of direction is shit. The last thing she needs is an angry, strung out, ineffectual werewolf pissing in the wrong corn flakes." She rubbed her face and ran her hands through her hair. "God, now *I* sound like Phillip."

"I'd listen to your girlfriend, Mr. Coldstone."

James looked up as Lacy wheeled around, her fangs and claws out instantly. The man in the suit stood a few yards away, his hands casually in his pockets, his mouth drawn up in a smirk. James tensed, made to rush him, but the man held his hand up. "I wouldn't."

"Who the fuck are you?" Lacy said. "Besides a potential snack?"

"My name is Agent Smith."

"I saw you in Charleston," James said. "What the hell are you doing here?"

"Watching you," Smith said. "You and I have a common interest."

James motioned over his shoulder at the wrecked yacht. "Did you do this?"

"I had to get your attention. You're a difficult man to refocus."

"So you threw a fucking boat at us?" Lacy said.

Smith nodded. "Sometimes, you have to do a little more than just tap someone on the shoulder."

"You have approximately thirty seconds to explain yourself," James said. "Then, I take you apart."

"There isn't time," Smith said. He pulled a manila envelope out of his suit jacket and held it out. "This is your next step. Think of it as your assignment."

"You're a spook?" Lacy said.

Smith's smirk grew into a grin. "You have no idea."

James moved past Lacy and took the envelope from Smith. He looked down at it and saw a name printed neatly across the top.

James Coldstone Assignment: Westenra Island. Numbers were written next to the label.

He looked up and started to speak, then closed his mouth when he saw the empty spot where Smith once stood.

"Wow," Lacy said. "Where did he go?"

"I don't know," James said. "He doesn't give off a scent." He looked at the envelope again. "But I'm fairly certain these are coordinates."

"I think Agent Cliché just helped us out."

James nodded. "Now we know where to go."

IV

WOLFHEART

1

A vacation on a remote island resort?" Lacy said as she stepped up beside James. "Yes, please."

"Phillip said the island wasn't on any map," James said. "I'm still trying to figure out how we managed to find a direct ferry there."

"It's a privately-owned island, Jimmy," Lacy said. "And it's man-made. They probably haven't updated the maps to show every single man-made island out there. Likely whoever owns the island owns the ferry, too. It's not unusual." She nodded to a group of people on the far side of the deck as they laughed loudly. "These people all paid through the nose to get here. They either know somebody or *are* somebody."

James Coldstone glanced sidelong at her. "We snuck aboard," he said. "Standing out here on the deck probably isn't the best idea." They'd managed to blend into the crowd boarding the ferry on the mainland, bypassing the boarding pass checkpoint after Lacy suggested that the two men working the checkpoint go take a break and sunbathe on the snack bar patio at port. James hadn't been worried about being able to afford it. The cost wouldn't have made a dent in his account any more than tossing a dollar or two into a vending machine. But payment had been via card only, and it was funny how quickly one could be traced by the places where they ran their Visa.

"If they thought someone was stowed away, they'd be searching the cargo holds and any other hidey-holes they could find." Lacy smiled.

"Relax. The best place we could hide is in plain sight. They won't think we're that stupid."

James laughed, and Lacy joined him, the sound musical in his ears. He caught a glimpse of her ice-blue eyes, their hue made brighter by her long dark brown hair moving in the breeze.

He turned away quickly. He had to focus. Mindy was out there. The memory flashed in his mind again: Mindy on her swing, laughing. Mindy standing in front of him as the Rock Hill SWAT team took aim at what they thought was a giant dog determined to eat the little girl.

Her pretty yellow sundress tattered and bloodstained as he'd clutched it in his hand back in Jacksonville.

It wasn't a rescue anymore. It was revenge.

James's phone rang, the sound of the *Police Academy* theme song loud in the night air. He answered the phone as some of the guests stared at him like he'd lost his mind.

"Hello, Phillip."

"I'm pretty sure I know where you are," Phillip said. "Give me a sec. Yup. I know exactly where you are."

"Are you tracking me?"

"All phones have a GPS, dumbass. I'm a cop. I have access to these things."

"Stalker."

"Someone has to keep you on a leash," Phillip said. "I'm calling because I've still got fuck-all on Westenra Island."

James rolled his eyes. "How enlightening. I'm glad you shared this wealth of knowledge with me."

"Yeah, love you too, dickhead."

James heard Phillip type something, then heard him grunt. "How's the leg?" James asked.

Phillip was back in Rock Hill and on bedrest, though he could still work remotely from his room at Piedmont Medical. They'd set him up at the Women's Tower due to the severity of his injury and the anonymous phone call from James's phone insisting that Phillip be placed in the much nicer and larger room rather than the small rooms in the main hospital unless there was a need more urgent than Phillip's. The surgery had been successful, and Phillip now had a steel rod in his leg and was undergoing physical therapy and recovery. James missed having him along, but he wasn't going to complain about Phillip being willing to call and help over the phone. Better than nothing.

"A bunch of guys met me out in a parking lot and broke my leg, I can't go home because I can't walk around on my own yet, and I was up all night because a woman went into full labor next door and my guess is they couldn't get her the epidural in time. Or she wanted a natural birth. Other than that, I'm peachy." More typing, then Phillip cleared his throat. "Okay, found something. Westenra Island *is* a private man-made island. You know that already. Here's what's weird: nothing."

"I thought you said fuck-all."

"Same thing."

"I like consistency."

Lacy smacked James lightly on the arm. "He's in pain, and you're antagonizing him? Wow, Jimmy." She plucked one of James's earbuds out and held it up to her ear. "Don't mind him, sweetie. He's pissy."

Phillip continued. "No record of land purchase, no building permits, no shipping manifests, nothing. It's like the place doesn't exist. No idea who even owns it, though I'm sure we can probably guess it's Wangenheim."

"Which is speculation all day long," Lacy said. "Vampire politics aren't all that different from human politics. Like him or not, you accuse a vampire master of shady shit, you'd better have the evidence to back it up."

"Whoever owns this place doesn't want anyone to know about it," James said as he took another look around at the passengers on the ferry. He estimated at least three hundred people aboard. "So why have the crowds?"

Something caught his eye. A young man strolled along the deck, glancing around as he went. He stopped, stared at James for a moment, then kept walking.

"Good question," Phillip said. "I'll keep digging."

"You do that," James said, not taking his eyes off the kid as he went into the indoor passenger hold. "I think I'm going to follow someone who looks like he's up to no good."

"Try not to do anything stupid."

"No promises."

Phillip sighed. "I hate dogs." The line went dead.

"Someone?" Lacy asked as she handed James the earbud. She looked in the direction he was looking. "Who?"

"Stay here," James said as he started toward the hold.

"Where are you going?"

"To disappoint my best friend and do something stupid."

The lower levels of the ferry were dark, the air damp and cool as James stepped down off the stairway and looked around. The wolf enhanced his vision, and he searched the area first with his yellowed eyes. Dozens of cars sat parked in the lower levels, all luxury vehicles, all clean and in pristine condition.

Something made a scratching noise, maybe a boot on rough concrete. James's body tensed as the wolf heightened his hearing. The low thrum of the diesel engines grew louder, the sound drowning out everything else. He pushed the wolf back and shook his head.

"Well, that isn't helpful," he said. He moved out farther into the garage, glided between the parked cars as he sniffed the air. Oil. Gasoline. Saline. Tire rubber.

Blood. Rot.

The wind left his lungs as the kid tackled him and threw him into a parked car. James hit the windshield hard enough to cave it in, but the spiderwebbed glass and plastic managed to hold enough to keep him from falling into the car. He took a second to regain his breath, rolled off the car much to the ire of his aching human body, and faced his attacker.

"A tap on the shoulder would've been fine," he said, wincing as he rubbed his back. "I hope they have a chiropractor on the island."

"You won't be making it that far," the kid said around his long fangs. "Master Wangenheim doesn't like dogs."

James shot him a look. "You know?"

"I could smell you the minute you and your species traitor boarded." The kid laughed. "You weres. All morons who think they can hide from us."

"We try," James said. "Where are the girls?"

"Already on the island," the kid said. "Out of reach."

"Challenge accepted."

The vampire grinned as his eyes flashed red. "Good. I was getting bored."

James shifted, his clothing shredded within a second as he rushed the vampire, the aches and pains from his argument with the windshield gone in an instant. The kid ducked James's charge and countered with a savage punch to the ribs. James staggered, recovered, and lashed out with his claws. Sparks flew as they raked up the passenger door of a Ferrari where the fanger had been only a second before. James felt the thing climb his back, felt teeth try to puncture through his thick silvered fur. He grabbed the vampire by the neck and flung him into a black Lotus coupe hard enough to cave the vehicle roof in completely.

The kid recovered and charged him again, jumped into the air and spun, his foot connecting with James's jaw and sending him sideways. He tried to lunge at the vampire again, but the fucker unleashed a flurry of punches into his stomach and finished off with an uppercut that made James's teeth clack together. James shook it off and brought his fist down like a hammer, felt the vampire's clavicle bone snap.

Relentless, the kid lunged at him, his left arm limp from a broken shoulder. James caught the vampire and yanked the bastard's head off. He tossed the crumbling body aside and took in the mechanical carnage. The wolf panted in his mind, sending an urge of joy and playfulness.

Of course, you had a good time, James thought back at him. *Breaking things can be satisfying.* He surveyed the area with his eyes, looking over the damaged cars. *Good thing most people turn off their car alarms during transport.*

A loud, long horn sounded from above deck. An announcement followed, the captain droning on about off-boarding procedures and how to get the cars off the ferry. James heard footsteps on the stairs accompanied by the sound of people chatting.

Oops, he thought. He darted through the parking area to the other side and stopped as more people came down the second staircase. He looked around. Why were people coming down here? *We must be close to port. Shit.* He went low and sprinted between the cars toward the front end of the ferry, keeping to the wall and using the cars as cover as people went by. He stopped when a man stepped into view.

"Right?" the man said. He was tall and wore a suit that looked like it cost as much as the cars in the garage. He was on the phone. "No, honey, I'm just going to be here a few days. Kiss the kids for me. Yeah, business meetings. Boring shit. I'll be inside a damn hotel conference room all weekend. Yeah. No, I don't know that there's much to do here. Pretty low-key place."

James swallowed a growl. A private luxury island not even on a map was boring? He wanted to slash the backs of the man's knees open with his claws, the lying sack of shit.

"What the fuck happened to my fucking car?!"

The shout came from several rows down. James peered up through the passenger windows of the sedan that served as his hiding spot and saw people grouping in one of the areas where he and the vampire had argued only minutes ago. Random cries of "Hey, my car got hit, too!" and "Report it! Goddamned vandalism!" rang out in the area. Lying-Shit-Sack went to join the crowd, and James used the opportunity to grab him by the ankle and jerk him back behind the car. He gave a quick yelp before James smacked him over the head. Lying-Shit-Sack went still, and James shifted to human form and turned the unconscious man over to check the interior labels on the suit. *This might fit,* he thought as he came across the coat size. *Maybe.*

M y, don't *you* look dapper," Lacy said, surveying James up and down. "Damn, Jimmy, you look good in a suit."

James adjusted the tie and glanced sidelong at her. He'd made his way to the seating area upstairs after stripping the unconscious asshole and getting dressed in a suit that barely fit him, the shoulders too snug and the legs ending well above his ankles. Small price to pay to keep the attention on the vandalized cars and off the naked guy walking around the ferry.

James pulled his phone out of his pocket. He'd managed to grab it up on his way out of the parking area while people were looking over the damage. He sent Phillip a text message telling him what happened. His phone rang a few seconds later. He held it up to his ear, and Lacy moved in closer so she could hear as well.

"James, this is bad shit," Phillip said the second he picked up. "The ship is required to report to the Coast Guard when fuckery goes down."

"I'm guessing they haven't?" Lacy said.

"I've got nothing here," Phillip said. "Not a damn thing."

"It makes sense if they're trying to keep things quiet," James said.

"James, no the fuck it doesn't. I just sent in an official request for a port log from your point of departure. There's no record of that ferry going out. It means everyone aboard is there for a reason, and not a good one."

Lying-Shit-Sack's words bounced around in James's mind. *Yeah, business meetings. Boring shit. I'll be inside a damn hotel conference room all weekend.*

"Buying little girls." It was out of his mouth before he could stop it.

Sickness and rage danced in the pit of his stomach. He wanted to shift and kill everyone on board.

"Hey," Lacy said, giving him a nudge. "I see that face again. Stop it."

Pissed-Jimmy-face, James thought. *Right.* He shook it off, though he couldn't make the fury go away completely.

"You gotta keep your cool, Coldstone," Phillip said. "I'm sending up an email now to make sure we've got eyes and ears with you. Don't hold your breath. There's a chance you're alone on this." There was a pause, then James heard Phillip sigh. "James, this is shit that gives people nightmares for life. The cleanest cops have ended up junkies just trying to get the images out of their heads. No one deserves this. If you wanna bail, I've got your back. You could stow away on the ferry, take it back to the mainland."

"I can't do that," James said instantly. Lacy moved away and stood in front of him, looking up at him. He met her stare, his eyes locked on hers. "I can't walk away. Not now."

Phillip sighed again. "Okay. Let's do it then. Oh, and James? I just got an email from the forensics guys."

"I'm listening."

"The blood on Mindy's dress? It wasn't hers."

2

The crowd moving off the ferry by foot wasn't as dense as James thought it would be, though it was still enough for him and Lacy to blend in. Lacy had taken the liberty of mind-jobbing a woman in much nicer clothes than a pink t-shirt and cutoffs and had let the woman know that the water was perfect for a swim. The nudist going for a late-night dip was enough to distract the crew while James and Lacy made their way ashore.

"Wow, I lucked out," Lacy said as she adjusted the skirt and blouse she'd acquired. "How about this chick was the *exact* same size I wear."

James tried to breathe shallow enough to avoid sending a shirt button flying, his shirttail threatening to go free of the slacks at any given moment. He rolled his eyes. "Yes, how fortunate. Right down to the underwear. Lucky you."

"Oh, hell no," Lacy said with a laugh. "Bra, sure. Panties? Don't know, don't care. Eww."

James blinked, the wolf panting in his mind as the crowd moved off the ramp and onto the docks. A couple of men in suits stopped people as they went, handing each person a manila envelope. James and Lacy stopped as the larger one held up his hand. He wore sunglasses even though it was dark, and James saw two bite marks on his neck. The guard was sweating, and his girth threatened to burst his suit at the seams.

The wolf growled inside.

Smell him, he thought at it. *He's human. Probably a blood slave. Down.*

The scent of body odor, cheap cologne, and onions mixed with garlic filled James's senses. The wolf panted in his mind, its way of laughing.

I fucking hate you, James thought. He swallowed back bile as Lacy spoke to the guard.

"Hey, sweetie. What's that?"

"Key," the man said, his voice distant as he stared at her through his shades. "House."

"I'm pretty sure you're going to give that to me," Lacy said, patting his shoulder. "And I know you didn't see either of us."

"No, ma'am," he said as he handed her an envelope. Lacy took it and looked it over.

"I'll take this one."

"Enjoy your stay," the guard said as he stepped aside. "Welcome to Westenra Island."

Lacy and James moved past him and followed a group to a fleet of small cars. He sighed again, breathing outward.

The blood on Mindy's dress? It isn't hers.

Phillip's voice said it repeatedly in his head, each time filling him with both hope and unrelenting terror. She was alive. She had to be. But being alive meant she was still in danger. Why wasn't her dress on her body? The thought of any reason why she wasn't wearing her clothes made James sick to his core.

And hellishly angry.

J ames let Lacy do all the talking, and the driver was happy to take them directly to their quarters without question. The roads were paved and small, canopied by trees that nearly touched at the top and allowed little more than glimpses of the starry night sky. As the motorized golf cart drove toward the small house, James saw several other houses, each set a considerable distance apart, each lot separated by trees and foliage.

Can't be a witness if you didn't hear anything, he thought.

"All of them look the same," Lacy said. "That makes it easy. Not." She held the envelope up as James turned his head to stare at her. He saw the large "G" on the front of the envelope along with coordinates. "I've already put the coordinates in my phone. I'll do yours when we get there."

"How do you know I can't program them in myself?"

"Because I've known you long enough to know you probably don't know how to use your phone beyond texting and calling."

James shrugged. "I've never had a reason to do much else."

"Same reason you don't drive?"

"That's different."

"You don't have a driver's license, do you?"

James glanced up. "Look, we're here."

The car stopped in front of one of the small houses. White like the rest of the houses, it had a set of stairs leading up to the small front porch. It sat on stilts, hoisted a good three feet off the ground, which told James the island had flooded before up to at least a foot of water. Blinds covered the windows, and the light on the front porch was on. Back in Rock Hill, the place would've fit right into what he'd heard realtors refer to as "cookie-cutter" neighborhoods as yet another run-of-the-mill tiny home. However, it being a cabin on a remote tropical island gave it a more luxurious air. Lacy stepped out of the cart, and James followed as she closed the back door and stepped up to the driver.

"Where's the police station here?" she asked.

"Police," the driver said, Lacy's influence heavy on him. "No police."

"Security? Law enforcement? Batman. Is Batman here?"

"Security. All for the Master. Use phone to call."

James looked at her. "Wangenheim's own private security force? Phillip's going to love that. I'll text him now." He pulled his phone out and held it up. "See? I'm good for something." He texted Phillip as Lacy finished up with the driver. He pulled their bags out of the back of the cart while she spoke to him.

"You've had a long night. Go home. Don't worry about checking in. They'll get over it."

The driver put the cart in gear and pulled away without another word.

"Just so you know," Lacy said as she picked up her bag, "I get the bottom bunk. I bet you chase cars in your sleep."

The front door opened into a small living room with a futon couch on one side and a television on the opposite wall. A false fireplace sat underneath the TV, and a kitchenette and hotel-sized refrigerator occupied the same wall a few feet down. A doorway at the back led into a bathroom just big enough for the tub, sink, and toilet, and an alcove with a hanger bar and a dresser sat next to the bathroom. The place was immaculately clean, the rich hardwood floors polished to a near mirror finish, and

James figured the bedsheets would be expensive enough to entice someone with a lot of money and not a lot of common sense. They'd passed a few other cabins along the way, some extravagant, others small and simple like this one. Even though the extremely rich tended to like ritzier digs, there were also those like James who preferred humbler surroundings.

"Well, the futon looks comfy," Lacy said as she peeked into the bedroom. "Looks like I get the bathtub. Fuck it. I've slept in worse."

"Take the bed," James said. He looked at Lacy as she turned to him. "I'll figure something out."

"I really don't mind the tub, Jimmy. It's sweet of you, but it would be easier than trying to rig the windows to not let any sunlight in." She stopped and stared at him. "You okay?"

He stared at the futon and wondered how many of the people staying on the island were Wangenheim's customers. How many other people had stayed in that very cabin, slept on that very futon.

How many little girls had been bought and forced to spend a sleepless night on that very futon.

"No," he said, not looking back at Lacy. "No, I'm so fucking far from okay I can't even describe it."

Lacy approached him, placed her hand on his cheek, and gently turned his head to face her. "You're better than anything that's happened in here because you're here to stop it. That matters."

James started to speak when his phone rang, breaking the quiet. He put Phillip on speaker.

"James," Phillip said, not giving him the time to speak, "you two are in place?"

"Yes," James said. "It's a hellhole."

"That island is owned by someone who makes you look like a pauper."

"It's a very nice hellhole."

"That's a little more believable. Is Lacy with you?"

"No," Lacy said with a snide grin. "I decided to go out for a wild night of feeding on tourists and bored cops."

"Oh, she's got jokes," Phillip said. "She's cute, James. And I wanted to make sure you two were settled in. We've had a few reports of people going missing on the island. You two need to watch yourselves."

"How are you getting reports?" Lacy asked.

Phillip paused. "What do you mean?"

"I mean I mind-fucked our driver and he told me there's no law enforcement of any kind on this island. Just Wangenheim's personal security detail."

"Oh," Phillip said. James furrowed his brow. Phillip was usually a lot quicker on the wit. James noticed his pause right away, caught the tone in Phillip's voice that sounded more like he'd said something he shouldn't have. "Right. No, nothing from the island. But people have been filing missing persons reports back on the mainland, and the victims have all been linked to Westenra Island."

James and Lacy glanced at each other, then back at the phone.

"We're at our cabin now," James said, trying to bring the call back from the awkwardness. "I'm assuming you want us to focus on the disappearances."

"Right now, I've got nothing in the way of details on what's happening there," Phillip said. "I've got people looking into it, but until then, we're flying blind. If you dig into the missing people, you'll likely find answers faster than I will."

"Okay," James said. "We'll call you if we learn anything." He ended the call as Phillip was talking. Something was off. The more Phillip talked, the more James wondered why he'd reacted to Lacy's question the way he did. Reports on the mainland? It didn't make sense. It wasn't unlikely that families were reporting missing loved ones. But they'd been in Florida for several days. Why was Phillip and his team just now finding out about the missing people? If he'd known sooner, James would've made a beeline to the ferry and bypassed the murderous sea siren he'd killed in Jacksonville a few days ago.

Which was probably why Phillip hadn't said anything. Or his superiors hadn't said anything. Did they know about supernaturals?

"Let's scout around before we turn in," Lacy said. "I want to get a good lay of the land. Get familiar with the area in case we run into trouble."

"Right," James said, setting his thoughts aside. "You're slightly faster than me, so you take the general area. I'll hang back and look around here. Be back in ten minutes?"

Lacy was gone before James could blink. He stripped, went outside, and shifted. He laughed at himself a little on the inside. *If the neighbors don't have a problem with a naked man on the porch, an eight-foot werewolf probably won't be an issue either.*

He moved into the night, the dark not affecting his yellowed vision in the least. The area was more of a clearing than a yard, giving the cabin an isolated feel. He could hear the surf on the other side of the woods behind the place, could hear the breeze moving through the tall palm trees. He crouched down and sniffed the ground. Boots. Cleaning supplies. Dirt. Vegetation. Gasoline. The grounds were as well-kept as the cabins. He stood and moved around the side. Something glinted in the moonlight. He stopped, looking up at the side of the cabin. He spotted a small shape tucked in the corner of the eave. He reached it easily, pulled it down, and examined it. The camera was tiny, narrow, the small red LED dark. It wasn't recording.

Yet.

He crushed the camera in his palm, tossed the pieces aside, and moved back into the cabin, ducking through the doorway as he went. He scanned the room, thankful for the vaulted ceiling. He didn't want to have to share his human vision with the wolf.

He wanted the beast to have it all.

He spotted the small rectangle in the corner tucked in underneath where the rafter met the wall. He turned, following the direction the thing was aimed, his eyes settling on the futon. A wave of revulsion ran through him as he reached up and easily yanked the camera off the wall. Lacy walked in through the front door as he crumpled the device and tossed it aside.

"What was that?" she asked.

James shifted into human form. "I believe they have the cabins here set up for a show." He motioned to the spot where he'd pulled down the camera. "I found one outside, too. I don't know where the recording equipment would be, though."

"Shit," Lacy said. "Were they on?"

"No," James said. "I would guess they wait until whoever is staying in here has something incriminating. Blackmail can be quite effective." He didn't want to think about any other reason someone would watch what happened in that cabin.

Lacy moved over to the dresser and looked down the side of it next to the wall. "There are some hookups here. USB and HDMI cables and stuff. Looks like whoever stays for the weekend has the option to record themselves." She stood and faced him, shuddering. "Gross."

James looked back at the futon, anger welling in his gut. "I'm not sleeping on the futon."

"We won't both fit in the tub, Jimmy," Lacy said. "I mean, I like you and all, but it's a bathtub. I get why you don't want the bed, but it's all we've got."

"I'll sleep on the floor."

"Jimmy, just sleep on the futon."

James shifted. Lacy stepped aside as James smashed his fists into the futon repeatedly, springs, stuffing, and parts flying in all directions. He didn't stop until it was a pile of twisted metal and torn fabric on the floor. He shifted back to human form and looked over his shoulder at Lacy. She stared at him, her expression solemn.

"I can't," James said. "It's broken."

Lacy turned and walked toward the bedroom, talking as she went. "I'll see if I can find you some blankets."

3

The island appeared much different in the daytime. The pine trees were tall, lush, and full, creating a canopy over the ground. Sunlight shined between the branches, the shafts coming through to the shorter palms around the area before settling on the ground. James could hear the ocean in the distance, the sound of waves crashing on the shore mixed with the breeze singing through the trees and seagulls calling at each other over whatever scraps they'd found. The air smelled rich, floral, and clean.

James grunted. "Clean" was the last word he'd thought to use when it came to this evil island.

He glanced at the pile of scrap that used to be a futon as he rubbed his aching shoulder and stepped out onto the front porch. He hadn't slept well at all, the floor proving uncomfortable even though Lacy managed to scrounge up some blankets and pillows in the closet. She'd offered to find another cabin and "convince" the occupants to swap out, but James turned her down. He had no regrets.

He would get used to the floor.

He blinked as he spotted the gas-powered golf cart sitting in the yard in front of the cabin. Every alarm in his head went off as he looked around. He nudged the wolf in his mind, the beast stirring and grunting sleepily at him. If one couldn't sleep, the other was out of luck.

Wake up, he thought at it. *We might have company.*

The wolf got to its feet, yawned, and pushed its will at James. His vision enhanced; his hearing sharpened. He sniffed the air, the scents of pine, palm, and swamp deeper than they had been a minute ago. Gas fumes and oil from the golf cart. Tire rubber. Grass. He moved closer to it, body tense with caution. The keys still hung in the ignition, and a piece of paper had been folded up and clipped to the steering wheel. James pulled it free and unfolded it, surprised by Lacy's eloquent handwriting.

I made a pit stop while you were searching the yard and told our driver to bring us the cart. Should have plenty of gas. Let me know what you find. And make sure to stop for cookies. Lacy.

She'd drawn a heart next to her name.

The wolf panted in his mind, its way of laughing at him.

Shut up, James thought. *She doesn't know.*

James spun at the sound of rustling in the woods. The driver from last night wandered out, zipping his pants up as he went. He looked at James and tipped his hat at him.

"Morning," the man said. James blinked, looking him up and down. He wore khaki cargo shorts, sandals, and an open Hawaiian shirt over a white tank top. It reminded James of Panama Jack. Shades, mustache, and all.

Plus some swaying. Lacy must have hit him hard the night before.

"Morning," James said, keeping his guard up. "I'm guessing Lacy hired you?"

"I'm supposed to drive you," he said, his tone distant and dreamy. "Anywhere you want."

"How much?"

"One day costs one pack of cookies."

James laughed. *Only Lacy.*

The Cookie Monster stepped past James, got into the cart, and started the engine. "This way, sir. The cookies await."

Westenra Island reminded James of Hilton Head Island in South Carolina. It was as if they'd taken Harbor Town, a small port area made up of yachts and name-brand designer shops, and expanded it to include several high-end restaurants and tours, and doubled the number of people. A main road split the island down the center. A few turns here and there led down into the wooded areas behind the strip that catered to those who wanted to get out and eat, shop, or mingle with their fellow super-wealthy before heading back to their cabins. A port sat at the end of the island opposite the entry point where the ferry had dropped them off. It was a stark contrast to the rest of the island, the docks and walkways cold modern concrete rather than the rustic island motif the rest of the island was going for. It was large enough to accommodate one cruise ship from what James could tell.

One is all they would need, he thought. The wolf huffed in agreement.

"It's strange," James said, trying to see if Cookie would be willing to offer up information given his fugue state. "I've not seen any police around the island."

"No police," the driver said, just like the night before. "Security for the Master."

"Use the phone to call," James said. "Right. Why no police?"

"Why police?" the driver responded. "Don't need them. If the Master can afford his own security personnel, he doesn't have to answer to anything else."

Like procedure and protocol, James thought. *Great.*

The drive around the entirety of the island took about an hour, and James had Cookie pick a spot to stop for lunch. The shop was a small bakery just off the main road and sat between a bar and a clothing shop that carried shirts priced at Phillip's annual salary. The market was rustic-looking, but James could tell it was intentional, a way to add to the visual aesthetic of the place being a tropical getaway. Every store dealt in designer merchandise, one store advertising a blowout sale on a pair of shoes recently marked down to a mere ten thousand dollars. James nodded at the driver and handed him a twenty. He glanced at the menu posted outside, noted the advertised "Handcrafted Desserts" and some of the prices, and handed him three more twenties.

"Go get your cookies," he said. "I'll be in after I make a phone call."

Cookie nodded and went into the bakery. James pulled his phone out and dialed Phillip.

"You look like shit," Phillip said on the video call, looking closer at the camera. "Damn, James. Did you sleep?"

"In a way," James said, sidestepping the question. "Lacy mind-jobbed a driver for me. I've been touring the island, getting an idea of the land. There's not much here."

Phillip typed on a keyboard, then looked at something offscreen. "Nope, you're right. Satellite images show a shitload of trees, a few shops, and a port at one end for the ferry. The other port is larger. Probably for the cruise ship."

"That was my thinking," James said. "I asked again about the lack of law enforcement. Guy gave me the same answer. Says all they need is security."

"He's right," Phillip said. "It's a private island. He doesn't have to have any kind of publicly funded law enforcement at all. If some shit goes down, the Coast Guard or the FBI can step in, but that's it. Even private security firms have to follow the law."

"Perfect. How's your leg?"

"Groovy. Ran a race today. Think I'll try pole-vaultin' this evening." Phillip typed again, then looked back at James. "I've got a location I need you to look at. You'll probably need your girlfriend, too. It's a stakeout. We think it's the next spot that might get hit by whoever is making these people disappear."

James sighed. He needed a reprieve.

"I was hoping to unwind."

Phillip blinked. "Are you fucking serious?"

"I'm working a lot lately."

"You're on an island run by vampires who are selling underage girls."

"I'm sure they still have drinks with those little umbrellas."

Phillip glared at him. "Quit making jokes and finish up your tour with your new buddy. You need to be familiar with the terrain. I'm shooting you the coordinates now. Put them in your phone GPS." He paused. "On second thought, have Lacy do it. She gets along with tech better than you do." Phillip typed again, and a text message appeared on James's phone. "I'm off. It's time for my bath."

"Fall into the bedpan again?"

Phillip's middle finger filled the screen just before the call ended. James looked up to see the Cookie Monster leaving the bakery with a large paper grocery bag of cookies in his left arm while he munched on the impressively sized cookie in his right hand. He grinned at James with bits of sugar cookie falling from his mouth.

James sighed and pulled out his wallet as he stepped up to the door and walked past Cookie. "Save me a couple."

This is the best cookie I've ever had," Lacy said. She took another bite. "Oh, my God. *Yum.*"

James gave her a sidelong glance as they walked on the beach, then turned his attention forward. A few people sat around on the sand; a couple made out under an umbrella. Other than that, the beach was fairly empty at night. The tide was in. James and Lacy made sure to stay at the highest point to avoid the surf. Vampires and saltwater didn't mix well.

"So, this place is on the beach?" James asked.

"Yeah, that's what the coordinates Phillip sent say," Lacy said as she finished her cookie. She pulled her phone out and brought up the GPS. They were on the right track. "Looks like we're not far. Maybe a quarter mile. Said it's a small place like ours. We totally could've used my driver."

"You forgot to tell him to use the bathroom every now and then. Food is a rental, after all."

"Oops." Lacy laughed. "Not complaining. I like long walks on the beach. It's romantic."

James's heart skipped a beat. The wolf let out a happy-sounding bark and panted. He scrambled, tried to think of something to say.

"Do you also like drinks by the fire?"

"Yup. I'm that kind of sap."

"Dogs and cats?"

"They don't taste as good as humans, but I won't turn them down."

James's phone rang. He pulled it out and answered. "Yes, Phillip?"

"You two need to get to that house *now*," Phillip said, his tone urgent. "*Hurry!*"

James broke into a run, Lacy following close behind. "What is it?" she asked.

"C'mon," James shouted over his shoulder as he cut left and leapt over the dunes and into the brush. The wolf went on high alert, James's vision yellow and bright against the darkness as he made his way into the clearing where the cabin had once stood. He stopped, held his arm out to stop Lacy as she approached. She breathed out as she spoke.

"What the fuck...?"

James tuned her out as he surveyed the carnage. The cabin lay in complete ruins, wood and debris scattered everywhere. Swaths of blood covered the grass and foliage, red spattered over some of the wreckage. Body parts were strewn about, some half-eaten, none lending any clue to the identity of the person or people who'd once occupied the dwelling.

"Somebody had fun," Lacy said. "Damn, Jimmy. I've never seen vampires do this."

"They toyed with them," James said, squatting to get a closer look at a severed head he'd seen peeking out from underneath part of what used to be a front door. The face had been torn off completely. "This wasn't about younglings feeding. Whoever did this had a purpose."

"Good God," Lacy said from behind him. "Just found someone's head. They tore the face off."

"This one, too," James said, standing. "Something tells me they didn't want anyone to know who these people were."

Lacy picked up a hand and held it up. "They even chewed off the fingers."

Something glinted in the moonlight, the small reflective surface catching James's eye. He moved to where a large section of the roof lay and got down on his hands and knees. The wolf urged him to shift, but James pushed it back.

"Shit, what about the cameras?" Lacy asked.

"We'd have to know where the feed goes," James said as he reached for the object. "I never did find a hard drive at our place. Think it's safe to say these are wireless, too."

He plucked the object out of the rubble and stood, holding it up where he could get a good look at it. The wallet was flipped inside out, the item attached to it gold and shiny.

"Federal Bureau of Investigation," James read, saying it almost as if it were a question. He looked at the ID card next to the badge. "Agent Smith."

"How many Agent Smiths are there?" Lacy said as she walked up. "That dude does *not* look like the Agent Smith that sent us here."

"No, he doesn't," James said, studying the photo of the young man staring back at the camera with a serious expression. "But why would the FBI be here without us knowing about it? Phillip is working with them."

"Maybe he doesn't know either," Lacy said. "It wouldn't surprise me if they were doing something on the side. Kind of a pincer attack."

"No, they can't do that." James shook his head. "They'd still have to coordinate with Phillip. He's the lead." He looked back at the badge, then surveyed the area. The cicadas were howling, and he could still hear the ocean. Someone shouted and laughed a ways down the beach. He looked at Lacy. "The island has quite a few cabins. Why this one?"

"I don't like it either," Lacy said. "It's like they knew exactly where to come and who to take out. And how to make it impossible to tell who they were."

James held up the Federal ID wallet. "It appears they've made a mistake." Something clicked in his mind. He gazed at the ID again. It read that Agent Smith worked for the FBI, but there was another department listed. *Supernatural Crimes Unit.*

He felt a flash of anger as the wolf pushed a memory at him.

People have been filing missing persons reports back on the mainland, Phillip had said, *and the victims have all been linked to Westenra Island.*

James pulled his phone out.

"What's up?" Lacy asked as James pressed the "Call" icon on the touchscreen.

Phillip answered right away, his expression anxious. "What did you find?"

"The cabin has been completely destroyed," James said, keeping his anger down. He glanced at Lacy. Her eyes widened as she mouthed "Pissed-Jimmy-Face" at him. "The victims were all mutilated."

"No way to ID anyone?" Phillip asked.

"No. Not right away."

"Damn." Phillip sighed over the line. "Dental records take too long."

James held up the ID and flipped it open, not taking his eyes off Phillip. "You could use this."

Phillip looked away from the camera. "Fuck," he muttered, rubbing his face. "James, I can explain."

"Do tell," James snapped, his anger growing. "I'm simply dying to hear what you've been hiding from me."

Phillip leaned in, his face filling the screen. "James, you have to understand how sensitive this is. This thing could turn into a fuckin' shit-filled dumpster fire if it goes sideways."

"I'm still waiting for you to tell me why there are Federal agents on this island, why you knew we had to check out this particular cabin, and what the Supernatural Crimes Unit is."

"James, you need to stay focused and follow my lead here. You do not want to fuck with these people."

"What people?" James asked. "The people you're working for? Supernatural Crimes? So that's why you were so easy to convince when I asked Lacy to join us. Why I was able to talk you into this in the first place. How long have you been using me?"

"James, I need you to cool off," Phillip said, his voice rising. "I don't need this shit off you right now. Get it together."

"You lied to me." James shook his head. "For all I know, you're lying now."

"James, listen—"

"No," James snapped. "*You* listen. I'm done. I quit. Whatever superior you need to talk to, make sure you tell them that I've kindly asked them to kiss my ass."

"So you're giving up on Mindy?" Phillip said, shouting. "That's it? You get a little pissed off at me and you give up on a little girl—no, *two* little girls who need your help?"

"No," James said, putting the phone close to his face, his vision yellowed, his canines slightly elongating in his mouth. "I'm giving up on *you*. I'm doing this on my own. Stay away from me."

Phillip started to speak, but James ended the call. He put the phone in his pocket and calmed the wolf, his canines retracting back as he glared at Lacy. She shrugged.

"If it helps," she said, "I enjoyed our walk on the beach."

4

J ames and Lacy returned to the cabin in silence. While they hadn't known each other long, Lacy had apparently already figured out not to try and talk to James when he was angry. He had a horrible temper. He knew this about himself. It wasn't that he didn't like Lacy. It was that he needed time to think. He didn't want her to say anything to him in case he might accidentally lash out at her.

He was just too furious.

Phillip's betrayal hurt more than anything he'd ever been through. Finding out his father was a killer, finding out that his ability to keep his humanity during the shift was a deal made with druids, none of it bit him at his core more than finding out someone he'd essentially adopted as his own brother had been using him. For how long? Since Mindy was taken? Since Anderson's killing spree around Rock Hill?

Since before then? When vampires had been attacking Winthrop students, Phillip called James. When a giant bat creature terrorized Chester County, feasting on the area's livestock, Phillip called James.

They were back at the cabin just as the dark sky began to turn a deep purple. Lacy stepped onto the porch, and James could see her start to sweat as she turned to him.

"I'm sorry," she said. "About Phillip. I had no idea."

"Not your fault," James said. "You need to get inside."

Lacy looked at him, nodded, opened the door. She began to step inside, then stopped. James blinked as she put her arms around his midsection and hugged him tight. She was drenched as if she'd been running a footrace all night long, her sweat soaking through his shirt. He put his arms around her, his heart pounding. He didn't care if she was sweating. Her voice, her holding him, it was soothing to his nerves.

She pulled away and smiled up at him. "You needed a hug. I need to not burn in sun-induced hellfire. I'm going to lay down. Sorry about the sweat." She turned on her heel and went inside, leaving James on the porch with his arms still up and the front of his shirt soaked and sticking to his skin.

The wolf rolled over in his mind, groaning as it panted at him, its belly and loins exposed.

He had to take a moment to make himself not agree with the animal.

James muted his phone and slept for four hours before he woke up and stretched on the cabin floor. He sniffed the air, the smell of musk mixed with blood and vanilla heavy in his nose. He grabbed the front of his shirt and sniffed it, the scent overpowering.

He didn't mind, but he needed to bathe if he planned on touring the island again.

He went outside and around to the back of the cabin. A garden hose hung coiled on a hook and connected to a spigot on the side of the building. A notice above the hose advised tenants to please wash the sand off before entering the cabin. He went back inside and slowly opened the bathroom door.

She's a light sleeper, he thought to himself. He peered in and saw the ornate, Victorian-looking claw-foot bathtub to the right. The curtain was pulled closed, but he could see through the small space between it and the wall. Lacy lay curled up on her side, fast asleep. He stood there for a second trying to get his heart to stop beating so loud. *Down, Coldstone. You've got other shit to worry about. Like finding soap.* He saw a bar of what looked like handmade soap on the tray right above where she slept. *Great.*

James had started to close the door when Lacy's hand suddenly jutted out through the gap he'd been staring through a second ago, the bar of soap clutched in her hand. "Here, Jimmy. It's not flea-and-tick, but it should help you not smell like ass."

James took the soap. "Thanks." He shut the door and went outside. He stripped and turned on the water as the *Police Academy* theme began to blare from his shorts pocket on the ground. He picked up the phone, sent Phillip to voicemail, and tossed it aside. *I'll deal with you later.*

He washed off with the garden hose, dressed, and texted the Cookie Monster to come pick him up. Cookie drove the gas-powered golf cart into the market area and straight to the bakery where they'd gotten cookies the day before. James remembered from yesterday that it also doubled as a coffee house, and he needed caffeine. He found a table in the back while Cookie perused the display of fresh-baked chocolate chip yummies in the case at the front counter.

"Oh right," James muttered to himself. "It's a coffee house, not a restaurant. Good one, Coldstone." He rolled his eyes as he began to stand and stopped midway out of his seat as someone placed a cup of hot coffee on the table in front of him.

"Good morning, Mr. Coldstone," Agent Smith said with a slight British accent. He was smiling, his eyes covered by dark sunglasses. He gave James a curt nod. "No need. I've taken the liberty of buying you breakfast. The bagels will be a moment. They're making them now." Smith took the seat across from James as he sat back down. "Have you ever had warm bagels fresh off the line? It's a different world. Quite satisfying."

"That's why you came to talk to me, Agent Cliché?" James said, invoking Lacy's nickname for the spook. "To buy me coffee and a warm bagel? I usually like a full meal before I put out. I've got standards."

Smith gave a smirk as he took a sip of his coffee and sat it back down on the table. He leaned forward. "You found something last night."

"I did," James said. "I'm guessing the pieces of human around that cabin used to be your agent?"

"Correct."

"I thought you FBI-types liked your secrecy."

"I can be a little relaxed with my information considering your status in this affair."

"What do you want, Agent Smith?" James narrowed his eyes as he added some sarcasm to his tone. "*If* that's your real name."

"Of course it's not," Smith said, sitting back. "But it's what you may call me."

"Funny story," James said. "The ID on the meat pile I found at that house also said Agent Smith."

"Have you ever looked up the name Smith in a phonebook?"

"Fair point."

"I don't have much time. Considering your unfortunate argument with Supervisory Special Agent Brown, I've had to escalate matters and have a face-to-face meeting with you."

"Supervisory Special Agent?" James laughed. "Phillip? So, the FBI provides weaponry, intelligence, and delusions of grandeur?"

Smith took his sunglasses off and nodded to the barista who approached the table. She put a plate down in front of James, smiled, and walked off. James looked down at the bagel. It smelled like maple syrup and butter.

"Okay, so I'm officially impressed," James said. "You know what my favorite foods are. Do you also know my pants size?"

"Thirty-six waist."

"Touché."

"The disappearances here on Westenra Island have all been our agents," Smith said, pushing forward. "The island is owned by Victor von Wangenheim. He's a count out of Germany. Nobility, if you will."

"I'm aware of who owns this island," James said. "But why are they targeting your agents?"

"I run the Supernatural Crimes Unit of the FBI," Smith said. "We began sending in agents to gather intelligence here weeks ago. Our only guess at the SCU is that the agents were made, and action is being taken."

"I'd say that's a fairly accurate guess."

"Indeed."

"And *Agent* Brown?"

"He's been doing his job," Smith said. "Keeping you under control while making sure we have the local LEO's cooperation in this matter."

James sighed. "I could probably guess, but why don't you tell me about the Supernatural Crimes Unit?"

"We handle matters that are outside of the human understanding," Smith said. "I believe you would refer to it as 'the thing under your bed.' In short, we police the thing under your bed."

"By using other things under my bed," James said.

Smith gave a curt chuckle. "Touché to *you*, Mr. Coldstone."

"Why are you here?" The conversation was getting on his nerves. He wanted to sit at the table comparing dick sizes about as much as he wanted to sniff a public toilet for evidence of what the last user had for lunch. "I get it. You're top secret. There are bad guys here killing your people. What do you want from me?"

"We need you to find out who and why. And then we need you to stop them."

"I'm trying to figure out where the auction is and find a bunch of missing little girls," James said. "I'm fairly certain figuring out who is butchering your people isn't part of that."

"You'd be mistaken," Smith said. "It has everything to do with it. We've no other reason to be here. Wangenheim does not have his hand in the drug trade, money laundering, or any other criminal network that we are aware of. If our agents have been made, then it makes sense to wipe them out before they can report in."

"But they're already reporting in. That's how you know about the disappearances."

"Which means our communications have been intercepted." Smith stood and straightened his tie. "I must see to an issue on another part of the island. I trust you and your new companion have matters under control?"

James looked around Smith. Cookie sat at a table with a plate of his namesake in front of him. He ate hungrily, stopping only every now and again to wash things down with his tall, iced coffee.

"He's the very best," James said. "Nothing gets by him."

"Impressive," Smith said, his tone dripping with sarcasm. "Reconcile with SSA Brown. You need a partner who doesn't have a cookie fetish." Smith turned on his heel and walked out of the bakery. Cookie looked at James and grinned stupidly.

James shook his head and started on his bagel.

James decided to go search the destroyed cabin again. He needed more clues. Even though he saw his new task as yet *another* distraction from looking for Mindy and Marianne, Agent Smith had a valid point: finding the attackers would likely put him much closer to Wangenheim's group.

He put together his plan in his mind as Cookie drove the golf cart down the shaded street. He'd have to go in and shift to get everything. Having the wolf put its senses on it fully, having a fresh set of eyes and sense of smell, could only help him.

Cabins went by as they drove down the road, each yard maybe a half-acre to keep things nice and separated by the dense foliage around them.

James used his wolfen vision to search the trees as he went by, seeing sunlight glint off the small metal objects mounted in the trees and watching the yards. Why not look at the cameras?

Shit, James thought. *I could just do that. Check the debris for the server. Maybe I just missed it at my place? It's not like it's piped out anywhere else. Or is it?*

Either way, having the hard drive could be something. He could get it over to Phillip somehow and—

He stopped himself short. It would mean speaking to Phillip again. The thought brought up a new wave of emotion he had to push back, most notably anger.

Cookie stopped the cart and stared straight ahead. "We're here."

James looked around. A clearing sat before him, the grass undisturbed and tall. A couple of Blue Herons picked through the grass, and insects flew around in small swarms here and there.

"There's nothing here, Cookie," James said. "This isn't the place."

Cookie pulled out his map and pointed to it. "This is the right place," he said in his monotone drone. "You told me to bring you here. I brought you here."

"Have you stopped to consider that you might be reading the map incorrectly?" James reached over and plucked the map out of Cookie's hands.

"Nope," Cookie said. "Been here for years driving clients for the Master. Know this place like I know my hat."

James ignored him, opening the map and looking it over. It was haphazard, sketched. He wasn't surprised since the island was private *and* supposedly a den of evil. "How can you read this?" he asked. "The handwriting is horrible."

"It's my handwriting," said Cookie. "I drew that map. See?" He pointed at a mark near the far edge. "We're here. Go down this road here and turn left at the coffee stain, and that's the market. Keep straight up to the grease mark, and you'll hit the northern port."

James pointed at a smudge near the center where Cookie had pointed out the market. "What's that?"

"Oh, that's jelly."

"No, I mean the mark next to it."

"The bakery. Speaking of which, can we go get more cookies now?"

James glanced sidelong at him. "You're going to get a stomachache."

"Hey, but what a way to go."

James turned back to the map. "If there's a port at the north, then that means the ferry came in here." He pointed at the west side of the island. "Then the cruise ship comes here?"

"Yup," Cookie said. "Damn thing is huge. It's the Master's." He snatched the map out of James's hand. "I brought you to the spot."

James started to argue again when something caught his eye. The sunlight glinted off an object in the trees. He engaged the wolf and enhanced his sight, focused on the object.

On the small camera.

James got out of the cart. He sniffed the air. Other than the typical smells of the beach and marshlands, he found nothing out of the ordinary. He moved through the grass, looking up at the camera as he moved closer to the tree where it was mounted. More smells wafted his way in the breeze. The wolf opened his senses more. There was something...different.

Wood. Blood. Soap.

James squatted down, and the scents grew stronger. He surveyed the area again, his eyes falling on the gap in the trees he and Lacy found the night before. He stood and moved to the gap, walked the short way through the brush until he stepped out onto the dunes at the top edge of the beach. The tide was out, and people walked along the beach, played in the surf, or were sunning on towels. James turned and made his way back to the clearing. Cookie sat in the cart, waiting patiently as James walked over the lawn again.

"It's gone," he said to himself. "What the hell?" He stopped. The ground shifted slightly under his feet. He squatted and ran his hand over the grass, noting the water rising up in a near-perfect line down the yard. "Sod?" He turned to Cookie. "They put down sod?"

Cookie shrugged. James dug his fingers into the crack and lifted the section of grass. He looked underneath the dirt and grass blanket and saw something sticking out of the ground. He dropped the sod, stood, and walked back to the cart.

"Where to?" Cookie asked.

"I've got another question," James asked.

"Shoot."

"Do human fingers grow wild on this part of the island?"

5

J ames knocked lightly on the bathroom door. He heard Lacy stir inside, grunt, and eventually mumble something. He knocked again.

"Jimmy," she called from inside, "I like you, and that'd *better* be you, but I like sleep more."

"We need to talk," James said.

"Fine. Can I sleep while you talk? I'll listen, I promise."

"They cleared the cabin away," James said. "There's nothing there."

Lacy was quiet for a minute. He almost thought she'd gone back to sleep when she spoke again. "Seriously? When? It didn't take that damn long to walk back here from there."

"I don't know," James said. "But they even managed to put down sod. It looks like the lot never had a cabin on it in the first place. And unless human fingers are among the exotic plant life here on Westenra Island, I'd say they did a fairly good job cleaning up the scene."

"They didn't want anyone to see what'd happened," Lacy said. "I'm guessing you went back to see about finding the hard drive for the cameras?"

"Nothing. They left one of the cameras in place, but it looked like an accident. They must have cleaned the place in a hurry. I also ran into our friend Agent Smith."

"And?"

"He apparently works for the organization called the 'Supernatural Crimes Unit.' Same place as the agents we found last night."

"Federal spooks." Lacy shifted again and chuckled. "Cool. I always wanted to be in a spy novel."

"His agents are the ones getting attacked. Apparently, they've gotten closer than we have. He thinks there's a connection."

"He may be right. This could be directly linked to our traffickers. It's also possible not everyone on this island is here to buy little girls. It might actually be a resort as a front." She sighed. "I'll bet Phillip could pull up something. Not even vampires can hide from a satellite."

"We don't have that luxury."

"You might just have to put on your big boy pants and make up with your boyfriend, Jimmy," Lacy said. "We need him."

"I have no time to deal with liars."

"You don't have time to deal with much of anything. If they're taking down Federal agents, that means things are probably going to move faster than we thought."

"I can handle it."

Lacy snorted. "Right. I can't be outside in the sunlight, so you've only got help at night. You need adult supervision, sweetie. Around the clock."

James pulled his phone out of his pocket. He'd even turned off the vibration feature. He had at least ten missed calls from Phillip, and twice as many text messages. The most recent sat at the top of the stack on the screen.

I know you're angry. I can't help that. But we need to talk. The girls are more important.

James sighed.

"Just do it outside, babe?" Lacy called from behind the bathroom door. "Let a girl get some sleep."

James nodded as another video call came in on his phone, Phillip's caller ID displayed across the screen. He moved out onto the front porch and answered. Phillip blinked on the screen as if surprised by James answering.

"I guess you got over it?" he said.

"What is it, Phillip?" James said, his tone short. "I've got things going on here."

"I've got information you might want to hear. Have you been to the northernmost part of the island yet?"

"I've not had a reason to, no," James said. "But Cookie told me there's a rather sizable port there for a cruise ship."

"Cookie?"

"He's my new best friend."

Phillip shot James a look. "Are you serious?"

"Yup. He drives me around the island and doesn't yell at me."

"Is he the driver Lacy mind-fucked the other night?"

"Don't judge him."

"Is he *still* under her control?"

"That's not important. He doesn't lie to me."

Phillip closed his eyes and sighed, obviously taking in James's jab. "Okay, I deserve that. I didn't have a choice, James." He opened his eyes and leaned in close to the camera. "I was under orders."

"How long have you worked for them?" James asked, pushing the subject forward. "No more lies."

Phillip sighed. "Since after college."

James almost hurled the phone across the yard, then stopped himself, his grip tight on the device as he fought down his anger.

"They recruited me in my senior year," Phillip continued. "After I applied to the Academy, I had to put down a reference, and you were the first name I thought of. Agent Smith met with me at lunch the next day."

"And you couldn't be bothered with telling me?"

"It's the darkest organization in the FBI," Phillip said. "The Rock Hill Police Department doesn't know I'm an agent for the SCU. As far as they know, I'm just a member of the force who also acts as a liaison to the FBI when they're needed for a case. And I had to earn that status just like everyone else."

"So, when do you do anything for the SCU?"

"When *you* need to get involved."

James stopped for a minute, processing what Phillip was saying. He fought to push out his next question. "You've been using me this whole time?"

"Yes." Phillip shook his head. "Not gonna sweeten it. I didn't have a choice. I'm supposed to be your handler. They're particularly interested in you."

"Why?"

"Because you keep your humanity when you shift." Phillip shook his head again. "And because of your father. The Wolf Man Murders were on their radar long before I came around. I didn't want to lie to you, James. I had to. And I won't ask you to forgive me because you have the right not to. But there are two little girls out there hoping you'll come to their rescue, and God knows how many more on that ship who need you."

"Ship?"

Phillip nodded and typed something on a keyboard. He looked away from the phone, probably at a computer screen. "That port at the north side of the island is big enough for one ocean liner. One of our people on the island reported in this morning that they've gotten intel on the auction. They do it on the ship."

"Why there?" James asked.

"Because if they do it in international waters, there's two things anyone can do about it: jack and shit."

"Surely there are laws in place for that. I can't imagine one could simply commit any crime they wanted to on the high seas."

"They can't," Phillip said. "Once you're twenty-four miles out from the shore, you're in international water. The domestic laws for whoever's flag flies on the ship apply. But here's the reality: you're looking at weeks before anyone agrees to who's got jurisdiction, and more weeks for them to investigate. By the time anyone's ready to do anything, it's a moot point. Besides, if this asshole owns his own country, we're screwed and he's looking at a clean getaway."

"Which means Mindy and Marianne would be long gone." James sighed. The news never seemed to get any better.

"Sorry, but that's just real talk," Phillip said. "Maritime law is hard shit. They've been trying to nail it down for years, but it's not like there are lines someone can go out and mark in the water. It's not a perfect system, but it's a system."

"So, they likely meet up with another ship out in the water and offload the sold girls there," James said.

"There's probably an offshore port they meet at," Phillip said. "I doubt they go ship-to-ship. They aren't pirates."

"They kind of are."

"You watch too many movies."

"In other news, I went back to the site where the SCU agents got wiped out," James said. "It's clean. Nothing there. If you don't find the cracks in the sod they laid down, it's like the place never existed."

Phillip frowned. "That's weird. That's really weird. So far, you're the only registered supernatural we have on the ground out there." He started typing again. "I'm shooting an email to Agent Smith. In the meantime, get to that port and figure out how you're going to get on that ship. Don't let it reach international waters."

"Right," James said.

"Hey, James?"

"Yeah?"

"It's all out there now. No more lies. I promise."

James nodded and ended the call.

I think it's sweet that you two lovebirds kissed and made up," Lacy said, grinning at James. Cookie guided the cart down the road through the market area and toward the northern port, humming quietly as they went. Both James and Lacy sat in the back seat, an attempt to look like a couple on an evening tour of the island.

James glanced at her sidelong. "He had information. Besides, I missed the abuse."

"I could abuse you," Lacy said.

"It's different coming from Phillip."

Lacy leaned in and gave him a sly look as she licked her lips. "Yeah, but it's a lot more fun coming from me."

James rolled his eyes as she laughed at him. "You're worse than most of the guys I went to college with."

"Oh, loosen up, Jimmy," Lacy said. "Gotta have a little fun here and there. Otherwise you'll go nuts."

"I'm fun."

"You can be kind of a dud sometimes."

"I believe the term 'one-man party' has been used before."

"You have to be able to have fun to be a party, Jimmy."

"I'll have you know that I put the F-U in fun."

Cookie pulled the cart to a stop. "This is the place."

The port was a stark contrast to the rest of the island. Large concrete pylons lined the concrete docks, the steel cables between them acting as railing to keep hapless walkers from falling into the drink. It was a large enough area to accommodate a sizeable cruise ship. People walked around the docks chatting, some pointing out over the water while others laughed and drank with their groups. James saw a small building off to the side with a countertop and open window. A bartender served drinks while speakers perched on either top corner of the booth played Jimmy Buffet songs.

"I've never really liked piña colada," Lacy said. "Tequila sunrises are okay."

"Tequila makes my clothes come off," James said as he got out of the cart. Lacy laughed as she joined him.

"There you go," she said. "I knew you had a sense of humor!"

James looked around the area as he began to walk toward the bar, listening in on conversations as he went. The wolf grunted in his mind as it pushed out and enhanced his hearing. Most of the conversations were mundane. Some complained about having to go back to work on Monday, others about how their office didn't have a good view. An older couple bragged about their kids getting elected to local political offices while a couple of men laughed at a joke that would've offended even Lacy.

"Someone around here has to know when the ship comes back around," Lacy said.

"Phillip sent me a text earlier," James said. "We're almost twenty-four hours out from the next auction."

James's eyes fell on a helipad that sat on the far side of the port. Security guards were roping the area off, politely asking partiers to clear the way as they closed off the pad. James stretched his hearing up, the wolf even closer in his mind. He caught no sound of a helicopter.

"Hey, let's check out the bar," Lacy said. "I could use a drink, you could *definitely* use a drink, and the barkeep might know something."

"Why would the bartender know anything?" James asked, looking at her.

Lacy shrugged. "Because he's a bartender. Knowing things is part of the job."

"I fail to see how serving alcohol makes one an oracle."

Lacy shook her head and took his hand. "Jesus Christ, James, you have *got* to watch more TV." She led him over to the bar where the server, a young Black kid with long hair done in braids, finished shaking up a canister before pouring the martini and handing the glass over to a woman. She tipped him a couple of hundreds and went about her way. The kid looked at Lacy, smiled, then looked up at James.

"*Weh Yuh ah seh*, lovebirds," he said in a thick Jamaican accent. "What can I get for you?"

"Got beer?" Lacy said. "We like to keep it simple."

The kid grinned. "I like simple myself! Two beers, one for the gent and one for the pretty girl! What kind? We got a few."

"IPA," Lacy said. "It's hot as Satan's ass crack out here."

The barkeep poured two beers from the tap and slid the glasses across the counter. James pulled a hundred out of his wallet and handed it over. The kid looked up at him and smiled again. "You look like a man who needs a little more than beer, *bredren*."

"You seem wise for your years," James said, noticing the bartender's name tag. Bart.

"Shee-it," the kid said. "I'm all of forty, an' I don' let my body show it. Not allowed. Gotta keep 'dem girls flockin'." He leaned in and spoke, his accent gone completely. "Keeping up the Bob Marley act works, too." He winked and stood up straight again, resuming the accent. "Whatcha need?"

"Information," James said. He pulled out another hundred. "On a cruise."

"Everyone on this island gets on that ship," Bart told him, dropping the accent again. "Comes with the package."

James pulled out another two hundreds. Bart's eyes widened. James gave a smirk as Lacy picked up her beer and took a sip. She smiled as she finished and spoke, her eyes flashing red. "My boyfriend's loaded. What's your price, sweetie?"

"You didn't have to pay him, you know," Lacy said. "I was about to mess with his head."

James looked at her. "I'm not going to feel a few hundred dollars."

"I swear," Phillip said over the video chat. "It's like watching a Loony-Tunes cartoon with you two."

Lacy and James sat on a bench across from the heliport, the streetlamp above casting a soft glow onto them as partiers milled about on the docks. The line at the bar was up again, and Bart was furiously making drinks, still grinning ear-to-ear at having made eight hundred dollars cash only a few minutes ago.

"According to Bart, everyone on the island gets to board the ship as part of the package," James said.

"Great," Phillip said. "So, we get to pilfer through over hundreds of people to try and find ones who like 'em young. Whatever would we do without this brilliant intel?"

"Well, that's where it gets interesting," Lacy said. "People have to have a boarding pass. They deliver your packet to your cabin the morning of departure, and there's a badge inside. Kinda like comic-con."

"You know about comic-con?" Phillip said. James rolled his eyes. Phillip was always dragging him to science fiction conventions around the Southeast. Not that James didn't enjoy geeky stuff, but Phillip was far more social than James and handled himself better in crowds. He'd taken Phillip to a rather large one in Atlanta a year ago for his birthday. Ninety thousand people later, James found himself sleeping off the mania in his head on the trip home while Phillip complained about not being able to see out the rear windshield of his car because of all the stuff they'd bought in the vendor building.

"Honey, I'm a hundred years old," Lacy said. "You think I've been a shut-in over the years?"

"Bart told us there are different badges," James said. "Most everyone gets a red badge. But there are a select few who get a blue badge."

Phillip nodded, eyebrows raised. "The ones wearing the blue badges may be our bidders." He took a note and looked back at the camera. "I'll make sure I send this up. James, it's a safe assumption the island isn't going to turn up the girls. I'll bet they're already on that ship."

"Then we need to get on board."

"Hold tight, Jimmy," Lacy said, making a T-shape with her hands in a time-out signal. "We're not even supposed to be here. And we're not getting on that ship without badges."

"Besides," Phillip said. "Red badges will just get you the cruise. You'd need blue badges to actually get where we need to be."

James's ears perked as the low thump of helicopter blades sounded in the distance. He saw security guards moving people farther away from the helipad as the thrum grew closer. "I'll call you back," he said, ending the call as Phillip started to protest.

"Guess someone took the express lane in," Lacy said, looking up at the sky along with James. "A diplomat of some kind wouldn't come in with the rabble on a ferry."

James nodded. "I think we may have found our chance for some blue badges."

6

James and Lacy stayed on the bench and watched as a helicopter flew overhead, its ground lights bright as they shined over the helipad. A few of the guards on the ground waved orange wand-lights around to signal to the pilot, and one of them stood to the side, watching intently as the chopper hovered overhead and began its descent, finally landing on the helipad and slowing its engines. The chopper was jet black, small. James watched the supervising guard step up to the bird and open the side door. An older man in a business suit waved to him as someone from inside handed out a walker. The guard assisted the old man down, helped him to the walker, then guided him across the helipad. More assistants crowded around the gentleman, some talking in his ear as they walked away from the helicopter.

"I wonder who that is," Lacy said.

James shrugged. "No idea." His ears perked, and he turned toward the conversation. A couple stood nearby, watching the scene unfold as the entourage made their way to a black SUV.

"Who is that?" the woman asked.

"Some movie producer," the man said. "I think I've seen him before."

James watched as the SUV pulled away, another following behind. The guard who'd escorted the producer looked over his shoulder, his eyes briefly meeting James's before his attention turned to another guard who'd walked up to him and started speaking.

"We may have been made," James said.

"How can you tell?" Lacy asked.

James nodded at the guard. "That one, there. The tall one. Just looked directly at me. Keeps glancing back at us. We need to go." He stood, holding his hand out to Lacy. "Keep the optics. Come on."

Lacy took his hand and also stood, glancing over her shoulder. Skippy the Guard looked at them again. James turned and led Lacy down the docks toward where Cookie sat with the parked cart. Cookie waved at them, a bag of Oreos clutched in his other hand. "Did you two have a good time?" he asked, talking around the cookie in his mouth.

"Enchanting," James said as he and Lacy climbed in the back. "Get us back to the cabin."

Cookie gave him a salute, put the Oreos down, and cranked the engine on the cart. "Damn fuel's low," he said as he shifted into reverse. "We'll need to stop along the way."

"Whatever we need to do, sweetie," Lacy said, flashing her eyes at him again. "Just get us out of here."

Cookie put the cart in gear and drove off. James looked over his shoulder, saw the guard standing in the spot where they'd been parked only a moment ago. He watched after them, not moving. James could almost feel the man's eyes on him. He turned back to Lacy.

"Is he back there?" she asked.

"He knows," James said. "I don't know how, but I can tell." He pulled his phone out and sent Phillip a text.

What do you mean made? Phillip texted back.

I mean discovered. Busted. Blown.

Wow, James.

You know what I mean.

By who?

One of the island guards.

Shit. Lay low.

James smiled as the wolf panted in his mind. *You know me better than that,* he thought.

Cookie took a corner, and James saw something flash in one of the rearview mirrors. He leaned over to get a better view. He saw the headlights in the reflection, turned, and looked over his shoulder again. Another cart was behind them, this one covered, also motorized, and pacing them. "Lovely," he said.

"You want me to have Cookie lose him?" Lacy asked.

"No, we need to keep making it look like we don't know what's going on." James leaned in close to her as if whispering in her ear. "They're just pacing us. Seeing where we're going."

Lacy nodded. "Cookie, how far are we from the nearest gas station?"

"Got a pit stop just over there," Cookie said, pointing ahead. It was a small gas station, only enough for the motorized carts that populated the island along with the few luxury cars here and there. There was no price on the sign, indicating the fuel was also part of the stay on Westenra.

Cookie pulled the cart into the station and had barely stopped before James leapt out and ran to the corner. The wolf came forward, stood at the ready for the change. The cart containing the guards stopped at an intersection a hundred yards away. James heard Cookie humming to himself as Lacy called out.

"Hear anything?"

James listened for second. "The Panthers lost again."

"Crap. I had money on that game."

"Now what?"

"They saw us pull off and kept going." James narrowed his eyes at the cart. "I say we see how they like being followed. They might have some answers on what's going on here."

"Great plan. You think of that one all by yourself?"

"Lack of better ideas."

"Fair."

The other cart yanked to the left, tires dragging on asphalt, and disappeared down another street. James headed back to the cart. "Cookie, we're following them."

"Yes, sir!" Cookie jumped into the cart and turned the engine over.

James clenched his fists, readied himself for a fight, clothes be damned. *Let's do this.*

He jumped onto the back of their cart and held on as Cookie pulled out and took off down the street the other cart had taken. James climbed into the back seat with Lacy and stripped as Lacy leaned forward and spoke to Cookie. "That's their brake lights up ahead. Stay with them but be discrete."

"Yes, ma'am," Cookie shouted over his shoulder. He pressed down harder on the gas.

James leaned over and tumbled out of the cart as Cookie took a corner a little too sharp. He let the wolf take him, his body massive and muscular, covered in silver fur as his shoulder hit the pavement, the force sending

332

him into a roll. He easily regained his footing and loped down the street. He saw the other cart swerve, saw a shape fly off to the side as it hit a curb and veered back into the road. He moved past Cookie and Lacy on all fours, the other vehicle coming closer in his sights. The cart in front of him moved wildly, the canopy flapping on the driver's side where it hadn't been zipped up. James slowed his pace as the cart jerked, the front wheels locking to the side. It flipped and tumbled, parts and debris flying everywhere as it hit a lamp post and stopped. The post fell over in a shower of sparks and breaking glass, caving in the driver's side. James stopped and stood over the wreckage, looking around, a low growl of frustration rumbling in his throat. *He's not going to be able to talk to us if he's dead,* he thought at the wolf as Cookie and Lacy pulled up. *Fuck.*

"Well, shit," Lacy said. "That's one way to park."

James crouched and sniffed the ground, the stench of gasoline overpowering. He saw the open flap on the driver's side. He grabbed it and tore it away, ready to pull what was left of their pursuer out of the vehicle.

"What the hell?" Lacy said. "Where is he?"

James shifted back to human form. He turned and went back to where Cookie had parked. The driver's eyes went wide. "You're naked," he said.

"It's Tuesday," James muttered as he pulled his clothes out of the back seat and got dressed. He turned to Lacy as he pulled his shirt on. "He had to have jumped out when he took the corner."

"No way," Lacy said, shaking her head. "The cart would've crashed before that. I guess these things have some sort of cruise control?"

"Yup," Cookie said. "Makes tours easier."

"I think he jumped out back there," James said. "But I barely saw him. Just a blur. How does someone evade two supernaturals like that? He was in plain sight."

"Unless he's a supernatural himself," Lacy said. "Keep up, Jimmy. We're not alone here."

"What would he be then?"

"Maybe we have another demon on our hands?" Lacy shrugged. "Considering we killed a succubus, that's not too far-fetched."

"And a siren," James said.

"Nope," Lacy said. "Not a demon. Sirens are mythical creatures. Completely different. They're living, breathing things. Demons are a physical manifestation of emotion, usually anger and hate."

James glanced at Cookie, who nodded along as if conversations about monsters and demons were typically discussed while passing the home fries at dinner. "We need to head back before the island security guards see us standing next to this."

The theme song from *Police Academy* sounded from James's pocket. He answered the phone, surprised Phillip was voice calling rather than doing a video chat.

"James, what happened?" Phillip said on the other end. "Never mind. I'm sending you coordinates now."

"What are you talking about?" James said. "What's going on?"

"Another attack. It's in progress right now. I've got you on GPS tracking; you're not far from there!"

James felt a tweak of anger. "They're FBI agents. If they can see it coming in time to call it in, can't they handle it themselves? We just had a run-in here."

Phillip sputtered. "Look, goddammit: you can be pissed at me. Fine. Be pissed at the FBI. I don't give a fuck. These agents are good people here, trying to help you. Some of them have families. Tell me about the run-in later, but save those people!" The line went dead, and James looked at the phone and saw the text message. He opened it, tapped on the coordinates, and the map application opened.

Phillip was right. James was angry. At Phillip. At the SCU. But James also knew his temper. He needed to control it. It wasn't worth more people dying.

The fight was between James and the FBI, not the agents who were just doing their jobs and offering support.

He showed the phone to Cookie. "Do you know where this is?"

Cookie slowed the cart as one of Wangenheim's security guards stepped out onto the road, motioning for them to stop. James watched as the guard approached and held a flashlight up, first on Cookie, then on Lacy.

"Evening," he said, looking Lacy up and down. "Can I help you folks?"

"We're heading back to our cabin," James said. Lacy smiled and leaned into him, giving the guard a sly stare.

"Right," the guard said. "And which cabin are you in?"

Lacy smiled up at James, then back at the guard. Her eyes flashed bright red as she spoke to him. "Whichever cabin we come to first. Why are you stopping us, handsome?"

The guard's face slackened, his shoulders slumping as he stared back at her.

"Had a thing," he muttered.

"A thing?" Lacy said, pouting playfully as she leaned toward him. "Well, that's not very helpful, Barney Fife."

"Looking for someone," he said, his speech slurred as if he were half asleep. "Had to stop them…from calling…"

Lacy turned to James. "Something's up with this one. He's been mind-fucked by someone else. And I mean *hard*."

"You seem to be holding your own," James said.

Lacy shook her head. "He's not gonna give us anything." She turned back to the guard. "The vampire that did this is way older than me. This guy's brain is banana pudding."

The guard grinned stupidly at her, then shook his head and resumed his former professional demeanor. "I'm going to have to ask you to turn around, folks. Nothing to see here."

Lacy grinned. "Come here, sweetie. I wanna see your credentials before I let you order me around."

The guard stepped up and flashed his badge. In the time James took a breath, Lacy grabbed the guard by the arm, jerked him hard enough to pull him off his feet, and slammed his head into the side of the cart before throwing his limp body to the ground. "He's gonna need an ice pack when he wakes up."

They got back into the motorized golf cart and Cookie started it back up. It rolled forward a few feet, then sputtered to a stop. James tapped Cookie on the shoulder. "What happened?"

"Ain't moving."

James looked at Lacy. "I thought you barbecued his brain the other day?"

"I did."

"Outta gas," Cookie said, turning to them. "I didn't get a chance to tank up all the way before we chased that other cart earlier."

"Fuck," James muttered.

"Place is straight ahead," Cookie said, pointing down the road. "Can't miss it."

James stripped and took off down the road at a run, the wolf rushing in, changing his body as he went. He was on all fours, fighting to stay out of his wolfen speed. He didn't want to accidentally pass the place. Lacy paced behind him, the run not even causing her to breathe heavier than normal. They passed a couple of cabins. Something crashed in the distance; James's ears perked up at the sound. He barreled toward the noise, the trees whipping by faster. He slowed as the wreckage came into view.

The house had been pulled down, the roof still relatively intact but now sitting on the pile of debris that used to be a cabin. Dark splotches of blood caked the grass in spots, and a human leg lay on the ground a few yards away from where the back door would've been. He moved around past the leg and spotted entrails strewn across the lawn toward the woods. A torso lay in the brush, the stomach torn open.

"Well, this sucks," Lacy said. James looked over his shoulder and saw her squat and reach into the debris. She pulled out a human head and held it up. "This one's face is torn off."

James shifted to human form and walked toward her as she stood and tossed the head to the side. "Someone doesn't want us to be able to identify these people."

"But that's stupid," Lacy said. "If the victims are SCU agents, then the SCU will know who got hit and who isn't checking in."

"It means that our killer doesn't know how these things work," James said. "That, or the killer is trying to send a message to the Agency."

Lacy's phone began to blast the theme from *Dragnet*. James raised an eyebrow as she pulled it out of her pocket and gave him an innocent shrug. "What?" she said. "I can have a ringtone for him, too." She pressed the icon on the screen and held up the phone for the video call. Phillip looked back at them, then shook his head.

"You're standing in a yard. James is naked. I'm guessing you didn't make it in time?"

"I told you he was observant," James said to Lacy.

"Great," Phillip said. "Shit. That agent only called about ten minutes ago."

"This place is a wreck," Lacy said.

Phillip glanced off-screen, then back at the camera. "That's weird."

James blinked. "Your best friend is a werewolf, and we're working with a vampire hunting down criminals *led* by a vampire. You need to be more specific."

"The agent that was staying there," Phillip said. "The GPS on his phone is still active. And it's showing it right where you're standing." He typed again. "In fact, it's showing just a few feet from Lacy's phone. Putting in a call now."

A phone rang from inside the destroyed house. James shifted into wolf form and began to clear the way, pushing aside large scraps of wood and walls like they weighed nothing. He grabbed the edge of the roof and shoved, sending the structure forward more as the ringing grew louder. James lifted a wayward door and tossed it to the side, peering down between the boards that used to be flooring. A hand gripped the ringing cell phone. He reached down and pulled the hand up, finding quickly that it was severed at the wrist. The fingers slid from the phone, and the hand dropped to the ground as James returned to Lacy. He shifted into human form once he made it to the grass and held up the phone.

"Huh," Phillip said. "Yup. That's an agency phone. I've got a record of the text messages here. Looks like Agent Smith was undercover as a bidder at the auction."

"Wait, Agent Smith?" Lacy asked. She looked at James. "Shit. We didn't even get to know the guy."

"No, not *that* Agent Smith," Phillip said. "Another Agent Smith. He was working with Agent Smith and Agent Smith on getting onto the cruise ship, apparently. He was supposed to meet Agent Smith on board so they could get in and make a path for you."

Lacy blinked and looked at James, her face drawn in utter confusion. James shook his head. "Long story. I'd recommend just going along with it."

"Looks like Agent Smith made it in as an invitee for the auction," Phillip continued. "The last text he got was from one of the organizers. Pretty cryptic. Something about making sure he was in his cabin when the courier arrived with his VIP pass."

James gestured back at the carnage in front of them. "This one's face was torn off as well. Just like the last one."

"Huh," Phillip said. "Maybe they're trying to make it hard to identify the victims?"

"I had the same thought," James said. "Lacy pointed out that their identification was left behind, which could indicate that they're aware of who is here looking to cause trouble for them."

"Probably," Phillip said. "It's pretty obvious now that they know you're here."

"Good," James said. "I was beginning to feel unwelcome. Getting room service is a nightmare."

7

James moved through the brush and found himself standing at the edge of the trees overlooking the empty beach. He stood tall, his massive chest rising and falling as he sighed deeply, the action causing a low growl in the back of his throat. He looked to his left and saw the small wooden steps leading from the sand onto a pier that stretched back into the palms. That walkway would end right behind the cabin where he and Lacy were staying. He knew if he went to the steps and dug underneath, he'd find the bag where he'd stowed his clothing.

Lacy stepped onto the beach from the other side of the walk as James made his way over. He shifted into human form and pulled the bag out from underneath. He was dressed by the time she approached him.

"I'm guessing you found the same two things I found?" she said.

James grunted. "I'm inclined to believe you're referring to our friends: Jack and Shit."

"Whoever wrecked that cabin is long gone." Lacy shook her head. "Damn. I've never seen anything like this. Vampires don't do this kind of thing. We'll drain you dry and tear you apart, but we're not going to take the time to eat your face."

"The parts were all chewed on," James said. "Maybe another werewolf, but I didn't smell one. In fact, I didn't smell anything unusual. Not even a vampire."

"Really?" Lacy said. "That's weird. You told me a while back that we smell like blood and rotten meat."

"Not all of you," James said before he could stop himself. He pursed his lips. *I shouldn't have said that,* he thought to himself.

Lacy looked at him, smiling wryly. The breeze came through, her hair moving slightly away from her face.

Nope, he thought. *Definitely shouldn't have said that.*

"What do I smell like, Jimmy?" she asked, moving closer to him.

"Um," James said, the vanilla and blood scent mixing in his senses, the wolf inside intoxicated as it slumped over and rolled onto its back. His heart began to pound; his stomach clenched.

He never thought he'd feel relief at the sound of the theme from *Police Academy.* He pulled his phone out of his pocket and answered it.

"I'm guessing you found jack shit," Phillip said over the speaker.

"That's just creepy," Lacy said as she moved beside James so she could see Phillip's face on the screen. "Jimmy took the southern part of the island and checked the cabins. I hit the north. Market, port, resort area, all of it turned up nada."

"Something about all of this is off," James said. "I can't smell anything at the scenes other than blood and building materials. Nothing that indicates the presence of anything or anyone who would do something like this."

"You don't think we have another shifter on our hands?" Phillip asked. "Maybe that's why?"

"Wade Anderson still had a scent," James said. "Even in his other forms, a person can't hide the smell of their groin." Lacy looked up at him, her eyebrow raised and a look of slight revulsion on her face. James glanced back at her. "Don't ask."

"Chances are the site will be cleared by morning," Phillip said. "Just like the last one. Shit. That cruise ship will be in tomorrow if your intel with that Jamaican kid pans out. We can't be split in two different directions on this."

"I can stay here and look for whoever is going after the agents," Lacy said. "Jimmy can take the ship. Divide and conquer, baby."

"I hate to be the party pooper," Phillip said, "but the SCU wants the ship prioritized."

"What?" Lacy said. "Their own people are being butchered here."

"The hazard is part of the job description," Phillip said. "They have one more agent left on the island. We're locating him now. He's also in as an undercover creeper."

James turned to Lacy. "One agent is a lot easier to hide than ten."

"I've sent a warning to his phone," Phillip said. "In the meantime, it's a waiting game. I'll call you as soon as I have something."

"We've got ways to pass the time," Lacy said with a grin. "Besides, I'm hungry. I wonder what rich tourist tastes like?"

Phillip shook his head. "Ya' girl needs Jesus, James." The screen went black before flashing a message that the call was ended.

Waiting. James felt frustration push aside everything else. More waiting. More dead ends. He turned on his heel and headed toward the house, Lacy behind him.

"Jimmy, wait," she said. "What's wrong?"

"Nothing," James muttered. He stopped at the end of the boardwalk and breathed. "Just…it's nothing."

"You're worried about the agents being killed?" Lacy said, approaching him.

"I'm worried that this isn't going to end." James started walking again, Lacy close behind. He opened the door to the cabin and stepped inside, the cold air giving the sweat on his skin a chill. Lacy closed the door behind them.

"Good thing we don't need lights," Lacy said. James saw her point to her glowing eyes, two low-burning blue embers in the dark. "Night people. Gotta love it."

James nodded, went to the kitchenette, and splashed water on his face. He stopped as Lacy spoke again.

"It'll end, Jimmy. We'll find them."

James didn't look at her. He grabbed a towel and dried his face. "I'm glad you can be so optimistic."

"I take it you're not the type."

"As much as I dislike reality, I can't deny it." He turned to her finally, keeping the wolf pushed back, his vision human. The shafts of moonlight coming in through the two windows in the front of the tiny cabin gave the room a bluish hue. He could see well enough without his wolf vision, but he didn't want to call it back up. He also knew he wouldn't be able to take his eyes off Lacy.

Lacy sighed. "Would it kill you to at least *try* to have some hope?"

"I have hope," James said. "Otherwise, I would've gone home. Written it off."

"I don't think you could," Lacy said, moving closer to him, shaking her head. "James Coldstone writing off a little girl in need? Walking away from a friend with the same problem? Bullshit." She stopped, looking up at him. "No, it's bigger. I think you'd go after them even if you had no idea who Mindy was. You've got too much of a sense of...I dunno. Right and wrong?" She smiled. "You're noble. It's one of the things I like about you. That and you're adorably stupid."

"I figured you thought I was brilliant," James said, a lump in his chest, his stomach fluttering.

"Hey, Phillip's not around to call you dumb," Lacy said. "Someone's gotta pick up the slack." She moved a little closer. "You never answered my question, by the way."

"What question?"

"What do I smell like?"

It was out before James could stop himself. "Vanilla. Blood. But more vanilla."

Lacy laughed. "Okay, that's different. I don't use vanilla body wash or anything." The laugh faded as she drew closer. "You smell like...I can't describe it. Cedar wood? Maybe?" She shook her head. "I'm sorry. This is stupid."

"It's not," James said automatically. She looked up at him as he spoke again. "It's...it's not stupid." He couldn't move his eyes away from her. He touched her hair, brushed it gently out of her face. She reached up and grabbed his hand, and part of him was terrified that he'd overstepped.

That fear was laid to rest the moment she was on him, her body pressed firmly against him, her lips locked on his. He put his arms around her, returning the kiss, the wolf grunting happily in his mind as it flipped around and wriggled on its back. His own back started to strain from bending over to kiss her, his neck hurting. He lifted her, turned, sat her down on the countertop. She laughed before going back to kissing him, holding his head as she pressed harder, her tongue brushing his. She broke away, pulled her shirt off, tossed it aside, and tore James's shirt open. She pulled him back in, wrapping her legs around his hips, fiddling with the button on his shorts as his hands searched for and found where her bra clipped behind her back.

Lacy pushed him back at arm's length. James couldn't help but take in her beauty, wanted to go back to her.

Wanted *her*.

"James," she said, catching her breath. "I...stop."

"What?" James said, his stomach suddenly knotted in terror, the fear that he'd gone out of line stronger than before. He stepped back, just out of her reach. "Did I go too far?"

"No," Lacy said. She scooted off the counter and crossed her arms in front of her, straightening her bra strap as she turned away. "I...it's not you. I want to." She looked at him. "I can't. We can't."

"I don't understand."

"We just *can't!*"

James blinked at the sharpness of her tone. She reached down and picked up her shirt. James pulled the wolf forward enough to give him his night vision, saw the tears streaking her face as she turned and went to the bathroom.

"I'm sorry, James." She closed the door behind her. James stood there in the dark. He didn't need his wolfen ears to hear the weeping from the other side of the bathroom door.

It wasn't the first time his heart had ever been broken. But this one hurt more than the others. A lot more. But even more than that, he was confused. What'd just happened? Even in the short time he'd known her, Lacy hadn't been one to be cryptic. And she'd come back at him with the same passion. Right? Had she? Or was he reading too much into it and had pushed her too far?

The wolf spun circles in his mind, chasing its tail as it grunted and barked. *You're not wrong,* James thought at it. *I hate circles.*

James went to sit down and stopped in front of the pile of ruin that had once been a piece of furniture.

"Damn," he muttered. "*Now* I need the futon."

J ames was outside when the sun turned the sky a purplish orange as it rose from its night slumber. His sleep had been restless. It wasn't sexual frustration. He knew the difference. Self-doubt was a far worse adversary to rest.

He stood on the porch as the Cookie Monster brought the cart into the drive. James pulled out his phone to check the time and saw the notification from Phillip.

I'm showing the ocean liner approaching the north port. Go check it out.

James kept quiet as Cookie drove through the island, his thoughts replaying his encounter with Lacy last night over and over, wishing it hadn't ended. Even if they hadn't slept together. He'd have been fine just holding her, kissing her, feeling her against him.

Protecting her from whatever had her so terrified.

Cookie pulled the cart to a stop in the bustling port's parking lot. James got out and surveyed the area. Security was in full force, blocking off areas as dock workers flagged in the massive cruise liner. It looked like a more modern build of the *Titanic*, the red bow and black trim accompanied by two large orange smokestacks in the center on top of the ship. It sounded the horn as it slowed. The workers on both the ship and the dock coordinated, the lines from the ship to the dock being set in place while several ramps were wheeled in for the access doors in the side of the hull.

James's phone vibrated in his pocket. He'd switched it to silent. He stepped around behind a bathroom building and answered, peering around the corner at the activity as he spoke to Phillip.

"It's here," he said.

"Yeah, I know," Phillip said. "I've got it on satellite on my end. I won't be able to talk much today. My physical therapy's at noon."

"I don't see anything abnormal," James said. "It looks like a cruise ship coming into port."

"The weird shit will happen tonight," Phillip said. "Like I said earlier, our last contact on the island is also an undercover creeper. He's got a schedule." James heard Phillip type. "Looks like it's all aboard tonight around nine, and the auction is at midnight." Phillip cursed. "That's three hours. More than enough time to port out and get to international waters."

"That's not helpful," James said.

"Well *excuse* me," Phillip said, breaking into a mock Old Black South accent. "I'll try to be more he'pful, Massa James," he grumbled, going back to his normal voice. "Why are you ill? You know what, never mind. Dumb question."

"Lacy and I got complicated last night," James said. He needed someone to talk to. And he missed his friend.

"For real?" Phillip said, his tone perking up. "Damn. Can't say I didn't see it coming, but hey: guess she likes doggy style after all. Congrats, man. You two are good together."

"We didn't get that far," James said. "She...like I said, complicated."

"Oh. She still willing to help us?"

"Of course. Her niece is on that ship."

"I hate to be the asshole friend here, James, but you two are gonna have to work out your romance issues later. This thing is bigger than you burying your bone in your vampire roomie."

"Thanks," James said.

"For what?"

"Being a dick. I needed that."

"Part of my oath. 'To Protect and Be a Dick.' In the meantime, we've got another issue we need to deal with before that ship leaves out." James heard Phillip type again. "We've got the last Agent Smith on that island. I don't know how he's dodged being turned into a salad, but he's still checking in. He's top priority right now."

James bristled. "Top priority is getting on that ship and rescuing the girls."

"Not at this exact moment in time," Phillip said. "There's too many of Volkswagen's guards around that ship for you to go barging in."

"Wangenheim," James said. "And they need silver to kill me."

"But not to make you hurt," Phillip said. "We lose that Agent Smith, we're flying blind. We won't know anything about boarding that ship. We need him to keep us up on things and let us know exactly when the bidding starts. There's another thing, too."

"Go ahead. This just keeps getting better."

"The agent's phone needs to be plugged into the ship's computer so the SCU can hack in and alter the course."

"That's a thing?"

"Shit, you really think it's still a dude at the helm givin' orders and calling everyone scallywag?" Phillip snorted. "Welcome to the future, James. Most of it's automated now. The captain just steers the ship where the system tells him. The SCU has him routed to spin circles around Westenra Island, and no one will know what the hell is going on 'til they're bein' boarded by the Coast Guard."

"Sounds like a plan."

"Yeah, and a damn good one as long as you don't let whoever is wiping out our agents take out the last one."

"I'll make sure to get him before he gets Agent Smith."

"Speaking of which, Agent Smith wants the killer alive."

"So, he doesn't want me to kill off the person coming to murder him?"

"No, not *that* Agent Smith. The other Agent Smith. The one in charge." James sighed. "You people need to figure out a better way to do this."

"The confusion is the point," Phillip said. "Just nail the bad guy and keep the agent alive. He's likely to have intel we need. Don't fuck this up, James. A lot's at stake here."

8

James spent the day at the docks watching the activity. He was able to get a better look at the name painted on the hull toward the bow. The crew disembarked the *Empusa* along with a swarm of tourists. James sat casually on a bench near the bar, sipping on a beer while he watched the passengers go through the customs gate and mill about the docks, many of them lining up for drinks at the bar while another fair number lined up at food tents that had been erected. The area smelled of grilled hamburgers and smoked barbecue. James kept to himself, letting the wolf rest near the forefront of his mind so he could hear the scatterings of conversation.

The wolf flashed an image: Lacy's tear-streaked face staring up at him just before she locked herself away in the bathroom.

I don't know, either, he thought to the wolf. The beast grunted, sent another image at him, this time one of her laughing at him, smiling. *I know. But we've got to focus. We'll deal with it later. On her terms.*

The conversation around him was mostly dull. Beautiful island. Best cruise ever. "How much did that girl end up costing you, Edward?"

James's blood went cold. He scanned the crowd, saw two men standing about three spots in line back from the bar. They were dressed casually, tacky Hawaiian shirts and cargo shorts. They looked like they had a good ten years on him, possibly a little over forty-five.

"Three grand per half hour," Edward said, rubbing his bald head, his shades large on his face and reflecting the sun. "Worth it. She was a hellcat."

James gripped the glass in his hand, forced himself to keep calm as the wolf growled low in his mind.

"Did you get her at that event they had in the ballroom?" Edward's friend asked. "That invite-only thing?"

"Yup," said Edward as the line moved forward. They were closer. "She was up first. Dunno how I got into that one. I applied and thought for sure I'd get turned down."

The line moved again. They ordered drinks. James looked at the ground. It was ten feet of concrete between him and the two bastards. He could close it quickly. Change, have them both mauled and torn to pieces in seconds.

Down, James thought to both himself and the wolf as the beast moved closer. His muscles tensed, his bones urging to shift and move into place.

"She was down with it," Edward said as he paid for his drink. They walked by James. "It was a party. Weird shit, though. As soon as I won the bid, the help all but booted us out the door. Real turn-and-burn thing. Hell, I'm not complaining. Girl was in her twenties, eager, and kept me up till the sun rose. I was asleep the whole way back into port!" Edward laughed. "Certified virgin, they said. Yeah, right. No virgin would do what this girl was up for."

James didn't flinch at the quick, sharp pain in his hand. He looked down, saw blood dripping from his fingers to the ground, the sun glinting off the shards of glass. He opened his hand, saw the large piece of glass sticking out of his palm.

"Hey, buddy," Edward said, looking at him. "Oh, God. Charlie, go see if the barkeep has a first aid kit." Edward moved closer to James, sat down next to him. "Hey, man. You okay?"

James ignored him, his jaw set as his blood roared in his ears, hot with anger and hatred. He pulled the glass out of his palm, the pain nauseating. He didn't let himself react, didn't show how much it hurt. Edward gagged next to him. "Holy *shit!*"

James threw the shard to the side as Edward reached out for him, asking if he needed help. James glared, his vision yellowed as the wolf snarled on the inside.

"Don't fucking touch me."

Edward's eyes widened in terror as James towered over him, his fists clenched, his fingers wet as blood poured from the open wound in his hand.

"What the fuck is up with your eyes, man?" Edward said, his voice wavering.

James growled at him, moved closer. He could do it. Break him. Make him suffer. He wanted to hear the pervert scream. Wanted to hear him beg for the pain to stop.

Then the whole island would be on to him. *Fuck.*

James spun on his heel and walked off.

It was nightfall by the time James had Cookie drop him off at the cabin. The sun set at eight thirty, which meant Lacy would be up and about. He'd need her if they planned to board the ship at nine.

James startled a little when the door opened before he could grab the doorknob. Lacy looked just as startled to see him.

"Hi," he said.

She gave him a weak smile. "Hey." She shook her head.

"Look, I'm sorry," James said. "I—"

"Don't," Lacy said. "It's not you." She breathed. "Just...let's not right now. Okay?" Her eyes fell on his hand. "Oh shit, Jimmy, what happened?"

James looked down at his hand. The blood was dried on his fingers. "Nothing," he said. "It'll heal when I shift." He pulled out his phone. "Phillip just shot us coordinates to the cabin where the last Agent Smith is staying."

"They need a better system," Lacy said. "Okay. I'm ready if you are."

James handed her his phone, stripped, stepped out into the yard, and shifted. Lacy moved up next to him and held her phone up. He looked at her again, his heart aching a little.

"Okay, Lassie," she said. "Keep up if you can." She darted off through the woods toward the beach. James hunkered down and sprang off on all fours, taking to his wolfen speed as he burst out onto the shore and headed in Lacy's direction, her scent still strong in the air.

Still intoxicating.

Get it together, Coldstone, he thought. *You're working.*

A sound up ahead caught his attention. Lacy's blur darted left into the brush and he heard a shout. Something crashed. James pushed himself harder, followed Lacy's trail. He found himself in a yard within a second.

He stopped next to Lacy and stood to full height as the figure in the dark held up a human head. The man turned and looked at the two supernaturals watching him.

Well, shit, James thought.

"It's Skippy from earlier," Lacy said. "The one you said was staring at you."

James growled as the man stepped down off the back porch. "Looks like you caught me," the guard said. "Guess I can't let you two leave, either."

"He's a vampire," Lacy said, nudging James. "Be careful."

"Yes, very careful," Skippy said, smiling. He wore shades despite the dark, and James could see his eyes glowing from behind the tinted lenses. "You don't know anything about me. I could be only a few years old." His grin broadened as he leveled his shaded gaze at James. "Doggy, right? Isn't that what she calls you?"

"No, doggy! Don't leave me!"

James blinked at Mindy's voice tearing through his mind, cutting him. The panic in her voice. The terror. James's vision turned red. The wolf charged in, melded with his own consciousness, instinct combining with hatred as his blood boiled over.

Lacy's shout was muffled in James's ears as he rushed the vampire, reached for him. Skippy stood his ground and landed a solid blow to the wolf's face, sending James backward through the air. He caught a glimpse of Lacy as she used the split second to attack. James rolled to his feet and charged again as Lacy traded blows with the vampire. She raked four bloody trails across her attacker's chest. He countered by grabbing her head and smashing her face into the back wall of the house.

James attacked, lifting and slinging the vampire into the yard and away from Lacy, who recovered and launched forward again. Skippy landed on his feet and swung; his fist connected with Lacy's head and sent her to the ground. James moved in, tried to grab him, but the bastard was too fast. He nailed James with a roundhouse kick, heel slamming into his temple. James felt the second hard blow on the other side of his face when he hit the ground. His head spun; his vision blurred as Skippy went back to Lacy. He kicked her in the ribs. James's chest ached at the sound of her grunt as the force of the kick rolled her over. She tried to crawl away, get to a place where she could get up. Her breathing was rasped, short. James saw the pain in her eyes. The kick had broken her ribs.

"Silly little bitch," Skippy said. "Looks like I'm done here. Oh, wait a minute." He raised his foot and brought it down on Lacy's lower back. Her scream drowned out the sound of her spine snapping. James barked, tried to shake off the dizziness from the blow he'd taken. The vampire just smiled down at him. "Now I'm done here. I'll give you a minute with her." He disappeared in a split second.

James forced himself to his feet, shook off to clear his head, and went to Lacy. She waved him off with a weak gesture. "Go," she said, her breath ragged, her voice harsh as she forced the words out. "I'll be fine. *Go!*"

James sniffed the air. Blood. Vanilla. Rotted blood. That way.

The world blurred by as he followed the scent, his wolfen speed maxed out as he dashed toward the market. He saw Skippy ahead, the sonofabitch walking casually through the market area as tourists moved up and down the strip. Carts jerked to the side, people screaming and running as James plowed through the area, charging down his prey. The vampire saw him and fled, turning a corner to the right. James went after him, the road heading toward more shops and bars, the traffic heavier. Skippy slowed long enough to yank a driver out of a cart and sling him over his shoulder with no effort. James leapt, caught the screaming man, and dropped him into the back seat of another cart as he landed and kept up his pace. The vampire jerked another cart sideways, and the driver and passengers bailed out just before James slammed through it. He caught the front end of the spinning cart and slung it forward, the weight barely taxing his muscles. The vehicle slammed into Skippy's back and sent him sprawling. He tried to recover, but James landed on him. He clamped his jaw down on the vampire's pinned arms, biting through meat and bone. He jerked his head and sent his enemy's arm flying. More people screamed and scattered, abandoning carts, and clearing the street.

Skippy struggled to buck James off, but James sent his fist into his enemy's ribcage, bone cracking as the vampire's scream turned into a wheeze thanks to a punctured lung. James stamped down on Skippy's knees, shattered the joint with ease. The vamp screamed in pain and fury. His shades had been knocked off, and his eyes were full of hate as he glared up at James.

James shifted into human form. "Start talking, Skippy. Why were you killing agents?"

"I knew that man was an informant," said Skippy. "I couldn't risk him getting on the ship."

"Why did you tear their faces off?"

Skippy blinked. "What?"

James grabbed Skippy by the hair and jerked his head up. "Don't play with me! You killed every agent on this island and stripped off their faces. *Why?*"

Skippy shook his head, coughed up blood as he tried to breathe with one lung. *He has no idea what I'm talking about,* James thought. *New question.* "Fine. Where's the girl? Is she on the ship?"

"You'll never find her," Skippy said, grinning. "But go to the ship anyway. The Master has plans for you."

James stood as the vampire pulled a plastic pill of clear liquid from a pouch on his belt. It looked like it could've been a vitamin supplement of some kind. James went to grab it as Skippy popped the pill in his mouth and bit down. He started screaming instantly as smoke billowed from every orifice in his head, his skin melting away. It was ten seconds before Skippy's head was nothing but mush on the pavement.

James looked around, noticing the crowd of people watching him for the first time. Many of them had cell phones out, cameras pointing at him. "Shit," he muttered.

The wolf pushed an image of Lacy at him. *Fuck,* James thought. *Lacy.* He shifted, the crowd reacting with shrieks and gasps as he turned and loped back down the road toward the cabin where he'd left Lacy. He felt his speed increase as he blew through the night, hoping he wasn't too late.

He took corners, trailed through woods and yards until he was on the beach. It would be a more direct route. Sand kicked up high as he moved across the beach, Lacy's vanilla scent locked in his senses, growing stronger. He turned and dashed up the dunes to the trees and stopped. The cabin was quiet, the dead body on the porch still bleeding out from the stump where a head had once been. James looked down, saw a patch of blood in the grass where he'd left Lacy. His vision sharpened as he went to all fours and sniffed the blood. Definitely Lacy's. He saw the dark streak across the grass. She'd dragged herself toward the cabin. James heard a dog yelp inside, a grunt, then silence as something solid hit the floor.

Something larger than a dog.

9

James moved up onto the porch. He looked down at the dead body, saw the bite marks on the corpse's exposed shoulder. He followed the trail of Lacy's blood into the house, shifting to human form so he could fit inside. The wolf stayed prominent enough in his mind to keep his vision yellowed as he searched. This cabin was larger than the one he shared with Lacy. It had a separate kitchen and living room, and two doors off to the left that were likely bedrooms. James saw the blood trail on the floor turn in the living room. She was in one of the bedrooms. He started to make his way there when he heard his phone ringing. *Police Academy.*

He found it underneath the kitchen table. It must have fallen out of her pocket while she'd been crawling. He picked it up and hit the green button on the screen. Phillip started talking immediately.

"James, did yo—"

"We were too late," he said as he walked to the living room. "Lacy's down."

"Holy shit," Phillip said. "Was it another supernatural?"

"A vampire," James said. "Stronger than her. He messed her up bad. I need help."

"You're on your own, James," Phillip said. "Fuck. That Agent Smith was the last one. The boss left a few hours ago to oversee the Coast Guard intercept."

James cursed as he opened the bedroom door where the blood ended. Lacy lay on the floor, a dead dog in the corner of the room. She lifted her head and smiled at him, the motion obviously taking every bit of her strength.

"Oh, hey, Jimmy," she said in a weak voice. "Tell Bacon we fucked up."

"What happened?" Phillip said over the phone. "Dammit, James." He hung up, and the phone rang again almost instantly. James answered the video call and turned the phone around so Phillip could see. "Holy *shit*."

"J-James," Lacy said. "Hold me."

She never calls me James, he thought. James dropped his phone, Phillip shouting and asking what the hell was going on. He went to Lacy as she tried to move again. She gripped his arm, tried to pull herself up as he knelt. She cried out, and he caught her and helped her onto the bed.

"Stop trying to move," he said.

"I tried to feed," she said. "I...I needed to feed. Not enough...blood." She lay on her back, looking up at him. "I'm sorry. You need to catch that ship."

"I need your help," James said.

"I need blood. There's no time." She sighed, the sound rasping in her throat. She reached up and touched James's cheek. "Just go, Jimmy."

James shook his head. "I respectfully decline your request."

She laughed, the gurgled and ugly noise a far cry from the musical sound James had to admit he loved to hear. "You always talk fancy when you're being a stubborn ass."

"I'm not letting you go," James said.

"I need blood," Lacy said. "A *lot* of blood. We don't...have time." She smiled. "I knew there was a reason I liked you."

The wolf mewled in his mind. James touched her hand on his cheek, held it. Her fingers wrapped around his. *No*, James thought to the wolf. He held his free hand out over Lacy's mouth.

"What are you doing?" Lacy said.

"Just do it," James said. "We don't have time to argue."

"No. I need way too much blood."

"I'll manage. I'll shift and heal right up."

"Go save Mindy. She needs you more."

James stood up off the bed, releasing her hand. "You don't get to argue. I lost Mindy. I almost lost Phillip. I'm not going to lose you." He set his jaw. "You need a *lot* of blood? Fine." He shifted into wolf form, the floor-boards groaning under his weight. He had to hunch low to keep his ears from scraping the ceiling. He bit down on his wrist, blood filling his mouth. He gently maneuvered his large paw on the bed to support her head and held his bleeding wrist over her mouth. She tried to argue, but the blood dripped onto her lips. Her eyes widened, and she gripped his arm with surprising strength and shoved his wrist into her mouth, grunting as she sucked hungrily on the wound. James felt as if his life was leaving him, his knees weakening as Lacy pressed harder. The bones in his arms strained under her grip, his head spinning as he dropped to one knee. She held on, sitting up as he went down. Her eyes glowed bright red, wide and insane as she feasted. He tried to pull against her, but she held fast.

She's going to kill me, James thought. The wolf barked in his mind, rushed forward.

The Lacy drank life. Wolf pulled against it again, but the Lacy held on. The James shouted and screamed from inside, but Wolf pushed it back. Needed strength. It forced itself to its feet, the Lacy following. It heard the Phillip screaming over the small noise box on the floor. Heart pounding in ears, whimpered as life was pulled into the Lacy's mouth. The Lacy stared at Wolf with hungry red eyes as it fed. Wolf touched the Lacy's head with nose, tongue lolling out of mouth, lightly touching face. The Lacy pulled away, dropped Wolf's arm as its body twisted, bone noisily snapping back into place, wounds closing. Wolf staggered backward as the James broke free of its bonds.

James fell backward into the corner as Lacy writhed on the bed, screaming. She rolled off and stood, her fangs out, her eyes glowing even brighter. James tried to stand, but his legs wouldn't work.

"I said god*damn*," Lacy breathed. "I've never...holy *shit*." She shook her head, her eyes still shining. She closed them, breathed deep, then opened them again. James could see her brilliant blues even in his yellowed vision, almost gleaming as bright as they'd been when they were red. He slumped back, feeling his body reel from being almost drained dry. He looked at his wrist, saw the wound starting to close as the wolf paced in circles in the forefront of his mind, barely giving him control. He could hear Phillip shouting over the phone, still asking what was going on. He tried to move his legs again, feeling some strength coming back to them as Lacy rushed over to him.

"Oh fuck, James," she said as she turned his large hand over, exposing the wound on his wrist fully. "Okay, wow. You're healing. Like really fast." She held up his arm as if it weighed nothing. James saw the fur growing back already. He shifted back to human form and winced in pain.

"Okay, I'll admit I may have done that a little too early," he said. The wolf grunted in his mind.

"Just rest a second, Jimmy," Lacy said. "That was stupid. I could've killed you."

"I didn't want you to die," James said, looking up at her. "I couldn't let that happen."

Lacy shook her head. "James, I'm not worth it. I made my peace with death a *long* time ago. You don't need me to bring down Wangenheim."

James nodded. "I'm sure I could take them down just fine on my own. But you're wrong. I need you."

A tear ran down Lacy's face as she smiled. "You don't give up, do you?"

"Not easily. Unless it's one of Phillip's video games. But that's different."

Lacy laughed, the sound musical again. Her smile faded. "It can't happen, James."

"I don't believe you."

"Well, you did just say you're persistent."

"I can be really annoying, honestly."

Phillip's canned voice sounded out from James's phone. "I'm still here. You know: the human guy *who doesn't know what the fuck is going on!*"

Lacy rolled her eyes and picked up the phone as James got to his feet. "Relax, Bacon," she said. "I'm okay. Jimmy's okay. How are you?"

"What the hell just happened?" Phillip said.

"Jimmy just saved my life," Lacy replied.

James took the phone from her. "We were having a moment."

"I know. I had to stop it before the sap shorted out the signal."

"Super Wolf always gets the girl."

"Dear God, not this again. I need you to not be a moron for at least ten seconds."

"You've got five."

"Good, because that ship is about to port out."

"What?"

"Radio chatter says they leave out in thirty minutes. You two think you can make it?"

J ames peered around the corner, being careful to stay hidden in the dark space he'd found between the bakery and the clothing shop. The market was alive, hundreds of people moving in and out of stores to make their last purchases before boarding the cruise liner.

I wonder how many of them are here to buy little girls, James thought bitterly. The wolf chuffed in agreement, forcing a low huff out of his own canine mouth. He looked over his shoulder as Lacy climbed the wall behind him like a human spider. She reached the eave and flipped herself onto the roof with seemingly no effort.

"Don't try this at home, Jimmy," she called down to him. "Seriously. This roof won't hold you when you're doggy-style." James looked up just as Lacy looked down from the edge. She grinned at him. "And yes, I'm calling you fat."

James rolled his eyes and scanned back out over the market. He saw security guards standing on corners and out in front of the busier shops, each wearing uniforms with the House Wangenheim insignia on the sleeves. The wolf sent an emotion at him.

Guilt.

He hadn't told Lacy and Phillip about Skippy's reaction to James's accusation of removing the victims' faces. And Skippy hadn't torn down the house, either. Not that James was holding back. Things were going fast, and he hadn't had a chance. Still, Skippy's confused reaction had James's mind going. If the vampire hadn't been the one tearing agents apart, then who? Or what? And back to the original question of why their faces had been torn off. Maybe Wangenheim had another hit-creature on the island. One that Skippy didn't know about.

Too much speculation, and it was making James's head hurt.

"Jimmy, look sharp," Lacy said from above. James tensed as a guard walked by the opening. The guy was older than James, but not by much. He could have passed for a wrestler if it weren't for his uniform, which threatened to burst at the seams under the strain of his muscles under the fabric. The guard's dark face looked chiseled from stone. James was thankful that he was as large as he was in wolf form. Tiny would likely break his human form in half and use the parts to hammer nails. He caught a glimpse of the name on the shirt: Tim.

Tiny Tim stopped, his fists clenched as he looked down the alley. His eyes narrowed and he stepped forward. He grunted, the sound rivaling James's own grunts and growls. He was in the alley, not at all far from where James stood. James saw Lacy drop down behind Tiny without a sound.

"Excuse me, sweetie," Lacy said. "I can't find my puppy. Can you help?"

Tiny stiffened and spun, glaring at her as he moved forward. James dashed from the shadows and stood tall as Tiny approached Lacy and spoke.

"You got no business in here," he said, his voice deep and resonating enough to give James Earl Jones a run for his money. His eyes flashed as he looked Lacy up and down. "What the hell happened to you? Who did this? Do you need help?"

James looked past the wrestler at Lacy as she walked toward Tiny. "It was terrible. He tried to mug me, and my puppy ran off. He was so scared, and he's just a little thing."

James cocked his head to the side with a grunt. Tiny started and spun around to find the eight-foot werewolf standing behind him. Lacy clapped her hands and cheered. "Oh, there he is! Hi, Jimmy! He's such a good boy!"

"Oh, *shit!*" Tiny shrieked, the shrill reminiscent of a young girl. He pressed against the wall, looking back and forth between James and Lacy. "You crazy heifer! That ain't no puppy!" James moved toward Tiny, growling, his eyes wide and his teeth bared as he put on his well-rehearsed "Psychotic Wolf" face.

"Oh my *God!* Please don't kill me!" Tiny squeaked.

Lacy shook her head. "Okay, this is sad." She grabbed Tiny by the shirt and held him against the wall. "We want on the ship. You're going to help us."

"Wait, the ship?" Tiny blinked. "You two must be…oh, sweet baby Jesus." He looked back at James. "You must be Coldstone. I'm with the SCU." He reached down into his pocket and pulled out a badge as Lacy let him go and backed away. "I'm undercover. I'm here to help. Name's Tim."

James shifted to human form. Tiny Tim's eyes widened as he looked James up and down. "Phillip told us all the agents on the island were killed," James said. "How would he not know about you?"

"Only been here a few days," Tiny said. "Been undercover with the guards. Different division." He nudged Lacy. "Your dude is scary as hell."

"Yeah, and he tastes like cocaine," Lacy said, moving into Tiny's line of sight. "Look, we need on that ship. Who else is here that can help?"

"I'm it," Tiny said. "I got a text message from Agent Smith to patrol this specific alleyway. Probably to meet up with you two."

Lacy looked over her shoulder at James, who shrugged and said, "Not like we couldn't use the help." He looked at Tiny. "Still need on that ship. How can you get us there?"

Tiny pulled two blue badges out of his back pocket. "I was told to make sure you get these. But you ain't gonna just board that ship." He motioned to the two of them. "Not with your naked ass walking up the ramp and your girlfriend looking like a used tampon. You need some clothes."

James nudged Lacy. "You brought my wallet, right?"

James brushed the lint off the shoulder on the sport coat and checked himself in the mirror. He straightened his belt and ran a hand through his hair as Tiny stepped up next to him clicking his tongue.

"Good lord, do I have to do everything?" he said. "Didn't your momma teach you how to dress? Unbutton them top two buttons, man." James did as he was told. Tiny stepped back and sized James up. "There you go. My man! You're gonna own that boat ramp!"

James glanced at the clock up on the shop wall. Tiny had snuck them in through the back of a nearby clothing store, distracting the owner while James and Lacy made their way into dressing rooms. It wouldn't have helped their plan at all if people noticed a naked man and a woman covered in blood and ripped clothing shopping for new duds. Tiny picked their clothes out for them, telling them the ship was semi-formal as he handed different outfits over the doors.

"He's got great taste in clothing," Lacy said from her stall.

James agreed. "I can't argue with his sense of color coordination and style."

Tiny laughed as James sat down in a nearby chair. "Mom had five kids, and I was the only boy." The dressing room door opened, and Lacy stepped out. James's lungs stopped working. Lacy straightened out the dress she wore as she looked at herself in the mirror. The dress crossed at her back, revealing miles of skin. She smoothed the black fabric over her form, the dress loose and slightly flowing around her legs. Her high heels clicked on the hardwood floor as she turned and checked her back. Tiny handed her a hairbrush and clapped his hands and laughed as she ran the brush through her rich and wavy chocolate-brown locks.

The wolf panted in James's mind. James didn't argue the creature's sentiment, reminding himself to breathe as his heart started beating a little harder.

"Lookin' good when you aren't covered in blood," Tiny said. "Can't say I don't impress myself sometimes." He clapped his hands again. "Okay, guys. Pip-pip. They're boarding."

10

The line of people boarding the ship was almost done by the time James and Lacy arrived. They wore the badges Tiny had given them as they made their way up the ramp. The guards at the top stopped them, pulling out metal detectors as they approached.

"Arms out," a younger one said to James. A woman approached Lacy and told her to do the same.

"I feel like we're going into a concert," Lacy quipped.

The guard rolled her eyes at Lacy. "She's good," she said.

James's guard finished the search and cleared him. Lacy took his arm, and they walked the rest of the way up the ramp and onto the ship.

The interior was extravagant. Wangenheim had obviously taken pains to make sure the ship looked as much like the *Titanic* as possible, right down to the mahogany trim and Victorian décor. The LED lighting and speakers set in the corners were the only telltale sign of a more modern build. The rich red color of the carpeting matched the polished wood, and the entryway they'd used to board led right into the main ballroom, complete with the grand staircase that went up to a second floor and overlooked the ballroom area.

"I suddenly feel the need to chart a course for the nearest iceberg," James said, not hiding his bitter tone. They could make the ship as beautiful as they wanted. It wouldn't change the fact James knew the purpose of having a luxury ship that could traverse international waters with no problem.

"Let's sink it *after* we save the day, Super Wolf," Lacy said, keeping her voice low.

James looked around at the crowd of people mingling in the ballroom, all chatting and laughing, many of them pointing out the décor and going on about how unique and wonderful it was to be on such a close replica of a romantic ship.

Romantic, James thought. *Not the word I'd choose.*

He listened as the speakers came to life, the area filling with a loud voice.

"Good evening, everyone! This is your captain speaking. Welcome aboard the *Empusa*. Your gracious host and owner of both this magnificent vessel and Westenra Island welcomes you aboard his prize project. You've noticed by now the *Empusa* is a close replica of the famous *Titanic*. Please enjoy your stay, and refrain from standing on the railing. After all, it's only a movie." The crowd laughed at the joke. James and Lacy glanced at each other as the captain continued speaking. "We are now porting out and heading to sea. We will reach international waters in a few minutes."

A man next to James pulled his phone out of his pocket. James saw the blue badge on his jacket and caught a glimpse of the phone screen as the man looked at an email from an undisclosed sender. *Smoking Room, Deck A, twenty minutes.*

"That's it," James said, leaning in close to Lacy and talking into her ear. "Five minutes, Smoking Room, Deck A. That's the auction."

"Shit," Lacy said. "We'll be in international waters by the time it starts, remember?"

"We'll have to figure it out," James said. "You brought that cell phone with you, right?"

Lacy patted the small pocketbook she carried with her. "I've got a cable, too. Phillip said to just find a USB port on the computer in the navigation room and the phone would take care of the rest."

A couple approached them, laughing and stumbling. James figured they'd likely spent some time with Bart at the bar before boarding. The woman, a middle-aged blonde in a red evening dress, hung on to the younger man as if he were the only reason she still stood erect.

"Oh, you two are adorable," she said loudly, waving around the glass of Scotch she held. She let go of Junior and moved closer to Lacy, reaching out and touching one of Lacy's curled locks of hair. "Oh, my god, you are *so* beautiful! I *love* your hair!"

"Thanks," Lacy said, smiling as she slipped easily into being a socialite. "Takes a lot of blood to make it shine like this, but it's worth it."

The woman laughed. "I'll bet is it...I mean it is." She laughed again. "Little heavy on the booze before I got on. Oh well. Bottoms up." She took an impressive swig of Scotch as James looked her partner up and down. Junior couldn't have been more than twenty-five.

"Is it just you and your husband this evening?" he said, taking a chance as he put on his best formal smile.

The woman laughed again, the sound high-pitched and grating on his nerves. "Oh, lord, no! Christopher is my son." She leaned in close to James as if speaking conspiratorially. "Though if your lady-friend here has a sister, I can promise you he takes after his father in lots of ways." She winked at him, and James nodded and laughed despite gritting his teeth at the awkward remark. Junior just groaned and shook his head.

"Thanks, Mom. I'm sure these people are so interested in my dick."

"My husband is off getting ready for the event," the woman continued as if Junior hadn't spoken. "He's a special...invite." She hiccupped. "Paid a...metric shitload of money." James swore she was starting to turn green as she patted Junior on the shoulder. "Bathroom. Oh. God."

Junior escorted his mother off as James breathed out. Lacy looked up at him. "She just told us about her son's..."

"Yes, yes she did."

"That was weird."

"Yes, yes it was. But she also told us her husband is one of Wangenheim's bidders." He tapped the blue badge on the lapel of his sport coat. "Which means he'll have one of these. If I understood her slurring correctly, the bidders are already lining up."

"That's weird," Lacy said. "They didn't follow any kind of protocol I've seen on the cruises I've been on."

"It's a private liner. Probably can get away with a lot." James looked around again. He saw an older gentleman smile and nod to his group, then make his way up the Grand Staircase. James caught a glimpse of a blue badge on his lapel. "Looks like we have someone to follow. When we get to the top, we'll split up. I'll go to the auction; you see if you can get a layout of the ship so we know where the nav deck is. We take it together."

Lacy moved into him and planted her lips on his, her hands on his face as she kissed him. She pulled away, leaving him breathless as she smiled up at him. "Good luck."

James watched her for a moment as she wound her way through the crowd toward a security guard, mingling as she went. He shook his head.

Women are confusing, he thought. The wolf grunted in agreement.

He glanced over and saw the older man reach the top of the stairs and turn right, walking along the upper level. James hit the steps and made after him, taking them two at a time and pulling his phone out to make it look as if he was checking the time and trying to hurry after Grandpa. A couple of younger boys ran past, both carrying large water cannons as they shouted about heading to the swimming pool. James side-stepped them, keeping his attention on his target. The crowd began to thin as they went down the corridors, the man moving along as if he'd been on the ship a thousand times.

Sickass, James thought involuntarily.

The man stopped at a set of doors and spoke to the guard. The guard acknowledged the blue badge, made a note on the clipboard in his hand, and waved the man in. James approached as soon as the door shut. The guard held a hand up. "Wait a second, buddy."

"Oh," James said, forcing politeness. "I forgot. My nam—"

"Isn't important," the guard said. "No names. Must be a first timer. Just let me see your badge." James stood straight as the guard made a note. "Right. They're about to start. Just keep quiet when you go in. Might not get the first bid, but you've got all night."

James went through the door, closing it gently behind him as he took in the room spread out before him. It was extravagant, the décor making it appear as if he'd stepped back into the Industrial Revolution. Dark wood, lush carpet, and intricately decorated glass made more ornate in the shadows of the low lighting as over a hundred men of various ages stood around the room smoking and drinking brandy as they listened to a man in the center speak. The scene looked as if it'd been ripped out of every vintage film he'd ever seen.

"Count Wangenheim bids you all welcome," the barker said. "Some of you are familiar, some are new. To those who are joining us for the first time, we ask that you refrain from bidding on the first item so that you may observe the process, as it is slightly different than most auctions. Not to worry, however. There are plenty of items to bid on tonight and tomorrow night." The man cleared his throat. "Well, I'm not one for grand speeches, so let's just get to it, shall we?"

"About time," a guy standing near James said under his breath. "Not gonna scratch this itch by myself."

James clenched his fist and fought the urge to shift and take the bastard apart.

Two security guards walked in through a set of doors on the opposite side of the room. A young girl came with them, dressed in a sequined evening gown that showed off her youthful frame. She had long, flowing brown hair and brilliant blue eyes. She couldn't have been much older than Mindy at all, maybe eleven or twelve. Her eyes darted around, terrified as she hunched shyly away from the men leering at her.

Those eyes.

Marianne, James thought. *Shit. She looks just like Lacy.*

"Our first item up for bid is a special one indeed," the barker said. "Twelve, has yet to enter womanhood. Certified pure."

"That means she's a virgin," James heard someone whisper. He looked over his shoulder and saw the older man he'd followed speaking to the kid he'd met earlier. Christopher.

"The bidding will begin at one hundred thousand."

Someone raised their hand.

"I have one. One is going once." Another hand. "I have two. Two hundred thousand dollars."

"A hundred thousand up," the old man scoffed. "Must be Harold. Cheap son of a bitch."

"Four hundred thousand," another man called from the group.

"Four, I have—"

"One million," James called, raising his hand. The barker blinked, looking his way as gasps and whispers hummed in the crowd.

"Um, thank you, sir. But I did ask—"

"Ask me if I give two fucks about what you asked," James said, focusing his fury on the barker as he kept his tone an authoritative growl. "I'm offering one million dollars. Do you want it or not?"

"Two," someone called.

"Five," James said, triggering gasps and low murmuring. Marianne looked at him, her eyes wide. He kept his gaze on her. *You're coming with me, tonight,* he thought. *I won't let them win.*

A tall man with reptilian eyes and a smug grin stepped forward. His haircut looked like something out of the fifties, and his large ears stuck straight out on either side of his head, making him resemble one of the Little Rascals in their geriatric years. He looked giddy at the prospect of a possible night with an underaged girl as he stepped closer. "I request a closer look at the merchandise before making a move to double the current bid," he said in a thick Old South drawl.

"You may inspect, but must refrain from physical contact," the barker said, nodding.

Clyde McInbreeding stepped up to Marianne. The girl whimpered, visibly shaking as McInbreeding leaned in close. He breathed in deep, sniffing her, the act causing James some nausea. The wolf tried to move forward, but James pushed it back. *If we shift, it could endanger her,* he thought at it. *And even if we save her, who knows how far out to sea we are?*

The wolf reluctantly backed away, its eyes staring back at his mind's eye with anger and need.

"I do believe I am feelin' generous this evenin'," said Clyde as he stood straight. "I'm afraid this young lady will be comin' with me tonight, gentlemen. I place my bid at fifteen million dollars for the company of this lovely young lady."

The room broke into grumbling and protests as the barker nodded. Clyde McInbreeding moved closer to Marianne as the barker collected himself and spoke. "The bid is fifteen million. Going once. Going twice."

It was only a split second before something dropped down from above and landed on McInbreeding. The shape tackled him to the floor, lifted him, and tore him in half, the auction space and people nearest to the scene drenched in blood and meat. Marianne screamed, backpedaling away, her face and clothes covered in blood.

Lacy tossed the halves of what had once been a rich redneck pervert aside. She looked around, her eyes bright red, her fangs completely out as she locked her stare on the barker.

"I place my bid on my niece," she said, her speech altered by having to talk around her fangs, her face twisted in feral rage. "Priceless."

Two guards charged in as the bidders scattered out of the way. James saw the guards leap at Lacy, their movement unnatural. *Vampires,* he thought. He called the wolf forward, his suit bursting into shreds as his body changed. He snarled at the group of rich men, plowed through them as he rushed toward the spot where Lacy fought the two guards. She grappled with one while the other reached for her, taking advantage of her being distracted by her assailant.

James grabbed the other guard by the head and slammed him to the floor hard enough to cave in his skull. The body went to dust as more rushed in. Gunfire went off, bullets peppering his flank, stinging and burning but not enough to slow him down. He saw the human guard firing at him, the kid backing away, his eyes wide as the smell of shit wafted up from where he stood. James swatted the assault rifle out of Rambo's hands and backhanded him to the floor, pulling the punch to keep from killing him.

"*James!*" Lacy called out. James spun and charged, assessing the situation as he closed in on the vampire guard who had Lacy pinned against the bar. James grabbed him and slung him into another group of guards rushing in, sending them all flying. Lacy leapt at James, kicked off his shoulders as she went over top of him and collided with another vampire mid-air hard enough to force him back down to the floor.

James grabbed a barstool and yanked it up, tearing the bolts free of the wood. He threw it at a human guard. Another human guard fired at him, but the shot only caught him in the shoulder, hurting just long enough to be annoying. James flew at him, connected, and sent the man backward. Lacy tore the head off the vampire she fought and hurled it into the back of another man's skull, dropping him like a sack of flour.

We've got to calm this down now, James thought at the wolf. The beast barked in agreement. James felt a swell in his chest, his muscles tensed as he reared back and looked to the ceiling. *What are you doing?!*

The wolf sent him an urge. *Trust.*

The James stepped back, letting Wolf have their body. Wolf held arms out as it called to Fenrir. It felt the wolf god, pushed the call harder. Humans and cold men clamped their hands over their ears, shrinking back, glass in room shuddering, cracking, bursting, sharp and hateful rain falling. One of the evil men in front of Wolf released its own howl, blood streaming from its ears. The doors to the room opened. The men swarmed out, their human barks and cries of terror humorous to Wolf.

James blinked as the wolf stepped back, felt its satisfaction as he looked around the empty, destroyed room. Lacy stood covered in blood, breathing heavily as she tossed a disembodied arm aside.

"That was different," she said. "Damn, Jimmy. Could've used that howl a couple times before now."

Didn't know I had that in me, James thought.

"The other vampires took off with the rest of the perv brigade," Lacy said. She called out. "Marianne? Are you here?"

James heard the soft sound of a young girl sobbing from behind an overturned couch. He made his way over and shoved it aside. The girl looked up, her eyes wide with terror as she pulled her hands away from her ears.

"Marianne?" Lacy said as she stepped out from behind James.

"How do you know my name?" the girl said, looking up at Lacy. "Please don't hurt me."

"No one's gonna hurt you, baby," Lacy said, her voice wavering as she clenched her jaw. James could see the rage in her eyes. "No one's ever gonna hurt you again."

James considered shifting to human form, then thought better of it. The last thing the girl needed was to see a werewolf turn into a naked man. He didn't know what she'd been through and didn't want to chance it. He woofed at Lacy.

"Right," Lacy said, nodding at him. "Jimmy, here, is looking for another little girl. Mindy. Do you know her?"

"The bad man in charge has her," Marianne said. "The one who owns this boat. He took her as soon as they brought us here."

"Wangenheim," Lacy said, turning to James. "I'm willing to bet he's a pompous enough ass to have the largest cabin on board. The captain's cabin." She pulled out a brochure and opened it to show a tourist's map of the ship layout. She pointed at the map, her finger landing in a large area marked "Captain's Quarters."

James growled low as he studied the map, his eyes tracing a route from the smoking room to the cabin and the nav deck. Lacy nodded at him. "I've got Marianne. Plan change. I'll get to the nav room and plug the phone in. You go get your girl. Sic him."

He took off, blew through the open double doors and into the main ballroom as people screamed and ran, diving out of his way as he crashed through tables and chairs, toppled other furniture as he rounded the corner at the grand staircase. He stopped, looked around for anything that would point him in the right direction. A sign on the wall with an arrow indicated the different locales down that corridor. Pool area. Chapel.

Captain's Quarters.

James scrambled down the corridor and up the steps to the outside deck. Crowds of panicked people. Security guards fired at him, bullets slamming into his hide and into the walls and ceiling around him. He ignored the stings, plowed into a guard hard enough to snap his spine and send him sideways.

A human, he thought. *I just killed a human.*

The wolf sent an emotion at him as he swatted another two people out of his way. He used the fear the emotion gave him, the bloodlust, channeled it into fury. Mindy was close. She was in danger. She was all that mattered.

These people were in his way.

He clamped his jaws down on a guard's arm and flung him overboard, charged ahead and slammed his fist into another guard's chest, felt bones cave in. He moved ahead, climbed the upper decks, and leapt the rail, landing in front of the nav room. A sign pointed to the captain's cabin. Down to the right. Crewmen populated the deck, running from him and shutting themselves off in the nav deck. James ignored them, moved down the deck and into another corridor. He stopped at a wooden door.

Captain.

The door splintered easily under the blow; James's fist barely felt the impact. He stepped into the tight quarters, still impressed by the size of the place. He roamed through the sitting area, saw the wet bar off in the corner. His ears perked as the scent of strawberries filled his senses. Something else. Blood. Rot. Pheromones.

James's chest clenched, white-hot rage turning his vision a deep amber as the fur around his eyes dampened with tears. He growled as he approached the door and inspected it. With no hesitation, he slammed his fist through the door and pulled it apart in a matter of seconds. Despite the tightness, he managed to crouch down and slip sideways through the opening. He glanced up, saw the ceiling and light fixture, and kept a gorilla stance, his shoulders hunched and knuckles on the floor as he moved in and glared at his target.

The old man's eyes were red around glowing yellow irises. Mindy struggled in his grasp, her dirty little body only covered by a small tanktop and shorts. Her eyes widened as she looked up at James.

"We finally meet," Wangenheim said in a thick German accent, grinning up at James as he stood tall. "I cordially invite you to dinner."

He was bald, his pale, wrinkled skin covered in liver spots, loose flesh sagging under his chin as he adjusted the red cigar jacket on his lithe form. He wore black dress pants and perfectly polished black shoes. His spider-like fingers were covered in various ornate rings, and an equally decorative amulet hung from a chain on his neck.

James stared hard at the old man, played every scenario in his mind he could think of to get Mindy away. Wangenheim wasn't simply old. James could see it in the crow's-feet-framed eyes. There was no telling how much history the bastard had seen. James had learned by now that for vampires, age equaled strength.

In every scenario, Mindy died before James could get to her.

"James Coldstone," Wangenheim said. "At last. You have been a constant problem for me. Always hunting. Always at my heels. My organization has lost millions because of your interference."

James stepped forward.

Wangenheim held up a finger, wagging it at James as if he were chastising a small child. "I would not, *Herr Coldstone*," he said. He lifted Mindy by the arm as if she weighed nothing, the small girl crying out in pain as he squeezed. He stroked her face with his free hand, running his long fingers along her cheek as his nails extended into inch-long claws.

"She is replaceable, and I will end her before you take another step." He smiled again as James stopped. "Now, I would disarm you. You will shift into your human form, *würdest du bitte.*"

James reached out, pulled the comforter off the bed, and wrapped it around his waist. He shifted to his human form, adjusting the blanket to keep himself covered. Mindy's eyes widened at the sight as Wangenheim sat her on the floor.

"Don't move," James said to her. "He's too fast."

"Doggy?" Mindy said, her lower lip trembling.

"Why isn't she wearing her dress?" James said, turning his glare to Wangenheim. "What did you do to her?"

"Nothing, I assure you," Wangenheim said. "Despite my business dealings, I am no monster. She was forced to change clothes so her dress could be used to distract you." He nodded at James. "I am much older than you think. I remember when Wallachia was founded and Lord Dracula reigned."

"I get it," James said. "You're strong. Out with it. Why the trafficking and murder? And why her?"

"*Geld,*" Wangenheim said. "Money. Wealth. Why do all businesses do what they do? If a few humans are willing to pay for their secret desires, who am I to turn away their generosity? But this one," he said, motioned at Mindy. "This one caught my attention, unlike the others."

"So that's why you had Wade Anderson take her?" James said. "Because she got your attention."

"*Nein,*" Wangenheim said. "I discovered her after. Unlike werewolves, shapeshifters are not sensitive to the Fae."

"Fae?" James blinked. He'd heard the term before, but barely knew what it meant. Phillip was more of a fantasy nerd than he was.

"Faeries," said Wangenheim, rolling his eyes. "*Christus,* the stupidity of you dogs sometimes." He patted Mindy on the shoulder. "She is not full, however. Only one of her parents. Her mother."

"I thought faeries were mean little bastards," James said, remembering Phillip telling him once that faeries were like insect-sized demons.

"All species have their black sheep," Wangenheim said. "And not all Fae are small or obvious in their abilities." He gripped Mindy's shoulder and pulled her closer. "And they taste delectable. Fae blood is rare, but this one happens to have a mother who can produce more if need be."

"There's about fifteen feet between the two of us." James clenched his fist. "Take your hand off of her, or I'm going to see if I can make it."

"You have no power here, *Herr* Coldstone," the vampire sneered. "Once I am done, once she is recovered, she will go to the highest bidder. It amazes me, the lust men have for children. They will pay money to me for her company, and she will learn to breed more of her kind for me and mine to feast upon."

"Let me go!" Mindy cried out, trying to struggle away. Wangenheim held fast, chuckling as the girl punched and kicked at him. James hesitated. The old son of a bitch could kill her in an instant. She'd be dead before he could finish the change.

"Quiet, child," Wangenheim said. "You are mine."

"Go away," Mindy shouted. James sucked in a breath as her hands began to glow. She put them against Wangenheim's side and shoved. "*Let me go!*"

Wangenheim was blown off his feet and sent airborne. James shifted into wolf form and charged as Mindy fell back out of the way. Wangenheim hit the wall and landed on his feet as James shoulder-checked him, sending them both through the wall and into the toilet. Wangenheim kicked James off him as if fighting an eight-hundred-pound werewolf was Tuesday. James recovered and charged in again, but Wangenheim was ready. He ripped the sink from the wall and clubbed James in the face with it. James staggered back from the blow; Wangenheim lashed out and left four bloody trails in James's chest. He grabbed James by the head and flipped him over, slammed him onto his back. James gasped, the wind knocked out of him. Wangenheim placed his foot on James's chest, holding him down.

"Mongrel," the old man spat. "You seek to fight *me*? I would expect more from the son of the Wolf Man Killer." James blinked as the bastard laughed. "Oh, *ja, mein fruend.* I know who your father was." He grinned as he leaned down. "He worked for me, making sure those who would interfere in my business would meet their end."

The Wolf Man Murders. David Coldstone had been killing for Wangenheim? James snarled and bucked, but Wangenheim pinned him back down easily, pressing with his foot. James felt his ribcage strain under the force, struggled to breathe. "You will rest now, *Herr* Coldstone. And I will possess this Fae child."

Wangenheim's face contorted, his fangs growing longer as his eyes glowed bright, his other teeth forming into sharp points as his jaw elongated. His skin grayed, his ears grew into bat-like points as his nose turned up, his nostrils now slits as a serpentine tongue licked out over the vicious maw that came closer to James, hot saliva dripping down onto his chest, the stench of burning fur wafting into the air and mixing with the odor of decayed meat. James tried to push back, but the force on his chest was too much. He could feel his heart pounding against his chest.

"Hey, asshole. Lay off my boyfriend."

James caught a glimpse of Lacy just before she sent a stream of water at Wangenheim. The vampire shrieked and backed away, covering his face as smoke billowed from the burns and lesions that opened in his skin where the water hit him. James rolled to the side, looking around the room for Mindy as Lacy started pumping the large water gun she held. She aimed and fired again, hitting Wangenheim square in the chest, the saltwater burning away flesh.

James felt his wounds healing, felt his strength coming back as he tried to stand, the tips of his ears brushing the ceiling and reminding him he needed to stay low. Wangenheim fell to the floor, writhing and screaming as his flesh melted away where Lacy had shot him. His arm fell away, and his knee turned to bubbling goop as he looked up at James, his eyes wide in pain. He spat something at him in German. James cocked his head to the side as Wangenheim repeated it.

No hablo asshole, James thought. He rammed his claws into Wangenheim's chest, bone shattering around his hand and wrist as he gripped the still heart and tore it free. Wangenheim shuddered in pain, his shocked eyes focused on the heart in James's hand as James closed his fist, blood and meat spewing to the sides and running down his arms. It began to go to ash as Wangenheim's body deteriorated, crumbled away, leaving only a pile of dust on the carpet.

"Jimmy," Lacy said, lowering the water cannon. "Are you okay?"

James barked, then looked around the room, sniffing the air. He caught the scent of strawberries just as Mindy peered out from the other side of the bed. She jumped up onto the mattress, crossed over the bed, and leapt at James, wrapping her arms around him as he caught her and held her close. The wolf mewled in his mind as he held the sobbing child in his arms.

You're safe, he thought to her. *I've got you.*

"We need to go," Lacy said, tossing the water gun aside. "I'm out of ammo, and the kid I swiped that from is probably looking for me."

James cocked his head to the side.

"What?" she said, shrugging. "The kid had a super-soaker, there was a sink and shitload of table salt handy, and I know how to network."

James moved Mindy onto his back, going to all fours so she could ride. He followed Lacy out into the corridor, moving quickly, but steady enough to keep the small girl from falling off. Lacy spoke as they walked.

"I tried to get to the nav room, but I got jumped," she said as they headed through the cabin and down the corridor back toward the open deck. "Then I heard the commotion in the cabin back there, and figured you found our buddy. Upside: he's history. Downside: the fucking ship is about two minutes out from international waters. Phillip just sent me a text. The Coast Guard is coming, but it won't matter unless we can turn this piece of junk around."

James nudged the phone, then the pocketbook she somehow still managed to have slung over her shoulder. Lacy looked down at it, then back at him. "Oh," she said. "I guess you're...yeah, I still have the phone. We need to get it plugged in right now." She gestured at Mindy. He could feel the girl's fingers clutching his fur. "Hey, sweetie. I'm Lacy. Gonna need you to not be around when Jimmy and I go to play with the people driving this dumpster fire."

"No," Mindy said, clutching James's fur tighter. "I'm not leaving doggy again. I want to be safe."

Shit, James thought. *I can't juggle a child while I'm going nuts in a small room.* He moved past Lacy and toward a storage closet right by the exterior door. He opened it, plucked Mindy off his back, and set her down inside.

"No, doggie!" she cried. "No, don't leave me again!"

James sighed, a low mewl sounding from the back of his throat. He touched his nose to her cheek, his heart breaking at the tears in her eyes.

"Okay," she said, nodding. James blinked. Had she...understood? "But hurry back. I'm scared."

Lacy moved in front of James and shut the door. She snapped the doorknob off, turned, and looked up at him. "I know how hard that was," she said. "Marianne is locked away, too. We can't risk them." She motioned at the door leading out to the deck. "The nav room is just to the left outside this door. Let's go see if the crew is wearing their brown pants."

The night air blew cool on his fur, the ocean scent soothing as he crept along the roof of the nav deck. He heard Lacy below as she knocked on the window. James heard steel on steel, heard a door open, heard a young man speak.

"Ma'am?"

Lacy's tone was hysterical. "Help me, please! I saw it! It's coming!"

"Jesus, get in here!"

James heard movement and the door shut. He breathed in deeply, then pushed it out slowly as the wolf braced in his mind, growling. He reached the edge, looking down the front at the observation window. He was in position. He ran over Lacy's plan in his head again.

That glass is probably about six inches thick, Jimmy. Might weaken it or break it with that new little trick of yours.

It would work. It had to work.

Okay, he thought at the wolf. *Go time.*

Wolf stood tall, breathed again as the James stepped back in its mind. Body was large, powerful. It looked to the sky, gnashing its teeth as it let the fire swell in its belly. It held the arms out to the sides as if to welcome sky, conjured howl from deep within, and unleashed Fenrir's battle cry with the fury of all wolfen brethren of North. Cries sounded from inside man room below. The James shouted, urged it harder, its cries lost behind the howl. Sound of glass cracking below was sharp, hateful. It stopped the call, took another breath, and called to Fenrir again, harder, stronger. The deck under its feet shuddered as the windows exploded outward, glass raining down on the rest of the ship as the James moved forward.

James shook his head, tried to move, fell over, his legs weak. The howl had taken it out of him. Where had that come from? Why did it drain him like this? It hadn't before. Had it?

He pushed himself up, forced some strength into his arms as he dragged himself forward enough to look over the edge of the nav deck again. He could hear Lacy fighting inside, could smell sweat mixed with vanilla and blood rot.

Vampires. Of course.

Lacy cried out, not in pain but in anger. Someone shouted, then James saw blood spatter out through the broken window and rain down on the panicking passengers swarming the deck below.

Damn, he thought. He saw the wolf stagger in his mind, then fight its way onto its feet. *We have to get it together. She needs help.*

The wolf barked at him, shook itself off as James took the cue to push his body, force his legs and arms to work. He mimicked the wolf, shaking off as he felt his strength come back. He jumped down to the balcony in front of the shattered observation window and leapt through as Lacy punched a hissing crewman in the face, knocking out one of his fangs. He howled in pain, covering his mouth as blood gushed between his fingers.

James lashed out, claws extended, and the vampire dropped to the deck, his body turning to ashes as his head rolled off into a corner. Human workers fled the scene as four of their vampire comrades charged Lacy and James. James picked one up by the face and slung him around like a ragdoll, smacking him into walls and control boards before throwing him through the open window. Lacy rushed James, hit the deck, and slid between his legs as the other vampires moved in after her.

"All yours, Jimmy," she said as she got to her feet behind him. "Need to plug this phone in before one of these assholes breaks it."

James snarled and lunged at the trio, clasped his hands together, and swung his arms like a sledgehammer. The group went flying into a wall together hard enough to dent the steel. One of them was dead from the impact, his body broken and bloody, but the other two shook it off and charged him again. James sent his fist through the chest of the nearest one, his large, clawed hand protruding through the vampire's back, covered in rotten blood. He could feel the heart burst as he lifted the body and hurled it to the side. The last vampire moved in, ducked James's swing, and sent an uppercut into his jaw.

Shit, James thought, reeling. *That hurt.*

The vampire removed his sailor's cap. James took a split second to size up his prey. The vampire was at least seven feet tall, his body rippling with muscle and covered in tattoos. He was bald, his scalp decorated with a tattoo of a black bird. He grinned at James and cracked his knuckles.

"Come here, puppy," he said. "Got a treat for ya."

James growled and hunkered down to attack. Before he could lunge, he heard Lacy behind him. "Now, Phillip! You're in!"

The ship lurched, leaned hard starboard, the force throwing James and Meathead the Magnificent off-balance. Screams and shouts rose from the decks below as the ship turned sharp off its course. James hit the deck and slid toward the window as Meathead held onto a railing. He laughed as James scrambled and tried to get to his feet.

"Need your ocean legs, Benji," the vampire said.

James saw him look at Lacy. She was holding onto a chair, the bolts that kept it in place pulling out of the floor from the force.

Meathead grinned as he started toward her. "Hey, hot stuff. Let Daddy show you how to work a throttle."

James pushed off the wall and crashed into the vampire, tackling him to the floor as he sunk his teeth into Meathead's neck. He tried to clamp down harder, but the muscle and bone were hard as steel. Meathead punched James in the jaw, causing him to release. James fell back as the ship steadied itself, then got to his feet as Meathead made for Lacy again. She kicked out at him, but the vampire caught her foot and shoved her down. His eyes widened appreciatively as he obviously looked down her dress when she hit the floor.

"Might keep you around for some fun," he said.

James made for him, grabbed him by the back of the neck, and plowed his head into the control panel. Sparks flew, smoke billowing as Meathead tried to fight back. James snatched him up by the shoulders and hurled him through the window. He heard the vampire's shout cut short. He moved to the window and saw Meathead's body turning to ash around the antenna he'd been impaled on.

"That's what you get for taking a peek at the goods, dickhead," Lacy said as she joined James at the window. "I think he had a few years on me."

James huffed. He heard a tinny voice shouting from the phone in Lacy's hand. He motioned to it, and she held it up and put it on speaker. Phillip's voice rang out loud and clear.

"The Coast Guard just radioed in the ship. You're back inside U.S. waters. Get the fuck out of there! They're about to board!"

"Aren't they on our side?" Lacy asked.

"You mean do they know that James is breakin' the leash laws and you like to snack on hemoglobin?"

"Fair point."

"*Get the fuck out of there!*"

"Where do we go, dumbass? We're still at sea."

James barked. *Mindy*, he thought.

Lacy shook her head. "We need to go get Marianne and Mindy. They're hidden."

"No time for that," Phillip said. "The Coast Guard will take it from here. *Go!*"

James barked again, one bark. *No.*

"Don't give me that shit, Lassie," Phillip said. "You did it. You saved the girl. Bail ass before things get more complicated than they already are! They'll get her home!"

Another bark.

"Goddamn, I *hate* dogs! If the Coast Guard finds you, this whole thing will be a shit sandwich!"

"Phillip's right," Lacy said, looking up at James. "We're the ones risking them now, Jimmy. We gotta move."

James gnashed his teeth. They were right. He wouldn't do Mindy any good by getting into a fight with the good guys. He heard shouts from below, looked out and saw uniformed men swarming the deck, some starting crowd control while others began arresting security guards. They grouped the crowd toward the front area while others headed for the bridge.

"Lifeboats," Lacy said. She pulled James's arm. "C'mon, Jimmy! Let's go!"

James kicked harder, pushing the inflatable raft along in the water as he fought to put distance between the lifeboat and the *Empusa*. His heart broke with every kick, every foot of water he plowed through as the thought of Mindy locked away in that closet played over and over in his mind.

He stopped, treading water as he looked back at the cruise ship.

"I think that's good, Jimmy," Lacy said. "Come up here and rest. You look dog tired."

Ha, ha, he thought. *I see what you did there. So clever.* He shifted to human form and climbed aboard, careful not to touch Lacy since he was covered in saltwater. He slumped down into the bottom of the raft, his body aching from exhaustion. The wolf grunted in his mind. *Then again, she may be onto something there.*

"We did the right thing, James," Lacy said. "There's no way we could've come out of that easy if the Coast Guard found us. It's better for the girls."

"You're unconvinced," James said.

Lacy looked away. "I don't have a choice because it's the truth. We can't be there for them."

"She's Fae."

Lacy looked at him. "Who?"

"Mindy. She's Fae. That's what Wangenheim said. She blew him across the room just by touching him. Faeries."

"Did you imprint on her?"

"I locked in her scent," James said. "I licked her face back home when the SWAT team was after me."

Lacy blinked. "Holy shit, James. That explains everything."

1 2

I t was an hour before James got the raft to shore. He'd rested for a bit, then gotten back into the water in wolf form and resumed being the outboard motor for the craft. He stumbled onto the beach, his fur heavy with saltwater as he went to his knees in the sand, his body sore and tired from swimming at wolfen speed, pushing the raft from a good two miles out from the shoreline.

Lacy leapt out of the raft to avoid the saltwater, landing solidly next to him on dry land.

"You know how to impress a date, Jimmy," she said, stepping in front of him and kneeling. "I don't think even Yamaha could top you for motor-boating."

Ha, James said. *Again with the jokes.*

James's phone rang from inside Lacy's purse. She pulled it out and put Phillip on speaker phone. "Hey, Bacon. We're back on the island."

"Yeah, I know," Phillip said. "I've been tracking you two with your phone. You need to get to the ferry and hide."

James shifted into human form and stood, taking the phone from Lacy as he went. He recognized Phillip's tone and didn't like it. "What is it, Phillip?"

"The Coast Guard has the *Empusa* on lockdown. The NSA, on the other hand, is storming Westenra Island right damn now. Not the SCU. The NS-fuckin'-A."

"That's what we wanted, right?" Lacy asked. "The feds to come in and take down the rest of the traffickers?"

"That's one group," Phillip said. "The other group is looking for a giant dog monster who may or may not be paper-trained."

"Oh shit."

"'Oh shit' is right. Someone sent video of Scooby-Doo storming the island earlier right to their damn social media page. The National Security Agency shut it down, took the video, and launched a task force on it. They think the Wolf Man Murderer is back."

"Lovely," James said. "Where are they?"

"I've got the island on satellite right now," Phillip said. "They're headed your way. From the west. You two need to go south and circle back up."

"Right," James said. "We'll text you when we get to the ferry." He ended the call and handed the phone back to Lacy. "Let's go." He shifted and took off down the beach, Lacy close behind him, both at full speed. The wolf pushed him, healed all his fatigue from his long swim as he sped by the dunes and piers, following the shoreline as the tide moved in.

Something slammed into his shoulder, sent him rolling to the ground. Lacy shouted out, ducked as more bullets sailed through the air. Voices shouted in the dark as James's entire arm burned in agony.

Silver, he thought. *Holy shit.*

He pushed himself up as Lacy got to her feet. A group burst through the trees, assault rifles aimed. James saw "FBI" on the front of their tactical gear. He rose to full height, his arm resisting with pain and tension as he clenched his fist.

"Freeze, motherfucker!" one of the men shouted, aiming his rifle at James. "Holy shit. It's real!"

Lacy stepped in front of James, her fangs out completely, her eyes glowing red. "I don't like it when people shoot my boyfriend."

Lacy vanished, moving so quickly she was barely visible. The agents shouted and cursed as their guns were swatted out of their hands. One went flying backward; another dropped to the sand like a sack of bricks. The last one standing looked around, then back at James. James hunkered down, growling, his eyes wide and psychotic as he let his jaw open, the growls turning into snarls. The agent yelped, fell backward, started scrambling away. Lacy appeared in front of him, picked him up by the nape as if he weighed nothing, and threw him back into the trees.

James fell over, his legs giving out. The pain had gone from his arms to his chest and down his side. He shifted to human form, saw the silver veins spiderwebbing over his body.

"Oh shit," Lacy said, running to him. She knelt next to him as he lay down on the sand. "Shit, shit, shit, *shit!*"

"I can't...think of much else to say either," James managed, finding it hard to talk as his breathing went shallow.

"Silver poisoning," Lacy said. "I've heard of this before. We've got to get that bullet out." She looked down the rest of his body. "Oh, god. James, it's all over."

"Must be...serious," James said. "Otherwise...I'm just Jimmy."

Lacy looked at his shoulder, put her hands on either side of the wound and squeezed. The pain almost made James vomit as he cried out.

"It's too deep," Lacy said. "Be ready to shift. You're not gonna like this." James screamed as she sank her vampire teeth into his shoulder and tore a large hunk of meat away. She spat it to the side, blood running down her chin and neck as she used her fingers to dig into the wound. James tried to buck, but his body was too weak. He felt her fingers digging around in his shoulder, felt something shift. Something hard. Each movement sent torrents of pain down his arm and spine. Lacy jerked the slug free and stood, moving back. "Shift, Jimmy! Now!"

The wolf charged in, and James screamed as his body began to change, fur pushing silver out of every pore as his shoulder started to heal. His strength returned as the wolf pushed his body, bone and sinew growing and moving, muscle reforming where it'd been eaten away.

James stood and looked down at Lacy, his body feeling new and powerful again. She held up the small silver bullet in her palm. "Here goes," she said. "You scratched my back before. Figured I'd return the favor." She threw the bullet into the surf.

James licked her face, causing her to laugh. "Ew, Jimmy! God, not in public! I'm modest, you know."

One of the men on the beach started to stir. James heard shouts coming from the trees behind the dunes. He barked at Lacy. *Time to go.*

Lacy ran down the beach, James taking up the rear as more gunfire rang out, rounds whizzing by or smacking the sand on either side of them. Lacy darted right, and James followed as she went through the trees, past the cabin where they'd been staying, and down the road toward the ferry. James spotted Cookie putting down the road in his gas-powered golf cart. He waved casually at them as they blew by him.

Goodbye, Cookie, James thought. He pressed on, staying behind Lacy as she slowed and moved past a row of gift shops at the ferry port. People were being herded onto the ferry, federal agents waving them along, some leading people in handcuffs.

"Feeling up for another swim?" Lacy asked.

James shifted to human form. "That won't work. I'm fairly certain salt-water kills vampires."

"I'll manage another way," Lacy said.

"No," said James, not looking at her. "I'm not leaving you alone. Too risky."

She looked at him, her mouth drawn in a smirk. "Aren't we chivalrous?"

James looked back at her. "They have silver bullets. They've been briefed as to what they're up against. Silver hurts vampires, too."

"It doesn't kill us," she said. "It'll be quicker if we split up."

"I don't care about being quick. I care about you."

Lacy blinked as if James had clapped in her face. He pursed his lips as his brain caught up with his mouth. He started as Lacy put her hands on either side of his head and kissed him hard. James could still taste some of his blood on her mouth, but he didn't care. He returned the kiss just as passionately, his heart pounding as the wolf turned over onto its back in his mind, its paws in the air.

Lacy pulled away, ending the kiss. She laughed a little, pointing at his mouth. "You've got…um, yeah."

James wiped his face. Something caught his eye. He looked up to his right, saw racks of clothing in the windows of the shop they hid behind. An idea came to mind.

"New plan," he said.

Lacy bit her lip playfully. "Wow, Jimmy. It's been a while, so don't go easy on me."

James ignored her, moving toward the window. He peered in, making sure the shop was empty before turning back to her. "I need to get dressed."

"Why?"

"So you can beat the shit out of me."

Help!" Lacy staggered a little to make it look like James's weight was too much on her small, willowy frame as she readjusted his arm around her shoulders. His face hurt where she'd punched him, his nose bloody and his eye swollen.

"Went a little overboard, didn't you?" he said. "I think you broke my cheekbone."

"Like you won't heal," she said under her breath. She went back to her staged hysterics. *"Help me, please!"*

Two federal agents in tactical gear came running. They pulled James off her, each one taking a side as they helped him walk. His left knee buckled where she'd kicked it out from underneath him. "What happened?" asked one of the agents.

"We were running this way when someone jumped him," Lacy said. "I thought they were mugging us, but they just beat him up and ran off."

One of the agents flagged down another. "These two were attacked. Get some men and get out there. Looks like we've already got some rioting."

The other agent nodded and said, "Sir." He took off, and James's two new friends helped him aboard the ferry. They sat him down on a bench near the front to make sure he was out of the way of the rest of the boarding process.

"I'm a nurse," Lacy said. "I can work on him if you can get me a first aid kit."

The man nodded and called for a first aid kit. Someone brought one to him, and he handed it off to Lacy before going back to managing the crowd with his partner.

"A nurse?" James said. "Really?"

Lacy shrugged. "About sixty years ago or so. It was a slow decade, and I needed something to pass the time." She opened the kit and went through it as the engines on the ferry started up. She poured some hydrogen peroxide on a gauze patch and began wiping off his face, touching carefully as he winced in pain. James's phone chimed in her purse. She stopped, pulled it out, and handed it to James. He saw the text message from Phillip on his home screen.

They found Mindy and Marianne. They're safe.

"Now what?" Lacy asked.

"We go home," James said, looking at her. "Both of us."

Lacy's expression saddened. "James, I—"

"My place is big enough," James said, cutting her off. "And you said you don't have a home. Not a permanent one. Let me at least give you that much."

She nodded, smiling at him. "Okay."

He couldn't help seeing the sadness behind her eyes.

EPILOGUE

Sun shafts gave the study an amber glow as the evening sky turned orange, the sun setting behind the trees on the far end of the fields that separated Coldstone Keep from the small plantation property next door. The air wasn't near as stale as it had been yesterday thanks to Phillip making the arrangements to have the power turned back on.

"You don't have an apartment anymore," he'd said during James's visit at the hospital. "And I live in a one-bedroom apartment, myself. You've got nowhere to go." He sighed, looking at James from the hospital bed as he winced in pain. "Damn rod. Shit hurts."

"How's the physical therapy going?"

"Nurse Nasty's a damn drill sergeant," Phillip said with a grunt. "That's why I call her Nurse Nasty. Woman has a temper. I think she got kicked out of the Marines for unnecessary roughness."

"At least she cares about you."

Phillip had responded with a snort. "Shee-it. That woman spends most of her day thinkin' about new ways to torture my ass."

James sat in the large chair behind his father's desk, staring out into the room as his thoughts forced their way back to Lacy. He looked down at the note still in his hand, Lacy's elegant cursive scrawled across the piece of tear-stained notebook paper. He read it again, her voice in his head reading along as if she stood next to him.

Jimmy,

I can't stay. You have to understand that. It's not that I don't care about you. I do. But this is best for both of us. You're a sweet, sweet man. And puppy. That's why I have to go. You didn't do anything wrong. This is on me. I'm so sorry.

Love,

Lacy

He couldn't get her image out of his mind: her smile and her bright blue eyes against her long curly hair. He'd felt heartbreak before, that pain in his chest and in the pit of his stomach, that feeling of despair and loss. But nothing like what he felt now. He stared at the letter, ran his fingers over the claw marks on the surface of the desk. He could still smell blood and vanilla around them.

He blinked at the sound of the doorbell. He rolled his eyes, stood, and strolled out of the study and through the main hall to the front door. Sheets still covered the furniture, and a thick layer of dust coated everything. He unlocked the double doors and opened the one on the right.

"You look like hell," Phillip said, standing on the front porch and leaning on his crutches.

"You have a metal rod in your leg and you're on crutches," James said, his tone flat. "I'm pretty certain I'm faring much better than you are."

"Can I come in, or are you gonna keep mocking the cripple at your front door?"

"The mockery is more fun."

Phillip rolled his eyes. "Let me in, jackass."

James stepped aside, opening the door as Phillip hobbled inside. He looked around the hall, then back at James. "Shit, James. You gonna clean this place up? You've been here a week."

James shook his head. A week. He'd been here a week. Lacy had been gone a week.

"Right," he said. "I keep meaning to. Been busy."

Phillip turned to him, the sound of crutches echoing in the room. "Look man, you're gonna have to stay here. Probably a while. Probably permanently."

"I hate this place." James walked past him toward the study. "I'd rather stand on the road and watch it burn."

"Well, no one knows you're back in Rock Hill," Phillip said, turning and following him. "Apartment hunting might be a bad idea." James sat back down at the desk, motioning Phillip to sit in the chair on the opposite side. Phillip sat, setting the crutches aside. "Besides, this place is registered as a historic landmark, and you still own it. No one can touch it, and no one can come here without a trespassing charge. You're safer here than anywhere."

James grunted.

"You're depressed, James," Phillip said. "You've got to go outside at some point. Or at least get this place livable."

"For who?" James asked bitterly. "It's just me."

"She's been gone a week, James," Phillip said. "Time to move on."

James looked away, not wanting to glare at Phillip. "Thanks. I'd almost forgotten."

Phillip sighed, rubbed his face. "I'm sorry, man. I'm an asshole."

"At least you admit it. How's the leg?"

"I'll be off the crutches in a few weeks." Phillip cleared his throat. "James, we need to talk. About the SCU."

James looked at him. "What about the SCU?"

The doorbell rang again, interrupting him. James raised an eyebrow at Phillip, who rubbed his eyes as he cursed under his breath. "I knew he'd be right behind me. Punk motherfucker."

James started toward the door, then stopped as Agent Smith walked into the room, his black suit perfectly pressed as usual. "Pardon the intrusion," he said. "I didn't want to wait on you to answer the door. Time is short, you understand." He motioned to the chair next to Phillip. "May I?"

James nodded, sat down behind the desk as Smith took his seat next to Phillip. "Good morning, Agent Brown."

"Just tell him why you're here," Phillip said. "He has about as much patience as I do lately."

"That's unfortunate," Smith said, and looked at James. "Though I understand completely. Seeing the darker side of human beings can have a rather negative impact on one's view of the world."

"What do you want?" James asked. "I saved the girl. Stopped the traffickers. I'm done."

"Far from it," Smith said. "You did save the Fae girl, which is a good thing. As she is a half-breed, she'll be able to lead a fairly normal life as long as she can keep her Fae side secret. It also means you'll be attuned to her since you imprinted on her. I'm sure you know that werewolves are the natural protectors of the Fae."

"You're telling me you want me to spend the rest of my life as Mindy Robertson's bodyguard?" James shook his head. "Yeah, her parents will *love* a grown man following their nine-year-old around after what she's been through. Not creepy at all."

"No, I'm telling you that you'll have to learn how to keep that separate from your duties with the Supernatural Crimes Unit."

James sat for a moment, staring at Smith and Phillip, waiting for one of them to laugh. He gave it a few seconds, then eased back in his chair and eyed Smith. "What in the *hell* makes you think I'd join a branch of the government? Especially one that's designed to take down people like me?" He shook his head. "I'm sure you looked at my finances. I don't need to work. I don't *want* to work."

"I'm afraid freeloading is a thing of the past for you," Smith said.

"Hey," Phillip said, turning to Smith. "James is a lot of things, but he ain't a freeloader. People know who he is."

"No one is going to want to work with the son of a man who butchered people in his basement or mauled them to death in their own homes," James said. "The murders Wade Anderson committed when all of this started brought up too many bad memories in this town. I'd rather not put myself out where people have access to me."

"Ah, but you wouldn't have to be in public to be at our beck and call," Smith said. "In fact, you wouldn't have to leave your—" he paused, looking around at the filthy room in disgust as he brushed a thick layer of dust off the desk, "*home.* Not unless you're specifically called to report to the office, which we would do under cover of night. You would work for us."

"So, you're telling me to be your bitch," James said. "Super Wolf is no one's bitch."

"Be serious for once, James," Phillip said. "I was going to try to tell you," he jerked a thumb at Smith as he emphasized the other part of his statement, "but *somebody* who doesn't know you like I do decided to drop by."

Smith stood and straightened his suit. "The other choice is to be outed by the agency. Doxed. Everyone knows this place. It's currently not to be touched or trespassed on as it is both private property and a historical landmark. That can change." He stared at James. "You'd put this entire city, and everyone in it, in danger. The national media would be all over it. Then what? There are groups that want you dead. Vampire houses, obviously. And we have a killer still on the loose who managed to take down almost every agent we had posted on Westenra Island, if your report to Agent Brown is correct."

"You told me the other day that the vampire had no idea what you were talking about when you mentioned ripping the faces off," Phillip said. "That means something else is going on."

"We need your help. You *will* help us. Or we'll force you."

"You're already forcing me," James said, standing up, his glare locked on Agent Smith.

"No," Smith said. "This is me asking. You have a choice in the matter. The right choice means everyone lives in peace, and you work for us. The wrong choice means things get complicated for this city, for you, and you still work for us." He pulled a cell phone from his pocket and placed it on the desk. "I'll expect a text message in exactly one hour. On the sixty-first minute, your information goes public. I'll see myself out." He turned on his heel and left the room. James waited until he heard the front door open and shut.

"I'm sorry, James," Phillip said. "I tried to talk him out of it. He said if you join, I'd be your handler. At least there's that."

James sighed, slumped back down into the desk chair. He surprised himself. Where was the rage? He knew he should've been furious. He was being strong-armed. He hated being forced into anything. Hated being cornered.

But he didn't have the resources he needed to find Lacy. He didn't know anything about searching for someone other than just going out hunting, and Lacy would've covered her tracks well. She'd had a hundred years to perfect hiding. And if vampire houses were after him, it could be that they were trying to get to her. But why?

He looked back down at the note on the desk. He read it again, Lacy's voice in his head drowning out Phillip asking him if he was good. He saw her looking at him, her eyes brilliant blue even in the dark. He felt the memory of her skin pressed against his that night in the cabin just before she'd pulled away. It made his heart hurt more.

He needed answers. He looked at Phillip.

"Do they offer dental?"

THE END for now...

ABOUT THE AUTHOR

Jason Gilbert is an avid reader, writer, and moviegoer who keeps busy with (probably) more projects than can possibly be healthy. He started his dream of writing stories in middle school and has been at it since. He lives with his wife and a rambunctious daughter who manage to keep him somewhat in line. Somewhat.

facebook.com/jasongilbertauthor
instagram.com/jasongilberauthor
amazon.com/author/jasonhgilbert

ALSO BY JASON GILBERT

Clockworks of War Series

Gaslit Insurrection

Gaslit Armageddon

Gaslit Revolution

Other Works

The Rifle Chronicles

FRIENDS OF FALSTAFF

Thank You to All our Falstaff Books Patrons, who get extra digital content each month! To be featured here and see what other great rewards we offer, go to www.patreon.com/falstaffbooks.

PATRONS

Dino Hicks
John Hooks
John Kilgallon
Larissa Lichty
Travis & Casey Schilling
Staci-Leigh Santore
Sheryl R. Hayes
Scott Norris
Samuel Montgomery-Blinn
Junkle

www.ingramcontent.com/pod-product-compliance
Lightning Source LLC
Chambersburg PA
CBHW050612110726
47899CB00001B/82